THE MOSCOW HORSE

Other Futura Spectaculars

John Denis

The Moscow Horse

Futura Publications Limited
A Futura Book

A Futura Book

First published in Great Britain by
Futura Publications Limited in 1978

ISBN 0 7088 1454 9

Printed in Great Britain by
Hazell Watson & Viney Ltd
Aylesbury, Bucks

Futura Publications Limited
110 Warner Road
Camberwell, London SE5

Creamy spittle-flecks bubbled at the corners of the fat man's petulant little mouth as he bent over the quaking body of the spy, his fingers stretching out to the unprotected throat.

Then he heard the loud, strange noise and looked up, peering uncomprehendingly through his thick glasses into the golden haze, and saw the bull come in from the sea.

Out of the blinding sun and glinting, winking surf it charged at them, bellowing with the noise of a hundred demons, jets of sand and spray spewing from its hooves, cruel horns branching from its fiery head.

The fat man had a vivid imagination, so that his brain chose the fantastic rather than the obvious, and the motorcycle, its rider almost horizontal over the handlebars, was on them before he realised the truth. He'd frozen over the whimpering spy, his eyes pierced by the sun, and the massive, screaming Yamaha took him squarely in the side.

It tossed him contemptuously in the air. The rider wheeled, slithered to a halt, took a Schmeisser machine pistol from its holster clip under the saddle, and stitched a vertical pattern of slugs into the second British agent crouching ten yards away in the sand, starting at the bridge of his nose as he struggled to his feet, and ending in the taut flesh of his groin.

The fat man moaned softly, blood coursing down his chin, his thin red hair clogged with sand, his eyes rolling vacantly back towards the stunned and silent spy. Another burst from the Schmeisser blew away his face.

Prologue

Sian heard distant voices, and put the binoculars down, covering them with the cardigan that she'd needlessly brought with her. She saw two hikers – one a girl – plodding along the path which skirted the celandine-strewn bank sloping down to the little headland where she sat on a bath towel with sunglasses, paperback book, thermos of lemonade . . . and binoculars, notebook and ball-point pen. The couple glanced towards her and the girl waved. She waved back – and breathed a sigh of relief as they carried on in the direction where the path itself dropped down behind the cliff edge.

She turned again and put the binoculars once more to her eyes. From the Trefynnon headland in the thumb-print on the coast of Wales called Cardigan Bay, it was less than two miles across the water to the Royal Aircraft Establishment at Tredogan. The headland was about the same distance from her home in Trefynnon village, and in the hot, heavy days of summer, when the school where she taught had broken up Sian Griffith regularly rode and pushed her bicycle up the cliff path to enjoy the sunshine and the solitude. The headland was really no more than a grassy knoll, an outcrop of rock at a lower level than the cliff of which it was a part. It was ideal for sunbathing – and perfect for seeing the new experimental rockets launched from the reinforced concrete pad at Tredogan, which jutted out into the sea, white and (to her) obscene. It was connected to the RAE above by a rail track dropping down the cliff.

Perspiration beaded her forehead and upper lip. She brushed her thick chestnut hair away from the binoculars, and her tongue peeped out as the slim silver dart of the rocket was raised to a vertical position on the launch-pad. It wouldn't be long now, she thought. It never was, after they'd got the thing upright.

Sian knew little of rockets, and cared even less . . . but for this one. This one, they had told her, was special; it needed watching. So she watched.

In the concrete bunker with thick glass windows that was the launch-pad control room, they knew all about the rocket. They called it ORBITMAN, and although it was incorporated in a regulation Skylark missile whose performance, specification and design were matters of public record, they would have agreed with Sian that the rocket was indeed special. So special, and so secret, that the British Government did not particularly mind people sitting on headlands and watching it being launched, since there was little or nothing that anyone could deduce from its propulsion into the sky. There had been five launches before this, and the experiment on that day was the second one to involve the property that ORBITMAN alone possessed, and that made it unique in the field of intercontinental ballistic weaponry.

For ORBITMAN carried in its tail a fuel source so powerful and compact that it must give missile mastery to whoever used it. The rocket was powered by a pellet of britium and deuterium, only a few grammes in weight, but so concentrated that when it was vaporised it created partial atomic fusion, provided it was triggered in the right way. And for ORBITMAN the trigger was mounted in a steel and concrete chamber sitting under the rocket on the launch-pad – a laser beam which heated the pellet of britium and deuterium and so produced a violent release of gases to a point fractionally short of nuclear reaction.

The gigantic thrust generated by the interaction sent the rocket soaring up into orbit. There, guided by a complicated Inertial Navigation Platform devised by one of the world's leading experts in computer sciences and electronic physics, the missile, with its hydrogen bomb warhead the size of a grapefruit, could be directed to any city or town on earth. And once the target was computer-set, nothing could interfere with ORBITMAN's progress. Nothing. Not even if the target were Moscow. Or Washington.

The rocket did not need a full-scale launch-pad as such. Something the size of a railway wagon equipped with a high-speed turbine, cooled by liquid helium and revolving at over 50,000 rpm, powered by a small nuclear reactor, exactly similar to the power unit of a nuclear submarine, was entirely adequate to create a laser-beam adapted to infra-red to penetrate the cloud cover. This gave ORBIT-MAN its second unique property. It was totally mobile. It could be launched from anywhere in the world, on land or sea.

But at Tredogan, the laser-beam was directed straight into the Skylark's tail, and the only physical evidence of the generation of such immense force was the explosion and puff of smoke caused by the ignition of the rocket. To Sian Griffith on the previous occasions when she'd seen it, it had appeared to be no more impressive than a distant firework. She took the glasses away from her aching eyes, mopped her face with the cardigan, pulled the bikini up over her melon-shaped, generously freckled breasts, and leaned back on her hands waiting for something to happen.

It did. In the observation bunker, the disembodied voice on the Tannoy was reciting the monotonous litany of the count-down. Tension lay heavy on the air; even without the new fuel system, when they were just testing the Inertial Navigation Platform in a close orbit over Llangollen (for the missile was exceedingly accurate), even then there'd been one launch-pad explosion. Nothing serious, but with the new fuel . . . 'Doesn't bear thinking about does it?' said one white-coated scientist to another. 'Can't happen, can it?' his friend replied. One of the three shirt-sleeved technicians at the radar console turned and gave a weak apprehensive grin. 'BOOM,' bellowed the first scientist throwing his hands in the air. The younger man's head jerked so vio-

13

lently that his headset fell off.

The other scientist barely had time to scan the monitor dials and say, 'Jesus Christ what's gone wrong with the fuel?' when the rocket exploded.

Sian saw the flash before the rolling wave of sound engulfed her. It was so terrible as to be almost beautiful. A sheet of horizontal flame, first white, then golden, then white and orange, then, like a sunburst, red and yellow, and finally orange again – a dull, dirty, smoke-laden orange. It was, in effect, almost – but mercifully not quite – a nuclear explosion. Of the three or four tiny, asbestos-clad figures she had seen crouching at the base of the cliff in an observation trench, two were picked up into the air and thrown aside, flaring like Bengal matches. Then she heard, for the first time, the blaring klaxon that had started to give a warning of the sudden instability of the fuel pellet after its first caress from the laser beam. She peered down into the water at the foot of the headland, only twenty or so feet below.

Even from that height, she could see quite clearly perhaps a dozen fish and seabirds cast up on the tiny beach. Each living creature within the ambit of that hellish blaze had been charred to a uniform, crisp, dark brown, in the intense heat.

Her green eyes smarting, her head throbbing and heart madly pumping, she picked up her things and ran up the bank to her bicycle parked by the style separating the two fields through which the cliff-path ran. She pedalled furiously home, made a pot of tea, smoked a cigarette (a rare indulgence for Sian), and picked up the telephone to dial a London number.

When the Russian answered, Sian Griffith told him what she had seen.

'That's fifty-seven "for" then,' announced the chairman, who was unimaginative and liked to have things in order, 'and fifty-five against. Very well, gentlemen – we are on strike.'

And so two votes cast at a mass meeting of helicopter pilots in Stavanger, Norway, on a cold autumn morning, unwittingly started a chain reaction of events which opened the way to the Soviet Union gaining world dominance in nuclear warfare.

News of the dispute spread rapidly among the North Sea Oilfield crews waiting to be lifted off the rigs for their fortnight's shore leave. On SEDCO TRIPLE THREE in the Ekofisk Field, they cursed and they raved, because it was in their natures to do so. And the toolpusher summed it all up with a wave of his big hand that took in not just the helicopter pilots but the rest of the world as well. 'What else could you expect from that lot?' he demanded scornfully. 'They don't think like us, do they?'

And they fell to wondering how they were going to tell the bargemaster that he wouldn't be going to Stavanger after all, but most probably to Scotland. The bargemaster, they all agreed, was a difficult man . . .

One of the paradoxes of life on an oil rig is the existence of a spurious permanency, even solidity, that life on dry land long ago lost. There are no distractions, no temptations, no brazen alternatives to doing quite simply what you have been put there to do. For two weeks at a stretch, rig life is a shared experience of close intimacy for seventy-two men. There is nowhere to walk away from the job at the end of a gruelling, twelve-hour shift unless you have webbed feet and a spare set of gills.

You have to talk to the men working with you, because if you don't you end up talking to the wind or the paraffin budgie, which is the oilman's pet name for a helicopter. Men work on oil rigs because they cannot afford not to, and gradually they learn that to be confined on one very small world can somehow be more dignified and even more fulfilling than being free to roam at the careless mercy of an infinitely larger one. The crew of SEDCO TRIPLE

THREE were no exception.

In the mid-nineteen seventies, oil fever turned the North Sea into a liquid Klondike. The Ekofisk Field, just past the median line between the coasts of Britain and Norway, was one of the richer fields, and SEDCO TRIPLE THREE was a lucky rig. Like oil rigs the world over, it was a haven of noise in an ocean of peace . . . the walls were of resounding steel, the floors of echoing quarry tiles. In the crew's quarters, with four men to a room Boxing and Coxing on the day and night shifts, there were just four lockers and two double-tiered bunk beds, and no pin-ups, and the windows were taped over to help the night shift men sleep. As for the noise, if you couldn't adjust to it, you quit the rig; there was no other way.

So for the roustabouts (the general labourers of the rig), the roughnecks on the drilling floor, the derrickman, the driller and his crew, the toolpusher and his crew, and the swarm of support staff – cook, medics, engineers, motormen, painters – for the totally interdependent members of this busy little anthill on the wild, cold sea, SEDCO TRIPLE THREE was home. They did their jobs and ate their meals and slept, played cards, read books, and drank milk or tea or cocoa or coffee, and they lived their artificial lives as they wanted to live them.

They had their own language. When they wanted a hammer they asked for a 'clooring stick', and if they wanted to put something into a hole – even the mighty, carbon-steel, diamond-tipped drill – they talked of 'pluffing it in'. There was one usage nobody could explain; 'chattie' meant anything and everything – all things to all men. Silly, really, the crew thought, yet they would no more think of dropping the word than they would consider missing the relief helicopter which on this day, even now, they felt so sure was on its way to pick them off and take them back to the real world outside.

They talked and argued and finally picked the smallest

16

roustabout they could find to tell him, for he was about as close as you could get to a loner in their monastic society, and a dangerous man to cross. He was allowed to be an almost-loner for two reasons. First, he was the barge-master; he commanded the rig, and he had immense power in his tiny domain; and secondly, he was the biggest man most of them had ever seen.

His name was Michael Patrick Gresson, and he was American by birth and Irish by instinct and conception, for he'd been born five months after his parents emigrated from Sligo. His father had often said that if the family had waited out the wife's confinement in Ireland, Mick would have been a foot shorter, since his height would have been extravagantly out of place for a Sligoman, but as an American he was just big.

More by accident than design, the Gressons ended up in the tenements of the New York waterfront, generally on the wrong side of the bread line. Mick was big and poor, an unhealthy combination until his size was so great the poverty no longer mattered because his strength and bulk were marketable commodities. His bitterness at his father's failure, his resentment of rich America which rented his body and used it to crush others, his loathing and detestation of imperial England; these prepared him for a creed of nihilism and hate as surely and thoroughly as the Jesuit ministry would have done for the Church. He was a gift to the sharp and canny Communists who infiltrated the docks; they got him at the age of fourteen, and kept him for life.

They ran him not as the field agent he'd have liked to have been, but as the industrial saboteur he so obviously was. They used him sparingly but well, and finally they sent him from the waterfront to the water just before his twentieth birthday, when the offshore oil industry started to boom. Now, at the age of thirty-six, he was an oilman to his fingertips. Promotion to bargemaster had come easily, and the American Communists handed him on to their masters in the Soviet Union, who found all manner of uses for him and paid him more money than he'd ever dreamed he'd see in his life. If anything, it made Gresson even more bitter that both of his parents had died before they could share in his prosperity.

He was a fundamental, gut Communist without knowing why, and the KGB were anxious to keep it that way. His freedom of movement was a priceless asset – but no one had any reason on this day to predict how immensely important it would become.

He stood by himself (as he invariably did) at the rail, the almost-loner Gresson, and the diminutive roustabout tapped him on the arm and said:

'Message from Company. The budgie drivers are on strike for more kroners, so we ain't going to Stavanger this time, we're going to Scotland.'

Gresson looked down thunderously at him. 'Scotland? Aberdeen? Is this some kind of a joke.'

'No, Mick, honest,' the little Londoner said. 'Strike me stupid, it's true. I mean, you can always go to Stavanger from Aberdeen, at Company expenses of course, but they say there won't be a plane until tomorrow,' he finished timidly.

As every man aboard knew – but never mentioned to his face – Gresson had a girl in Stavanger, a Junoesque Viking if such a breed existed, from whose body he was reluctant to emerge except for air, food and rig duty. To keep Mick and Kirsten apart was a pastime for fools; to draw attention to the fact would have been suicidal.

'Piss off, Squirrel,' Gresson said to the roustabout, whose name was Nutcombe. It was true what the little man had said; it would only be for a day, he could easily get a flight to Norway from Aberdeen. He'd never been to Scotland (or any part of Great Britain for that matter), and it might be useful to have a contact there, or at least a working knowledge of the oil town.

Nutcombe scurried back and told his friends it hadn't been all that bad – you just had to know how to handle the big, thick pillock. He almost passed out when he thought Gresson might have overheard him, but the big man had veered off to check in his quarters that he had his passport.

He waited with his gear on the steel deck of the rig for the helicopter to come, endlessly scanning the horizon to the south-west. The small, black dot that somebody hailed grew larger, took on a shape, and gradually became a British Airways helicopter which began its lazy descent to the rig. The bright red, blue and white Sikorski hovered like a giant dragonfly, only yards from the landing pad for a moment or two, and crept slowly in. The cold of the day intensified as the blades created new gusts of wind, and the air was filled with the shrill whine of the engines and the stench of paraffin.

The pilot let his aircraft sink on to its wheels, and then throttled the engines back to idling speed. For those on the rig it was a beautiful sight, not only because of its shape, but because it was their contact with the real world.

The platform was soon alive with activity. Refuelling got under way, and the roustabouts dashed to and fro with crates and boxes. They waved to the relief crew who were just visible through the windows of the helicopter, peeling off their normality and their sexuality with their orange survival suits to begin another fortnight of bearable, and remunerative, celibacy.

The budgie never waited around for long, and within twenty minutes they were up and climbing away, leaving the rig looking about as impressive as a single character of type on a blank sheet of newsprint.

An hour and a half later Scotland stole into view – the east-facing cliffs of Aberdeenshire, picked out as always by the permanent white fringe of foam where the normally green-grey sea boils against the granite. Low cloud and poor visibility deprived Gresson of a sight he didn't know was there – the majesty of the eastern Highlands rising in the background. The patchwork of green and brown fields tilted alarmingly, and the American could see the concrete and tarmacadam scar of Dyce Airport. The big square buildings, he supposed, were hangars, and the still, symmetrical insects marshalled in neat ranks around the perimeter were cars in the car-parks.

The airport was desolate and windy, and Gresson and the others trotted over to the single-storey terminal. Inside the double doors it was warm and steamy, smoky and noisy, a mass of oilmen – Gresson's type – in denims, donkey jackets, tartan shirts and thick woollen sweaters, covering bodies of perhaps a dozen different nationalities with one thing in common, their love of oil and the money it brought them. Gresson took out his passport and his identification papers, and picked his way through the throng searching for the customs and immigration barrier.

He didn't find the barrier, but he saw a door marked EXIT and that was where everyone else seemed to be going, so he went, too. The man in front – Squirrel Nutcombe – held the door open for him, and he strode through to the open air.

He was in Scotland. An American, with his passport in his hand, he'd walked unhindered into a foreign country and no one had even so much as asked his name.

Gresson stood there stupidly, a smile of bemused incredulity on his lips, men pushing impatiently past him, jogging and bumping him, and he didn't notice. He shook his head and gave a dry chuckle, and walked on.

The real significance of what he'd done struck him late that night, twisting uncomfortably in his too-short bed in the Station Hotel. If *he* could do it – travel from a rig to a country having flourishing off-shore oil interests, without any kind of check on his identity, merely because he was presumed to be an oilman – why couldn't another Russian agent . . . or several . . . or any number . . . carrying anything they liked – because neither they nor their effects would be searched – why couldn't they do it? No Customs, no Immigration – no police, even. Oil was king and oilmen princes – sacrosanct; or above suspicion?

There was no doubt in Gresson's mind that he'd penetrated the security of Great Britain with ridiculous ease, and he reckoned it was simply because rig owners were trusted to know precisely who and what was aboard their chartered helicopters. Naturally a rig owner wouldn't permit a foreign agent or, for example, arms and ammunition, to be carried on his helicopter. Unless, that is, the rig happened to be owned . . . by the KGB.

Gresson put the idea on paper and passed it to his Stavanger contact when he reached Norway the following day.

Within a year, a high department of the KGB bought a rig through unimpeachable nominees in Dublin. Six months later it was plying for hire in the offshore oilfields of the British North Sea, with Gresson in charge.

Although they didn't realise it at the time, Gresson had prepared the ground for the most breathtaking and audacious Soviet espionage strike in the history of the Communist master-State.

Target

ONE

Just as patriotism, according to Doctor Samuel Johnson, is the last refuge of the scoundrel, so treachery, he might have been heard to observe, is frequently the first refuge of the greedy, the fanatical or the fearful. It would have been a perceptive remark, and indeed prophetic in the case of the three people who came to Moscow in that December for each exemplified one of these fatal characteristics to the extent of wearing it like a second skin.

Roger Ainley, a marginally successful career diplomat in the British Foreign Service, was cursed with an appetite for money and the things it would buy which his background, salary and expectations could never begin to satisfy. He was blessed with a remarkably retentive memory and an utter lack of conscience, and he embraced espionage as another criminal might turn to forgery or fraud.

Sian Griffith was doubly dangerous . . . a fanatic for two causes. A few years younger than Ainley's forty-eight, she was a Welsh Nationalist by virtue of her birthright and the burning conviction she'd held since she was old enough to despise the English. She was a Communist by instinct and design. Her commitment was more cerebral than Gresson's, but equally as strong. If she were ever to be asked, though, to choose between the two causes, Russian would take a poor second place to Wales.

Paul Miernek was a Pole, and Poles have no love for Russians, nor Russians for Poles. The Russians kept Miernek's loyalty and services as an agent in Britain by holding the lives of his parents and their granddaughter – Miernek's child – in thrall. Miernek was forty-three, and had worked for his masters for fifteen years.

Ainley, surprisingly, had served the Soviet Union for

nearly twice as long. His character had been formed as the sneak of the minor public school which had only just accepted him. It was a talent that never deserted him, and since it was the only one he had, it seemed natural to turn it into a profession.

He was recruited to Communism in the Cambridge of the early 1950s when it was fashionable to be a fellow-traveller, and the influence of the insouciant Kim Philby, and the debonair homosexual Guy Burgess, were all-pervasive. Ainley's amorality, combined with a sometimes over-powering charm, made him an obvious candidate as an occasionally hyperactive sleeper. It never occurred to him to reject the university cell's advances once it became clear that money was involved. Ainley himself cheerfully admitted that it was unusual to meet anyone remotely as venal as he was.

Sian Griffith could claim almost to have been a founder member of Welsh nationalism in its modern, militant form. Both her parents were of that generation of Welsh children at the turn of the century who had been often – and some-times cruelly – punished at school for the crime of speaking the language they were born to, and which they used to the exclusion of any other until their English-style education commenced.

Through the old Free Wales Army she'd formed connec-tions with the hard men of the IRA – those whose younger brothers and sons would later create the Official IRA, the Marxist revolutionaries for whom Irish republicanism was merely the machinery with which to fashion a Green Socia-list Republic. She learned guns and bombs in the back streets of Ireland, and taught languages and literature in the schools of rural Wales. She taught hatred, too, but so subtly that it was made to merge with historical perspective.

Ainley arrived in the Russian capital legitimately with a British trade delegation; Sian Griffith quite properly with a mostly English package-tour, on a ticket she'd paid for herself. Miernek was the problem.

He was now a naturalised Briton running a hotel in Earls Court, catering to casual Central European traffic who were delighted to deal with a multi-linguist. The place doubled as a safe refuge and clearing house for anonymous KGB operatives either working on field projects or just passing through. He was well-liked and even respected, but as a native Pole he would needlessly arouse suspicion if he attempted to visit the Soviet Union, whose tyranny he had ostensibly fled.

Miernek could, however, go to Warsaw more or less at will, and the KGB unit that employed him used one of these trips to smuggle him into Russia. A telephone call before midnight in his Warsaw hotel (he wasn't permitted to stay with his parents) told him that a car booked by the State travel agency to take him on a tour combining sightseeing (obligatory for returning exiles) with a visit to his parents and daughter, would be waiting for him at seven the following morning.

The chauffeur didn't even look round as he got in, and after driving less than a mile they turned off the shopping street, and he was decanted into an underground car park. There he was transferred to an airport catering van of the type used for direct loading into an aeroplane's hold, when the whole body of the vehicle rose on hydraulic ramps to be swallowed up in the aircraft's belly. Barely twenty minutes later, the back doors of the van were thrown open, and Miernek walked out into an Illyushin 17 of Aeroflot, empty but for the flight crew.

The grimy grey cloud covering most of Northern Europe that day parted at the right moment to give him his first magical glimpse of the vast, snowy plain blanketing the approach to the Soviet capital. Tiny clumps of birch trees were the sole islands of relief in the monotonous patchwork of hundred-acre collective fields. Then the pattern was abruptly broken by the broad black ribbon of the three-lane highway that led to Moscow and, far away to the right, the dirty white outline of the city itself, merging so completely into its surroundings that it looked like a monolithic snow-drift fashioned by a regiment of demonic architects.

The Illyushin landed at Vnukova Two, the airfield to the south-west of the city reserved for VIPs and Government flights, a haven of order and peace compared to Tscheremotov, the recognised international airport. Miernek peered curiously at the terminal, apparently deserted behind its plate-glass windows. He was halfway down the steps leading from the plane when a big car, a Zim, with tinted rear windows, pulled up on the tarmac. A uniformed chauffeur got out and marched smartly round the bonnet to hold open the rear door for him. After the surly Warsaw driver, thought Miernek, the Russian was a prince of his calling.

The capital was initially disappointing, for the entire suburban sprawl seemed to Paul to consist solely of glaring white eight- and nine-storey flat blocks which effectively hid any sight of the old city. Soon the road widened into a dual carriageway, lined with dwellings built in the older, red-brick style, with shops at ground level.

Immediately above the shops the authorities of a bygone age had decreed that complicated decorative cornices should adorn the masonry, and many of the buildings now had nets suspended at first-floor level to catch the weighty fragments of crumbling stonework, which made walking under them slightly more hazardous than Russian Roulette.

The two lanes became eight, and they swept through the gates of the old city, across the stone river bridge, and up the hill past the Kremlin and the Twenty-fifth of October Square. A left turn took them into Gorki Street, and half-way down the Zim wheeled right, then immediately left through a narrow tunnel, and squealed to a halt in the dingy courtyard of a grey and forbidding pre-revolution house. The chauffeur saluted, Miernek nodded, and walked through the open front door. A hatless Red Army private took him up the ornate marble staircase and across a wide, quiet landing to a pair of polished oaken doors with heavy gilt handles. They opened inwards without any obvious human assistance, and he walked alone into a big, handsome room overlooking an inner – and infinitely more prepossessing – courtyard. The room had a high ceiling and contained three dominating portraits – of Vladimir Ilyitch Lenin, Leonid Brezhnev, and Yuri Andropov, the head of the Russian Bureau of State Security.

Underneath the portrait of Andropov stood the man he had come to see.

Nikita Ivanovitch sat, or rather stacked himself, behind the tiny desk, which served the dual purpose of storing only the most innocent and public of his correspondence, and of making him appear larger and even more grotesque than he already was. It was in any case a superfluous gesture, because he converted anything regular or symmetrical into a sympathetic ambience for his own shaggy bulk.

By an unhappy accident of nature (or the indulgent inbreeding of his aristocratic forebears), Ivanovitch bore all the natal characteristics of a misshapen dwarf while standing six feet four inches in thick woollen socks, and weighing in at eighteen stone on his groaning bathroom scales.

But the Head of the Special Task Force (an autonomous sub-division of the Second Chief Directorate) of the Komitet Gosudarstvennoi Bezopasnosti (the KGB), was not a man whose appearance could be lightly mocked. He held the power of life or death over ninety-nine out of a hundred of the men and women who trod the path to his little desk, the time-servers and party hacks, the grand functionaries of the State or the earnest departmental luminaries, the innocent and the guilty, the proud and the humble. His master, Yuri Andropov, was an obsessive bureaucrat, and Ivanovitch, by contrast, an adventurer, a soldier of fortune, who ran his department – sited well away from the main KGB complex – like a pirate ship.

With justice, few men were more feared in all Russia.

He might as well have left his bargain-price, furrowed, brown-serge suit on the peg off which he bought it for all the definition it lent his gross body. The dominant feature was the huge head, with hair so closely cropped it seemed in the first stages of recovery from an all-over shave. His nose jutted bluntly from a face cast out of a collection of uneven spheres, like a pyramid of fruit in a greengrocer's window. Sunk between ridges of fat under his shaven brows were the intense, burning, dark-grey eyes, mirrors of the fanatical zeal of a man still trying to atone for his aristocratic blood, in a Russia which had been torn by revolution ten years before he was born. As if to compensate for all the natural disasters visited on his person, he had splendid, even teeth and sweet breath.

Ainley, urbane as always, his legs crossed neatly, lolled in an armchair in the corner. Miernek was in a matching chair, but pressing on the hard edge of the uncomfortable seat. Sian Griffith sat stiffly and looked levelly at the Russian, challenging his gaze to penetrate beyond the thick lisle stockings and pleated tweed skirt. Ivanovitch took his time. For once he was unsure of his ground, driven into a course of action his instincts told him was wrong. Besides, by the very act of bringing together the three agents, he had increased the risk to all of them . . . perhaps beyond the point of recovery. But there was, he reasoned, no alternative. He was facing an appalling crisis.

He remembered previous holders of his job who had resorted to far less grandiose strategies than he proposed, and had paid unthinkable penalties for their failure. But in this case the balance of World power could – indeed, would – change unless he could prevent it. This time, it was failure that was unthinkable.

'We have discovered,' he said, 'that the British have developed a new –' he paused to clear his throat '– a new weapon; or, to be precise, a new version of an old weapon. It is a rocket capable of delivering a nuclear warhead to any point in the world. It is called ORBITMAN.

'The range is unlimited, because it is designed for orbital flight, and when I tell you that they have also discovered a new compact fuel source, making the device many times smaller than anything in production elsewhere, even in China, you will perhaps realize its true potential.'

He leaned forward; the cannonball head lifted slightly from his squat neck and mighty shoulders. A tiny bead of perspiration formed on his forehead and began to trickle and tickle its way down to his eye. It made him irrationally irritable, and he fought to regain control. 'Like the American "Cruise" missile, it is impossible to stop this weapon once it is launched. Worse than that, its very smallness,' his hands clawed into a cradle, as if they held the rocket, 'means it can be delivered from a mobile site – a ship, an aircraft – even a trailer. It doesn't need a concrete silo; therefore you cannot destroy it, even on the ground. And if you did by some chance discover a way to damage it directly, you would still have to find it. And it could be anywhere . . . anywhere.'

He drew back, folded his hands again, cracking the knuckles and seeing the delicate wince flit across Ainley's face. He picked up a long, black lantern-lecture pointer.

'We know that this weapon is being produced at the Royal Aircraft Establishment on the Welsh coast. Here'. He swung half round and slapped the tip of the stick precisely on Cardigan Bay on the wall-map. 'We also know that, probably to avoid drawing undue attention to the place, security has not been overtly stepped up. We intend, therefore,' the thick lips folded into a lupine grin, 'to take a sample from the more than adequate stocks they have there.'

Ivanovitch paused, intently studying the three faces as his words sank in. Miernek was a picture of mingled disbelief and fear. Sian Griffith uncrossed her legs and sat up, her mouth half open, her eyes alight, hissing out her breath, a bloom forming on her cheeks. But it was Ainley, whose expression never changed, that spoke first.

31

'You must be out of your mind.' His under-lip noticeably trembled. 'We'll all be caught. You're going to invade . . .? Christ, there'll be international dysentry. What the . . .

'Shut up,' snarled Nikita Ivanovitch. And then quietly, but with infinite menace, 'Shut up.' He saw that Miernek, too, was close to panic, so a third time, 'Shut up,' grating the words out with terrible deliberation.

'Listen to the plans we have made. All right,' he conceded, 'it is an outrageous scheme, but if properly executed, it will work,' Miernek relaxed slightly. Sian Griffith shot Ainley a look of deep contempt.

'As you know,' the Russian continued, 'we are always investigating the weak spots in any country's defences. Through our study of the North Sea Oil operations, we've found exactly what we're looking for.

'Nobody,' he held up a stubby finger, 'nobody monitors the movements of people travelling to and from an oil rig. There are no customs or immigration checks, because it is presumed that anyone returning to, say, Aberdeen from a rig must originally have left from Aberdeen to get to the rig.

'They cannot, in theory, have been anywhere else except out to the rig. Their presence, ostensibly coming back from a rig, is taken for granted. Therefore, if you have a way of getting people on to an oil rig secretly, you can bring them ashore without difficulty, at any time you choose.'

Ainley looked thoughtful. The old sod, he mused, had done it again. Ivanovitch allowed himself a brief, but genuine, smile.

'Obviously, you can also transport people, and merchandize, out of the country in the same way, because nothing and no one is checked – ever.'

Sian said, 'What are you going to do?'

'We are going to station a rig in the Irish Sea which has the facility to dock a submarine against one of its submersible pontoons. We shall transfer men and equipment from the submarine to the rig, and from there to the Welsh shore. We have devised the modern equivalent of the

Trojan Horse. The classic weapon.'

Miernek, he saw, was calmer now, Sian ever more wound up, and Ainley . . . well, Ainley was – Ainley; whose imperturbability would never shield his cowardice, whose greed and gullibility had led to his recruitment all those years ago at Cambridge. Ainley, who lacked even the smallest trace of fanaticism or commitment, was always the weak link, yet curiously competent and resourceful. He had a difficult and taxing role in the operation, and he would have to be persuaded. Ivanovitch decided to instruct the other two first.

'Miernek, we are going to need a base for surveillance, and I think there's no better place than a local hotel which has just come on the market. You're an established hotelier in London. You're a Pole, you speak several European languages, and your hotel has a reputation as a refuge for stranded foreigners. That's why you work for us.

'It would not, I think, seem unnatural that you should move to Cardiganshire, where soon there will be all manner of foreign nationals drifting about, to cash in on the Celtic Sea oil boom. We can then put our own people on the staff by recruiting through Poland in the normal way, and the rig team can also use it as a transit hotel. The money will be made available to you through discreet channels, and we're buying your London place with a nominee company.' Miernek nodded.

The glistening dome swivelled to Sian. 'Ms Griffith.' He was careful with the form of address, which he knew she appreciated.

'You will provide the local liaison for Miernek. You've lived in Cardiganshire, I believe, all your life?' She dipped her head in assent. 'And I've no doubt your friends in the Free Wales Army, who so love the English, can help with the explosives? As they did in the Irish matter a few years ago?' 'Yes,' Sian said, confidently.

'You may, if you wish,' Ivanovitch went on, 'have the Official IRA as well. It can be arranged.'

33

'No. We'll handle it,' Sian replied. 'There'll be some action, of course,' she said.

'Of course,' Ivanovitch nodded. 'Why don't you and Miernek go next door and see Marko? He has all the details. There are some things I want to discuss with Ainley.' They got up and left.

The Russian turned his enormous resources of guile and charm on Ainley, whom he despised. 'I wanted just the two of us to discuss this matter, for it is not for the ears of those on the lower rungs of the lader. It is a task which will demand considerable skill, tact and subtlety, and I am sure you will perform it supremely well.'

Ainley was impressed, but not overmuch. He knew the gloss only served to deodorise what was to come. Still, it was a bit much, coming from Old Nik; suddenly he felt better. The Russian's dislike of him grew as each sycophantic word found its target.

'You will already have appreciated,' Ivanovitch went on, 'that the crux of the problem is to get our rig stationed on one of the drilling blocks relatively close to the Cardigan Bay coast. I think our luck is in. The company which has the rights on Block 109, the most suitable site, is Pura Petroleum. They are, however, dragging their feet, and they haven't drilled for more than a year. I require them to restart at once – but not themselves. They are to sub-let the block to the drilling company we have already formed. This, of course, will only be possible with the consent of the British Department of Energy.

'You have been useful, very useful, to me in the past, Ainley. But do this, and the moon and stars are yours. You know what I want.' Ainley did. 'That marvellous period when you were at Cambridge, when austerity was retreating, when Britain basked in the post-war esteem of the world, still a Great Power. What a time that must have been to be young, and gifted, and what giants your year produced, did it not? Statesmen, politicians, prime ministers of at least three colours, industrialists, artists, millionaires, even a billionaire. Is that not so?' and Ainley agreed it was so. 'And among them . . .'

'Among them,' Ainley interrupted, 'Lindstrom and Canterwell.'

'As you say,' the Russian answered. 'Lindstrom and Canterwell. With you friend to all of them. Guide, counsellor, confidant.' He always spoke English with Ainley, which was strange because Ainley was a fluent Russian speaker. 'How assiduously you cultivated them. How carefully you watched them. How greedily you explored their little peccadilloes, their peculiarities, their kinks. They all trusted you, didn't they, Ainley? They were young, wild, brash and carefree. And now that they're older, wiser, successful, important, they've forgotten, haven't they? But not you, Ainley; not you.

'Since we recruited you, we've made you rich; and you and that priceless store of reminiscence coupled with your natural . . . flair? – for corruption . . . you've repaid us many times. It was one of the best day's work my illustrious predecessor Comrade Beria ever did to recruit you while you were still at college, and in the full flush of your discriminatory powers.'

Ivanovitch pulled a bulky file from his briefcase, to which his secretaries never under any circumstances had access. His eyes flickered over the fist page. 'Twenty-five years ago, wasn't it?

'Twenty-eight.'

'So it was,' Ivanovitch grinned again. It was not, Ainley thought, a pleasant sight. 'Goodness me, how time flies. But then, it was your very first . . . success, wasn't it?'

Ainley nodded. It was. Quite by chance, too, though of course he'd known about Lindstrom and the boy from Trumpington. They'd been seen having tea together at Grantchester. But Canterwell; brilliant, commanding, aggressive Canterwell . . . he'd been a surprise bonus. Just as well, Ainley thought as his mind strayed back, that he'd gone to the May Ball. Even though he was, in a sense, on overtime . . .

TWO

Tiny speckled moths played tag with the fairy lights strung along both sides of the river and across the triple-span bridges linking the meadows and Backs to Clare College, Trinity and St John's. Anyone with a senstive ear standing on Trinity Bridge could have been assaulted by at least three, if not more, near and distant strains of music, for the May Ball – by quirky tradition falling on the first Saturday in June – was not one dance, but many. At Trinity there were marquees in the Library quadrangle green, and on the bank of the Cam outside, and on the lawn leading down to the opposite bank, which sported the biggest marquee of all. It was the social event of the year, and the May Ball of 1950, with post-war austerity still biting deeply into the national conscience, bred a kind of desperate, defiant gaiety that was almost Edwardian in its innocence.

The fairy lights, of course, were certainly pre-Second World War. So were the vast majority of the full evening dress outfits worn by the gentlemen (no dinner-jackets at Trinity; tails, or you stayed home); some were said unkindly – but truly – to be pre-First World War. One ancient Professor sat huddled inside a moulding frock-coat with moth-eaten reveres which he was happy to acknowledge was purchased by his grandfather to celebrate the downfall of the Paris Commune in 1871, but since his memory was as elusive as his command of Horatian tags, a certain amount of doubt was cast on the veracity of his claim. Did he perhaps mean 1771? somebody asked. At any rate, he caused a mild sensation by dancing a veleta and revealing a pair of Cuban-heeled, button-up boots which quite genuinely belonged to one of his grandsire's happily less fecund mistresses.

The ladies – and how ravishingly they looked! – bought their dinner gowns if they could, and if they couldn't they practised the honourable wartime philosophy of 'make do and mend'. Their ingenuity was boundless, their complexions flawless, their corrugated coiffures seamless. And to young men fresh from military service, where dinner was poured on to a tin tray by greasy WRAC slatterns in repulsive denims and heavy duty clogs, their elegance was stupefying. To be young and beautiful on that night was to own the world.

The musicians – many of them gifted soloists in their own right – played Old Time for the old timers in the Library green marquee (not a few venerable ankles threatened dislocation in the St Bernard Waltz), and the very latest swing hits for the young bloods and their poppets on the big lawns. The sparkling, bobbing lights turned the towpath willows into droopy Christmas Trees, and on the grass outside the marquee across the Cam from Trinity, a string of glowing braziers barbecued sausages, chops and even gristly hunks of steak. On the facing lawns, outside the Library and New Court, coatless, black-trousered waiters shimmered between festive tables with lukewarm bottles of hock and sauterne and, just occasionally, ersatz champagne.

On the river, the punts which would later form perilous flotillas down to the Red Lion at Grantchester for breakfast, now paraded, bedecked and festooned, from college to college, ball to ball, lover to lover. It was extravagant and joyous and altogether beautiful, and it was no place for a murder to happen – but then, where is?

Trinity itself was ablaze with light – the Library green, New Court and Nevill's Court, the Hall and Great Court beyond – all but the chapel. Looking at the college from across the river, the towpath to the right led to a single-arched bridge and the punt moorings underneath it. It was the furthest extent to which dancers could walk, because in order to get to Clare you had to leave the grounds of Trinity and rejoin the main road along the Backs. Unless, that is, you went by water.

To the left, however, people were walking along the bank at the foot of the Trinity lawns and marquee, and where the river made a right-hand bend a canal had been cut, crossed by a quaint little iron footbridge. If you followed the path there, you came to the glorious vista of St John's College, with its three-arched bridge affording entry to the college itself and, a few yards upriver, the closed and mysterious Bridge of Sighs.

Roger Ainley was on the lawn in front of the Library, sitting at a table recently vacated by an obviously wealthy party of six. By draining all the glasses and the assorted near-dead or half-dead bottles into one, he'd assembled three-quarters of a bottle of interesting, if eclectic, wine. He ordered the table to be cleared, and sat in solitary state waiting for inspiration, or a victim, or preferably both. Ainley was old in the ways of treachery, innuendo and extortion. He was now dabbling in their application to the cause of Communism.

He pinpointed his targets immediately they came in view and, being the single-minded young man he was, never doubted that the evening would be profitable. They walked past his table from the direction of the college, obviously intending to cross the bridge and make for the marquee on the lawn. He followed about twenty yards behind.

He knew two of them well . . . or at least he knew of them; they were not his friends. He didn't have friends, yet he wasn't by any means unpopular. He just made it his business to know everybody, and thus spent no appreciable length of time with anybody. He was easy to talk to, dangerously easy. People told Ainley things they didn't tell their friends; unlike the man in the fable who could not tolerate the burden of a dreaded secret and whispered it to a hole in the ground, the Trinity undergraduates of Ainley's year whispered their secrets to him. Sometimes he didn't even have to ask them.

He greeted perhaps a dozen young men crossing the bridge, and a dozen more before he reached the marquee, and nearly everyone he met inside, including the Master of Trinity. The Master's wife said, 'What a charming boy,' and the Master nodded benignly but didn't reply, because he'd known both Kim Philby and Guy Burgess, and he had a feeling about Ainley that he was never, alas, to put into words. Ainley sighted his quarry, and bided his time. The band finished 'American Patrol' and started 'Moonlight Serenade' and Ainley decided to dance. He liked the foxtrot; he liked the freedom it gave his hands, the feel of a girl dancing really close to him, the smell of her hair, the scent of her breath, the delicate pressure of her body.

Because he was young and slim and boyishly handsome with sleek yellow hair and laughing blue eyes and perfect manners it took him about twenty seconds to find a girl who would let him stroke her bottom to Glenn Miller (freely adapted). Her name was Cynthia and she brushed his erection eleven times before the dance ended. He looked around for the men he'd followed, and they were still there. Suddenly they got up to leave, and Ainley bade Cynthia a reluctant farewell.

The elder of the two with whom he was acquainted was fractionally taller than he was; an impossibly beautiful man called Hugo Lindstrom, eighteen months older than Ainley, rich and acute and talented, with jet-black hair over an exquisitely chiselled, aquiline face, slim shoulders and a narrow waist. With him was Lewis Canterwell, Ainley's height, rugged and square, a formidable athlete and scholar, middle middle-class, and not nouveau enough to be riche. That both were homosexual – Lindstrom ardently so, Canterwell hesitantly but then demandingly – had not even been suspected by each other until Ainley thoughtfully introduced them. He was continually helpful to people in that special way of his.

All the previous summer he'd watched and followed them, observing, noting, planning. He saw them together, and separately, and together with other boys, and separately with different boys again. He once caught Canterwell with a girl and told Lindstrom about it, but she turned out to be Lindstrom's sister. The boy who was with the two of them now, in close-fitting hired tails, had been with both men many times. He was sweetly pretty, his name was Robin, and he worked in a cycle repair shop in Trumpington.

What made Ainley stick so closely to them on the night of the 1950 May Ball was the total certainty that something – he didn't know what – was going to happen. Over the spring months both men had individually told him that Robin was getting to be a problem. He was indiscreet, talkative and modestly avaricious. His greed didn't bother Lindstrom, who had money and lust in abundance to satisfy his little friend. Even Canterwell didn't mind the occasional treat, provided Robin's smooth white flanks came as the pay-off. But neither man was prepared to submit to outright, vicious blackmail, and neither could face the prospect of exposure, disgrace, and the likelihood of a stiff prison sentence. They had, they thought, even then too much to lose. Canterwell, a budding idol of the Union and a brilliant debater, was poised for a career in politics; Lindstrom was confident that his money and his charm would bring him prestige and power in the City. What, Ainley wondered, would they do about little Robin? What could they do?

When they walked from the marquee to the strains of 'In the Mood' they went to the river bank and turned left along the path. The punts drifted aimlessly by, the fairy lights glowed warmly in the willows and lit the suddenly, maddeningly deserted bank. If Ainley followed then now, and any of the three turned round, he'd be spotted for sure.

He cursed feelingly, and broke into a run. He made the bridge and pushed through a jostling, laughing crowd of richly drunk Rowing Club hearties, then sprinted past the

Library and through the Great Court to the main entrance of the college in Trinity Street.

He cannoned into a startled porter, who said, "Ere, 'ere, young gentleman,' which was a porter's traditional form of reproof, out onto the street, spun left, and a couple of hundred yards further on turned left again and in at the front door of St John's. He knew the college well – he had acquaintances there – and it took him less than a minute to wheedle his way on to the Bridge of Sighs, where he crouched in one of the four stone-latticed arches and saw Canterwell, Lindstrom and Robin reach the triple-span St John's Bridge. There, because of the bend in the river, they were invisible to the remnants of the Trinity Ball taking a breather and to the revellers of St John's, for the lawn ran steeply down to the Cam where the three young men walked.

There was no path on the opposite bank: just the grey walls of one of the minor buildings of the college. Just enough light came from the college and the marquee on St John's lawn to show the three stopping by an enormous beech tree low down on the bank. Canterwell was crouching within a couple of feet of the water. He was pointing at something in Ainley's general direction, and Ainley ducked his head for a second before he realised that it couldn't be him; he was well-concealed. A punt came under St John's Bridge containing a furious girl with a torn dress who was methodically beating a young man over the head with a ukelele. Canterwell straightened up and beckoned to Robin, pointing once more . . . at the bridge itself.

Now Ainley knew what it was. The light would be just sufficient to see it, a mark on the stone and a date, March 14, 1947 – the day on which the Cam, swollen by spring rains, had flooded to that precise point. Robin had obviously never seen it before.

The boy took Lindstrom's hand and allowed himself to be lowered down the bank in the shadow of the huge tree. The fairy lights still twinkled and the bands still played and the distant dancers still danced and laughed and sang and ate and drank, as Canterwell caught Robin by his neatly fashioned bow tie and hauled him into the river.

He struggled more than Canterwell thought he would, and when an empty punt bumped into a pillar of the bridge and veered over towards their banks it forced him to loosen his grip. Robin's head was still more than half under water, and Canterwell seized the long punt pole and jammed the rounded wooden end into the hollow between his shoulder and neck, where it crushed the starch out of his collar and the life from his body, because he didn't come up for a long, long time.

Canterwell got to his feet, plucked the handerchief from his top pocket, and sponged the water on his trousers. Lindstrom, who cried easily, was crying. Canterwell put his arm around his lover's shoulders and guided him back to the Trinity May Ball.

Roger Ainley could hardly believe his luck. He went back into St John's and found his way quickly to the bridge. The revelry was going strong on St John's lawn, and a marvellously evocative sight it was, Ainley thought. He sauntered across the bridge, then ducked down at the far side and slipped over the edge to the bank.

The punt was still there, its prow stuck in a patch of soft earth. Ainley prudently left it in place, and arranged the pole against the bank at what he hoped was an artistically convincing angle. Robin was floating face down in the water, and Ainley pulled him on to dry land. He searched the boy thoroughly and took everything he could find in his pockets and, as afterthought, a signet ring from the wedding finger of his left hand. Then he stood up and gently rolled the body back into the river with his foot.

He put his prizes into he pocket of his tails, and he, too, went back to the ball. Cynthia was still there, and greeted him warmly, if a little drunkenly. She proved to be only a mildly interesting lay, though willing to learn, she assured him.

Later, by arrangement, he joined Lindstrom and Canterwell for breakfast at Grantchester, and they solemnly agreed what a splendid night it had been.

THREE

The hands on the short-case Bristol clock crept round to
10.20 . . . 10.35 . . . 10.40. The reception room of the
banqueting suite in the Collingwood Hotel at Milford
Haven was awash with Pura Petroleum executives. The talk
was animated, and of business. The room was stately and
sombre with age, solidly rather than tastefully furnished,
the carpet deep-piled, the drapes of weighty, red-on-red
patterned velveteen, and the low beams, architraves and
dado of gleaming black.

Executives (senior) tittered dutifully at aldermanic
quips; executives (upper management, but not senior)
brayed in support; executives (middle management) hooted
like consumptive seals; executives (junior) bid fair to wet
themselves deciding which was the best noise to make.

Only Lindstrom – indisputably the Chief Executive and
therefore not bound by the rules – found his eyes straying to
the clock. The First Citizen was an amiable enough fellow,
he thought, but scarcely incandescent. He allowed himself
an occasional weakening of the structure of his mouth
which then lapsed into, rather than formed, a smile. It was
an almost unconscious reflex, the vaguest of polite reactions
as the First Citizen droned relentlessly on – 'Milford Haven
this, Milford Haven that, oil basin, prosperity, good for
trade, wonderful to have your new refinery' – and Lindstrom nodded and smiled, nodded and smiled. He would
possibly not have bothered had he appreciated that it was
his feeble gestures to minimal courtesy that triggered the
chain reaction of manic hilarity among his subordinates as
upper took the cue from senior and passed it to middle, who
tossed it to junior, who savaged it and shipped it to PR and
advertising (the base of every management pyramid).

There it rested uneasily in cryogenic animation until Lindstrom chose to revive it.

10.52 – Canterwell was late. This time the Mayor noticed the movement of Lindstrom's eyes.

'Secretary of State's a bit behind-hand,' he said, eyeing the unopened bottles of champagne in the ice buckets, and the crisp white cloths forming a miniature Andes over the no doubt succulent buffet luncheon.

He downed his fifth whisky and remarked, 'Still, we've got to see this lot off – ' nodding at the advance guard of gin, scotch, vodka, martini and campari, waiting patiently (but not for long) on the bar – 'before we can get round to that lot – ' indicating the champagne.

'And open our new refinery – don't forget that, Mr Mayor,' Lindstrom said with a chuckle.

The result of such genuine and spontaneous warmth on the Chief Executive's part could well have been cataclysmic and might easily have led to multiple bladder strangulation in the lower ranks, had not MacLeish (engineering) tip-toed up to Lindstrom and whispered, 'He's downstairs,' which wiped the smile from his face.

Lindstrom's feeling of unease always nagged at him when he was due to meet Canterwell. But why was it so strong today? Like so many people, he was a devotee of astrological predicition, and susceptible to premonitions and omens. He had been touched by the stirring of a premonition a few days before and he'd only just realised that it might have been an extra-strong emanation of Canterwell-phobia.

Something particularly bad was going to come out of today's meeting, this he knew with absolute certainty. Yet it was an irrational fear. Never once during their infrequent encounters had Canterwell even mentioned Cambridge, let alone that fateful May Ball night. He may indeed have forgotten it . . . but no, Lindstrom thought. No, one does not forget an act of murder.

But his anxiety, logic told him, was misapplied. Canterwell and he, after all, were a threat to each other, so neither could be a danger to either. Could he?

Lindstrom relaxed fractionally and composed himself. He was in his fiftieth year, and wore his age well. Discreetly used make-up helped shade the scores left by the whips of time. He was still an aggressive seducer and sometimes brutal lover. Simon – he of the chestnut curls and tender, flawless buttocks – would betray genuine fear at the force of Lindstrom's ardour which served only to excite Lindstrom beyond restraint, and then it was all tears, contrition, gold watches.

Lust fleetingly transfixed his lean, classically sculptured face, with the grey temple wings carefully moulded over his perfect ears. But he checked the spasm, and it was replaced by a frisson of dread as Canterwell came into the room, flanked by his toadies.

The years, Lindstrom decided, had dealt kindly with the politician, too. He was upright and beautifully proportioned, bouncing with confidence, his chin firm and his belly flat, the creases from his nose to the corners of his mouth emphatic and symmetrical rather than disfiguring, the honey-brown eyes shrewd and penetrating, and the lines of his strong, square face and the crisp waves of his dark, abundant hair untroubled and unruffled, either by age or modest depravity. 'Still the best I ever had,' Lindstrom reflected.

Canterwell bounded across the floor like a well-dressed kangaroo. He grasped the Mayor's outstretched hand and pumped it ecstatically.

'Mr Pugh, isn't it,' he said, with obvious pleasure at their reunion. The mayor basked in the glow of recognition. The aide with Canterwell grinned his relief. He hadn't been sure the boss had caught the whispered name that followed the query Canterwell hissed at him in the doorway: 'What's this Welsh twat called?'

The politician turned to Lindstrom, and with just the right soupçon of reserve when addressing an industrialist, said, 'Hugo. Good to see you. You're well, I trust?'

'Very well, Minister, thank you,' Lindstrom replied.

Downstairs at the reception desk, another man whom twenty-eight years had treated with tolerant affection passed a credit card over the counter to pay for his two nights' lodging.

I have some business in Milford Haven today,' he told the clerk in his brisk, indefatigably superior voice. 'It would suit me very well to leave my case in your excellent care.'

'Of course, sir. Our pleasure.'

'I'm obliged,' the man said. He made to leave, but then turned again to the desk.

'What's going on upstairs?'

'Ah, big do today, sir,' the clerk said, the Welsh lilt creeping back into the carefully modulated neutrality of his cadences. 'New oil refinery opening for Pura Petroleum in the Haven. They're all there,' jerking his well-groomed head heavenwards. 'plus,' he leaned forward confidentially, 'the Energy Minister, Mr Canterwell. Just gone up, he has.'

'Hmm,' the man said. 'Glad I missed him. Can't stand the fellow.'

'Quite frankly, Mr Ainley,' said the clerk, who made a point of agreeing with everyone, 'Neither can I.'

Driving his own car for a change (and enjoying it), Lindstrom entered the warren of little streets off the Earls Court Road, passed the Indian restaurant Ainley had specified, and parked around the next bend. The restaurant was one of a cosmopolitan family of eating places, varying in decor and persuasion from garish to blatant. Only the Indians – who all came from Sylhet region of Assam, in what had been West Bengal, and was now Bangladesh – had any real class.

Ainley, sitting at a corner table on a raised platform at the rear (it was like being in the circle of a tiny, aromatic cinema), thought that the only common identity in the street was struck between the Indian restaurant and the launderama opposite, in that both managements sought to take their customers to the cleaners. But the food was genuinely excellent as well as expensive, and Ainley valued the place for important contact dinners in surroundngs of total discretion.

There was another reason why he'd chosen it. The serving staff seemed to be uniformly possessed of appealingly diminutive stature, satin-smooth dark ivory skins, delicate, fragile features and alarmingly cocquettish eyes, and since they were all men, the prospect should suit Lindstrom admirably. The wallpaper was the mandatory orange flock; ornately carved (and slightly dented) brass plates, jugs and figurines winked dimly in the low lighting; and above and to the right of Ainley's head, in a back-lit alcove, was an unusual bust of the goddess KALI, unusual because the deity whose trademark was six sinuously-poised arms, in this representation had none at all. A sort of Venus de Kali, Ainley mused. Obviously an oversight.

How easy it had all been, he thought yet again. Almost as if Lindstrom was prepared for his approach – or at least prepared for something to happen that concerned himself and Canterwell. At Milford Haven, Ainley had endured (uninvited) the tedious ceremony at the refinery, and afterwards mingled (uninvited) with the guests at the Collingwood. It needed barely a minute of conversation with the briefly unchaperoned chief executive to leave Lindstrom in no doubt as to what Ainley wanted, and that he was serious when he threatened exposure of that long-past instant of criminal folly. Ainley hadn't been subtle, he hadn't had time to be. 'I'll be in touch,' he'd warned, giving Lindstrom a broad wink and standing with his back to Canterwell as the Secretary of State loped over to bid his host goodbye.

'Now,' he thought, watching Lindstrom mount the dais and make for his table. 'Now for the reckoning.'

'Hugo,' he said, getting up and smiling warmly, 'how good of you to come.'

'Had I any choice?'

'No, you hadn't.'

They agreed to share sheema kebabs, chicken tikka, rogan josht, aloo dag and pillau rice with side bowls of lady's fingers, and fresh mangoes to follow. The lager was exorbitant and the coffee foul. During the meal Ainley explained in more detail why he wanted the drilling rights on Block 109 in the Celtic Sea sublet to Taraco Ltd.

'It's not going to worry you, Hugo old boy,' he said. 'Drop in the ocean – sorry, unintended – but it is, for you, isn't it? I mean, even if they strike oil, it won't matter, will it? Besides being micks they'll probably think it's treacle and have it all made into toffee.'

Lindstrom smiled faintly. He could, he felt, afford to. Ainley was right; it wasn't a difficult proposition. The Pura board might even applaud him for negotiating a sub-lease. Like most oil multi-nationals they were (precisely as Ivanovitch had said) dragging their feet in both the North and Celtic Seas until the woefully insubstantial fabric of the British National Oil Corporation crumbled, and the pickings became richer under a right-wing government.

'Agreed,' he said. 'But of course, it doesn't finally rest with me.'

Ainley sat back, dabbed at his mouth with a hot, scented flannel handed him by an epicene waiter using a pair of iron tongs, and said, 'No. Lewis has to be in favour, too. Am I right?'

'You are.'

'Then that's simple. You will persuade him.'

'That,' Lindstrom said, 'I'm afraid I cannot do.'

'Cannot?'

'Will not.'

Ainley leaned forward, put his elbows on the table, picked up a paper packet of sugar and, without opening it, dropped it into Lindstrom's discarded cup of lukewarm coffee. It splashed the oilman's Italian silk tie.

'Oh yes you will, Hugo,' he drawled. 'Indeed you will.'

Gresson leaned on the rail of TARACO FIVE, and gazed moodily out over the grey expanse of water. The rig was a hundred and fifty miles from landfall and the horizon was unbroken. Even in the best of weather, the big man thought, the North Sea kept its cold, slate colour, and when the sky was blue (as it was today) it served only to make the sea appear by contrast more inhospitable.

He pulled himself off the rail, turned, and half sat on it, looking up to the peak of the swaying derrick. It wasn't the grinding monotony of life at sea and the routine of the rig that depressed him, but the certainty that TARACO FIVE would leave the North Sea and the service of Caledonian Explorations Inc. without striking so much as a gas deposit, let alone oil.

Gresson waved automatically as the bearded face of Larsen, the toolpusher, showed briefly at the window of his cabin above. The Dane flapped a hand at him.

Whatever else he may have been – and mere men, he knew had called him many things in his life, but never to his face – Gresson was first and foremost an oilman. His commitment to the cause of his Russian paymasters was (unlike Roger Ainley's) fierce and unswerving. He'd always known TARACO FIVE was *the* rig – the one for which Ivanovitch was planning something special, the one commissioned by the KGB as soon as Gresson's observations on unrestricted movement had filtered down through the Kremlin. So it was no surprise when the order came to tow the rig to a dry dock in Pembroke for a refit, to prepare it for its new role in the Celtic Sea. But it was the additional inference that annoyed Gresson – the North Sea operation was to be abandoned as a dry well.

He took it as a personal affront, yet the logic was incontrovertible. They'd drilled more than twelve thousand feet before the petroleum geologists shook their heads and said it was pointless going on. Still Gresson hadn't quite accepted it. Still – against all the scientific evidence – he had the intuitive feeling that just a little further down there was something there.

A call from the toolpusher's cabin snapped him out of his black mood. Glad of something to do, he took the steel steps at a run and within seconds was standing on what would be equivalent on a ship to the bridge.

Larsen sank back down in the swivel chair which gave him a commanding view of the entire drilling operation. He looked pensively over the top of an impressive communications console, linking him to intercoms, telephones, control switches, and a relay display of all the essential information available to him, particularly of the expected movements of wind and weather – very often decisive influences in the North Sea.

The toolpusher was comfortably huge and shaggy – not aggressively so, like the giant bargemaster. All the same, Larsen was one of the few people Gresson made a point of never shoving around. There was only one man alive that Gresson truly feared. Nikita Ivanovitch.

'Vell, Mick,' Larsen said in his fractured English. 'Eversing goes damn OK, ja? No?'

'I thought you were going to have the roustabouts off by this morning,' the bargemaster replied, brusquely. 'It's not going to leave us long for our test if the tugs get here on time day after tomorrow.'

'Ah don't vorry, Mick, I tell you, don't vorry.' Larsen said soothingly, tugging his beard with a hairy, spatulate hand. 'Ve shall have ze rig clear by tonight. Ze helicopters have been ordered, and zere vill be plenty of time to finish tinks off before your precious submarine gets here in ze mornink.'

Gresson grunted and turned to go back down the stairway, but then Larsen chuckled and boomed. 'If you really vant somezink to vorry about, chust tink how you're going to explain to ze people in ze dry dock vy it iss you have a pressure lock in one of ze pontoons.'

Gresson looked over his shoulder and grinned. 'Listen, fungus-face,' he said, 'the explanation – though I doubt whether a knucklehead like you would appreciate it – is not only credible, but true. It so happens that the pressure chamber doubles as a release point for divers in bad weather. See? It's so simple – and so efficient – that I'm surprised nobody's thought of it before.'

Larsen gave a long, appreciative whistle. He was impressed. As well he might be . . . the idea had been another master-stroke on Gresson's part, providing an obvious and acceptable answer to a seemingly insoluble snag.

At dawn the periscope of the Russian submarine *Slavyanka* broke the still, cold surface of the sea. One of the older members of the Soviet fleet, built in the mid-fifties, she had been retired to research duties. Indeed more than half of her class, known to NATO by the codename 'Whisky', had been progressively withdrawn.

It was the designation 'VA' alone that saved the *Slavyanka* and one of her sister ships from the same fate, and launched them on a new career as oceanographic research vessels.

They earned this life-saving classification because both were fitted with external hatches to enable them to release divers under water. It had not taken long for Ivanovitch and his boffins – acting on Gregson's brainwave – to search out a sub that matched his description. They then modified the device to allow it to mate with the one on the rig pontoon, and so enable men to walk unhindered from the boat on to the rig.

It took an hour and forty minutes of careful manoeuvering, with the aid of the underwater television cameras and the rig's two resident divers, to line up the steel flanges, and insert the bolts to make the connection airtight. The water was blasted out in a matter of minutes, and it was time to put the theory into practice.

Gresson gingerly unwound the securing bolts on the watertight hatch, conscious that at eighty feet below the surface, a break in the seal could destroy both rig and submarine. If there had been the slightest error, the hatch would give under the force of a monster tidal wave and engulf him. But when he looked down, holding his breath, he saw the equivalent of only a few cupfuls of water splash on to the steel floor of the pontoon. Then he brought his head up again and stared straight into the eyes of a young, fair-haired Russian submariner, who'd been performing the same operation on the other side.

Gresson was not an imaginative man, and only rudimentarily educated, but on an impulse he raised his arm in a mock salute and intoned, dramatically, 'Hail, warrior of Greece.'

The Russian, who'd actually read his Homer, looked at him in utter mystification. But Gresson didn't care. He chuckled, then laughed, then roared and spluttered, 'Don't you see, Ivan me boy? Don't you see? The Trojan Horse. It works, lad, it works.'

A beatific smile of comprehension split the serious young seaman's face. There in a man-made tunnel not far from the ocean floor, the American and the Georgian danced a frantic, whooping czardas.

FOUR

Canterwell rose to his feet in the third quarter of Question Time in the House of Commons and said, 'Yes. No. Three years. Eighteen million pounds on contract, but we've agreed to to underwrite a possible increase in the price of beryllium. Yes, there are penalty clauses.' He sat down.

The question to the Rt. Hon. the Secretary of State for Energy had been framed by the Hon. Gentleman and Member for Medmenham (North) in five parts, and was intended to elicit new information, impress his constituents that he was both well-informed and diligent, confound the Minister, and gain publicity for the Hon. Gentleman.

The speaker called his name for a supplementary, and he got up automatically, opened and closed his mouth a few times, finally stammering a request for the Rt. Hon. Gentleman to tell the House the unvarnished truth about this latest Nuclear Reactor Contract, only for Canterwell to rise again and say, 'I just did.' (Laughter). The Hon. Gentleman sat down, acutely aware that he'd achieved none of his objectives.

Three-thirty arrived, and the Minister of State for Education and Science resumed his seat, after taking the last quarter of Question Time. He dabbed his brow with a patterned handkerchief. The sartorial infelicity, coupled with his poor showing over the past fifteen minutes, virtually ensured his removal in the next reshuffle. Canterwell glanced at Miles Paulfrey on his right, and Paulfrey nodded. It was often said that in Cabinet the Energy Secretary and the Prime Minister were almost telepathic in their understanding. Elsewhere, too, Canterwell thought.

The Speaker intoned 'The Prime Minister', and Paulfrey rose and made a statement on Phase Two of the Contract for

National Unity. The Leader of the Opposition and various Shadows, with the Chancellor and Canterwell backing up Paulfrey, turned it into a spirited half-hour, and the Prime Minister even stayed to hear Canterwell's own statement on the prospects for the Celtic Sea Oilfield. They left the House together.

Talmidge, Canterwell's Parliamentary Private Secretary, travelled back in Canterwell's car to the tower block on Millbank which housed the Department of Energy.

'Not a bad show today, sir,' Talmidge observed, using the respectful form of address for the sake of the departmental minion in the front passenger seat. Talmidge had long ago decided to hitch his waggon to Canterwell's ascending star, and he'd not yet regretted the liaison. In private he was on first-name terms – a privilege granted by Canterwell in return for Talmidge's services as PPS, informer, hatchet-man and (on four occasions) pimp.

'Gave as good as we got, Mark,' Canterwell replied. 'Truth to tell, they're not much opposition these days.'

He looked at his watch. 'Anything urgent for me back at the office, do you know, Chambers?'

'I believe not, Minister,' the Department's deputy chief press officer replied in his clipped, prissy voice. 'I checked before I came to meet you down at the House.' (Like many Whitehall hangers-on, Chambers employed an extraordinary affection with this particular phrase, so that it came out almost as 'dine at the Hice').

Canterwell winced; Talmidge grinned. 'And?' Canterwell asked acidly.

'The only communication which could be classified as remotely urgent was a personal message asking you to telephone Mr Hugo Lindstrom, of Pura Petroleum. I believe he's the chair . . .'

'I'm perfectly aware of his position,' Canterwell broke in. 'Did he say what it was about.?'

'I wasn't informed so, Minister. The message from your secretary was that you should be told as soon as possible.'

Astonishingly, Chambers was addicted to writing racy handouts on oil (when he was permitted to), and had an encyclopaedic command of oilfield jargon. A few of his unedited efforts, smuggled out of the Department by a disloyal and short-lived office junior, were collectors' items in Fleet Street.

'Probably the Celtic Sea oilfield,' Talmidge suggested.

'Hm?'

'Lindstrom, sir.'

'Oh – eh, yes. Possibly.'

Could it be, he wondered? Could it really be something as innocent as the business of taking oil from the seabed – something as unimportant as politics or high finance? Could the man who was capable of singlehandedly destroying everything Canterwell had worked for, striven to build . . . position, his reputation, his impressive charisma – even his marriage – have telephoned with no more than a simple request for assistance from a Government department?

No, Canterwell decided as the big limousine purred into the car park at the tower. Something unprecedentedly grave must have happened, because in the process of unmasking Canterwell – should it come to that – Lindstrom would, of course, destroy himself. Even though Canterwell was bitterly aware that Lindstrom possessed an asset which would cushion him against the effects of ultimate disaster, his immense wealth.

Something must have occurred – of that Canterwell was sure. For by the very act of 'phoning, Lindstrom had broken a mutual embargo that had lasted twenty-eight years. The contacts between the two men were as infrequent, brief and formal as they could decently observe, and dictated by chance or by the course of events.

But never once, since they left Cambridge had either actively sought to summon the other. No calls, no letters, no assignations – at no time, ever, a bilateral attempt to break the silence.

Until now.

Canterwell had said, 'It's my private office line. You can talk freely.' And Lindstrom did.

Now they faced each other in the Energy Minister's study at his home in Kensington Gore, and it was eight minutes past midnight. Lindstrom had come from a select dinner party which followed a visit to Covent Garden where he'd entertained an Australian mineralogist to an evening of opera.

'*Otello*,' he told Canterwell. 'You know, Verdi. It seemed appropriate for someone about to be involved once again in a conspiracy.'

He revealed the substance of Ainley's proposal.

'I don't even remember him,' Canterwell said. 'Can he do what he says he can do?'

'Implicate us absolutely, you mean?'

'Yes.'

'I think he can, yes. He saw it, you know. He was on the Bridge of Sighs.'

'Doing what?'

'Watching us.'

'Why?'

'That's the kind of thing he did,' Lindstrom said, spreading his hands and fluttering his fingers vaguely. 'He watched people, learned about them, studied them, found out about them.'

'Does he have proof?'

'He saw Robin and me, Robin and you, all three of us, at various times. He's got dates, places.'

'He's just a dirty little nark, then.'

'For God's sake, Lewis, he saw us kill Robin. He's got my signet ring – the one I gave Robin. He knows, Lewis, he knows.'

'He's got to be able to prove it, Hugo. Otherwise, nothing doing.'

'All right. He says there's something else – irrefutable. I don't know what it is. Even without it, he could cause an enormous amount of trouble.'

58

'And how do *you* know, Hugo,' Canterwell asked, 'that he won't? Even if we agree to the oilfield concession. How do you know that he won't go on – and on – and on?'

'I would guess he's being well enough paid for what he's doing. I wouldn't think there's anything else that could possibly persuade you or me to go any further than we are prepared to go at the moment. I've already decided to do as he wants with the Celtic Sea block. Normally, if a company such as mine wishes to sublet in this way, approval from your Department is virtually automatic. Why shouldn't it be so in this case?'

Canterwell slumped back in his chair, ruffled his hair and stroked his hand down the length of his face to pinch the cleft in his chin and form into a decisive fist.

'All right.'

Lindstrom was immensely relieved. 'You couldn't take the chance of exposure, Lewis,' he said.

Within a fortnight the Department of Energy had agreed to the subletting of the oil drilling rights on Block One Zero Nine in the Celtic Sea, leased by Pura Petroleum Incorporated, to Taraco Limited, of Henry Street, Dublin, Republic of Ireland.

The following day a neatly wrapped little package arrived at Lindstrom's house. Inside was a note saying, Many thanks for your help – Roger.

Lying on a bed of cotton wool was a slim gold signet ring bearing the initials RS. Engraved on the inner face were the words HUGO TO ROBIN. FEBRUARY, 1950.

FIVE

Sleightley twisted his torso to the required angle for near-side rear viewing. He eyed the parking space speculatively, played the clutch and eased his second-best car – a 1932 Lanchester – uncertainly back. As usual, it took him two tries, but his temper remained serene. It was a fine spring day. He glanced in either direction, and with studied non-chalance – and just a smidgeon of shame – slipped into the meter one of the special tokens devised by Pond. It not only shot the indicator round a full two hours, but wouldn't release it by so much as a minute, and then inevitably a perplexed traffic warden popped a plastic bag over the meter's head and called an engineer to unjam it. Sleightley used the tokens only twice a week. As a senior Civil Servant, he thought that was just about right. Pond, who didn't own a car, regarded the whole proceedings with lofty disdain from their secretaries' front-facing office.

Sleightley looked up – he always did – at the handsome salmon-pink shell over the front door of the remarkably gracious building. He pushed the door open and walked in. Upstairs, Pond waited for the sound of the tightly furled umbrella hitting the pimply tin floor of the hall stand. Sleightley's homburg enveloped an unoccupied branch above it, he coughed delicately to signal his approach, and started up the broad, oaken staircase.

The cough never ceased to amuse Pond. In the wildest stretches of his imagination he could not fathom what communal activity between himself, Miss Bunce and Mrs Costello Sleightley feared he might one morning interrupt if he didn't cough to announce his arrival. He turned from the window, placed his hands behind his back, and beamed expectantly. Following his invariable practice, Sleightley

60

pushed open the door, poked his head into the room, and said 'Ah.'

'No, we're not,' said Pond.

'I beg your pardon?'.

'We're not engaged in some complex oriental exercise in sexual troilism.'

Sleightley regarded him gravely. 'If I had the slightest idea what you're talking about,' he said, 'I should without doubt be as outraged as Miss Bunce and Mrs Costello must be at that grossly unseemly suggestion. Good morning, ladies.'

'Good morning, Sir,' they said, totally indifferent to the ludicrous exchanges.

'Now, unless you wish me to summon medical assistance for you,' he turned to Pond, 'I suggest we go into the office and review the current – ah – business.'

'By all means'.

Mrs Costello mouthed to Miss Bunce, 'Perhaps you would kindly bring in the contents of the morning box when they are duly assembled,' and broke off as Sleightley peered around the door again and said, 'Perhaps you would kindly bring in the contents of the morning box when they are duly assembled,' and she replied, 'Yes, sir'.

Like most experienced and supremely competent secretaries in the upper echelons of the Civil Service, they regarded their departmental heads with affection and resigned tolerance. Neither of them ever entered the electronically sealed, sound-proofed office where Sleightley and Pond worked without being expressly invited. But they were not fools. They knew they worked for British Intelligence, they'd both signed the Official Secrets Act, and they were acutely aware that Department RE (Research and Evaluation) was not only clearly unorthodox, but also highly important.

Beyond that, they had not the slightest conception of the real functions of the department they served so loyally and efficiently. They trafficked in names, places, supplies and travel arrangements, not in clandestine electronic surveillance and murder, and outside the building they were discretion itself.

Only one thing bothered them. None of their wide circle of friends in the Service knew anything about Department RE, either. And one always learned more about one's employers in the Civil Service from outside the department than from daily contact with one's bosses inside. Furthermore they felt they were not contributing to the essential circulation of inspired gossip. While Miss Bunce and Mrs Costello (who emphasized the first syllable of her name, after the Irish fashion) received their due quota of chit-chat about other offices — especially from Miss Parminter at SIS – they were unable to repay their informants in kind. It was annoying, and they longed for the day when Sleightley or Pond would let something of value slip. But they never did.

One of the few affectations their masters maintained was their resolute refusal to use each other's names. Miss Parminter had paid four chocolate eclairs to learn that Sleightley called Pond 'C' after his decoration (Commander of the Order of St Mı˙ ˙ ˙el and St George), while Pond referred to his colleague – ı. ˙˙oments of stress or intimacy – as 'K' (Knight Commander of tne Order of St Michael and St George. Sleightley was sometimes almost offensively aware of his seniority). Neither man freely acknowledged that the two orders were commonly rendered by the decreasing number of Civil Service wags as 'Call Me God' and 'Kindly Call Me God'.

The Lamson hydraulic tubing behind Pond's desk said 'Kerflup' and shot a cork-tipped, spring-loaded, transparent plastic container in to a wickerwork basket on the floor: Sleightley glanced balefully at the receptacle. 'Before you ask,' Pond remarked, reaching down and retrieving the canister, 'whether it's possible to instal a more expeditious and seemly was of passing messages to and receiving signals from our monitoring staff – no, it isn't.'

'We have a lavishly expensive computer,' Sleightley said

heavily, 'VDU scanners for field summaries, agent's progress reports and monitoring abstracts – closed-circuit television which I know you periodically adjust to receive five-day cricket commentaries. Why is it that we have to resort to emissions of supercharged wind to be delivered of routine monitoring dispatches.?'

'It's safe, and it's cheap,' Pond replied, smugly. He rapped the lip of the metal cap at the end of the tube so that it fell open, inserted the canister, and listened fondly as it rattled out of the office and down to the basement to the Chief Monitor.

Sleightley raised his eyes to heaven and inquired what Intelligence Monitoring were presuming to offer. Pond thumbed through the roll of paper he'd taken from the container.

'Top level conference at the Department of Industry,' he replied, leafing through the report slips, 'the Chancellor's thoughts on Phase Three of the Contract for National Unity, the CBI's thoughts on Phase Two – the Prime Minister made a statement to Parliament about it this afternoon – oh, an interesting little snippet from the SIS man in Teheran. Hard-working chap, obviously, though I think he's off beam this time.'

'Really?'

'Yes. And a newspaper clipping.'

'A what?'

'A cutting from a newspaper – the *Financial Times*.'

'Is that why we've assembled an electronic surveillance network without parallel in the world, so that our monitors can sit down and read the popular press? Sleightley asked.

'I understand that the *Financial Times* is not regarded as coming precisely within that categorical description,' Pond observed.

'Really.'

'Yes. More *Daily Mirror*, or *Sun*, if you know what I mean.'

'I do,' Sleightley assented. 'The readership appeal of the

organ in question is not, however, a matter of consuming interest. What does the cutting say that we could not have learned through the medium of the costly apparatus of our trade?'

'It says,' Pond read 'that the production and testing of the ORBITMAN missile is being transferred in toto to the Royal Aircraft Establishment at Tredogan, in Cardiganshire. It's a very short paragraph.'

'Isn't the ORBITMAN already located there? The major part of the programme, anyway? You had something to do with it, didn't you?'

'I helped out a little,' Pond replied, modestly. 'I designed the computer for their Inertial Navigation Platform. But the real point of ORBITMAN is the fuel system. God knows how it works, they wouldn't even tell *me*. And when I suggested that it might have something to do with, say, a britium and deuterium pellet, they got miffed and clammed up. Unfriendly lot, if you ask me – although to be perfectly fair to them, they didn't deserve that spot of bother last summer.'

'The accident, you mean,' said Sleightley.

'Did you hear about that.' Pond asked, curiously. 'I thought they tried to keep it quiet.'

'Oh, they did,' Sleightley remarked airily, 'but as you know we have our little ways of finding things out.' Pond was about to interrupt, but Sleightley carried on, a little too quickly, possibly to cover his embarrassment at being found in possession of intelligence that he had not passed to his colleague. 'You see I was interested in Tredogan anyway. The place always seems terribly vulnerable to me. That explosion more or less made up my mind to do something about it, and in point of fact I've put certain – ahem – precautions in train.'

'HMG can't be too desperately concerned if they go plastering the place all over the public prints,' Pond pointed out, not unreasonably.

'My dear fellow,' Sleightley said, 'when the Government,

and particularly the Special Intelligence Service, display so manifest an unconcern for one of their supposedly clandestine ventures, that surely is the time for this Department to start worrying.'

It was all too delphic for Pond, who unnecessarily rearranged the cushion in the Lamson tubing basket, closed his eyes and fell to thinking about a cardigan a maiden aunt was knitting for him, such were his simple processes of word association. With a conscious effort, he wrenched himself back to reality as the import of Sleightley's remarks sank in.

'We don't actually know the Russians are going to try anything, do we?'

'No, we don't. We merely suspect it. We must suspect it, because it would be unnatural if they didn't.'

'SIS aren't worried,' Pond remarked.

'SIS,' Sleightley replied, a shade pompously, 'have the remarkable facility of not worrying about anything until it's happened, by which time it is generally too late.'

'Still . . .'

'My dear fellow,' said Sleightley, 'you are as aware as I am that the weapons being manufactured at Tredogan are unique. As you say, you yourself contributed, did you not, to the guidance system? Quite. We must, I repeat, assume that the rockets, and therefore the station, will become targets. Security at Tredogan is good, but it can be breached. Not to anticipate that would be criminally negligent. If SIS', he jerked his head in the general direction of France, 'wish to ignore the possibility, let them. We cannot.'

Sleightley held no high opinion of the British Special Intelligence Service, and in the case of the Tredogan Royal Aircraft Establishment he was more than half right. The SIS – as Department RE knew full well – had reinforced security at Tredogan to the extent they considered advisable – that is, up to the point beyond which markedly increased activity would itself have aroused suspicion. What Sleightley didn't know – but was soon to learn – was that British field agents behind the Iron Curtain had already reported that the Soviet Union almost certainly knew about the rocket system anyway, and the SIS chiefs, despite this, still maintained that Tredogan would be under no direct threat, simply because it was inconceivable that it should be. Department RE, on the other hand, regularly conceived the inconceivable.

'They're right about one thing though,' Pond said, with satisfaction. 'The plans by themselves will be of no value to an enemy.'

'I agree.'

'So how could anyone steal the rocket itself?'

'I don't know,' Sleightley replied. 'But I am reasonably certain they will try'.

'And?'.

'We send an agent to the area. Now. Undercover. To find out what's happening – if anything is happening – to indicate that something might happen, if you follow me.'

'Oh, yes. Whom do you think? Vengan?'

'No, Scott would be better. Vengan's still on that other affair, and besides Scott would have better cover there. He's a trained pilot . . . 'planes, helicopters, and suchlike. There are several oil rigs out in the Celtic Sea now, and they're serviced by a firm called, I believe, Cambrian Helicopters. Air Vice Marshal Sault has kindly agreed to persuade an old friend who knows the chairman of the Group which own Cambrian Helicopters to ask them to take on Scott as a pilot. He's going down this weekend, if you agree.'

'Yes. Yes, indeed. Anything else?'.

'No, but I think you're right that we'll probably need Vengan soon. Is the Salonika business nearly finished?'.

By which he meant, had Vengan dealt with the Greek whose interests Pond had reluctantly decided were antipathetic to British security.

'Yes, it's – uh – finished.'

'Splendid. Perhaps Vengan can be brought back at some stage, then.'

'I'll tell Miss Bunce. She can send a cable.'

Sleightley, who'd been reading the *Times Literary Supplement* from the moment he sat down at his desk, looked Pond straight in the eyes for the first time, and said, 'Splendid.'

The buzzer on Pond's desk had been refined by him to imitate a French horn sounding middle 'C' and at that moment it did. He flicked a key.

'Are you ready for the box, sir?' Miss Bunce asked.

'We are,' said Pond. 'Two lumps, please.'

The day's mail, divided into more or less equal piles, came in with Miss Bunce, the coffee with Mrs Costello. She poured two measures into bone china cups. Cream for Pond, black for Sleightley, two lumps of sugar for Pond (he varied his daily order between one and six lumps to sustain Mrs Costello's interest), none for Sleightley, Royal Scot biscuits (two) for Sleightley, none for Pond, who knew where to draw the line. Pond sipped his brew and riffled through the stack of letters and folders in front of him. At the very bottom was Cristal's file.

He opened it almost fondly. He was more deeply attached to Cristal than to any person in the world, except (but sometimes including) his irascible colleague, Sleightley. For one thing, she was startlingly (overwhelmingly in Pond's experience) beautiful. He had once confided to Miss Bunce that if he'd been a foot taller and thirty years younger, he'd ask Cristal out to dinner. Three night later an urgent 'phone call, ostensibly from Sleightley, called him to one of the most expensive and select restaurants in Mayfair. Cristal, nearly wearing a mind-shattering creation that caused the maitre d'hotel to ruin a flare-pan of crepe suzette, was seated at his table. She entertained him to a delicious meal in the most exquisite company any man could have wished. She'd taken him home, tucked him up in bed, and given his forehead a daughterly kiss.

She had been in her twenty-third year when the file was

started; she would now, he calculated, be twenty-seven. For four years they had known her, yet neither Sleightley nor himself had ever really understood why she was as she was, why she had elected to serve Department RE as posssibly the most accomplished and ruthless field agent they had ever recruited.

Pond scanned the first page of the file. Where was she born? Some outlandish place, wasn't it? Ah yes, Samarkand. Her schools, family background and connections were there, her known political affiliations (none), academic distinctions (impressive), languages (several), health (excellent), personal wealth (considerable). Her evident suitability for recruitment was logged, along with her extraordinarily high agent potential, and so on.

'Good Lord,' he said.

'What?' asked Sleightley.

'Eh – nothing.'

Pond had just noticed that she had one sixteenth Asian, or possibly negroid blood. 'Funny I didn't spot that before,' he mused. What did that make her? A double octaroon? A quadruple quadroon? A sextodecimaroon? Anyway, she was well-born, nobly, as Sleightley had pointed out before they had even met her. 'Cadet branch of an earldom – see?'

Pond's first impression of her had been that she must be somehow incomplete. An extraordinary and abundant human being without even a shred of humanity, totally lacking in compassion or pity. He had put it tentatively to Sleightley, 'Perhaps her creator felt He had been overgenerous with her physical and mental attributes, and resolved simply to leave her – well . . . emotionally unfinished?'

However, as Pond had grown to know her, he realised his initial judgement was wrong. Cristal could and did feel uncertainty and remorse, and pain, and horror – and tenderness.

So the enigma remained that this astonishing girl, so warm, so vital and alive, had chosen to dedicate her beauty

68

and her body and her brain to the most soulless and hazardous way of life (and death) that could ever have been offered to her. Why? Pond wondered, for the thousandth time. She'd dropped curious, fleeting half-hints that night at the restaurant, he recalled, but he had been to bemused (and replete) to appreciate their significance.

'Perhaps we'll never learn,' he said, softly. 'Perhaps it's better that we don't.'

'Don't what?' Sleightley inquired, still engrossed in the TLS.

'Find out what makes Cristal . . . well, as she is.'

'Cristal,' said Sleightley, reflectively. 'No. No, that, I feel, would be a mistake.'

Pond sighed and closed the file. He depressed the lip of the Lamson delivery chute again to annoy Sleightley, succeeded, and drained his cup of coffee with every indication of complete contentment.

SIX

It was a soft and seductive July evening in NW1, and the party matched the mood. The union boss remarked to the flaxen-haired, bespectacled, boring correspondent of South German Radio how odd it was that Monk's parties exercised a magnetic attraction for the greatest luminaries of the land (including, by implication, himself), and not a few gifted foreigners as well (a courteous after-thought which the young German totally failed to appreciate). He was unarguably the cleverest and most detested trades union leader in the country.

Sir Ranulph Monk was chairman of British Steel and as if that were not enough, occupied a vast, fourteen-roomed flat (actually a maisonette, or what the American ambassador was fond of calling a 'superduplex') off Regents Park. It afforded an unrivalled view of Lord Snowdon's birdcage at the London Zoological Gardens in the Park and, at Monk's spring and summer soirées (which started at 4pm), an interesting study of the mating habits of the large mammals on the Mappin Terraces.

Among the facilities provided at the monsastery (as the apartment was fondly known to the cognoscenti) was a rank of pedestal telescopes thoughtfully placed at intervals along the three 20ft wide picture windows in the reception rooms. A mere 5p in the slot enlarged to an astonishing size the already grotesque organs of generation of the gentlemen polar bears. Sir Ranulph, in an Old Shirburnians' blazer with a pre-war 'bus conductor's cap, would trot happily up and down the queues servicing the telescopes himself if any of them stuck.

'I mean,' said the union man 'look at this lot. Captains of industry – and a few sergeant-majors – ' (patting himself

70

clumsily on the back and spilling his drink over the radio man's new Hush Puppies) ' – sorry, old boy. But look at them. Politicians, film stars, television chaps . . . there's one cabinet minister talking to another, and they don't even do that in cabinet . . . And God knows how many ex-ministers. Or perhaps,' he sniggered, 'the Archibishop of Canterbury knows. He's here, too. And why do we come?' he damanded truculently of the by now alarmed German, since the 'Sergeant-major' was perceptibly drunk.

'Why? Because we bloody well have to, that's why. Though a combination of eckshtraordinary sircumshtances – I say, can I borrow your teeth? – Monk'sh made himself indispensable. He's the host with the most. And it's a death sentence – a bloody death sentence – not to be invited to at least one a year of old Ranulph's shebang. Life was so uncomplicated when it was just the Queen and Vic Feather you had to be nice to.'

The earnest young broadcaster was about to draw, in encyclopaedic detail, a precise parallel with a noted social climber of Bismarck's day, when the Gen. Sec. spun on his heel, lurched to the corner of the room and vomited over a large rubber plant.

At the buffet table in the drawing room, Pond was building a gastronomically repellent combination of tiny white onions, Maraschino cherries, gherkins, Gruyère cheese squares and seedless grapes on an extra-long cocktail stick he'd brought to the party himself in a Havana cigar tube. He walked over to the window and tapped Sleightley on the shoulder. Sleightley looked up from the telescope and said, 'Well?'

'May I offer you a savoury?' Pond said, tendering the revolting delicacy. Sleightley took one look and resumed his absorbed contemplation of the resolutely comatose fauna. The party continued around him, until Pond said, 'I say.'

'What do you say?' Sleightley inquired with ponderous deliberation. 'Those chaps over there,' Pond said, pointing to the far side of the room. Sleightley looked at the men deep in conversation in a shelf-lined recess designed to show off an impressive display of early Venetian and later Chelsea and Bristol glass. The recess was not illuminated.

'Those two?'

'Those two. Lindstrom, isn't it? The oilman. And the one with his back to us is Lewis Canterwell. I'd know that back anywhere. I've seen it any number of times on television vanishing into the front door of Number Ten.'

Sleightley contained his patience with difficulty. 'It would indeed,' he sighed, 'appear to be the Chairman and Managing Director of Pura Petroleum and Her Majesty's Secretary of State for Energy.' He glanced back at the telescope. 'Blast,' he said. 'Could you lend me five pence, please?'

'Try this,' Pond suggested, handing him a green plastic counter with a serrated edge.

'Thank you,' Sleightley said. 'Ah, good. Very good. In fact, splendid.' He concentrated on the focus mechanism and was silent; then without taking his eye from the telescope murmured, 'Is the point you're trying to make that they ought not to be together?'

'I suppose it is,' Pond admitted. 'I mentioned something about it the other day, didn't I? I was looking through Canterwell's file – remember?' Sleightley remembered.

'You see,' Pond continued, 'they were together at Cambridge. They were good friends . . . if anything, more than that. That's the point I believe we established from that speical piece of research I commissioned when Canterwell got his big ministry. At that time – Cambridge, I mean – there's every reason to suspect that he was – ' Pond coughed delicately, ' – one of them. Those, I mean.'

'I'm aware what you mean,' Sleightley said. 'Kept it jolly quiet, hasn't he?'

'Yes,' Pond conceded. 'And Lindstrom has.'

'Him too?' Sleightley inquired.

'Apparently, yes. Mind you, he looks like he might have

been one, doesn't he? And possibly still is.' He did, Sleightley decided.

'I don't believe anyone else has got a sniff of this,' Pond went on. 'but there's another aspect to it. There was a hint – the barest hint – of a serious scandal. Some local boy, found dead in the river. Homosexual, of course. And he knew both of them, and they him. In the biblical sense as well, I imagine.'

'Really?' Sleightley said, transferring his interest from the vigorous performance on the Mappin Terraces to the more subtle scenario in the corner.

'Of course, nothing was ever proven,' Pond went on, 'but the curious thing to me is that – as far as I'm aware – Lindstrom and Canterwell just haven't been close since those days. Obviously they meet occasionally, they'd have to, wouldn't they? But from memory, I would say that neither man's file – either ours or SIS – lists the other as a friend. Yet here they are rabbiting away as though they're bosom pals and the future of the world depended on it.'

'Did we cause any warning to be leaked when Canterwell was appointed Secretary of State?'

'No,' Pond said. 'You were away, and I decided to let it ride. No reason to suspect, after all, that he's still – uh – bent. But this – ' gesturing at the pair ' – is odd, wouldn't you say?'.

'I would. I would indeed. I'll go further . . . it may well bear watching.'

Lindstrom and Canterwell were unaware that their behaviour had aroused such interest, although Canterwell had been reluctant to start the conversation in which he was now engrossed. When Lindstrom had sidled up to him and whispered discreetly, 'I must see you,' he'd glared at him and hissed, 'Why?'

'The bastard's blackmailing me,' Lindstrom replied.

'Ainley?'

'Who else?'

Canterwell motioned with his head to the corner recess.

Lindstrom followed him and Canterwell switched off the display light. 'Blackmailing you for money, you mean?'

'Yes. I think he's going to have a go at you, too.'

'For God's sake, Hugo. I can't afford that. I'm not a millionaire, like you.'

'I'm not at all sure I can afford the kind of payments Ainley's demanding.' Lindstrom said, hotly.

Canterwell looked around anxiously. 'Keep your voice down,' he urged. 'There are all sorts of people here.'

'Very well.' Lindstrom said, lapsing again into a whisper. 'But we're going to have to do something about him, Lewis, sooner or later.'

'And what do you suggest?' Canterwell sneered. 'The same as we did before when we were threatened with exposure? Me again, I suppose? Shall I invite him up to Cambridge next weekend for a college reunion? Though I doubt honestly whether he'd come.'

Lindstrom flinched at the venom in his voice. He went on:

'At any rate, he wants to see us both again – together, this time. For dinner. This week.'

'Out of the question.'

'Argue the point with Ainley. He's phoning you tonight.'

'How much have you paid him, Hugo?' Canterwell asked, not wanting to hear the answer.

'So far?' Lindstrom said. 'About eighty thousand.'

'Jesus,' the Energy Minister whispered.

The Canterwells weren't permitted to have a foreign au pair, and couldn't afford an English one. Eve Canterwell picked up the 'phone herself the minute her husband walked into the house. 'It's for you, Lewis.' she said. 'A friend, he says. Personal.' She grinned, with a 'what have you been up to?' look on her face, then left him alone.

'It's Roger Ainley,' the voice said.

'Just thought I'd let you know – I've booked a table for three at Thor's Restaurant on Thursday. I may say in all seriousness, Lewis, that you dare not refuse to come. I expect you know the place. Near Marylebone High Street. Table's reserved for nine o'clock in my name. My treat, of course.'

'I'll see you in hell first, you loathsome shit,' Canterwell said, savagely.

'Not before I see you at Thor's at nine o'clock on Thursday.' Ainley replied imperturbably, and put down the telephone.

The Special Intelligence Service electronics man who'd been listening in on Canterwell's line 'phoned Pink, the crusty and – at a quarter past one in the morning, evil-tempered – SIS chief.

'It's about Mr Canterwell, Sir,' the operative said. Pink grunted dangerously.

'You said you wanted to be kept informed,' the eaves dropper added defensively.

'Well?'

'The man Ainley phoned at – ' he consulted his notes – '01.08. He wants to see Canterwell and somebody else in a restaurant called Thor's at nine o'clock on Thursday night.'

'Very well,' Pink barked, and slammed the receiver back on its sellotaped rest. That was the third contact Ainley had made with Canterwell and Lindstrom, he reflected; he imagined the other man at the dinner party would be Lindstrom. It was almost unknown for a multinational executive to call a Cabinet minister direct, and Chambers, SIS's man at the Department of Energy, had reported Lindstrom's message. Pink had smelt a rat and put a tail on the Minister and, for good measure, ordered a tap on his home telephone.

Sleightley, who bugged Pink's private line as a matter of course, massaged his tingling ear-drum, and made an entry in the Boot's DATADAY diary on his bedside table.

Ainley ate, with apparent relish, turtle soup and pheasant, with an agreeably rough claret, which Lindstrom considered bad form. It was a cheap evening for Ainley, because neither Canterwell nor Lindstrom ordered more than one course. Canterwell consumed a great deal of brandy, which Ainley insisted he should pay for himself, since it wasn't in the terms of the original treat. Canterwell tossed him a crumpled five-pound note, and accepted the change, along with a brace of excellent Armagnacs pressed on him – as a distinguished guest – by the restaurant's shrewd owner.

'I understood our business was concluded,' Canterwell said, icily.

'Not from me you didn't, Lewis,' Ainley said, draining his brandy balloon.

'You've got your drilling licence, and as far as I'm concerned, that's that.' Canterwell declared flatly, spreading the fingers of both hands in the air across the table-top. 'Any financial arrangement you may have made with Hugo is your affair, and his. You'll get nothing from me.'

'Oh?'

'No. Frankly, I don't consider that the so-called evidence you produced of our joint – ' he pursed his lips, 'error of judgment, is in any case real proof of our complicity in a crime.'

'Oh?'

'No.'

'How about this, then?' Ainley drew from his pocket a piece of paper and tossed it carelessly over to Canterwell.

It was a photostat of a diary entry for Saturday, June 2nd 1950. The writing was unmistakably Robin's delicate, spidery hand.

It read, 'I'm to go to May Night – the last part, anyway – with darling Hugo and lovely Lewis Canterwell! What exquisite fun!! Shall I be Queen of the Ball???'

'Culled from the same source as your ring, darling Hugo,' Ainley said.

'Robin's body? My God, how could you?'

'As easily as you and Lewis killed him,' Ainley replied.

There was a long silence. Canterwell sat back in his chair,

ran his fingers through his unruly hair (a gesture Lindstrom doted on at one time), then sat forward again and placed his arms on the table, clasping his powerful hands.

'No,' he said, quietly. 'Screw you, Ainley. Screw you every fucking way there is. But the answer's no. I'm not giving you one solitary, single penny.'

This time Ainley leaned back and his eyes moved from face to face of the two men opposite him. The waiter brought three more Armagnacs.

Ainley sighed with what seemed to be real regret.

'Very well,' he said. 'I'd anticipated this. I need money badly – very badly. Unwise investments, you understand? So you leave me little choice.'

And, quite simply, he told them. He told them all about the Russian scheme to steal the British wonder rocket. He explained with brutal clarity that the plan was only possible with the willing – indeed, avid – cooperation of the Chairman and Managing Director of Pura Petroleum International and Her Majesty's Secretary of State for Energy.

Canterwell's tongue was so dry that his mouth refused to close. Lindstrom held his head in his hands, and blinked back sudden actual, tears. Somehow Canterwell found the strength – and it was a conscious effort – to lick his lips and expel his breath.

'You . . .' he started. 'You . . . you . . .'

'I'm a shit, I expect you're going to say, Lewis,' Ainley rejoined smoothly. 'And I've made a traitor of you. Of you both.'

Lindstrom quivered as if he'd been struck. And the full realisation of what Ainley was saying sank in with frightening swiftness. The divided hands blanketing his face were now wet and shaking.

'Pull yourself together Hugo.' Canterwell ordered, and Lindstrom snuffled and snivelled, and apologised.

'How much?' the practical politician demanded.

'Oh . . . well,' Ainley mused. 'Can you run to, say, ten?'

'If I sell my villa in the South of France, possibly, yes.'

'Ah well, it's the wrong end, anyway, isn't it? Hardly San Trop?'

'You'll get the money.'

'Good, let's drink to that.'

'Get fucked,' Canterwell said. 'Have this one on me,' and he threw the contents of his glass into Ainley's face, where the spirits dripped disconsolately off his wiry moustache.

'Thank you, Lewis. I enjoyed that.' Canterwell stalked out.

Lindstrom couldn't get a taxi, and wandered into Marylebone High Street and up Thayer Street to Oxford Street. It was, he felt, distinctly off. As well as being a traitor, he was a multimillionaire who couldn't get a taxi. Then a battered cab drew up, and Lindstrom gave Simon's address rather than his own, without really knowing why.

The taxi pulled off Old Brompton Road, and Lindstrom settled with the driver. Simon was sleepy, sulky and resentful.

'This is my place,' Lindstrom reminded, gently. 'I have a right to come here, I would have thought, at any time I choose.'

Simon, who looked gorgeous and smelt delicious when Hugo kissed him, came out with the 'Don't I have any rights? bit, and Hugo kissed him again, and slipped his hand under Simon's silken robe (gift of Hugo) and stroked Simon's silken skin (gift of God).

'I love you, Simon,' Lindstrom said, more intensely than he ever had before. 'Let me show you how much I love you.'

But the boy regarded him curiously and slipped out of his grasp. 'I know you love me, Hugo.' he said. 'But tonight I do believe you actually need me as well. And that's not like you, Hugo. Not like you at all. So something's happened – something's gone wrong, and I want to know what it is.'

So Lindstrom told him. Not the details – just the rough outline. He was being blackmailed – and he was a traitor. It was bound to come out. He needed love, compassion, understanding, help, love, love, love.

He walked towards Simon, his arms outstretched, his eyes wide with fear and pleading.

'I've never asked you for anything that it wasn't my right to possess and that you weren't glad to surrender,' he said. 'But now, Simon, now – yes, I am begging you to help me. I have to have a friend, I have to get away – you must see that. Simon, darling Simon. I've given you so much. Don't deny me this, for pity's sake, don't.

But the boy backed away again, across the wide hall of the flat that Lindstrom maintained, felt for the bedroom door, turned it and slipped into the vaguely scented lilac-coloured room, snapping on the light switch.

He stood looking at his protector for several seconds, and then he shrugged off the lilac shot silk robe and stood naked.

Sudden hope leapt into Lindstrom's eyes, and he almost ran into the room . . . The girl could have been no more than fifteen.

Lindstrom had started to babble, 'I know we can work something out, Simon. It'll be diff . . .' his voice trailed off into a silence of disbelief and horror.

She was naked, and asleep with her legs apart. She had a pert little chestnut-coloured pubic triangle and lusciously firm, tip-tilted breasts on which it would be a crime not to balance fifty pence pieces, just for the fun of it.

'You weren't meant to see her, Hugo,' the boy said, 'but perhaps now it's just as well. Believe it or not, but her father's quite well off, so I shan't starve. I've enjoyed everything we've had together, and I'm grateful to you. But this trouble you're in – it's bad. I know. But it's no concern of mine. You shouldn't be so selfish as to expect that I'd compromise myself by trying to help you. So I'm getting out, whether you mind or not. Goodbye, Hugo. I'll come for my stuff tomorrow. Please stay tonight if you wish. I hope things work out all right for you.'

It was the longest speech Lindstrom had ever heard him make. He felt almost proud. The only think he could think of saying was, 'I see. Well then – goodbye, Simon. Goodbye.'

The boy dressed quickly, and walked over to the bed and gently shook the sleeping girl's shoulder. She lazily opened her eyes and said, 'Oh.' Lindstrom felt a stab of jealousy as he saw the genuine fondness in Simon's gaze.

The girl turned from her boy and saw the man. She said, 'Oh,' again, and sat bolt upright on the bed. Her incredible breasts bounced like a couple of ping-pong balls on jets of water at a fairground shooting gallery.

'Congratlulations, Simon,' Lindstrom remarked. 'Her speech is somewhat limited, but her equipment is truly amazing. And rich, too, you say. Hmmm.'

'What's 'e on abaht?' the girl asked, and Lindstrom left the room.

When they'd gone he drank nearly half a bottle of Courvoisier and cried himself to sleep. He awoke at four o'clock in the morning and took the tasseled cord from Simon's dressing-gown and hanged himself from the bars of a small grille set high up on the wall of the second toilet.

Simon and the girl found him the next afternoon, and Simon fainted.

The inquest was widely reported, but press follow-ups did not penetrate further than the fact that Lindstrom was a secret homosexual. Simon gave evidence, and never once mentioned what Lindstrom had told him. It was not, as he told himself, his problem.

SEVEN

' – and if they don't like it . . .' Canterwell's tones were heavy with implied menace. He didn't trouble to finish the sentence.

'Yes, well, they're not pushovers like some of the other unions,' Spurgeon, his senior civil servant, replied. Eleven years as a Permanent Secretary – first at Power and then at the new and bloated Department of Energy – gave him assured command of the lofty heights from which penetrating advice (and sometimes quiet contempt) could be dispensed to obdurate Secretaries of State. Canterwell, however, didn't react kindly to advice from any quarter – of which Spurgeon was well aware.

'I know how to deal with the power union, thank you,' Canterwell said, icily. 'and I know that they can make brass monkeys of us at Christmas time, but I think you can safely leave the politics of this department to me, Sir James.'

It was a cutting and unmerited rebuke, and to do Canterwell justice, he would not have delivered it unless he and Spurgeon had been alone. Spurgeon blinked and stiffened; he was about to frame a suitably tart rejoinder, when the intercom buzzer came between the two men like an anxious referee at a boxing match.

Canterwell flicked a key, and snapped, 'Yes?'

'It's the Prime Minister, Sir.'

'Just a moment.'

'Perfectly all right, Mr Secretary,' Spurgeon said, edging towards the door. 'Perhaps we can take it up again later.'

'Yes, Sir James,' Canterwell said, levelly. 'We need to settle it.' Spurgeon left the room, and Canterwell picked up the green telephone.

Paulfrey said, 'Lewis, could you come over to Number

Ten, please? There's something I want to see you about.'

Canterwell was genuinely dumbfounded. 'I beg your pardon?' he asked.

'I know what you're thinking, Lewis,' Paulfrey said. 'But you must accept, please, that for the moment it's necessary. Obviously, were it something we could discuss over the scrambler, I should be only too happy to do so. But it isn't. I shall be free at ten thirty, and I'll expect you then.'

'Very well, Prime Minister,' Canterwell said. 'Ten thirty.' They hung up simultaneously, without saying goodbye. It briefly disturbed both of them, because they were good friends.

On his way to Downing Street in his official car – he was damned if he'd sneak in round the back – Canterwell's brain raced furiously. It was obvious what Paulfrey wanted to see him about – the oil rig. It could only be that. And why the Prime Minister had no choice but to summon him to Number Ten. Canterwell appreciated that matters of this sort – or questions affecting, possibly, the security of the state – could only be dealt wiht by personal contact. Both men would have to take the risk that the sudden arrival in Downing Street, during a period of relative political inactivity, of a senior Cabinet minister, would not excite too much uninformed press speculation.

The point that bothered him was, how much did the PM know? Paulfrey was an exceptionally clever man. Canterwell had sccn him on previous occasions, playing suspects like a master angler. Paulfrey would use his bait sparingly and shrewdly until he caught his man in a trap very often of the poor fish's own making. The PM was a remorseless and singleminded logician, with a calculating, permanently active mind. Canterwell had once got no further than 'Good morning' before Paulfrey accused him of changing the subject.

The policeman at the door saluted Canterwell, and he was shown into Paulfrey's study. The Prime Minster was alone. As usual, he came straight to the point.

'It has been put to me, he said, gravely, 'that you may have compromised yourself in some way. Is this true?'

There was a fractional pause, then Canterwell said, 'Yes.'

'To what extent, and in what way?' Paulfrey asked, revealing nothing, putting the burden of lying on Canterwell.

'I am being blackmailed,' the Energy Minster said, 'by the man whose name is written on your notepad.'

Paulfrey glanced at the block of paper. Roger Ainley's name was inscribed in large, clear letters – not at all like the PM's usual barely decipherable scribble. The instant he had seen it there, Canterwell knew he was safe. Paulfrey was trying to be helpful; therefore he'd decided not to sacrifice his friend. Furthermore, he'd intended that Canterwell should be aware of it. Such were the unfathomable processes of Paulfrey's brain, it was probably also a commanding hint to tell the truth. Canterwell's relief was enormous, but not obvious. That would have been a mistake.

'What connection do you have with this man Ainley?'

'I knew him at Cambridge.'

'And?'

'He is able to prove,' Canterwell said, weighing each word with the utmost care, 'that at that time I was an occasional practising homosexual.'

'Nothing more?' Paulfrey's expression had not changed by so much as the barest flicker of surprise, even though the statement was, to him, alarming. Not because he felt revulsion for homosexuals but for the reason that he thought he knew Canterwell intimately, and now realised he didn't.

'I was involved in an incident with another man which led to a tragic accident. Ainley saw it happen.'

'The other being Lindstrom.'

'Yes.' Paulfrey indicated he'd like full details of the 'accident' at a later date. Canterwell replied, 'Of course.'

'You're paying him then?' Paulfrey continued.

'I am. Yes.'

'Nothing else?'

'What do you mean?' Canterwell asked.

'Do not prevaricate, Lewis. You know precisely what I mean.'

'I beg your pardon, Prime Minister. Security, of course.' Careful, he thought, careful. 'No, there is no security aspect. It was, and remains, a straightforward blackmail transaction. My conduct' (he got to the hair-shirt bit) 'is, I realise, unforgiveable. I shall, of course, tender my resignation.'

Paulfrey allowed himself a thin, humourless smile. 'Either you are excessively naive, Lewis, or you believe me to be, which is considerably more upsetting. You will by now have appreciated that I do not wish you to resign.'

'You will protect me?'

'I will protect myself, Lewis. The process of protecting you has already commenced.'

'What do you wish me to do?'

Paulfrey leaned back in his chair and clasped his fingers over his superbly cut waistcoat. 'Take a few hours off,' he said, enjoying Canterwell's momentary discomforture.

'I'm sorry?'

'You like cricket, don't you, Lewis?'

'Yes.'

'Good. Then off to Lords with you. Row 'P' in the Mound Stand. Ask for seat 32. I'm informed it will be waiting for you at the turnstile. In seat 31 you will find Admiral Pink of the Special Intelligence Service. I believe Somerset are playing Middlesex in the Benson and Hedges Cup. No doubt Middlesex will win, and that should at least afford you some incidental pleasure.'

Canterwell chuckled, and made one of the most serious errors of judgment of his political life.

He said, 'I'm deeply grateful, Miles. Thank you.'

Paulfrey looked up at him; his gaze was totally without warmth, and while his expression was neutral, Canterwell sensed the boundless contempt he felt.

'I think in future Lewis,' he said, 'you had better call me Prime Minister.'

Twelve words, the Energy Minister thought as he climbed back into his car. Twelve words that meant, without any shade or vestige of doubt, that he would never sit in the chair from which Paulfrey delivered them. He was now a permanent outsider; the Establishment – his own Establishment, for God's sake – would close its ranks against him.

Selvey was bowling to Rose, who was three not out, when Canterwell sank on to the wooden bench. Pink said, 'What's this bugger got on you, then?'

Canterwell replied, 'I expect you already know.'

No one who'd fenced for twenty years with Miles Paulfrey should have the slightest trouble with the likes of Pink, he considered.

'Yes. Bum-boy, were you?'

Canterwell flared up, instantly. 'Watch your dirty tongue,' he said, then clamped his lips together angrily as the Admiral winked at him with massive deliberation, and he realised he was being baited.

'Not such a fool as you thought I was, am I?'

'No,' Canterwell said. 'I'm sorry.' Without being asked, he repeated the story he'd told Paulfrey.

Pink said, 'Excellent,' and started clapping. Canterwell was baffled until he saw Rose walking towards the pavilion, and Wayne Daniel having his back slapped by Brearley. 'Clean bowled the sod,' Pink said.

'Commie, is he? Ainley?'

'No,' Canterwell said, firmly. 'Nothing like that. Believe me, nothing.'

'I believe you,' Pink said. 'Right then – leave it to us.'

Canterwell gathered to his astonishment that he was being dismissed by an imperious wave of Pink's meaty, mottled hand.

'What will you do?' he asked.

Pink turned full-face to him, and Canterwell realised that he'd made his second error. The Admiral scowled. He didn't like homosexuals, he didn't like Canterwell, and he saw no reason to conceal his distaste.

'We'll do what we have to do,' he said. 'And when we've done it – if I consider it advisable to tell you – you'll be told. If not, you bloody well won't. Now fuck off.'

Pink said, 'Hope the buggers kill each other,' as Daniel started bowling at Vivian Richards, and stumped out of the stand.

Back in his office, he said to Savage, 'Get Swaine.' Swaine wa the SIS's top field controller. Like Savage, he was a first-class operator. Also like Savage, he was totally unappreciated by Vice-Admiral Sir Sacheverell Pink, who ruled the Specal intelligence Service with the exquisite subtlety of a Sherman tank knocking over a brick wall. Now aged fifty-eight, Pink was just under six feet tall and almost the same around. No man more sweetly matched his name, for Pink's puffy, craggy face was permanently rosy, the result of an inherited choleric nature and gross over-indulgence.

Swaine, who was older than the stylish and deceptively willowy Savage, was briefed in the outer office.

'What do you want us to do about Ainley, Sir?' Swaine asked, when he and Savage had gone back to face their master.

Pink pulled out a solid gold half-hunter watch attached to a chain girding his midriff.

'I want to find out everything there is to know about this,' he said gravely. 'Then we'll have a conference here at four o'clock. And after that, Mr Swaine, I'll tell you just what you will do about Roger Ainley.'

Sleightley stood at the putative Adam fireplace, his back to the room, studying the framed reproduction of Velasquez's extraordinary mirror-image painting of the daughter, ladies-in-waiting and household pets of King Philip IV of Spain. As always, he bounced his words off the wall. Sleightley avoided looking at people unless it was totally imperative that he should.

He asked Pond if the RE monitors were listening to SIS. While Pond consulted a schedule on his desk, Sleightley transferred his attention to a neat, oblong text embroidered on a plain white background, also tastefully framed, executed by one of Pond's legion of maiden aunts. It read *Quis custodiet ipsos custodes* but without the question mark, as though it were a statement rather than rhetorical query. Pond had wanted it that way, overriding the objections of his ancient, but classically meticulous, relative, Miss Begonia Archbold. It was, Pond said, a department motto. Sleightley thought it frivolous, but tolerated it.

Pond eventually replied that the monitors didn't appear to be plugged in to SIS at the moment, but he could arrange it if Sleightley were absolutely certain he wished them to. The fraying ends of Sleightley's weak, iron-grey moustache took on an independent life, and he said that yes, he did wish it. He knew, in any case, that the Special Intelligence Service were being recorded, like all the other vital listening points in the Department's complicated and far-flung surveillance network.

'Possibly you could put them on the board now, if you don't mind, that is,' he said to an exquisite little Byzantine icon on the mantlepiece.

'Not at all,' Pond assented, and pressed a key marked '%' on a desk calculator. A voice said, 'Yes, Doctor Pond?'

'Could you put up SIS please, if you're not too busy?' Pond requested.

'Of course,' the monitor said.

Department of RE's operations in electronic surveillance were of a type and on a scale that would have astonished and delighted even the Russians. In point of fact, one of Pond's few failures was their inability to penetrate the sophisticated jamming field around the Soviet Embassy in Kensington Palace Gardens. But apart from that, the Department were supreme at their chosen task. They could, if they wished, catch the Prime Minister in mid-fart.

A tiny green cue light flashed on Pond's desk, which had a bad case of woodworm, but couldn't be removed because of the mass of electronics embedded in it. He knocked down a switch on a standard, grey internal telephone console of the key-and-lamp variety.

A panel slid back on a short wall of the roughly hexagonal room. Behind it was a miniaturised concentration of the largest and most efficient listening post in the western world, housed in the labyrinthine basement of the building and staffed night and day by multilingual monitors, whose task was merely to log and pass on information. The most important lines – and the SIS were high on the priority bugging list – could be transferred direct to the master board in the office.

The electronic components of Department RE's stock-in-trade had been manufactured by specialists in seventeen countries, each one allocated one small, disparate function. The complex was designed and assembled by Pond.

Along with his fellow don, Sleightley, Pond had been persuaded nearly thirty years before by an astute and far-sighted chief of the Imperial General Staff, to cooperate in the formation of a watchdog department. Their function would be to oversee the overseers of the nation's security. Where they found lapses, misjudgments or straightforward villainy, they were empowered to carry out corrective action.

They were funded by special subventions from a number of Government departments. The Permanent Secretaries of those departments authorised the payments of the subventions to an account controlled by the Head of the Civil Service and the Chief Secretary to the Treasury. They, in turn, credited the index-linked sums to the Chief of the

General Staff (the 'Imperial' having been dropped in the interests of good Commonwealth relations) under the vague heading 'Intelligence Research'.

Admiral Pink, at SIS (directly across the street from the Department), referred to them disparagingly as 'that lot over the road', rather in the way the House of Commons designates the House of Lords as 'another place'. He was, however, shrewd enough to be sometimes frustrated by his complete ignorance of whatever it was the Department RE actually did.

He would have been surprised to learn that their executive powers were practically limitless, and included an express injunction to form an elite squad of people frivolously termed by Pond as 'asset strippers'.

The monitor's voice crackled across the intercommunications system. 'SIS, Doctor Pond.'

'Line Two' Pond said, pressing the key marked 'B' on his portable electric typewriter. Pink's voice flooded into the room.

'. . . told the Prime Minister just the bare facts,' Pink was saying. 'It's totally beyond me why we didn't pick up this homosexual thing about Canterwell years ago. Not that we could have suspected it, he seems straightforward enough. But a few discreet inquiries among his old Cambridge buddies today – of whom this creature Ainley was apparently one – convinced me that we're quite possibly the only people in Western Europe who didn't know about it.

'At any rate, we can't have Ainley suborning Ministers of the Crown and Chief Executives of multinationals, even when they're pooves like Canterwell and Lindstrom. I want him got out of the way, Swaine. Dispose of him.'

'Termination?'

'That's the usual form, isn't it?'

'It is.'

'Then do it,' growled Pink. 'And no buggering around. Do it quickly.'

'It shall be done.'

Pond switched off, and Sleightley turned from the Velasquez and said 'No. We cannot permit that.'

Pond looked baffled, and Sleightley apologised. 'I forgot you were not completely up to date with this affair,' he said. 'I believe it may be connected with Tredogan, but I could be wrong.'

He explained that Departmental bugging of SIS and Pink had yielded the link between Ainley, the Energy Secretary and the Chairman and Managing Director of Pura Petroleum International. SIS, who obviously did not suspect a connection with the ORBITMAN programme, were about to remove the only lead, Ainley.

'And what do we know of Manley?' inquired Pond.

'Not Manley, Ainley,' Sleightley sighed. 'He's a junior in the Diplomatic Service. I've looked him up. Iron Curtain places, mostly, Warsaw, Bucharest, Moscow . . . he was there in Moscow with a trade delegation at the end of last year. Apparently blameless, insignificant even, but he has a lifestyle that seems to have been overlooked.

'The point is, he was with both Lindstrom and Canterwell at Cambridge. Clearly he knew they were homosexual, as you had discovered and Pink has now confirmed. He's blackmailing them both, and killing him will not reveal the reason why. I have to know what he wants from them – provided it's not just money, and I suspect it isn't.'

'Why?' Pond interjected.

'No more than a feeling, perhaps, 'Sleightley admitted. 'But it's a very strong feeling. Why has he chosen this moment to surface? What can it have to do with energy or the oil business? To me, it sounds like a Soviet game – and if that is the case, then it may well be Tredogan. If it is, it's infinitely more serious than our friend Pink believes.'

'Yes,' Pond observed. 'It would be.'

'Quite,' said Sleightley. 'So Ainley must not be allowed to die, merely to slake Pink's blood lust.'

'No,' Pond agreed.

Sleightley, six feet one, poker-thin and with what might

generously be called an academic stoop, had a face hatched like a relief map of the Lake District with lines and creases. He was known – unoriginally but not inaccurately – as 'Ever So' Sleightley to his secretary, Mrs (relict of Algernon) Costello. His colleague – corpulent, benign, sleepy, bald but for a despairing fringe – had been dubbed 'round' Pond by Miss Bunce the day after they met.

Sleightley pressed Roman numerals on the music-tone dialling platform of a futuristic-looking telephone Pond had made, and when a voice answered, said, 'I have something for you to do.'

EIGHT

Cristal put the 'phone down, and considered for a moment how decidedly odd it was that a Department RE agent should be allotted the task of specifically keeping someone alive. There was, she thought, no accounting for the foibles of Sleightley and Pond.

The written instructions, when they arrived by despatch-boy an hour later, shed little light on Ainley, who was no more than a name to Cristal. AINLEY, Roger (the data said): age, 48, description: 5′ 10″, 11 st 13 lbs, good condition, thinning fair hair, blue eyes, gingery-brown moustache (the accompanying picture was in monochrome), well-dressed (sub-Savile Row). The curriculum vitae, besides listing various diplomatic and foreign postings since Ainley entered Government service after Cambridge, hinted that he liked high living and, though unmarried, had had a fair number of orthodox relationships with women.

He was, Sleightley's crabbed script explained, more than likely a traitor, and possibly in the pay of the Russians. There was reason to believe that he was bringing some kind of pressure not only on the British Energy Minister, Lewis Canterwell, but also on Hugo Lindstrom, the Chief Executive of Pura Petroleum International.

SIS, Sleightley wrote, had decided to eliminate Ainley. Department RE had resolved to stop them. He had not mentioned their reasons for wanting to keep Ainley alive, and Cristal wasn't concerned enough to inquire.

She thought Sleightley was probably right in assuming that once Pink had given the order to dispose of Ainley, the SIS 'executioners' would reach for their guns without even 'phoning to say they'd be late for supper. It might, in fact, already be too late.

The Department considered all SIS hit men to be either cowboys or hip-shooters, and frequently both. One, whom Pond called 'The Lone Ranger', was highly dangerous with a gun – sometimes to his target, but always to himself, and generally to anyone else who happened to be around. Pond had arranged for him to have a fairly serious accident to protect the rest of the population, but he needn't have bothered. The previous Sunday, the Ranger had shot off his own left foot during an otherwise uneventful stake-out in Salford.

But even SIS, the Department reasoned, wouldn't be stupid enough to try to take Ainley at (or near) the Foreign Office, which was where the spy ought to be at this time of day, so presumably the attempt would be decently delayed until nightfall, and would be made at Ainley's mews house on the wrong side of the Park in W2.

'PS', Sleightley had written. 'If you look out of your window you will see a 5cwt blue Thames van, drawn from the Department's motor vehicle pool, which should afford you unobtrusive cover. It will be accompanied, I trust, by a driver, who will leave you the ignition key. Kindly wear the overalls, etc, provided.'

Cristal, who was temporarily lodged in one of the Department's sprinkling of South Kensington flats, pulled aside the curtain. Directly beneath the window was a 5 cwt, blue Thames van. Standing beside it, gazing up at the block of flats and waving aloft a bunch of keys, was one of the most affirmatively nondescript men the agent had ever seen. He have a lopsided grin of sheer idiot delight when he saw the window open, and shook the bunch of keys even more vigorously.

'For Christ's sake leave the keys in the ignition and bugger off, you twit', she hissed at him. The little man's face fell a mile, but he did as he was told, and slouched sniffily away down the road.

The van was totally devoid of information apart from its licence, the name-plate announcing its make, and a handy little sign stuck behind the windscreen saying, DEEP FREEZE ENGINEER ATTENDING EMERGENCY in neatly printed red capitals, underlined in blue (why blue, Cristal never discovered). The overalls, off white and none too clean, unfortunately fitted, so she kept them on, and wore the large peaked cap as well for the drive through Hyde Park to the street where Ainley lived.

The spy was at home – but only just. His car was ticking over outside the white-painted Georgian-style front door, standing open to show the narrow stairs to the upper storeys. Altogether, Cristal decided, quite a nice little place, even down to the well-designed wrought-iron flower baskets flanking the first-floor window, with its tiny panes of chunky glass.

Ainley emerged with a big, dark-green suitcase, dropped it in the boot of the three and a half litre Rover, and checked the 'up and over' door of the built-in garage. She parked just beyond the end of the mews, got out and strolled un-concernedly in Ainley's direction, and was almost level with him on the other side of the little street when the spy slammed down the tail-gate of the car, jumped in and drove off at a pace that left the RE agent flat-footed and feeling distinctly foolish. Pursuit was out.

At least, Cristal thought ruefully, Ainley had got away from the SIS as well, and since he'd taken a suitcase he would, presumably, stay away for some time. His absence, though, would not deter the SIS guns from making their bid tonight, since they had no way of knowing he'd flown the coop.

A couple of other points on the credit side occurred to her. The mews house was difficult to protect with Ainley's cooperation, so he was better off out out of it. And secondly, his not being there would provide an excellent opportunity both to search the place and bug it into the bargain, and then Ainley's return could be monitored without the embarrass-ment of clumsy and – in that quiet street – obvious sur-veillance.

Cristal, who thought it might be fun to watch the SIS at work again, walked back to the blue van, and drove to Paddington Station for a beer, a cheese and tomato sandwich, and a read of the *Evening Standard*. She caught a glimpse of the paper's contents board at the entrance to the station. TYCOON IN DEATH DRAMA it said. The front page lead gave the obvious explanation for Ainley's flight – Hugo Lindstrom had killed himself.

Cristal 'phoned Sleightley – who, surprisingly, didn't know about the oilman's suicide – and just after dark, piloted the Thames van back into Lancaster Mews, stopping opposite Ainley's house and switching off the lights. An hour passed, and no one came or went. She decided it was safe to break in, and the barrel lock on the stout but decorative front door yielded to the first delicate touch of the agent's American Express card.

The bugging process was simple, and the planting sites self-evident; one in the base of the old-fashioned brass telephone in the hall; another under the saddle of a vintage racing bicycle gathering dust and cobwebs in the corner of the garage; a third inside the plastic cover of the bell chimes on the landing; the fourth hidden in the air-freshener in Ainley's bathroom. The fifth she concealed behind the heavy, possibly immoveable, mahogany wardrobe in the bedroom – a curiously out-of-place hulk in such a small and well-furnished house.

Cristal left the bedroom and crossed into the large, open-plan lounge at the front over the garage, to plant the final bug. Just enough light came through the lacy curtains from the fake gas lamps in the mews to show the outline of another telephone – modern orthodox this time – on the window ledge. She unscrewed the mouthpiece and had just finished fitting the tiny transmitter when a black Austin Princes nosed into the street and took a vacant space right next to the Department's van.

She saw it immediately, and waited for someone to get out – or in. But five minutes passed, and nothing happened, except for a brief flicker of flame that started on the near side, travelled over to the driver's seat, and vanished, to be followed by the occasional red glow of cigarettes.

'Get on with it, for God's sake,' Cristal said, a little louder this time. And they did.

Both front doors of the car opened, and the interior light didn't come on, which earned the SIS a 'Full Marks' commendation from Department RE. Two shadowy figures flitted across the street to Ainley's house.

Silently, Cristal left the front room and padded down the carpeted steps, passing through the connecting door into the garage at the very instant that the door chimes pealed discreetly and musically at the top of the stairs.

She pushed the door to, and it clicked softly over to lock. There were no lights in the house, so obviously the SIS sensed that Ainley was either hiding or – more likely – wasn't there at all. Nonetheless, they waited another half minute before pressing the bell-push again, and then five more minutes until one of the two produced an Access card and got in the same way Cristal had.

The RE agent heard them go up the stairs, and the muffled sounds they made while they searched the place, and then a barely audible creak from the staircase as one – or both? came back down to the ground floor. The handle of the communicating door began slowly to turn, and Cristal trained the Walther PPK just to the left of it.

The door squeaked as an SIS agent pushed it, but the lock held. Just as slowly, the handle returned to the horizontal. She breathed and relaxed, but only a fraction. Then the sound of a hushed voice came through the door.

'That just leads to the garage,' one of the killers whispered.

'Yes, it's locked,' the other said – obviously the one with his hand on the door.

'I wish to Christ the sod would come home,' the first man growled. 'I got a bit stoned last night, and I'd be a lot better off in bed with my lady wife than stuck here waiting for

Mister Roger fucking Ainley to ditch his bit of stuff and get back from his night on the bleedin' town.'

'Keep your voice down,' the other urged. From the sound of him, Cristal thought, he was a cut above his colleague, but that was nothing new for SIS. They often sent out oddly assorted pairs – one, as it were, Winchester and Oxford, the other Bethnal Green Secondary Modern and Borstal. If they had a single target, they normally took it in turns to do the actual killing.

Judging from the fact that it had been Winchester and Oxford's hand on the door, it was his turn tonight. He'd have been the one to come springing through at the crouch, blasting at anything that moved with his silenced gun (Beretta?), otherwise he wouldn't have tried to open the door. That was how Cristal worked it out, anyway.

'Well I'm pissed off as well as hung over,' Bethnal Green and Borstal said.

'Oh, let him have his fun,' Winchester and Oxford replied. 'After all it's his last night, isn't it? "Eat, drink and be merry, for tomorrow . . ."' he didn't need to finish the quote. 'I really think you might be a little more sympathetic to our – er – clients at times like this. It may not have struck you, but they're almost never uncharitable about us, are they?'

'Don't even see us, do they?' his partner said.

'We'd better stay another couple of hours,' Winchester and Oxford decided. 'It's . . .' he squinted at his watch, '11.20-ish now. If he's not home by, say, one-thirty, we'll assume he's either away for a few days – and I'll be annoyed if he is, because somebody should have told us – either that, or he's holed up for the night somewhere with a no doubt compliant lady friend.'

'Yeahrokay,' Bethnal Green agreed, moodily. 'Do we have to stay here, though?'

'No. We'll go out to the car. It's more comfortable, and we can watch the street as well.'

'Yeah,' Bethnal Green said, then hissed. 'Hey.'

'What?'

'Hadn't we better leave a bug? You know what they said back at HQ.'

'Don't worry, I've done it.'

'Oh. Where did you put it?'

'Under the base of that big table lamp in the upstairs room. If he doesn't come back tonight, we'll tell HQ,' 'Winchester' said, 'and they can draft in another team tomorrow. They'll have the job of following Ainley once the bug's picked him up.'

'Bethnal Green' – or somebody, Cristal didn't know which – checked the street, and she heard the door close softly behind them a few moments later.

The desk sergeant at Paddington Green Police Station took her call, noting the number – an anagram of Ainley's digits following the correct exchange code.

'What did you say?' he demanded. 'Two men, both armed? You're sure now?'

'Of course I'm sure,' she replied.

'And what are they doing?'

'Look, I've told you what they're doing. They came out of a house near me in Lancaster Mews, and they're sitting in a big dark car – I think it's an Austin but I can't see it very well.'

'And where's the car?'

'In Lancaster Mews. Where else would it be?'

'Right. Now, can I have your name and address, caller?'

Cristal pretended not to have heard the question, and instead replied, 'Yes, I can see it better now. Somebody's just switched a light on three doors down. The car's a black Austin, and I believe its a Princess. Anyway, the registration number's QPR 136R.'

'Right, I've got that,' the sergeant said. 'Now then, could I please have your name and address . . . you know, just for the record?' But there was no reply. His caller had hung up.

Cristal cradled the big brass 'phone, and started to snigger, then had to run upstairs and hide in the bathroom before the giggle could mature into a laugh.

'Jesus, I'd love to see Pink's face tomorrow when two of his pet goons come up in court.' She was almost crying by now, but the spasm receded, and the front window made a good vantage point for watching the fun.

'Ello,' 'Bethnal Green' remarked, 'someone's having a busy night.' The wail of at least two police sirens sounded in the distance, and seemed to 'Winchester' to be drawing closer.

'It'd be a laugh if something was happening around here,' he said.

'Cramp our style a bit, though, wouldn't it?'.

'Yes, you're right, it would. We'd better keep our heads down.'

And they did, literally, sliding low in their seats – 'Winchester, the passenger, actually kneeling on the floor, and they were still there when the first Triumph 2000 from Paddington Green screamed into the Mews. It slowed to a halt on the smooth cobbles twenty yards from the Princess, its headlights, on full beam, illuminating the big car as though it were Nelson spotlit on his column.

'What the bleedin' 'ell's 'appening?' shrieked 'Bethnal Green'.

'Oh, Jesus fucking wept,' sighed 'Winchester', who already knew.

Explosions like thunderous cymbals bounced off the walls of the wakening Mews as a second police car drew up and a Chief Inspector blew three times into the microphone of his public address system.

'We,' he announced, unneccessarily, 'are police officers.'

'What else could you be?' 'Bethnal Green' moaned, because now he also knew.

'We are armed,' the Chief Inspector said.

'Hoo bloody ray,' 'Winchester' commented. Although neither of them could see him, the Chief Inspector held up a long-barrelled police issue revolver to demonstrate the undoubted truth of what he said.

'Will the occupants of car registration number QPR 136R, please open the nearside front window, and throw their weapons into the street. Will you then,' his voice, he thought, came over awfully well, 'get out of the car, and place your hands on the roof.'

'Winchester' edged his body up the back of the seat, and dimly made out behind the blazing corona of light the figures of at least six helmeted, flak-jacketed policemen, each kneeling on one knee, and carrying at the aim a police marksman's rifle.

'Shit, it's the SPG,' he said.

'The Specials?' 'Bethnal Green' said. 'Oh, fuck it, that's all we need.'

A sergeant of the Special Patrol Group, kneeling to the left of the Chief Inspector's feet, whispered urgently to him. 'What?' the officer inquired. The sergeant repeated it. 'Oh yes, of course.'

'I'm sorry,' he said into the public address microphone, and wished he hadn't, because it sounded daft, 'You have ten seconds to comply.' He started counting, and again regretted it because it was strategy, but he had to carry on.

At 'eight', delivered in a firm, uncompromising baritone, two Berettas arced out of the open car window and clattered on the cobbles.

'Right, then,' said the Chief Inspector, but realised he was broadcasting again and covered the microphone with his gloved hand, which made an appallingly grating noise that set everyone's teeth on edge, and shook a sensitive budgerigar in the second house clean off its perch.

'I think there's something else, sir,' the sergeant said. The Chief Inspector, who'd been about to say 'Forward, men,' stared unbelievingly at the Austin Princess.

First a Browning sub-machine gun shot through the window and bounced into the pool of light. Then a knife – no, two knives! – a pair of nasty little rubber coshes, and finally a wickedly winking brass knuckle-duster.

'Christ,' a young SPG man ventured, a trifle nervously,

'who are we arresting, the Bengal bloody Lancers?'

The Chief Inspector was about to ask the occupants of QPR 136R if that was all, but luckily he appreciated in time how idiotic *that* would appear, and instead observed, almost avuncularly, 'we're waiting for you.'

The doors opened, and out stepped the SIS men, hands clasped behind their heads. They removed them, leaned forward in utter resignation and defeat, and the next sound Cristal heard was the despairing, staccato slap of four sweating palms on the cold roof of the car.

She had been in serious danger of choking. When the police cars came and the lights went on, She had slipped down behind the wall under the window and followed the rest of the proceedings by ear, crouching on the floor and racked by paroxysms of stifled laughter.

'Oh, Jesus . . . Oh, God Almighty . . . Oh Christ, this is too much, it's just too much.'

The show, though, was nearly over. The SPG advanced in line and covered the SIS. The Chief Inspector, who'd at last succeeded in immobilising the microphone, marched up to the agents as the cuffs went on their wrists, and said:

'Well, my lads. You've got some explaining to do.'

'You're right,' 'Winchester' moaned softly. 'You're so right.'

NINE

Ainley had been too preoccupied to notice the figure in cap and overalls walking towards him down the Mews when he made his untimely exit. The news of Lindstrom's death – which he picked up off the three o'clock IRN summary on London Broadcasting – had shaken him more profoundly than he could have believed possible.

As a relief Warsaw Pact desk officer at the Foreign Office – which was his none too serious, 'between postings' job – he had a fair amount of time to kill. The lunch 'hour' – 12.30 to 2.30 – had been gainfully spent at the Savages' Club (where his membership rested on a relentlessly trivial tract on Öst-Politik), in visiting his Jermyn Street shirt-maker, and calling at Airey and Wheeler for a second fitting for his latest suit.

He'd made his way reluctantly back to the office, and was seated at his desk reflecting on last night's excellent dinner at 'Thor's, and wondering how large Lindstrom's next 'subscription' would be, when the squawk of the cheap plastic transistor told him, in so many words, to start looking elsewhere.

'The trouble is,' he said to himself, 'there isn't anywhere else to look.' True, there was Canterwell, and Canterwell was paying, but he wasn't in the same league, financially, as Lindstrom.

Ainley had reached for the phone, then drawn back his hand. There was no point in telling the Russians about Lindstrom's death, because they'd already know. Besides, it would be bound to lead to awkward questions from Balchinsky. Ainley bit his lip, shook his head, and said, 'Sod it.' Not for a second did he feel even a flicker of sympathy for Lindstrom. Just annoyance.

He could imagine the implacable Russian spy-master grilling him. 'But you must have some idea, Roger. Surely. You had dinner with him last night. Was the meal so ineffably bad that he felt driven to go off and hang himself? Did he give no indication that he had an intolerable problem? In any case, Roger, why were you dining with him? You're hardly in his social register – and his part in our little plan had been completed, had it not? Our rig is in operation, and with Pura Petroleum's blessing. Is that not so?

'Could it be, Roger, that you were – how do you English say it? – "moonlighting?" Now don't play the innocent, Ainley. You know very well what I mean. You were putting the black on him, weren't you? And Canterwell, too? It wasn't in the plan, Roger, and Comrade Nikita will be very angry when he learns that someone on our side has – shall we say – screwed up the plan. You follow me, Roger, don't you . . . ?'

No, it didn't bear thinking about. He just couldn't face it without a cover story. 'And that's something, chum, that you just don't have,' he murmured. And added, 'Yet.'

Every second longer that he stayed in London – and available, either to the Soviets or British Intelligence who, Ainley decided, must be sniffing by now – he was putting his head further in the noose.

'It's off for you, Roger my lad,' he'd said, with as much humour as he could muster. 'Off to bonny Scotland and up the lot of them.'

He picked up the phone. 'Martin' he said, just short of ingratiatingly, to his departmental chief. 'Martin, you know that leave I've got coming before my next assignment.' Yes, Martin did, though not with any great interest.

'Well, look, old boy, something's come up.' Oh, yes? 'Yes. Look, eh, Martin – I wonder if I could start it more or less straight away? It'd be doing me a positively vast favour. I won't forget it, old chap.'

Ainley snapped off the radio, collected his briefcase, winked at 'Miss July' on the Penthouse calendar (a present from Balchinsky) and shot out of the building.

The phone rang just as the door slammed behind him.

Cristal perched on the 'difficult' Chesterfeld in the corner of Department RE's spy factory. Pond had designated it as 'difficult' for the simple reason that wherever you sat on it, it was difficult to achieve any real comfort. Cristal didn't seem to mind.

Sleightley was reading a tedious private letter from the Prime Minister to the Foreign Secretary's wife, and Pond was at his desk, his head in his hands, shaking with convulsions of silent laughter. 'We must,' he managed to get out between stifled guffaws, 'listen in. We really must.'

Sleightley glanced up disapprovingly. 'Our considerable electronic resources,' he said stiffly, 'were not installed to provide field staff with light entertainment. However, if you feel it would be useful . . .' he waved a limp hand vaguely at the wall.

'What's the time?' Pond said.

'Ten-oh-three,' Cristal answered.

'Just about right,' Pond chuckled, attacking his key-and-lamp console and portable typewriter with vigorous precision. The 'wall' disappeared into itself, and the nest of furiously active bugs once more unerringly selected the big house across the street. After a few preliminary whirrs and cheeps, Savage was heard to say, 'He won't like it.'

Swaine, who had personally accepted the assignment of Ainley's removal, echoed the sentiment feelingly. 'He won't. Indeed, he won't.' Pond felt rather sorry for Swaine; he was one of the more human and genuinely talented members of Pink's staff.

Pond was also more conscious than Sleightley seemed to be that Department RE might one day interfere once too often in the affairs of the Special Intelligence Service, and compromise a really important operation. Sleightley totally lacked even a grudging respect for the orthodox intelligence arm, whereas Pond was ready to concede that *they* got all the dirty jobs.

The eavesdroppers heard the SIS maestro, whose entries were always unmistakeable, burst into the room. He was, for once, genuinely and justifiably furious.

'What happened?' the Vice-Admiral thundered. 'Swaine. You. What bloody happened?'

'As far as we can make out, sir,' Swaine said, 'the police at Paddington Green had a call from a householder to the effect that two men, who appeared to be armed, were acting suspiciously somewhere near Ainley's place, and the law simply – er – picked them up.'

'And told the press,' Pink said, bitingly. 'And made a bloody laughing stock of this Service, of me, and of all of you. Gremlins again, Mr Swaine.'

'Either that, or appallingly bad luck, sir.'

'Or appallingly bad management.'

'It seemed straightforward enough, sir. Unless an outside agency intervened, there was nothing that could go wrong. Our men were as discreet as they normally are. It was a good team.'

'So what,' Pink demanded, 'are you doing about it?'

'We're already on to it, sir,' Swaine said. 'Savage?'

Savage uncoiled himself from his perch on the corner of a huge mahogany bookcase, and said:

'Our chaps are off the hook, Admiral. The press have been fed some fetching yarn about sensitive foreign nationals larking around off bounds – sheikh's bodyguards, in fact. The sheer – ah – weight of armaments in the possession of the police has been successfully concealed, and the stuff's in process of being returned. With any luck, we should get away with it.'

'Luck, Savage?' Pink boomed. Then his voice grew quieter, and the volume to the RE monitors automatically adjusted itself to pick up his words.

'Outside agency, you say, Mr Swaine. Yes, I think you may be right,' he said, slowly, thoughtfully. 'I'm sure it exists.' He looked up sharply at Swaine and Savage. 'But they're making one big mistake. They're assuming I'm bloody fool enough to believe that all these coincidences are some kind of divine intervention, or gremlins, or 'luck'. And gentlemen, I'm not.'

Miss Parminter – Pond deduced from the adenoidal sniff that floated over the wire – brought in the coffee. Pond made an elaborate mime of pouring something into a cup, and guffawed loudly as the clink of glass and palpable 'glug' confirmed that Pink was lacing his brew with Remy Martin.

Then Pink asked, 'What about Ainley?'

'Our chaps never saw him, sir,' Savage replied. 'He's obviously gone to ground.'

'Find him,' the Admiral said, flatly.

Swaine merely nodded.

'Not the same team of idiots, either,' Pink growled.

'That's a little unfair, sir,' Swaine protested.

'I'm not trying to be fair, Mr Swaine. I'm trying to remove a nuisance.'

Swaine glanced at Savage, who said, 'We had anticipated you wishes, Admiral. We already have another team on it. The best.'

'That pervert Hawker – and what's the other chap's name . . . Fielding?'

'That's the pair, sir' said Savage.

'Good,' Pink grunted. 'They don't make mistakes, do they?'

Pond switched off, and Sleightley remarked, 'No. Hawker and Fielding don't make mistakes.'

Pond sighed. 'You're right. Indeed they don't'

Marko knocked respectfully at the door, and waited to be told to come in.

'Well?' Ivanovitch said.

'Ainley, sir,' Marko said, hesitantly. 'He's out of contact.'

'Who told you?'

'Balchinsky. Ainley's given him the slip. He's up to something.'

'So?'

'One of the two men Ainley was . . .'

'I know about Lindstrom.'

'Balchinsky is worried, sir,' Marko said. 'He thinks Ainley may have been engaged in some kind of – unofficial operation.'

'Lining his pockets, you mean.'

'Something like that.'

Ivanovitch put his hand to his mouth, then smoothed back his shaven dome, and with his hands clasped, cracked his knuckles. Marko had learned from sometimes bitter experience never to interrupt one of these intensely private trains of thought.

'Tell Balchinsky nothing is to happen to Ainley. I want him found, but not harmed. Tell Balchinsky it doesn't really matter about Lindstrom, but if Ainley's been squeezing Canterwell, too, he must be wasted. I cannot, above all, have any suspicion drawn to us at this – uh – delicate stage. You follow me?'

Marko said, 'Yes, Colonel. I will inform Balchinsky.'

'If I know Ainley,' Ivanovitch continued, 'and I do, then he'll have gone to Scotland. Somewhere up near a place called Perth. I want him traced, but he needn't reappear yet. He will have covered his tracks with the British Foreign Office, he always does. He's probably negotiated some special sort of leave. The Embassy must contact him, find out what he's done – especially about Canterwell – and he should return to duty on schedule. Then he can join Miernek up at Tredogan, and if he's playing games with Canterwell, we'll find out. But don't hurt him – yet.'

'As you say, Colonel.'

Marko turned to leave, but Ivanovitch grunted peremptorily, and his assistant froze in his tracks.

'Why are you in such a hurry?'

'I – I – thought you wanted me to . . .' he trailed off, pointing vaguely in the direction of the radio wing.

'Marko, I will tell you when I want you to do anything. Until I do, your job is to do nothing.'

'Of course, sir.'

'What about the rig?'

'TARACO FIVE?'

'How many others have we got?'

'I don't believe we have any, Colonel.'

'Then it follows I mean TARACO FIVE, doesn't it?'

'Y-Y-yes, sir,' Marko stammered.

'Good. What about it?'

'It's going well, sir, I believe.'

'What do you mean?' Ivanovitch said very distinctly, leaning forward and hunching his shoulders so that his huge, simian bulk seemed to loom before Marko's eyes like a too-close camera image. 'What do you mean, going well? And I presume that is not an intentional pun?'

'No. No, indeed, sir.' Marko was appalled by the very idea.

'Tell me, you irrelevant little foetus. You have something to tell me that you're afraid I won't like, haven't you?' Marko nodded, miserably.

'Tell me, then, yak's whelp,' Ivanovitch thundered, 'or you'll be straining salt through you drawers in Siberia next week.'

Marko closed his eyes. 'We might be close to oil,' he said. There was utter silence, and then Ivanovitch threw back his huge head and bellowed and spluttered himself into a coughing fit that brought the two less agreeable of his three female secretaries into the room, their eyes wide with alarm, their bosoms theatrically heaving.

The KGB chief waved them away weakly, but changed his mind when his third – and distinctly more comely – secretary streamed in behind then, her superb breasts playing tag under the thin woollen jumper. He beckoned her forward. She bent over him. 'Closer,' he urged, still gasping and groaning.

She bent lower. He rubbed his ear-lobe surreptitiously against her nipple, and slipped his hand up the back of her legs, on the flimsy pretext of having to hold on to something. She'd not worn underwear since the day she came into his office three and a half years ago for a preliminary interview that lasted twenty-seven hours.

Then he pounded the desk with his fist. 'That, Marko,' he roared, 'that is the best news I've had in God knows how long.' And he laughed again, uncontrollably. Natasha burrowed her stiff nipple even more deeply into his ear and slapped him soundly on the back.

Marko's face was a picture of disbelieving relief. 'I thought you'd be furious,' he said, 'because we'd have to give the oil to the British.'

'Give it to the British,' Ivanovitch spluttered. 'Give it to the British, he says. No Marko, we don't give it to the British. When we leave,' he choked, and and wiped his eyes on his sleeve. 'Oh, my God. When we leave, Marko, we'll blow the whole bloody field up – that's what we'll do.'

Ivanovitch was used to being right, and it would not have surprised him to learn that he was corrct about Ainley.

To the left of Perth, south of what would become the 'Road to the Isles', is an area of gentle hills, mountains, lochs and glens surrounding the Lake of Menteith. An old school friend of Ainley's – and there wasn't one alive who hadn't had cause bitterly to regret their friendship – had a superbly appointed and expensively furnished cottage there – a dream hideaway far removed in style from the spartan crofts of further west. The owner liked nothing more than to spend part – most, if he could – of his summers in the comforting isolation it afforded him and his cherished family.

He was there when Ainley 'phoned from the Newport Pagnell service area on the M1. He asked Ainley to spin the conversation out long enough to enable him to think up a good enough excuse for the cherished family, but it didn't once occur to him to refuse Ainley's demand that the cottage should be empty by nightfall. Too much – far too much, he thought with a shudder – was at stake.

'Thank you, then, Frank,' Ainley said. 'I'll be eternally in your debt.'

'Not at all, Roger,' he replied. 'It's I who am in your debt.'

'And don't you just know it baby,' Ainley whispered.

There was a barmaid not four miles from the cottage with the tightest, smoothest ass Ainley had ever goosed. Her name was Fiona, and six days later, in the cool of the morning, with fifteen couplings behind him, Ainley was squatting on the bank of his favourite stream, eyes closed, pleasantly exhausted and at peace with the world, casting a speculative line amongst the bounding trout.

The still air vibrated with the crack of a shot, and a big, brown, speckled beauty leapt out of the water and lay quaking in the sandy shallows near Ainley's feet. Across the stream, Balchinsky blew carefully into the barrel of his gun, and said, 'Strange. We thought you were playing bigger fish than these, Roger.'

TEN

Night fell with almost Mediterranean suddeness and the air was hot and still and heavy, but no cicadas chirruped where Gresson stood, looking out on the calm, black sea. He thought there were yet fingers of grey-blue where Ireland lay and the sun lingered west of Sligo, and he settled his great frame against the door of the toolpusher's cabin and gazed almost with longing towards the land he'd never seen but where his fathers were born and where he was conceived. He lifted the plastic cup to his lips and drained it, and then his mood broke as he spat out a gobbet of half-melted sugar impregnated with the dregs of cold, machine-made coffee.

Larsen, the tool-pusher, leaned back in his chair and chuckled. 'I thought you Americans liked coffee, Mick.'

'This?' Gresson said, crumpling the plastic cup and slinging it away. 'Jesus, if only the so-called coffee was as hot as the weather, it'd be something.'

'Ya, it iss hot, Mick, it iss sure hot. Not like ze North Sea, huh?'

'I never heard you complain there,' the bargemaster said jokily. 'Your patch, ain't it?'

'Sure, I come from Denmark, you know zat, Mick. So ze North Sea, ya, she iss home for me.'

'And the Irish Sea's home for me, Gresson replied. 'My folks came from there,' he nodded to the west.

The phone rang and Larsen heaved his bulk forward to pick it up. Gresson wasn't interested in the outcome; he was off-shift, and whatever it was, someone else could take care of it. He strolled outside again, and looked out on the rig. It was ablaze with light and noise, and yet he felt strangely lonely. The reflections from the blinding arc-lamps flickered eerily on the water. Below deck – where Gresson himself ought to be by now – the day shift tossed, sweated and turned in their bunks and tried to shut out the constant but ragged hum of the machinery. There was always noise and clamour and sweat on an oil rig, and the day shift's only consolation was that it would be infinitely worse for the night shift when they tried to get some sleep in the morning.

'Surrounded by thousands of miles of nothing,' Gresson murmured, 'and half of us have got claustrophobia. Does that make sense?'

His eyes took in the deck without really seeing it; the frenzied but always purposeful activity, the shouted commands, the grinding crunch of the drilling machinery, the clatter of discarded piping, the sudden flow of men towards the drilling derrick . . . he straightened up, and his scrutiny became searching and deliberate. Why were they running to the derrick – why were the roustabouts chatting animatedly to men with whom they normally exchanged only apathetic grunts – why were they stopping each other on the catwalks, exchanging winks and secret handshakes? Why had the mood, the whole atmosphere of TARACO FIVE, subtly, yet perceptively, changed? Larsen supplied the answer.

'Ya, Ho-kay, I fix it now,' he roared into the phone and slammed down the receiver. 'Mick,' he yelled to the bargemaster. 'Zat vas ze damn geologist. Ve haff struck oil, Mick. Oil! VE HAFF STRUCK OIL. YAHOOOOO-OOO! And he jumped from his creaking chair, siezed the giant American round the waist, hoisted him in the air and whirled him in a clumsy, elephantine pirouette that ended with both of them crashing to the floor laughing like lunatics. Even Gresson, the forbidding almost-loner, caved in gracefully to the gut-wrenching emotion of an oil-strike.

There was a buzz of frantic tension while the news spread, and then the cheers rang out, and men who dared not ordinarily talk to him when the evil mood was on him ran up and slapped him brazenly on the back and screamed,

'We done it, we done it,' in at least four languages. The heat and the monotony and the tedium were forgotten, and for a moment each roustabout was a ten-foot tall king. They were oilmen, and the sea had paid them their price in the only coin that oilmen recognised.

Gresson shrugged them off and slipped away to a deserted stretch of rail, spread his arms and hung his head over the side of the rig. He was as delirious as any of them – with one crucial difference. Their only purpose and raison d'être was to find their precious oil, but he had another objective. He'd cancelled out the disappointment of a dry well in the North Sea and soon the screens would go up round the derrick, the geologists would take over, the roustabouts and big Larsen and his men would be taken off . . . and TARACO FIVE would be left to Gresson and those members of his crew who could now speak their native Russian without fear, to fulfil the rig's real and ineffably more crucial role.

Eighty-five miles to the east, and twenty-four hours later, Ewan Scott sat in the lounge of the Carreg Wen Hotel, which lay just off the road that led to the village of Tredogan and his own home in Trefynnon, one of the little fishing hamlets that dotted the broken coastline of Cardigan Bay. The Carreg Wen was under new – and interesting – ownership. The advertisement in his local paper announcing the licence tranfer from a now defunct Tredogan pub had named the buyer as Paul Tadeusz Miernek. Scott hadn't bothered to work out the nationality yet; it was enough for him that the old, rambling guest house had been a new lease of life as a functioning hotel, because the road alongside the Carreg Wen ('"White Rock" it means, see,' he'd been told) – that road lay between the air base of RAF Tredogan and the Royal Aircraft Establishment next door. And RAF Tredogan housed Britain's entire stockpile of ORBITMAN missiles. Like Vengan and a few other people who were just names to him, Ewan Scott was an agent for Department RE.

Scott rented a small whitewash-and-slate fisherman's cottage in Trefynnon, the end one of a row that faced directly on to the pebble and grit beach. It had very little charm, and a broken chimney-pot. An oil-fired Aga doubled for cooking and heating, and Scott had had a telephone installed. From there he drove each day to the corner of the airfield at RAG Tredogan leased to Cambrian Helicopters, and flew an S 61 N Sikorski on pick-up and delivery runs to the rigs in the Celtic Sea oilfield. The air was clean, the work functional rather than demanding, the natives friendly – and the big Sikorski a joy to fly in every way. He'd also fallen in with a rich local farmer who owned a private airstrip, and there Scott was able to garage the little monoplane which had years ago become part of his life.

The assignment, too, was going well. He was amazed to discover how much was freely talked about and circulated through the comprehensive grapevine of a small Welsh village. It was the holiday season, and since Trefynnon was geared to the tourist trade, strangers were accepted into the little community, and included in the traditional Welsh pastime of malicious gossip. Scott moved freely throughout the area, and looked, and listened. Several things were in his favour . . . he was an expert in a glamorous occupation – the locals were consumed with interest in the desolate piles of ocean iron-mongery which were his customers – and more important, perhaps, he was a handsome and eligible bachelor. He hadn't gone short of female company since he arrived in Trefynnon, and the fiery, passionate girls were duly grateful. He liked the place, and he liked the people, and his thoughts had strayed lately into the unlikely reaches of where he might settle down after he'd had his fill of flying and spying. Trefynnon? Could be, but not for a long time – a good long time. Scott wasn't finished with life yet – and the job had to be done.

If he had a prime suspect in the presumed scenario of dirty work at the RAE, it was Sian Griffith, the local schoolmistress. Local in the sense that she'd been born in Tredogan and lived there all her life, though she taught the grammar stream of a comprehensive school in Cardigan. Her devotion to the Welsh Nationalists' cause was condescendingly tolerated as long as it wasn't translated into outright indoctrination.

But Sian – who'd been strikingly beautiful as a girl, and was still the best-looking woman he'd seen since coming to Wales – kept her special tuition for a hand-picked group of pupils and ex-pupils forming a Free Wales Army cadre of ultra-militant activists. At any rate, that was what Scott suspected. The talk at his own pub, The Ship in Trefynnon, was that she was up to something. Apart from rare appearances at public meetings – one was due the following week – she'd kept an unnaturally low profile in the past few months, as if she was no longer anxious to draw attention to her activities. Scott had no evidence, but he was playing a hunch that she would lead him to Tredogan.

Dark hints from garrulous patriots that she was committed to violence where the ends justified it, fuelled his determination to keep her under surveillance, and he'd dropped casually into her usual haunts night after night, and rarely failed to spot her playing an elaborate pantomime of studied innocence. She had never, to his knowledge, visited the Carreg Wen Hotel.

He drained his pint and saw that the bar was filling up with rather obvious oilrig types on the spree, so he decided to get another drink in before the surly and inarticulate young foreigner behind the bar (Polish, Scott thought) became so overwhelmed that he couldn't cope, which seemed to happen all too often. He'd cornered a yard of bar, and he was next – but the barman looked not at Scott but at a man who'd just come up with a ten pound note in his hand. Scott was about to protest, and turned to the newcomer with his mouth half open. His jaw dropped a further half inch, and stayed there, and he felt the pound note he was holding droop in a sympathetic wilt. He looked away and started a tuneless whistle . . . Scott was no coward, but he freely acknowledged that men who were built like the Post Office Tower with muscles usually got served pretty quickly in pubs.

There was an atmosphere of noisy release building up in the bar, and he thought he recognised some off-duty roustabouts from an Irish rig, TARACO FIVE, that he'd occasionally visited. They looked as though they'd something to celebrate, and it was, he supposed, more likely than not an oil strike, but being oilmen they were close-mouthed and wary when they were out of their element. The giant who was buying for them – his name was Mick, Scott gathered – had now turned and was leaning back against the bar, making it abundantly clear that it was his territory. Scott didn't feel like disputing the matter, so he strolled unconcernedly out swinging his car-keys.

He got into the Lotus and started the engine. Another car – a red Mini – was crossing the gravel car-park at the front of the hotel as he was backing out of his space. There was plenty of room at his end of the brilliantly lit parking lot, but the car swept straight by and made for what he knew to be a private yard at the rear. The driver was Sian Griffith, and Scott switched off his engine and waited until he heard her come to a halt. The car door slammed, and he caught the sound of another door closing.

More by instinct than any conscious design or reasoned deduction, he unlocked the glove compartment of the Lotus and felt around for one of a set of Pond's speciality line in barely detectable bugs. He slipped out of his car, crept round to the back of the hotel, and clamped the magnetized device to the underside of the Mini's bumper.

He realised as he doubled back to his car that Sian had now made the one positive move for which he'd been ing . . . unless she and Paul Miernek were closer than anyone thought, she could only have been sneaking into the rear entrance of the Carreg Wen Hotel for one reason – because she didn't want to be seen going in at the front.

He monitored the red Mini's movements for the rest of that week, and produced nothing more interesting than a shopping trip on Tuesday, a visit to the library in Cardigan on Wednesday – the school holidays were already well under way – and on Thursday a strangely well-planned and purposeful pub crawl ending in his own local, where she drank pits of bitter and refused to talk English. On Friday, though, his persistence paid off.

Pond's pet bugs contained two tiny transmitters, one sending out a continuous signal and the other broadcasting on a different frequency. The second transmitter was the more interesting of the two; it was beamed into a receiver which was always left 'on' at his cottage. It was activated solely by movement. As soon as the wheels of Sian's car started turning, the receiver emitted a piercing whoop which ended only when the miniature pendulum built into the device came to a rest and cut the noise off. By then Scott would be on the road himself, tracking her via the transmitter broadcasting to his car receiver. At seven o'clock on Friday evening, the cottage receiver shrilled in his ear just as he was wading through a tasty mixed grill he'd laboriously prepared on the Aga for high tea. He said 'Sod it!' and stuffed a piece of toast into his mouth as he ran out to the Lotus.

Sian was heading east into the heart of the wild, hilly country that started to rise a few miles inshore. Soon the road narrowed to single-track width, and hedges gave way to unfenced banks and bracken-strewn slopes. Scott started to slow down. The signal was loud and strong, and they'd been climbing steadily for miles along a road which had no turnings off it; he calculated they must now be close to a thousand feet above sea level. He changed down to take a particularly excruciating bend – and suddenly he was at the summit of a hill giving a breathtaking view of the tangled and desolate valley stretching out below. He jammed his foot on the brake-pedal, and followed the winding road down the other side of the hill with his eyes. Almost at the bottom the brake-lights of the Mini briefly pulsed, and the little car turned off towards an apparently derelict stone hut standing by itself at the end of a two or three hundred yard long track.

Scott decided he couldn't risk following her in the car, so he reversed behind a thick outcrop of bracken just off the road. He took his binoculars, went back to the brow of the hill, and dropped on his stomach just as Sian's car pulled up outside the hut. He focused the glasses, and saw her open the boot and take out a number of seemingly heavy packages, which she carried into the semi-ruined building one by one.

Then he caught the sound of a car engine, and swept the binoculars round to pick up a green Land Rover coming into the valley along the same road, but from the other direction. The track was dry and the driver was moving fast, trailing a dust-cloud in his wake. He, too, pulled off the road and followed the rutted path to the hut. The driver – it was definitely a man, though Scott couldn't recall having seen him before – climbed out and helped her with the last few packages. They stayed inside the hut for some little time, then both came out and went back to their vehicles.

Scott waited until Sian was on the move, then jumped up and ran back to the Lotus. He scorched off the bank on to the narrow road and drove like the hammers of hell for the first barely-remembered crossroads, turning down the right-hand branch and pulling into a field gateway as soon as he was out of sight. The flashing light activated by the bug showed the Mini drawing closer to the crossroads and then rapidly away again, back on the road to Tredogan. He did a six-point turn and, in the gathering dusk, headed for the stone hut.

It was derelict. Part of the roof had caved in, and his torch flashed on a bale of musty old straw and a dry, bleached and certainly worm-ridden bench that seemed to be the only artifacts the hut contained. He searched what remained of the ceiling, and then shone the torch on to the floor. The flagstones were dusty, cracked, and polka-dotted with little round, black sheep's droppings – all except one.

Scott fetched a hefty screw-driver from his car, and levered the flagstone easily out of its bed. He shone his torch down, and whistled. The stone covered an underground chamber about four feet deep and lined with bricks. Stacked neatly in the hole was enough stick gelignite to make Guy Fawkes green with envy. The explosives filled three quarters of the space, and the remainder was piled high with an impressive array of detonators and manufactured timing devices. Scott whistled again; this time through his teeth, a perky, self-satisfied little fanfarade. He resealed the arsenal with the flagstone, and moved the wooden bench to sit back over it again, as it had been when he'd first seen it. Then he poked his head out of the door, looked around, checked that he'd left nothing in the hut, and drove off up the hill. The bug receiver was silent, so he switched on the car radio and, it being Friday night, caught the Beethoven Symphony that formed the second half of the Promenade Concert.

The man from from the Land Rover, who'd been standing at the side of the hut with two sheepdogs at his heels when Scott left, couldn't see the intruder's face, but he groped in his anorak pocket for a chewed-up stump of pencil, and wrote the number and make of the car on a near-empty twenty packet of Woodbines. Dafydd had fallen early in life to Sian Griffith's spell; he was by no means a fervent Nationalist, but he didn't mind lending a hand. He was a shepherd from choice, and the hut was the base from which he made his late evening rounds. He always walked down from the hilltop because Sam, his favourite sheepdog, got fretful during the bumpy ride. Dafydd checked the explosives cache with his own torch, and then set off for the nearest telephone on the main road, the dogs bounding happily fore and aft of him in the knowledge that they were in for an early night.

At about the same time that Dafydd got through to Sian Griffith and broke the bad news, and Scott was humming his way into the recapitulation of the first movement of Beethoven's Pastoral Symphony, Marko, chief assistant in the Special Task Force of the KGB, was standing before Ivanovitch's little desk, shuffling his feet and clasping and unclasping his hands. He couldn't remember a moment when he'd ever felt uncomfortable in the Comrade Colonel's presence, and the nervous dread was now so deeply ingrained in his persona that he'd be lost without it. Finally Ivanovitch looked up at him and broke the oppressive silence.

'I'll go myself,' he announced. Marko was so staggered he almost forgot his overriding fear. 'You can't,' he gasped. 'You couldn't possibly.'

'I can't?' Ivanovitch inquired. 'Couldn't? Do you know what you are saying?'

'F-f-forgive me, Comrade C-colonel,' Marko stammered. 'It's just that – well, it's not done.'

'Well, it's going to be,' Ivanovitch said, reasonably. 'It's the only way, Marko. A lot's happening that I don't know about, and I cannot tolerate that. This operation must not be placed in jeopardy by anyone or anything, Marko. It is more important than anything I have ever embarked upon. Ainley is up to something, and I will have to know what it is. He will not lie to my face, so I will have him brought out to the rig and question him myself.'

'But how, Colonel – how will you leave? How will you get there? Comrade Andropov will not permit it. Suppose something should happen to you. It is not possible, Colonel, you are too valuable.'

'My value is greater, Marko, in ensuring that this mission is completed as planned. Yuri will see that – when I come back. It is not necessary that he knows I am going. It will worry him, and I do not want him worried, Marko. I shall leave in secrecy,' he rose from the desk and held Marko's gaze. 'Do you understand? No one must know. The whole affair is far too delicate.

'As to how I shall get there, that is simple. As you know we have a trawler standing by about two hundred miles off the British coast. It was intended as a back-up ship in case anything went wrong with the submarine or even the rig. It will now become my headquarters. The trawler is a converted fleet mother-ship and she is equipped with a helicopter. That will get me to and from the oil rig.

'You will have made ready for me at Leningrad one of our M-12 Tchaika amphibious flying boats, and make certain it is fitted with long-range tanks. Requisition it for departmental use, and no questions will be asked. The Tchaika can refuel from the trawler for its return trip, and when the operation is finished, I shall come back to Russia on board the submarine. Those are my orders, Marko. Make the arrangements. And Marko. Stop worrying, for God's sake. You'll give yourself an embolism if you carry on like that.'

'Yes, Comrade Colonel. Of course, Comrade Colonel,' Marko said. 'Are you absolutely sure,' he ventured, daringly, 'that it wouldn't be just as easy to use the method you just described to bring Ainley here to Moscow?'

'No!' Ivanovitch bellowed. 'I have told you, I have made my decision. It will be done as I wish.'

'But Colonel . . .'

'No, Marko, I tell you. It has to be done this way. It would take too long to bring Ainley here. You don't seem to realise the urgency. This operation may very well have to take place within a week from now.'

'So soon, Comrade Colonel!' Marko was aghast. 'I had no idea.'

'Well now you do, Marko. I must be at the rig not later than Tuesday. So get in touch with Balchinsky and tell him to fix a meeting with Ainley somewhere between London and Wales, and brief him so that Ainley can be at Miernek's hotel by Monday evening. Have you got that?'

'Yes, Comrade Colonel, yes,' Marko stuttered, wondering he'd ever summoned up the nerve to query his chief's grand design.

'Then do it, Marko. Do it!'

Mikhail Balchinsky flew back from Scotland to London leaving Ainley to drive down, chaperoned by an uncommunicative and single-minded member of the Soviet Trade Delegation in Highate, whose talents were anything but commercial. Balchinsky scanned the latest messages from Moscow. There was no hint in them that Ivanovitch himself was planning to join the party on the rig, yet Balchinsky – who was probably the shrewdest spy-master the KGB had ever employed – actually (and very privately, for it did not do to air such opinions) guessed the truth. He'd appreciated long before that the seizure of the rocket was so vital to the destiny of world Communism that if the plot failed, no one in Moscow who's been connected with it would escape the vengeance of Brezhnev and Andropov. Ivanovitch had made the Trojan Horse his own creation from start to finish; he had refused all offers of help, and merely dictated his orders and requirements. Balchinsky couldn't see the old bear sitting meekly in Gorki Street waiting for the axe to fall if the whole thing blew up in his face. Ivanovitch, Balchinsky was sure, would have a plan; Moscow wouldn't be a healthy place for him if his precious Trojan Horse developed colic and refused to leave the starting gate. He scanned the map of Wales to fix a meeting-place with Ainley, and decided that the south-western tip of Pembrokeshire looked a likely enough spot.

Ainley shook off his bovine shadow, checked his Mews for strangers, and decided it was safe to come home. There was no urgent mail, and a glance at the newspapers he'd bought at the motorway service area were evidence that

Lindstrom was no longer in the headlines. He felt certain he'd not been connected with the affair, and the only man who could expose him dare not do so, either now or in the future.

His instructions from Balchinsky were to keep in touch by ringing in from public kiosks at fixed times, and the following morning he decided to make a check call from Paddington station and collect the Sunday papers en route. He parked close to the main concourse, dialled the number and, feeling distinctly foolish, said – as he'd been told to – 'This is Pandora.'

No one had answered his first two calls, from the motorway and the Mews house, but this time a voice said, 'Wait,' then came back and reeled off a string of numbers which Ainley took down. The voice spoke again – just the one word, 'Clear'. Ainley whistled his surprise and hung up; the information wasn't even in code. Either the Embassy were supremely confident of the bug-proof jamming field, or the messsage was so urgent they didn't want to take the chance on his ability to decipher. Probably both, he thought. He drank a glass of beer, and separated the first eight figures – the map coordinates – from the date and time, which turned out to be the following evening. Balchinsky, he decided, was in a hurry to see him.

He got home and fished out his set of Ordnance Survey Maps. Unsurprisingly, the rendezvous was in Wales, which was the direction he knew he'd have to take eventually. It could only mean, he mused, that the operation – the big one – was close, very close.

Ainley decided he'd make what was for him an earlyish start – round about ten – the following morning, so he found a garage open to fill up his car in readiness for the trip. A small, plain blue 5cwt Thames van drew up at the opposite rank of pumps, and beat him to the elderly, sour-faced man who seemed to be the sole source of service at the filling station. But then a girl of about twenty with frizzy auburn curls, wearing a tee-shirt printed with a cartoon petrol pump on each attractively mobile breast, bounced out of the office and asked what she could do for him. He was tempted to tell her, but got a look of such profound disapproval from her boss that he merely asked politely for a fill-up. She tossed her pretty head at the sorely taxed old chap, who glared at her with concentrated venom and poured half a gallon of three-star down his trouserleg. The driver of the van burst out laughing, and the forecourt girl started an animated conversation with Ainley.

She wiped over his windscreen without being asked, and volunteered to check the water and oil. 'Might as well,' she twittered, lifting the bonnet, 'if you're off on a trip to-morrow. Going far?' Ainley said, 'Pembrokeshire, and then up-country.' She said, 'Ooh, That's Wales, innit?' and Ainley agreed that it was, indeed, Wales.

A broad grin appeared on the face of the driver of the plain blue 5cwt van, while the evil-tempered old man said, 'Bloody good riddance, an' all.' The van driver got out to pay at the sales office, but stumbled at the back of Ainley's car and dropped a handful of money, which Ainley and the girl helped to pick up.

The driver spotted a fifty pence piece rolling under Ainley's rear offside wheel, and leaned beneath the car to retrieve it, holding on to the bumper for support. Then they brushed down their respective trousers, jeans and overalls, settled for the fuel, and peace was restored. Ainley purred smoothly away back to Lancaster Mews, the girl painted her nails while her jealous employer ranted at her, and Vengan stopped at a phone box to tell Sleightley that Ainley was motoring to Wales in the morning, taking one of Doctor Pond's magnetic bugs under his rear bumper.

Countdown

ELEVEN

The new, dark-blue hatch-back Rover 3500 with upholstery the colour of a Lincoln biscuit nosed out of Lancaster Mews, turned left, left again into Craven Terrace and first left into Craven Hill. Ainley stopped at a tobacconist's, and bought a box of two hundred Rothmans International. The gold band at the base of the filter was distinctive, and matched his gold electronic Dunhill lighter. Ainley liked to be distinctive. He removed a beige leather driving glove and took out one of the dark blue and gold packets (they blended not only with his car, but also with the plain navy blue 12 oz Airey and Wheeler three-piece suit and suede half boots with deep fawn socks). A manicured nail picked ineffectually at the cellophane binding strip. Sensing he was losing presence, Ainley dug the nail in, making a crescent-shaped dent in the side of the packet, but then recovered a few points by stripping off the wrapping in one more or less continuous movement. His left hand was still gloved, but the opulent gold Rolex Oyster flashed discreetly through the gap beneath his sleeve.

'Olé', chanted the mop-haired, grinning pillar of acne behind the untidy counter. Ainley opened the packet, plucked out the gold-leaf foil, flipped the Dunhill and let his blue eyes fall unblinkingly on the boy as he lit the cigarette. It was a trick he had perfected, looking at someone while lighting a cigarette, or over a whisky tumbler as he drank. Most people looked down or into, Ainley across. He'd burned his dark ochre moustache twice and his nose once, and several times sent slivers of ice and droplets of Chivas Regal skittering down his Royal Yacht Squadron tie; but he'd persevered – with larger, chunkier glasses, half-filled, and the precisely adjusted Dunhill, and now

127

geographical errors were rare. It was, he felt, distinctive.

'Nice day, innit?' ventured the boy, still grinning inanely, which stretched a pustule on his cheek beyond the point of tolerance. Blood and pus welled up on the spot. The fastidious Ainley grunted, turned and walked out, balancing the box of cigarettes, the opened packet, the lighted cigarette, the Dunhill and the single glove as he fumbled for his car keys, kicking shut the glass door.

'An' fack orf ter you an' all,' shouted the boy when the door was safely slammed. 'Bleedin' poofter.' In which he was wrong. The elegant Ainley was an assiduous heterosexual lecher and an energetic lover, though not first thing in the morning. He flinched at powerful gusts of gamey female breath in his face. Even when he penetrated from the rear they generally looked round to say 'Thank you'. Not that he used the position much . . . his maternal grandfather had been a missionary, and anyway he never thought the polar bears at the Zoo seemed to be having much fun.

He reversed three feet from a metallic silver BMW 728 in front of him, put the Rover out into Craven Hill again, turned left into Leinster Terrace, and completed the square to Lancaster Gate before emerging into Bayswater Road, taking the one-way system round Lancaster Terrace to bring him into Hyde Park. The BMW, trapped at the Brook Street lights, caught up just past the Serpentine Bridge, and stayed with him as he went over on an orange light at the Alexandra Gate and started down Exhibition Road.

The two men in the front seats of the BMW – Fielding was driving, Hawker listening to the morning service on the Blaupunkt self-seeking car radio – didn't expect him to take the right-hand filter lane for Prince Consort Road, but Ainley did. They were not to know that by instinct and temperament he was a Kensington Road rather than a Cromwell Road man. So while he leaned into a leisurely right bend from Prince Consort Road to circumnavigate the Albert Hall, past the mansion block where Malcolm

Sargent used to live on top of, as it were, the job, Fielding was forced into an agonising 'U'-turn at the next break in the central reservation. He roared back up the other side of Exhibition Road, jumping the light in the direction Ainley had taken. This disturbed Hawker's concentration. His pleasure at hearing the hymn 'Let us with a gladsome mind' had in any case become alloyed by the persistent niggle of why the BBC should presume to have a Hymnal all to itself. The Yamaha XS 1000 purring on a double yellow line at the Albert Hall exit while its rider ate a Mars bar, didn't move as Ainley eased into Kensington Road, heading West.

It didn't move as Fielding, cursing with the window down, got there a minute later and screamed out in front of a taxi to a cacophony of klaxons. The Yamaha rider didn't know Ainley, either, but sensed that he'd prefer Kensington High Street and Olympia to the Great West Road and the Hammersmith Flyover. The Yamaha had taken up its station at the Albert Hall thirty-three minutes before. At ten forty-nine as Ainley was just on, and Fielding coming up to, the Chiswick Flyover, Hawker deeply engrossed in Morning Story, the Yamaha rider, in silver-buttoned black leathers and black crash helmet with an opaque, dusky visor, was satisfied no one else was joining the convoy. The engine swelled to full power, and the huge motorcycle slid effortlessly into the street. Just after the M4 turn-off to Windsor, the rider had both cars safely in sight, and sat in the middle lane a measured two hundred yards from the BMW's tail.

'Maidenhead', said Hawker. 'What?' said Fielding, irritably. He liked driving to be a private communion between himself, the car and the tarmac. 'Maidenhead,' Hawker repeated. 'Over there', pointing right. 'So fucking what?', Fielding replied, genuinely mystified. 'Just map-reading,' said Hawker, complacently.

'I don't need you to map-read on the sodding motorway'. Silence. Then, 'Can't we have something else on the radio?'

'*Round Britain Quiz*', said Hawker, Stiffly, 'like *The*

Times crossword puzzle, is a genuine intellectual exercise. A cerebral, if you like, gallop through the more interesting reaches of the mental process'.

Actually, he thought, the quiz was becoming dangerously precious these days, and he couldn't stand the London woman. For that matter he couldn't stand any woman, metropolitan or otherwise. Surprisingly, for a homosexual male, he'd even loathed his mother, who like Fielding, he mused, glancing at his companion, had had normal but voracious sexual appetites. She'd cultivated the (to him) distressing habit of absentmindedly but rhythmically pressing her clothed sex against the sharp corner of any table, kitchen working surface, newel-post or television set she happened to be standing alongside. Hawker found it repulsive, and invariably, when she'd left the room, wiped over the violated junctions with a damp cloth. He wouldn't let her near his radiogram. Also like Fielding, she hadn't been a fan of what was then the Home Service, now Radio Four.

'I would like' said Fielding, 'some music'.

'Crap, you mean. Mindless wallpaper'.

'Better than that turgid rubbish', Fielding snorted. 'Lot of stupid old fucking faggots and dikes giving wrong answers to ludicrous questions sent in by maniacs from Lemington Spa, Buxton or St Neots or somewhere'.

Hawker almost agreed. Sighing dramatically, he put the radio on to the long wave.

'Happy?' he inquired, smugly, as Pete Murray began to interview Cilla Black.

He settled his sixteen stones back in the padded seat, the safety belt straining over his bulging belly, and giggled in that funny, high-pitched way of his, the three chins quivering like descending scallops of pink blancmange. Fielding's sharp, lean, vulpine face showed his distaste, which made the fat man gurgle all the more hysterically, until the half-moon, rimless glasses popped off his little button nose.

'Jesus, you disgust me', Fielding grated.

'I know, dear heart, I know', squeaked Hawker, plung-
ing his hand under Fielding's seat belt.

'Get your podgy paw off,' Fielding snarled, 'or I'll stuff
that Browning up your fat arse'.

'Promises, promises,' Hawker breathed, ecstatically.

'Christ-all-bleedin'-mighty, how did I ever get tied up to
a slimy, poovy lard-barrel like you.'

'Twas fate, darling boy, fate,' shrieked Hawker, mercifully consigning *Open House* to oblivion.

'We were,' he gasped, wheezed, chortled and choked in
an alarming seriatim crescendo, 'We were . . . made for each
other.'

'Shut up, you fat pig. Shut up or I'll chop you, I swear I'll
fucking chop you.' Fielding's cultivated Southern Standard
English tended to slip into sub-Heckmondwike when he
got excited.

But it was true. They *were* a good pair. In Ankara, that
time, Hawker had started patiently to saw through a girl's
neck with the rusty, jagged edge of what had been a tin of
apricot slices, while Fielding forced her younger brother to
watch until he yielded the information they sought. Hawker
could have used one of three guns to kill the girl, or a knife,
or a wire garotte (his favourite), or simply the fearful
strength in his small, chubby hands. But he chose the
mangled tin. When they got what they wanted he finished
the job – with the tin.

He worked carefully, like a surgeon, his arms and chest
splashed with blood. It took a long time. As the girl died,
Fielding drove a broad-bladed knife into the back of the
boy's neck, severing his spinal cord.

'You really like it, don't you?' Fielding had asked. 'The
killing bit, I mean.'

'And you don't?'

'I do it because I have to do it,' Fielding said.

'Some men – ' Hawker intoned pompously, ' – make
electric toasters, some men hump bricks, pull teeth, cook
books, train horses . . . Us? We kill.'

131

Fielding had heard the speech before, but always with different job categories. Hawker's mind was a cornucopia of other people's occupations. 'But you enjoy it,' Fielding persisted.

'The man who trains horses enjoys training horses,' Hawker replied. 'What's wrong with that?' Fielding hadn't answered. He knew there was a limit beyond which it was dangerous to push Hawker.

They were, then, a good pair. Not the cold, unemotional, merciless sadists popular fiction might suppose them to be. Nor the glamorous, icily nonchalant matadors of international espionage with 00 numbers and 00000 bank accounts. Simply the most effective, painstaking and, in a curious way, honest assassins on the payroll of the British Special Intelligence Service. Vice-Admiral Pink called them 'Laurel and Hardy' at times, which was a very black joke. When jolly, roly-poly Hawker and his psychotic partner were killing – and particularly if the animal savagery so close to the surface of Hawker's affability gained the upper hand – they were in truth no laughing matter. And they were also reliable. When they promised to deliver, they delivered. Today they would deliver the traitor, Ainley.

TWELVE

11.58. Between Chippenham and the A429 turn-off to Cirencester and the Cotswolds. Still in the centre lane, because Ainley considered it pretentious to drive an expensive (more or less) car in the fast lane unless you were overtaking a more expensive one. The BMW slid past an old Morris Minor, and anchored in behind a Renault 14, five cars (sometimes three, or four, once none) from the Rover. Fielding was good. Ainley never once saw them.

'Where's the bugger going then?' growled Hawker, pushing the button for the news summary at noon.

'Wales?' he wondered.

'Bristol?' asked Fielding.

'Gloucester?' They looked at each other quickly, self-consciously.

They'd once killed a man in the packed courtyard of the New Inn at Gloucester immediately after a Three Choirs Festival performance of *The Dream of Gerontius*. Fielding had been unimpressed with Elgar's masterwork. Hawker fancied an epicene young cellist. The murder had been swift, bloody and clumsy. They'd only just managed to get away.

Ainley moved the Rover from the centre to the slow lane, and Fielding shot past him.

'Well done,' Hawker said, sarcastically.

'Balls,' grated Fielding, glancing in the mirror, then looking back, then into the mirror again. 'What shall I do?'

'First of all,' Hawker said, pompously, 'keep your eyes on the road. Then, when I tell you, indicate left and, should you still be capable of so doing, drive this heap into the slow lane and take the exit that's coming up and which I'm sure even you can see, which someone has thoughtfully engraved A429. Weedy little grey-haired men in county planning departments and Ministry of Transport Offices spent their entire lives providing you with succinct and exact directions and – '.

'For Christ's sake stop fucking rabbiting,' Fielding yelled. 'Why have I got to do this?' he demanded, surging into the slow lane ahead of a Pickford's van and snapping on the indicator.

'Because,' Hawker intoned, as if he were chanting the Versicles and Responses at Matins, 'that is what Ainley is doo-ingggg,' finishing on a phrase sounding not unlike a diesel-engine hooter in reverse.

Fielding shot off the motorway on to the slip road, came to a roundabout at the top of the hill, said 'Shit,' and took the right-hand outlet to Cirencester. He cut into a side road and skidded to a halt behind the startled owner of a farm tractor. Fielding jumped out, slammed the door, ran up to the tractor, crouched behind it, and with a feeling of enormous relief saw Ainley drive sedately down the road in the direction they'd intended taking. He doubled back to the car, did a three-point turn that decapitated a patch of cow parsley, and followed at a discreet distance. The Yamaha rider, who'd stopped off at the Membury service area for a Crunchie Bar, saw Fielding's braking lights at the first slight bend in the main road, and waved at the tractor driver as the big bike moved into top gear.

'What the hell's Ainley think he's doing?' said Fielding exasperated by now.

'What any gentleman does at lunchtime,' Hawker replied, folding his ands across his seat-belt and rubbing his tummy reflectively.

Ainley led them to the Badger's Sett, a South Gloucestershire country hotel with a comfortably middle-class farming and business luncheon trade.

'Drive past,' said Hawker, as Ainley walked in at the front door. 'He'll be an hour and a half at least.'

They went to the nearest little town. At a chrome-and-plastic cafe, Hawker consumed a double Wimpy-cheese-eggburger and chips, roll and butter, and thick Expresso coffee, with home-made apple tart and country farmhouse fresh cream as an after-thought. Fielding ate a plain Wimpy with a cup of tea. Ainley, at the Badger's Sett, chose mulligatawny soup, roast lamb with mint sauce, roast potatoes, carrots and greens, topped with an uninspired cômpote of fruit and single cream, strong black coffee (undrinkable), and a Remy Martin to balance the chilled Domecq La Ina dry fino sherry he'd ordered as an aperitif. The Yamaha rider scaled a wall into the garden of a large country house which that weekend would be open to the public, picked some strawberries and redcurrants, and ate them sitting on the lawn on the blind side of a drooping monkey-puzzle tree.

When they picked Ainley up again, Hawker was annoyed that they'd missed the *Archers*, but rather pleased that his first guess of Wales as the traitor's destination might turn out to be correct. He switched on Radio Three and caught the end of Schubert's Third Symphony, played by the BBC Welsh Orchestra, conducted by Boris Brott and the whole of Mozart's B Flat Major piano concerto, K.450, soloist Ingrid Haebler. The Yamaha rider, sharing some stolen raspberries with the now mollified tractor-driver down the same side turning, heard the music carried faintly on the breeze.

The last exit to Bristol or M5 spur to the South-West had come and gone. The Severn Bridge was just in sight. Ainley had scarcely ever dropped below 68 mph, or gone above 72 mph. Fielding paced him, sometimes erratically, always deliberately.

They crossed the Severn and Wye Bridges, and the Yamaha overhauled them east of Newport, near Caerwent. Ainley drove off the M4 then took the A48 to Cardiff and Swansea. Fielding now varied his speed more subtly than ever to prevent the slightest seed of suspicion growing in Ainley's mind. Neither driver (nor Hawker, who had his eyes closed, helping Boris Brott conduct the concerto) noticed the big bike pull off the main road at the Cowbridge Bypass and rejoin it at the other end. Ainley entered the motorway again at Margam.

'Swansea?' Fielding asked. No, not Swansea.

Then the Rover stopped for petrol, so Fielding decided to overtake and find him later. Hawker finished the Mozart with a magisterial flourish, and belched.

After Carmarthen, Fielding said, 'Christ, it could be anywhere.' Hawker mentioned that he was beginning to feel peckish again, and Fielding called him a greedy over-stuffed pig, which was fairly restrained for Fielding. Hawker was resigning himself to a lingering starvation when Ainley doubled back around the one-way system in Haverfordwest and pulled up outside a small, but select, hotel.

'Aah,' Hawker brayed, 'tea-time,' and gorged himself on cream slices and Welsh cake at a stuffy, timbered little restaurant with chintz tablecloths and ancient waitresses. Ainley had thickly buttered toasted teacakes, tiny smoked-salmon sandwiches fringed with cress and transparent cucumber slices, and strong tea from a metal pot that needed asbestos fingers to hold it. To add insult to com-parative injury, it leaked over his driving gloves, placed thoughtlessly too near the pot on the glass-topped, claw footed Victorian reproduction table wobbling on a patch of frayed, pseudo-oriental carpet. The tall, slender motor-cyclist went to the public convenience, and then bought a copy of the West Wales Guardian and a packet of Juicy Fruit at a newsagent's.

Even the Yamaha expected the Rover to turn North for Fisguard and Cardigan, but Ainley went West-South-West to Broad Haven and Marloes Sands.

'Beautiful', said Hawker.

'Got the fucker', said Fielding.

'Watch your step, now,' Hawker urged. 'He's bound to spot us'.

'Give me a stretch of open road with just us and him on it, and he can stop for a game of Travel Scrabble for all I care,' Fielding gritted. Hawker eased his coat away from the reverse-holstered .38 Beretta, then stroked the stock of the Browning almost as lovingly as he'd caressed Fielding's thigh.

'How?' he asked. They almost never laid detailed plans for a 'termination', as SIS quaintly called it; too much tended to happen at the last moment.

'If he goes to the beach, drown him,' suggested Fielding, tenser now than at any time since the row with his fat friend. Hawker glanced at the nearside wing mirror, looked away, then back. Fielding noticed the jerky movement from one whose neck was not constructed for oscillation.

'What's up?'

'Thought I saw that guy on the big bike – the one we passed in Haverfordwest.'

'The one you fancied. And?'

'Must have been mistaken.'

Fielding shrugged, but logged the tiny slip of information on the 'warning' side of his now cold, active appraisal of the hit.

Ainley reached the T-junction and turned left for Marloes Sands instead of right for Broad Haven. Balchinsky was renowned for his eccentric choices of meeting-places, and Ainley had not argued. Balchinsky was his wallet. Marloes Sands had been specified in the map coordinates, so Marloes Sands it was. It looked, Ainley thought, sufficiently isolated for Balchinsky who, though he was known to the SIS, preferred personal contacts because he distrusted passing messages by telephone. Ainley imagined that today's message would contain little more than the precise location of Miernek's hotel.

He parked the Rover, glanced left and right down the empty road, and started down the lane to Marloes. He thought it more than likely that he and Balchinsky would seem ludicrously inappropriate in their dark suits and city shoes, but at that stage he'd no idea how vast and empty Marloes Sands could be in the third week of August at the turn of the evening tide. Or that Welsh landladies and small hoteliers tended to serve dinner early.

It was nearly half a mile to the beach, and the lane was dusty. He came out at the edge of the sands and saw the rock outcrops, the pools, the vast expanse of beige-brown sand, the distant sea, the even more distant bulk of Skomer Island, and Balchinsky. He waved. The Russian didn't respond. Ainley hadn't expected him to. As far as he could tell, they were alone.

Fielding flattened himself against the hedgerow bank, and motioned Hawker back.

'There's another guy there.'

'So we take both.'

'A completely accidental double drowning?' Fielding asked sarcastically.

'We'll bury the other one.'

'What with?'

'We'll find something. Driftwood – anything. Get on with it.' In the last analysis, Hawker always took command.

'Who does what?' Fielding demanded.

'I'll take Ainley, you do the other guy. Don't shoot unless you have to.'

'You have my briefing?' Ainley inquired in Russian. Balchinsky nodded, and drew an envelope from his pocket. Ainley took it and opened it. He checked the beach again, then took out what to Hawker and Fielding appeared to be a large sheet of folded paper. They saw Balchinsky jab his finger at a point on the paper towards the left-hand edge.

Hawker whispered, 'Christ I do believe he's a contact,' then flattened himself into the dune again. 'The other guy,' he hissed to Fielding, 'I'm sure he's one of theirs. We've got to get them both – now. Ainley must be theirs, too. Move!'

'We can't,' Fielding argued. 'There must be other people

around.'

Hawker looked. 'Clear,' he rapped, 'Now!'

Fielding rose and ran at a fast crouch towards their quarry. The tide was coming in, and mussels, cockles, winkles and clams made tiny scars and indentations in the otherwise even and damp stretches of glistening sand. The sun burned low and fiercely in the west. Ainley and Balchinsky, deep in conversation, started to walk slowly towards the advancing waterline, then turned sharp left when they were parallel with it, away from the sun. Fielding swore and unholstered his Walther PPK. Despite Hawker's instructions, he was taking no chances. He could hear Hawker lumbering and wheezing behind him.

Fielding was perhaps ten feet from Balchinsky when the Russian saw his looming shadow. He half-turned, reaching into his coat, and Fielding knew he must get in the first shot if he wanted to stay alive. Balchinsky cannoned into Ainley as the British agent fired without aiming, and missed.

Ainley shouted 'What the . . . ?' until the shot, and then he rolled over and over in the wet, clinging sand, as though to bury his head in it so that no one would see him. Hawker puffed across to Ainley while Fielding steadied himself and fired once more at Balchinsky, hitting him in the left shoulder. The Russian ducked, weaved and stumbled. He dragged out his own gun and let off a round at the point where Fielding had been, but wasn't any longer.

Fielding dived to his left, straightened his lower arm for the impact, and snapped off three more shots, the second taking the Russian at the base of the throat. The pistol spun on Balchinsky's stiffened finger, he choked obscenely, pirouetted like a drunken puppet, fired once into the air and once into the sand, then pitched forward into a little rock pool that took on the colour of weak rosé wine.

Hawker was bending over Ainley when the bull came in from the sea.

Out of the blinding sun and glinting, winking surf it charged at them, bellowing with the noise of a hundred demons, jets of sand and spray spewing from its hooves, cruel horns branching from its fiery head.

Hawker had a vivid imagination, so that his brain chose the fantastic rather than the obvious, and the Yamaha, its rider almost horizontal over the handlebars, was on them before he realised the truth. He'd frozen over the whimpering Ainley, his eyes pierced by the sun, and the massive, screaming motorcycle took him squarely in the side.

The Yamaha tossed him contemptuously in the air. The rider wheeled, slithered to a halt, took the Schmeisser machine pistol from its holster slip under the saddle, and stitched a vertical pattern of slugs into Fielding, starting at the bridge of his nose as he struggled to his feet and ending in the taut flesh of his groin.

Hawker moaned softly, blood bubbles dribbling from the corners of his rosebud mouth, his thinning red hair clogged with sand, his eyes rolling vacantly back towards the stunned and silent Ainley. Another burst from the Schmeisser blew away his face.

Ainley shook with the terrible ague of fear, knowing he was going to die. The killer kicked him on the soft padding of his thigh, motioned him to get up, and nodded inland. Ainley peered uncomprehendingly into the impenetrenable visor, and stumbled to his feet, but stood rooted to the spot until a sharp, dismissive gesture of the Schmeisser sent him scuttling away. The killer had not spoken a word.

One of Ainley's driving gloves lay under Hawker's outstretched hand, and the spy had dropped the Dunhill lighter. The killer saw the curlicued monogram, and ground the lighter deeply into the sand with the heel of a slim, shaped, half-length black racing boot. Then back to the Yamaha for the black ruck-sack strapped to the frame behind the saddle, and off came the boots and the leather suit until the rider stood naked over Hawker's body.

And, on impulse, down to the sea, wading in until the water, red-gold in the rays of the sun, covered her thighs and the forest of jet-black hair on her mound, and lapped at her belly and the lower slopes of her breasts. She stood for a moment, a pulse beating fiercely at her temple, her hands plucking and kneading her chilling body, and she felt an almost physical sensation of the relief and tension flooding out of her into the frothing sea.

She turned, walked back and, without drying herself, put on a blue and white checked shirt and narrow blue jeans with rope-soled espadrilles that she took from the rucksack. She stowed her black riding gear away, along with the map Balchinsky had given Ainley, and the driving glove Ainley had dropped. She threw the Schmeisser down on the sand between Fielding and Hawker. When the tide was fully in, most of her tyre marks would vanish. The tracks she'd made at the end of the wide half circle she had taken some way down the lane and across the dunes to ride in out of the sun were already disappearing. The Police – and SIS for that matter – could make what they liked of the slaughter. She hadn't wanted to kill Hawker and Fieldng – unlike Hawker, she was a reluctant, though accomplished, killer – but there had been no alternative.

Her full name was Cristal Vengan, and she was Department RE's most highly prized secret weapon. She stood six feet tall, and her hair was a shining shoulder-length waterfall of the sheerest jet. Her eyebrows were well-defined, but not thick; her nose classically long and perfectly straight. She had eyes of a deep and fathomless dark blue, almost violet, and long, sweeping black lashes. She wore no make-up and her skin was clear but for tiny, impudent clusters of freckles at the sides of her nose. Her mouth was proportionately wide with full, deep-pink lips. She had a not unbecoming mole on her left shoulder. Sleightley and Pond judged correctly that men would find her so staggeringly lovely that they would not look for the immense power which had been ruthlessly drilled into her body in the four years she had served the Department.

As the Yamaha sped over the still deserted sand, she pressed a switch on the side of the rev. counter fastened to the handlebar. Another little toy of Pond's, it measured the mounting revolutions, but also emitted a weak, shrill bleep in regular tones, which was linked to the bug Cristal had planted behind the rear bumper of Ainley's Rover. He was still on the move. She took the road to St David's for the journey north.

THIRTEEN

A cockleshell fragment had entered the pad of hard skin on the big flat hammer toe of PC Glyn G. Davies's right foot. He was known as Glyn G. to distinguish him from PC Glynne T., Gwyn T. and G. Glyn Davies, all four comfortably shaped, unheroic stalwarts of the Dyfed Constabulary. If you went into their local and asked for 'Davies the Police' (which no one would dream of doing, except, perhaps an Englishman), five pairs of eyes would look up inquiringly from pewter pint pots, the aforementioned being in the invariable company of Sgt, T. Huw Davies, so-called to distinguish him from Sgt Ianto G. Davies, who never used the pub anyway.

But it was Sgt Ianto G. who followed on the bare heels of PC Glyn G. just as the sun was setting, their white, knobbly ankles breaking the gently rolling tide on Marloes Sands. Thick serge trousers were rolled up to just below the knees, and two pairs of winter-weight grey woollen socks were thrust into four identical black size elevens at the edge of the sand. Each man had also removed his cap, as though to balance enforced nudity at one end with deliberate undress at the other.

'Bugger me, Glyn G.,' Sgt Davies muttered in unconscious rhyme.

'What do you make of it, Ianto?' PC Davies said.

'Not for us, is it, Glyn G., man?' Sgt Davies decided. 'Let them that's paid to use their brains use 'em.'

'Right it is Ianto,' PC Davies agreed, and made a laborious sketch in his notebook. None of the three bodies was yet covered completely by the incoming tide. The young hiker who'd found them had been sick, but the water had dispersed her little puddle of vomit.

'These two haven't got faces, Sarge,' PC Davies remarked.

'Don't suppose they care much, now, Glyn G.' Sgt Davies said.

'That funny big gun, d'you think, man?' PC Davies asked, pointing to the Schmeisser.

'Probably,' Sgt Davies said, but then looked speculatively skywards. 'Mind you, though, the gulls do look might pleased with themselves,' nodding at the wheeling, squealing scavengers.

'That's not very nice, Ianto,' said PC Davies, who'd consumed nearly a third of a damson pie barely forty minutes earlier.

Sgt Davies finished making his notes, and snapped the notebook shut. As they turned for the shore, the first contingent of CID waved to them. They plodded splashily on.

'All yours, sir,' Sgt Davies said.

'Thank you, Sergeant,' replied Detective Chief Inspector Ivor Talfan Davies.

Things moved swiftly from then on, and it was barely eleven twenty when an ancient waiter called Mantle, clad in a yellow and black waistcoat with the top button missing, shimmered over to the largest and most comfortable leather armchair in the corner of the Smoking Room at the Porterhouse Club in St James. He bent low and whispered, 'Admiral, sir,' into the ear of the snoozing man. There was no reply.

He said it a little louder, but with the same result. Not wishing to lay hands on such an eminent member, he crossed to the neighbouring table, transferred some ice into a whisky tumbler, borrowed a swizzle-stick, and gently oscillated the mixture under Pink's nose. The Admiral awoke with a splutter.

'Your drink, sir,' said Mantle, 'and there's a telephone call for you. I'll bring the receiver over, sir, and plug it in here.' He pointed to the walnut panelling to the right of the empty fireplace, and left to fetch the telephone, carrying the tumbler of ice-cubes with him.

The voice said, 'It's Colonel Powell, Chief Constable of Dyfed, West Wales. Are you the gentleman I want to talk to, please?'

'How the bloody hell should I know who you want to talk to,' Pink growled.

'Please moderate your language,' the Chief Constable said. 'It is simply this. They wouldn't give me your name, for whatever reason I'm sure I don't know. But they said to ask for the Admiral, which I did. If you are the Admiral . . .'

'I am,' Pink said.

'. . . good, in that case your are, I understand, connected with the Special Intelligence Service.'

Pink grunted, and for the next five minutes uttered not a single word as the appalling story of the slaughter on the beach came out.

Then he said, 'My God.'

The Chief Constable went on, 'There was another car at the top of the lane. We managed to trace it to the Procurement Executive of the Ministry of Defence. After a bit of argy-bargy they said it belonged to your Department, and Mr –' he checked his notes, ' – Savage suggested we should inform you personally. He thought you might be here.' Pink scowled blackly, but conceded Savage had been right.

'From what we can make out,' Colonel Powell went on, 'the little tubby chap and the young dark one – we can't describe their looks because . . . Well, you know . . . anyway, we think they came from this car. The other chap we've traced to a taxi-cab that brought him out to Marloes from Haverfordwest Station at about six o'clock. We think, by the way, that he's Russian.'

'Russian? Why?'

'From a piece of paper in his pocket, and a plastic card in his wallet.'

'I'm grateful for all the trouble you've taken, Colonel Powell,' Pink said. 'I'm sorry I was a little short with you, but it's late, you know, and I was having forty winks.'

'No matter, sir,' the Chief Constable said. 'Oh, by the way,' he added, 'Mr Savage is on his way down here, with a Mr Connors. We've agreed to close off the beach until they arrive.'

Pink thanked him again, and phoned Swaine.

'Some bastard's declared war on us,' he said. 'It could be the Soviets, or it could be someone else. All a little bit too pat for me. But I want whoever was responsible. And I want that tricky little swine Ainley. He wouldn't have had the guts to do it. But he must have known who did, because he's gone. D'you hear, Swaine? I want blood for blood.'

Cristal ate a plate of Spam fritters, baked beans and chips at St David's, and called London from the kiosk near the tiny cathedral.

'Good,' said Sleightley. 'You're sure you weren't spotted?'

'No,' she said. 'And I never talked, not once.'

'And you really had no choice but to kill both of them?'

'None. They would certainly have killed Ainley, and probably me, too.'

'A pity. The Admiral thought highly of Hawker and Fielding,' Sleightley remarked.

'Were those their names?' she asked.

'They were.' She didn't reply.

Sleightley told her to link up with Ewan Scott, and gave her the address and phone number.

'He flies for a servicing firm called Cambrian Helicopters. I gather they actually have a corner of the RAF Base at Tredogan, which is roughly next to the RAE. This time of night, though, he'll probably be at his cottage. Trefynnon is just around the bay from Tredogan.'

'I know,' Cristal said. 'It's on the map I got from Ainley. It was given to him by the other man on the beach – the one SIS killed. He passed it to Ainley in a manilla envelope, and

146

I thought it was coded orders, but it turned out to be an Ordnance Survey Map for West Wales. That's all. Nothing else. I presume he was a contact, which could make Ainley Russian property.'

'Good work,' Sleightley said, warmly. 'In fact, excellent. If Ainley is with the Russians, it all ties in, doesn't it? It's got to be Tredogan. I hope to God SIS don't go putting their big feet in where they're not wanted. Is there anything on the map, by the way?'

'Yes,' she answered. 'A little circle, just off the road between what I take to be the RAF Base and the weapons station. It's on the way to Scott's village.'

'Splendid. Report tomorrow. Goodnight, Vengan.'

Past Fishguard, she pulled in occasionally to the side so that she could listen to the pulse from the rev. counter. The intervals between the flashing green light seemed to have been getting noticeably shorter, and she confirmed that the bleep was also more frequent. She was drawing closer to the bug on Ainley's Rover.

She turned off the main Newquay-Cardigan road to pass between the RAF camp and the rocket base on the road to Tredogan village, which also led to Trefynnon. She'd gone no more than three or four hundred yards when she stopped again and wheeled the big Yamaha on to the grass verge. The night was chill, and the sky occasionally starry; menacing clouds drifted across the hunter's moon.

Through a gap in the hedge she could dimly make out the shape of a large building with several chimneys at the end of a longish drive. She took a powerful torch from her saddlebag and shone it on a sign at the entrance to the drive. It said 'Carreg Wen Residential Hotel' in Gothic lettering, with no accompanying recommendation from either the AA or the RAC. The green light on the rev. counter glowed in one tremulous but continuous flicker, and the bleeper emitted a steady, unbroken yelp. The building matched the circle on her map. She had found Roger Ainley – or at least, his car.

Scott's mouth dropped open.

'You're *who*?' he exclaimed, in astonishment.

'I'm Vengan,' Cristal said. 'Why?' she asked, innocently, enjoying the confusion.

'It's just that I-I-th-thought you . . .' he stammered, then realised he was going to say something very silly.

'You thought I was a man,' she said.

He laughed, engagingly. 'No,' he said. 'Nobody could possibly think *you* were a man. I thought *Vengan* was a man.'

'And now you know I'm not?'

'You must be a truly remarkable woman.'

'Thank you. Where do I sleep?'

'Frankly,' Scott confessed, more than a little embarrassed, 'I've only got one bedroom. When London said they were sending you – sending Vengan, that is – I thought – well, er, "he", if you see what I mean, could bunk in with me, at least for tonight. Tomorrow I'll get a "lilo" or something.' He gave her a boyish grin, and blushed.

The cottage was lit by an oil lamp. Scott had an electricity supply there, but he preferred the lamp. It smelled good, and cast companionable shifting shadows on the rough-cast walls and the oak-beamed ceiling. In its unsteady light she saw a man of her own height in his mid-thirties, with becomingly long fair hair swept back over his ears, lively, questing blue eyes, and high cheekbones forming an upside-down triangle to the strong, blunt point of his jaw, where a little cleft made a matching pair with the indentation between his eyebrows above his nose. Her decision was among the easiest she had taken that long day.

'Of course,' he added, hurriedly, his flush deepening, 'that obviously won't be the case now.' He looked wildly around the room. 'I'll make up a bed for you – uh – somewhere.'

Spartans, she considered, would have felt at home in Scott's cottage. There was a scarred table, three chairs, a revolting and lumpy settee, a sideboard, and a chest of drawers bearing a record deck, amplifier, cassette recorder, and a neat rosewood speaker, whose twin was on the sideboard.

'The floor?' Cristal suggested, indicating the frayed carpet on the square slabs of stone.

'I'll think of something,' Scott said, miserably.

Then she grinned and moved towards him.

'Don't bother,' she said. 'And save yourself the money on the "lilo". Is the bed big enough?'

'Oh, plenty big enough,' he assured her, and bit his lip. He hadn't meant it to sound so salacious.

'Then it's fixed,' she said, quietly, her eyes holding him fast in a hypnotic embrace.

She touched him on the mouth and he took a finger between his teeth and gently bit it.

'It would be an outrageous and unthinkable lie if I said I wasn't attracted to you,' he murmured when he released her finger after nibbling at the nail.

'Naturally,' she agreed. 'Cocoa?'

He didn't reply for about a minute, then he blinked and said, 'I'm sorry. What did you say?'

'I said "cocoa"', Cristal replied. 'It means I would like some. Bachelors, which I assume you are, always make good, strong cocoa unless they're gay, when they don't.'

'Yes, of course. Forgive me, you must be hungry.'

'No,' she said. 'But I'd like some cocoa.'

'Yes, by all means.' His panic returned, and he bustled out to the little scullery to make the cocoa.

It came in big white china mugs, with Zodiac signs painted on them. Hers was Scorpio, his Libra.

'How did you know I was Scorpio?' she asked. 'That's very clever of you.'

'I could say I just guessed because the sign so clearly is you,' Scott answered with a grin. 'However, the truth is that it's the only other mug I've got. This one – ' he lifted it ' – is mine. Libra. And that is clearly not you.'

'Libras are supposed to be soft and nice, and Scorpios

hard and nasty,' she pointed out.

'And sexy,' he said.

They drank the hot brew. In the bedroom she asked him to undress first, and looked almost shyly at his powerful shoulders and legs, the matted dark-blonde hair on his chest and stomach, and the agressive swell of his male formation. Then she pulled out the blue and white checked shirt and unzipped her jeans and giggled when his eyes widened. 'Sorry. Forgot to put my knicks on,' she said.

She stood before him with her legs apart and her fingers intertwined awkwardly. She bit her lip and said, 'Like me?' Scott reached for her and she allowed him to pull her on to the bed. They kissed deeply and wildly, and it was the first of many kisses and cries and many laughs and some tears and hurts and a lifetime of indescribable pleasure for Scott that left his mind blown and his body drained and Cristal at peace.

She looked at him and said, 'Well?'

'Jesus Christ,' he breathed.

He smoked a cigarette. They sipped neat vodka, and she remarked that he wasn't the Western Hemisphere's most lavish host, and he blushed again.

'Never mind,' she said gently. He stubbed his cigarette out and asked if she wanted to talk business. 'OK,' she agreed.

He told her of his now definite suspicions concerning an active cell of the Free Wales Army in the area, and of the explosives he'd found.

'Are they on to you?' she asked.

'I don't think so,' he replied. 'When I ask discreet questions in the pubs, the locals are actually pretty forthcoming in a naive sort of way. Of course, they may be just having me on, but I don't think so. They don't mind talking to me, being a Scot, whereas I get the impression they probably wouldn't if I were English. Anyway, I'm sure something's on, and while it may not be Tredogan, it's in this area and up in the hills, the Prescellis, and it'll be worth investigating

150

whatever it turns out to be.'

She said, 'Did they tell you about Roger Ainley?'

'Yes, they did. Why?'

She paused and then said guardedly, 'I think he's around here somewhere.' She didn't explain how she knew; she was the senior agent, and there was much that Scott didn't need to know. He didn't press her, but merely said, 'Then it is Tredogan.' And she replied, 'Yes, it is.'

They talked on, and they were happy just to lie together, touching. They fell silent for a long while, and then he asked, diffidently, 'How did you – you know . . . start in all this?'

She turned to him sharply and said, 'You should know better than to put questions like that to me.' He said, 'I know. You don't have to answer.'

She was quiet again and he started to sulk, rather obviously. She looked at him, and touched him gently on his leg, and there was a sudden anxiety, a longing in her just to talk to someone without fear or without threat coming between them. For so long she had led a life of virtually total exclusion from genuine, warm human contact. She kept her fairly restricted circle of friends and saw her sister and her mother as often as she could, to preserve a facade of normality which in point of fact did not exist.

She remembered with a pang of wonderment standing before Sleightley and Pond in the office in St James for the fist time, on the day she had pledged her life to Department RE. 'You will live,' Sleightley had told her then, 'where we tell you to live. You will love whom we tell you to love. You will do precisely what we tell you to do. At all times. Is that clear?'

She had agreed, without hesitation, and had never for an instant regretted her decision. But throughout all of that time she'd had to subdue, ruthlessly, the simple and human urge to talk freely about herself and the way she lived, and analyse her emotions, with someone to whom the very possession of such knowledge would not be tantamount to a death sentence. But Scott surely must be safe . . .

So she told him. Of the early years in Haifa and Tel Aviv when Israel was new, of her Jewish mother and her wealthy English father, who indulged both his wife's deep concern for the infant State and his own passion for Middle East archaeological exploration. He'd been forty feet down in a desert dig at the site of a possible Essene settlement when the news that he had inherited his brother's peerage was brought to him. He died six years later in a rock fall on the Golan Heights. He left his wife a very great deal of money and a country house in Somerset, and to his daughters the inheritance of his own fierce awareness of right and wrong, of justice and injustice, tolerance and understanding. When her mother and sister left for England, the fifteen-year-old Cristal had chosen to stay in the home of her cousin, Scholem. In the following year, at the age on nineteen, Scholem died in the Six-Day War, and Cristal's world collapsed. She was a solemn, austere girl, tall, graceful and intense, and not yet overwhelmingly beautiful. That, like her selfless loyalty to the cause of Israel and its people, and her voluntary service in the Israeli Army, was still to come.

She left her adopted land without, in essence, truly adopting it. She had never embraced the Christian religion, and she found she could not grow easily into Judaism. She became uneasy, restless, tortured even. She had talents like the seven languages, including Arabic, which she had mastered, and the astonishing skill she had developed with weapons of all kinds, and the uses to which she could put her now mature and powerful body. She came gradually to realise that the heart of her dilemma lay in the one basic flaw of the life she had chosen: she was not Jewish, she was English. Once she had forced herself to acknowledge that fact, she left Israel, and she had never returned. After Oxford and a Classics degree, she took a flat in London and a job in the British Museum, and it was there that Pond first saw her. Contact had been made through an old friend of her father's, and although she had drawn back from the idea of death as a way of life, the fascination of becoming a secret and deadly international counter-espionage agent, supplemented by the characters of Sleightley and Pond, ensnared her in a subtle trap from which there was now no escape.

Some of this she told Scott, and then they fell asleep on top of the tickly white-fringed quilt. He cradled her head on his thighs, and she whispered, 'I'll have to tell Sleightley we've slept together.' He grunted and turned fractionally in his sleep, and she closed her thick eyelashes again and half-smiled cosily as his penis fell to lay along her cheek like a friendly snake.

FOURTEEN

Scott's alarm clock shrilled. Cristal opened one eye and shut it again quickly when she say what was blocking her view. Scott yawned and stretched, and then rolled gently over her face – which was a disturbing experience for both of them – and swung his body off the bed. He stopped the alarm, grinned at her and said, ruefully, 'Sorry. Must be about our masters' business.' Cristal sighed dramatically, pulled up her knees and swivelled round in the bed until her head was on the pillow. She murmured 'Bye-bye' and fell asleep again almost at once.

Scott gazed in astonishment at the big motorbike tucked against the side wall almost out of sight as he left his end-of-terrace cottage to drive to the airfield. 'That' he said to himself, 'has got to be some girl.' As he spun his Lotus into a tight turn on the patch of gravel at the end of his lane, he missed seeing the figure of a man sprint the last few yards and crouch concealed behind the wall of the first house in the rank. Scott's engine gave a throaty roar and a puff of smoke shot from his exhaust as he changed up and sped out to join the main road. The man straightened, took a dog-eared shopping list from his pocket, and wrote something on the back of it with a well-chewed stub of pencil.

Scott drove through Tredogan so that he could pass the Carreg Wen Hotel on his way to the RAF station. He caught a brief glimpse of Sian Griffith going into a cafe with two girls and a dark-bearded young man of about twenty, and Scott tried to register the man's face, but it came out as a hairy blob. As he drew near to the Carreg Wen, he slowed down to let a squat, broad-shouldered man cross the road into the gates of the hotel. The man was being pulled by a villainous-looking black dog straining at a chain-link leash, and he made no sign of acknowledgement that Scott had given way to him. It left the RE agent wondering why even taciturn foreigners (which was all there seemed to be on the staff of the hotel) needed Doberman Pinschers as pets.

He checked with the Cambrian Helicopters office, and by just after ten he was airborne. His trip was to a Shell Expro rig called SEDCO 700, in British waters south-east of the southern tip of Ireland. Scott freighted mail, an emergency order of cigarettes and cigars for the rig's little shop, newspapers and magazines (which were freely available in the mess rooms), 16mm films for the cinema, which were shown at various times of the day and night to the off-shift men, and video-cassettes of mainland television pro-grammes that could be slotted into mess-room sets and seen at will. Theoretically, a hooked roustabout could watch successive episodes of imported fodder until he dropped from sheer exhaustion. Scott also had two passengers – a reporter and photographer from a Cardiff paper doing a series optimistically entitled 'The Black Gold of Wales'. They were distinctly green when he dropped them on to the helicopter landing platform.

He got back just after two o'clock, and Cristal opened the door to him. She had news from London.

'Mrs Costello says we're invited for clay pigeon shooting tomorrow,' she said. 'Both of us. The bosses are giving us lunch.'

For Department RE agents, 'clay pigeon shooting' had two meanings. It was precisely what it purported to be – shooting clay pigeons – but it also meant that Sleightley and Pond wanted to see them for a field conference.

'Fine,' said Scott. 'Anything else?'

She said very quickly, spilling the words together, 'I told Doctor Pond we'd slept together, and he said it was all right by him as long as it didn't interfere with the operation, but he didn't think Sleightley would approve.'

He looked at her in astonishment. 'Did you have to tell them?' he asked, incredulously.

'Oh, yes,' she replied, earnestly. 'They absolutely insist.'

But then her eyes twinkled impishly. She whispered, 'So it's more or less legal then,' and unbuttoned her shirt.

He touched her, and she was good to touch. They were silent for a while, and then she said, 'Before you become unmanageable, there's some fish and chips in the top oven.'

Scott didn't get back to work that day.

Cristal tapped the barometer on the vertical beam supporting the bar canopy at the Ship Inn. The needle settled down at 'Sunny', which in no way matched the glare she got from the landlord, Idwal Evan Christopher, Licensed to sell Beer, Wines, Spirits and Tobacco. She riveted him with a calculated sexy look, grade one, full strength, and the glass he was wiping dropped and shattered.

'Clumsy twit,' his wife said. 'They're 40p each.' Cristal smiled engagingly at him, twitched her eyebrows and let her tongue wander along her full lower lip. Christopher pulled in his beer belly and undulated his chest. Then he cut his thumb on a piece of broken glass, and swore roundly.

Scott said to Cristal, 'Stop it. We don't want to attract any more attention than you normally do.' She pouted, and pulled a big, innocent sigh, nudging the pile of pennies next to the Doctor Barnardo's match-stand and almost unseating Mr Christopher's perilously popping eyes.

'Cristal, behave yourself,' Scott said, sternly. The Ship was their local. It had a good atmosphere and sympathetic decorations, with none of the jarring inconsistencies of a tourist trap to offend the eye. True, it sported the obligatory lobster pots, nets and floats, a weather glass and a handsome mahogany chronometer, but it was all so much in keeping that the magnificent red and green brass navigation lights seemed as though they'd guided the pub itself over the Seven Seas before anchoring it in its final berth in Trefynnon.

156

It was the end of another beautiful August day; outside in the bay the evening tide edged its way up the sandy beach and Cristal, who looked pointedly past Scott out through the open door, her nose disdainfully lifted and her lips set in a prissy line, saw the backdrop of inky-black sea, dappled in deep orange by the rays of the setting sun. The reflection cut a spreading swathe across the bay and bathed the concrete finger of the rocket launching pad in a warm, pink glow.

Cristal took a haughty sip of her Campari, and Scott pressed closer to her and blew softly in her ear, and when she turned sharply, kissed her full on the mouth and said, 'Home?' She grinned. 'I thought we had things to discuss.'

'We can do that too.'

'No. Now.'

'OK Cristal. Now.'

She liked the way he said her name, slightly rolling the 'r' in his posh, Edinburgh Morningside voice. He hadn't been born with it – Wester Ross speech is less suave and more musical – but public school and the University of St Andrew's had softened and refined his accent. She imagined him in a kilt, and giggled.

He raised his eyebrows inquiringly, didn't get a response, and said, 'I've been thinking of getting a weather forecast. If we're going "shooting" tomorrow,' pronouncing the word with studied emphasis, 'it might be nice to fly up to Northolt in my 'plane. We could leave a lot later.'

Neither of them saw the man who'd been standing at the bar with his back to Scott put down his unfinished pint and slip out. He was quite young, dark-haired and stocky, wearing a white fisherman's jersey and faded blue jeans and sandals. Next to the squeaking door marked 'Gentlemen', there was a pay phone, and he dialled his number and slotted in 2p. Sian Griffith answered it immediately in her customary abrupt way, and was slightly put out when all she heard was the urgent bleeping of the tone.

'Yes?' she demanded, again.

'It's Dafydd,' the young man answered. 'Your friend, the one you're interested in. Taking a little trip tomorrow. Northolt, he said. Going shooting, I think he said. With his girlfriend. At least, I suppose that's who she is. Tall, black hair, fabulous looking, big tits.'

'Don't be vulgar,' she said, in Welsh.

'Sorry. Just thought you'd like to know, that's all. Oh – and he's going in that little 'plane of his, the one he keeps up at the Flying club. Don't know what time. Nos da.' And he hung up.

Sian frowned at the dialling tone. Dafydd never wasted words. She's gained the impression he didn't quite approve of her. He was an occasional, though undeniably useful, operator, but it was just as well, she thought grimly, that he didn't know everything that was going on.

Her mind switched back to Scott, whose actions had aroused enough suspicion to persuade her to put Dafydd on to him. This could be a golden opportunity. If he was nothing but a harmless busybody, then he might genuinely be popping over to England for a day's shooting somewhere, but if he was an agent, his trip could have a far less innocent purpose. Either way, he'd be worth watching. She dialled a West London number, and spoke quickly and surely, in Russian.

The landlord of The Ship, whose thumb was still inconveniently sore, could have been proud of his weather-glass, because the next morning was bright, clear and sunny. Scott confirmed the forecast, and then phoned for a car to meet then at the airport and take them to the shooting school at Northwood. They drove to the local airfield in Scott's Lotus – or rather, Cristal drove, at her usual hair-raising pace.

'Must you,' Scott inquired with weighty sarcasm, 'strive always to emulate Jehu, the son of Nimshi?', as she squealed to a halt in the car park.

158

'The one who driveth furiously?' she asked, letting him know graciously that he hadn't got clean away with the Biblical quotation.

'The same.'

'Got here, didn't we?'.

'Just.' He looked at what passed for the runway. Three level fields belonging to a wealthy farmer and flying enthusiast had been joined into one long, wide strip by bulldozing the dividing hedgerows, leaving a tightly mown and rolled meadow-grass path, about six hundred yards long and forty yards wide. The farmer had recruited other potential fliers, and they'd installed a passable lighting system. The splendid and capacious Atcost building housing the four resident aircraft had been unsuspectingly subsidised by the Minstry of Agriculture.

The 'fleet' was two rather smooth new American Cherokees, one antique Auster, and Scott's own and much-loved little Victa Air-Tourer. He'd learned to fly in the Victa with his local club in the sixties, and he'd given his life savings to buy it when it was 'retired'.

Scott opened the padlock on the hangar door, slid it back, and picked up the towing handle attached to the Victa's nosewheel. Flexing his knees, he heaved the blue and white monoplane out into the bright sunlight. Sliding back the cockpit canopy, he motioned to Cristal to settle herself in the right-hand seat. He got back into the Lotus, parked it in the hangar, telephoned in details of his flight plan and got his clearance to land at Northolt.

Then the pre-flight checks, making sure there was oil in the Lycoming engine, running his fingers over the McCauley propellor, checking for nicks in the edges, inspecting the control surfaces, external linkages, tyre pressures, fuel. It was a daunting list, but absolutely vital. Secretly, Scott enjoyed it, not just because he had to do it, but for the additional reason that it afforded him the sensual pleasure of admiring and fondling his still most prized possession. Also it annoyed Cristal, who was obviously impatient. It wouldn't, Scott thought, do her any harm to have her composure occasionally ruffled.

Satisfied at last, and grinning at her intolerant snort, he clambered up on to the wing, dropped his flight bag into the luggage well behind the seats, and settled himself at the controls. It seemed slightly odd to be wearing (or at least taking) a tweed hacking jacket, white stock, cavalry twills and stout mid-tan brogues in an aeroplane, but it was acceptable shooting gear, he hoped. Cristal looked vaguely like Robin Hood, with tight, khaki-ish corduroy pants, brown, zip-up boots, a dark-green blouse inside a chic suede waistcoat with moccasin frills, and a suede head-band. All she needs is a feather, he mused . . .

The actions he now took were automatic, engraved on his mind like the alphabet or learning to swim; they had been since the first time he'd flown solo, in this very aircraft. Fuel on, throttle set and primed, brakes on; the propeller whirred into life, and soon the engine was idling sweetly. Scott checked Cristal's harness and kissed her impulsively but passionately, and his hand strayed under the waistcoat to cup her right breast. Their tongues met.

'What do I call you?' she asked. 'Skipper?'

'It's going to be a long day,' he whispered.

'Then get on with it.'

He licked the end of her nose, broke the clinch, then closed the Victa's canopy and taxied to the other end of the field for the take-off. His mind computed the pre-take-off checks: fuel, fuel-pump, trim, misture, flaps, hatches, harness. He checked the gyro against the runaway heading, looked at the compass, and pushed the throttle to its stop, the ball of his foot delicately counteracting the torque on the rudder bar.

The little plane accelerated down the runway, and at forty-five knots on the air-speed indicator he lifted the nose-wheel clean off the ground. The distance to the far hedge telescoped alarmingly but passing sixty-five, creeping up to seventy, Scott eased back the stick and the panorama of

Welsh countryside unfolded beneath them. The horizon tilted obligingly to the right as they set course for the radio beacon at Ammanford. He was a shade rusty on navigagion with ruler, compass and map, so he took the easy way out and flew under Green One, the main airway route. He dialled 116.3 on the NARCO and let the VOR needle guide them to Brecon. Chepstow came and went, and the silvery Severn, and he selected Woodley and started negotiating their complicated clearance with London Approach.

Half an hour passed. 'Northolt Radar, this is Golf Alfa Sierra Zulu Alfa, approaching you from the south-west, at one five zero zero feet, and estimating you at one five past the hour. Over.'

'Roger, Zulu Alfa, this is Northolt Radar. I have you in sight. Please turn twenty, two zero, degrees to your right to establish identification.'

The radar controller's words crackled loudly out of the expensive Sony multi-waveband receiver resting on the fascia shelf of the white TR7 parked on the grass verge outside the airport terminal, with its bonnet up. The driver was apparently making running repairs to the engine, while his passenger dozed in the front seat.

But as the radio, tuned to the control tower's wavelength, rasped out the message, the sleeper's eyes flickered, and the driver stopped tinkering with the wholly reliable carburettor and looked inquiringly through the windscreen.

Bornin nodded, without opening his eyes. The man they'd come to tail had arrived.

FIFTEEN

With unintentionally perfect timing, a red Cortina with a clashing orange TAXI sign on its roof, pulled up outside the main entrance to the terminal at the precise moment that the Victa crossed low over the road to land. The bonnet of the TR7 was still up when Scott and Cristal walked out. The passenger, Cristal noticed, was reading the *Financial Times*.

The taxi nosed its way out into Western Avenue and headed towards London. Vassily slammed the TR7's bonnet down, leaped into the driving seat, switched on the engine, and the little white car set off in pursuit. The Cortina turned off and threaded its way through the suburb of Ruislip, across a common, and out into open country, which ceased to be Middlesex and became Hertfordshire. On the fringe of a coppice with the inspired name of Mad Bess Wood, the car entered a narrow, tree-lined private road and vanished from sight.

Vassily swore, and his attempt to follow ended in a gravel-spitting halt. Bornin looked thoughtfully at the large, green-panted sign that said 'Holland and Holland' in a gilt-lettered arc, over 'Shooting School', in equally cursive script, below. He listened to the dull patter of explosions.

'Whatever they're doing in there,' he said in Russian to Vassily, 'it's marvellous cover for almost anything. I think we're on to something.'

'Do I go in?' Vassily asked. Bornin shot him a withering glance.

'Vassily. you have a Soviet Embassy identity card on you that you weren't supposed to bring, you do not speak English, and the gun you have is not the sort of gun they have. No. You do not go in.'

'Oh.'

Vassily parked on the verge. Bornin took out an omni-directional, long-range surveillance microphone and its transistorised kit, looked up and down the road, checked his gun, and jumped over the ditch. Vassily followed him.

The Cortina swept into a car park at the rear of a timbered building painted in lawn-mower green and cream, which housed the administrative staff of Holland and Holland's Shooting School for gentlemen (and occasionally ladies). The driver tipped his cap respectfully as Scott got out and held the door open for Cristal.

They walked up the verandah steps. Cristal approved. She whispered, 'Could be the polo pavvy at Ooty or Poona.'

Scott shook his head. 'Too big,' he said. 'More like the Long Room at Cawnpore.'

There was a pause. Then he said, 'Isn't that the boss's car?' pointing across the car park. She looked, and nodded.

'And that's the boss.'

For once, Sleightley's motor wasn't easy to isolate. There was a fat, self-satisfied Rolls Royce Silver Shadow next to it, and on the other side a gleaming, left-hand drive, CD-plated Lagonda claiming the interest of a brace of hardened afficionados. And in the far corner, a restored Black Label Bentley in regulation British Racing Green. Even a new Daimler making its debut hardly registered, which was why the enviably one-up pilot of a rakish Brantley Helicopter landing in the field next-door was sure he'd made the right decision.

Nonetheless, Sleightley basked in the certainty that he was still out with the leaders. He nodded politely to Cristal and Scott, nibbled a smoked salmon sandwich, and sipped the rather good, ice-cold Chablis from the hamper in the boot of his garish yellow Panther de Ville. It was a remarkable machine – or monstrosity – recreating the classic lines of the American automobile industry of the thirties. Its long bonnet ended in a burnished German silver radiator, squatting between a pair of massive, ugly headlamps. It had the original running-boards and, for want of a better description, a serpentine back. For Sleightley, it was an indulgence that swallowed a legacy from an aged relative, who would have been outraged had she known how her nest-egg had been squandered.

Pond had a jaundiced view of the Panther. Unaccountably, Sleightley behind the wheel suffered from delusions grandeur and performance which his driving skill in no way substantiated. Like most bad drivers, he thought everyone else was. Pond once remarked that the Panther only needed a couple of violin cases on the back seat to convince the SIS that Al Capone had taken up residence 'over the road'. The envious Pink had referred to it as a cross between an icecream wagon and a bumper-car, and when Pond sniggered, Sleightley was miffed for the rest of the day.

Sleightley put down the long-stemmed wine glass, raised a languid hand and said, 'Glad you were able to come. Do have some luncheon. We've just time before we go down to the butts.'

Cristal took a glass, said 'Here's to Fortnum and Mason,' and joined Pond in a chewy sliver of toast and paté de foie grâs. Pond, who still felt the residual traces of dyspepsia brought on by Sleightley's driving, coped manfully with the wedge of bread, and since he couldn't talk, looked at her instead. As always, appreciatively.

'Afternoon, Fanshawe,' Sleightley said to the man who met them outside the gunroom.

'Sir,' said Henry, then gave a repeat performance for Pond, and a slight bow to Cristal. Scott might just as well not have been there. Captain Henry Fanshawe had contrived to serve in the Royal Artillery, the Royal Engineers and the Shropshire Light Infantry in the course of an army career brought to an untimely end. He was impressively gifted as a small arms instructor, and could have taught field guns, too. Still only thirty-four, he was fair and lithe, and so neat that he managed to make the casual corduroys, sweater, open-necked shirt and elegant brown boots look like a uniform. Perhaps, Cristal decided, there was a shade too much shine on his toecaps, and wasn't his hair too perfectly sculptured? He was the Department's weapon training commander, and held himself to the style of a subaltern on parade, a habit ingrained not only by twelve years' service, but also by his boyhood in a country house ruled as a recalcitrant satrapy by the fiery Major-General who had sired him.

Fanshawe was proud of Cristal, who excelled with any sort of gun he put into her hands. Unlike most ex-Artillery men, he didn't mind saying 'gun' when what he actually meant was 'rifle' or 'pistol'. Except, that is, when the Major-General was around. He'd observed – but never once shown it – that Sleightley, whose background obviously included considerable experience on the moors, and in the covers, and notwithstanding his inheritance of a pair of identical twelve-bores made for his father in the thirties by Holland and Holland, was no match as a marksman for the podgy, unathletic and very myopic Pond.

Bored stiff on one of their earlier field rendezvous at the school, Pond had produced a cheap Spanish gun wrapped in brown paper, sighted on a clay and, as far as Fanshawe could recall, hadn't missed a single target from that day to this. Sleightley would regard him with aggrieved astonishment as he stood sloppily unbalanced, peering through his thick pebble lenses, and snapped off hit after hit. Some sort of pact with the Devil?, he wondered. What was that opera? *Der Freischütz*, wasn't it? Weber. No, Pond wasn't the type

. . .

They walked into the gunroom to chose pieces for Cristal and Scott. Scott took his time, and selected a magnificent twelve-bore chased with engravings of hunting scenes. Let into the underside of the polished French walnut stock was a gold disc bearing the initial 'C', surmounted by a coronet. Scott wondered idly if the gun was a hire-purchase re-possession, but quickly banished the heretical thought.

'Don't use it as a walking-stick, old boy,' said Fanshawe, deprecatingly. 'It's half of a pair worth eight thousand quid.'

Scott ignored him, then inwardly rejoiced when he presented Cristal with a lighter, single-barrelled .410, which shrieked aloud 'ladies' gun', and was a bad mistake for Fanshawe. He couldn't really be blamed, though, since when he wasn't training departmental operatives he was just an ordinary instructor at the school, and that was the gun he normally gave to a woman. Now he didn't have the gall to ask for it back, and watched in some trepidation as Cristal received it with icy reserve.

The range nestled among wooded slopes strewn with copses, thickets and hedges, perfect shooting country. It was a happy irony, which Cristal appreciated, that nothing living there was ever intentionally shot. She disapproved of field sports. Targets, she considered, ought to have an even chance. So the one small family of wood pigeons resident in the shoot, defying the constant sound and peril of gunfire, had been adopted as mascots, more carefully preserved than any legally protected species.

Their walk from the office took them past a large wheeled cannon at the crest of the hill, then down a crooked path, over a gate and into the adjoining field. The woods followed the line of the hedge at the bottom of their field and beyond that to the next one, and set behind the hedge of that field was a scaffolding tower about a hundred feet tall, shrouded in green canvas. It was used – in the appropriate season – for launching the clays that represented the high-flying varieties of birds.

Halfway up the slope to their left was the butt, made of sturdy timber, and resembling a box cut diagonally in half. A clump of bushes further up again concealed a trench, which both housed and protected the clay-operator. His task today would be to launch the simulated grouse in such a way that they would appear to rise quickly from the ground, and fly low and swiftly in the direction of the butt. Those who weren't shooting could sit at a safe distance on a green wooden bench and gloat. Sleightley closed one eye

166

and admired the clean, smooth rifling of the twin bores of his gun against the light. He was at the centre of the semi-circle of shooters.

'Very well, then,' he said. 'Perhaps you'd better finish your report.' Scott started to reply, but Sleightley fore-stalled him by nodding at Fanshawe, who took the whistle strung around his neck and blew a sharp warble on it. The launcher's hand was already resting on the lever, and his reaction was instantaneous.

The little black disc rose at speed from the undergrowth like a miniature flying saucer, and whirled over their heads at a height of forty feet. Two loud explosions were followed by a sullen grunt from Sleightley. A haze of blue smoke drifted about his head, the air was rank with the acrid, but not unpleasant, smell of cordite, and Sleightley broke the gun to reload it as the clay lost impetus and floated lazily to rest some eighty yards away.

'Right then,' Sleightley said, deliberately avoiding Pond's gaze. 'Let us summarise, Scott, the information you were kind enough to relay to us over luncheon. The Free Wales Army, you say, and in particular this person Griffith, are definitely up to something. You have discovered a cache of explosives which is presumably intended by them for some future subversive use. You cannot at the moment connect them with any activity directed against the Royal Aircraft Establishment at Tredogan, but the person Grif-fith is given to making inflamatory speeches, and thus cannot be presumed to be a devoted and patriotic citizen of the United Kingdon. Also she has been seen clandestinely entering an hotel, under the proprietorship of a dubious Polish gentleman and staffed by others of his ilk, so that place, too, is suspect. Is there anything else?'

'Not really, sir,' Scott said, 'just general suspicions.'

'And Ainley's car,' Cristal put in. Sleightley continued to contemplate the grounded clay with deep loathing.

'Ainley's car!' Scott exploded. 'Why didn't you tell me Ainley's car's there.'

167

'It may not be,' she said, soothingly. 'But it's close.'

'How do you know?' Sleightley asked, cutting off another outburst from Scott, whose blue eyes were boring angrily into Cristal's.

Pond gave a tentative little cough. 'I rather fancy,' he ventured, 'that Mr Ainley may have been carrying a passenger. Or should I say,' he sniggered, 'a stowaway.'

'Quite,' Cristal said, which drew a flicker of annoyance from Sleightley. He nodded curtly at Fanshawe, who wasn't watching.

'OK. So we *now* know,' Scott said heavily, 'that Ainley's bugged car, and therefore Ainley, could well be at the hotel too. Which makes it, I would have thought, worth looking at. I reckon they've got some pretty sophisticated equipment there, and I'll bet they're monitoring the rocket test trials. Perhaps . . . Cristal?' – he left the question on the air.

'Oh, please do, Vengan,' Sleightley said. 'Have yourself a holiday there'.

'Thank you, sir', she said, demurely.

'Send us a card,' Pond remarked, absently. Then his eyes narrowed behind the chunky lenses, which magnified the effect into a disconcerting two-way squint.

'On the other hand,' he suggested, 'd'you think – '

'Fanshawe,' Sleightley rapped out. 'Perhaps if I could obtain your undivided attention for, let us say, three seconds, you may care to favour me with another singular demonstration of breath control and provide a clay.'

Then to Pond, 'I beg your pardon. What were you saying?'.

'Perfectly all right,' Pond said affably. 'I was merely wondering whether . . .'

'Peeeeep' went the whistle, the release mechanism clunked, and Sleightley blasted away when the clay was directly overhead, shattering it and spraying the pieces over the butt party. Everyone ducked but Pond, who was still talking.

'. . . something really ambitious, like jamming the frequencies, and diverting a missile to somewhere where they could recover it themselves? They could do it, you know. Anyway, *I* could do it.'

'Could you,' Sleightley said. It was acknowledgment not a question.

'Well,' Pond continued, 'we agree they'd have to get their hands on an actual rocket to make anything they do there worthwhile. As I've remarked before, it's no good going after blueprints if you haven't got any fuel. And I still can't see them trying any sort of overt attack. I mean, that would be an act of war, wouldn't it?'.

Sleightley was obviously waiting patiently for him to conclude his rumination. 'It would,' he agreed, and blasted another clay out of the air, ducking smartly as the fragments rained down on them. 'Much better,' he beamed. 'Much, much better. Perhaps you'd like to shoot now, Vengan,' inclining his head to Cristal.

'I'm sure I'll be no match for you, sir,' she said, 'especially with a pea-shooter.' Fanshawe winced. Any intentions he might have entertained towards Cristal were, he thought, annihilated.

SIXTEEN

The sun was settling lower and the grasshoppers snickered as Cristal brought the rifle up and lodged the plate in the hollow of her shoulder with easy familiarity. 'Ready,' she snapped at Fanshawe, then wheeled sharply with the gun held perfectly straight and caught the clay just as it rose into the air. It disintegrated, and some of the pieces whistled back over the head of the launcher crouching in his trench.

'I think,' she said, a little petulantly, 'that this could get very boring.' She handed the .410 to Fanshawe, disregarded his worshipping gaze, walked over to the bench and sat down.

Pond cleared his throat and confided to Fanshawe, 'Our little tigress has sharp claws, Henry.'

'Yes, I daresay you're right, Dr Pond,' Fanshawe replied, and was gratified to get a sympathetic grin from Scott.

Scott took the next three clays at a more orthodox height, and hit all of them. Pond, meanwhile, was admiring his ancient rifle. He unnecessarily polished the pitted stock with his sleeve, and patted his pockets for the earplugs he always wore when it was his turn to shoot. His fingers traced the shape of his latest toy, a miniature bug detector of immense concentration and power, which he'd been working on for months to perfect. It was capable of pinpointing surveillance apparatus over a distance of possibly half a mile – his field trials weren't finished – and he took it out and switched on with no more urgent motives than idle curiosity and a battery check.

The indicator needle swung sharply to the right and stopped, quivering, three quarters of the way across its span. Pond's brow furrowed, and he looked up, then back down. He switched the bug-bug off, and on again. The needle, which was lurching back, swung out to its previous mark. The reading was unmistakable. Someone had them covered with a strong source. And it was inside the school grounds, not outside.

Pond turned the little box edgeways to get an elevation, and lifted it to eye-level. He squinted along the line of the needle, and his gaze met the top of the scaffolding tower. Unless the equipment was malfunctioning – which he did not accept – the electrical source was coming from the platform.

Pond snapped shut the bug-bug's cover and switched it off. He put it in his pocket, turned speculatively towards Sleightley, then compressed his lips into a thin line and shook his head. He could, after all, be wrong. He picked up his gun, looked at it for a moment, flicked the safety catch on and off, and made his decision.

'I suppose it would be better,' he said to no one in particular, 'if Scott and Cristal had a sort of – um, quarrel, up at wherever it is, otherwise if they're being watched, as they may well be, it'd look pretty rum if she just upped sticks and left him to go and stay in the Pole chappie's hotel. Don't you think?'

'I imagine she'll think of something,' Sleightley replied, both men now talking about Cristal as though she weren't there, which made her toss her head and stare moodily out into the distance. Sleightley regarded Pond curiously. He knew Pond better than any other person alive knew him; the only time his colleague ever consciously babbled was when he wanted to cover embarrassment or uncertainty. Which, Sleightley wondered, was it?

'Two, please, Henry,' Pond declared, grandly. 'Ah', Sleightley thought, 'embarrassment. Doesn't want to be caught showing off.'

'A trifle ostentatious, C.,' he said. Pond loaded from Fanshawe's pigskin cartridge bag, stood his ground squarely, nestled the gun into his shoulder, and laid careful aim. The scaffolding tower definitely wasn't in use at this time of year. If someone *was* there, he – or she – wasn't supposed to be.

Pond smiled thinly, blinked through his pebble lenses, and nodded to Fanshawe. A couple of shrill blasts on the whistle and two 'birds' rose up, one splaying to the right, and the other to the left. Pond let the left-hand clay pass over his head, watching it all the time, then shot it down with ease. He spun round to take the other, bent slightly forward, and waited till it sailed over to the sunlight now streaming directly at him above the tower, framing its gaunt, squat peak.

Only Fanshawe's experienced eye caught that Pond was leaving it late. And, Pond thought, a bit low, too, as he squeezed the second trigger and saw his shot rip through the canvas screen round the tower. The clay whistled unscathed a few feet to the right and died in a gentle parabola, rolling the last few yards to collapse in a cow-pat.

'How fitting,' Sleightley said. 'Told you, didn't I?' Then he sat bolt upright, and stared unbelievingly as the green canvas binding the tower started to bulge outwards. Pond, still looking along his gun-barrel, gave a small, satisfied sigh.

The canvas strained further, and a head appeared, hands clutching at its eyes; then Vassily's dark-suited body spilled out over the top. He screamed, and the short, thick, branch of an overhanging tree pierced his trunk, rupturing the spleen and jack-knifing him face down into a hawthorn bush that ripped weals across his cheeks and drove a thorn into his eyeball. He rolled off and lay spreadeagled on the hedge. 'Let it be the fall that killed him,' Pond prayed, because even from that distance they knew he must be dead.

Fanshawe was already halfway across the field with Scott at his heels and Sleightley bringing up the rear, when Pond waved to Cristal to stay. He was peering now at the base of the tower, and she followed his gaze. There was a break in the hedge at the foot of the scaffolding, and through it they could see a crack of light where the two sheets of canvas just failed to meet.

For almost a second it was blotted out as a shadow passed. Pond pointed and nodded, and Cristal broke into a run, covering the ground in long, even strides, her arms pumping rhythmically. She wrenched off the suede head-band and her released tresses bounced on her shoulders. She veered to the left of the tower, passing the group bending over Vassily, and leapt the hedge into the wood.

Bornin ducked under a branch, and cursed his painful stitch. He was a killer, not an athlete. He plunged on, the twigs brushing his face, his feet kicking up showers of fallen leaves and the occasional plump puff-ball. He was heading, he knew, in the right direction, and it wasn't much further, because he could faintly hear traffic noise – was it? yes, it was . . . it could only come from the main road. The English, he reasoned, were too busy with Vassily – 'Christ, I hope he's dead!' – to bother checking whether anyone else had been there.

He stuffed the omni-directional mike and pack into his pocket, remembered, with a brief flush of shame, his train-ing, and stopped – suddenly. Perfectly still, he listened. The light footfalls sounded clearly in his ears.

Swearing under his breath, Bornin tugged out his gun and snapped on the silencer. He looked round for cover, and chose an old, solid beech tree with branches that drooped almost to the ground. He crouched behind it and waited, straining his ears; but he was too late, the footsteps had ceased.

Cristal breathed deeply and noiselessly in the shadow of another spreading beech, and her ears picked up the sound she wanted to hear. Her eyes were screwed up in intense concentration, her hands lifting the hair from the sides of her head. The muffled rasp of the man's breath came towards her on the breeze.

She wheeled round and chose a circular path in a dainty,

high-stepping run, relying on speed to get behind her quarry, and not worrying if she crunched the occasional twig. Then she, too, stopped, switched direction, and advanced in a silent, cautious lope, moving trailing branches carefully out of her way, her eyes probing the green wall ahead.

Her tactics were correct, for Bornin had assumed she'd got further behind him than she actually had. He abandoned his shelter to creep round the other side of the tree and crouch some seven feet from the trunk in the shelter of a dipping branch.

Cristal heard him move. She was about a dozen yards away when she saw him, his back more than three quarters to her, arm resting on his knee, finger on the trigger of the silenced gun.

She changed direction again, moving to Bornin's left outside the circle of the leafy branches of his hideout. When she next became aware of him she was on his other flank, perhaps six feet from the kneeling man, and she saw his sharp, un-Slavonic profile and dark greasy hair. He peered intently at the bole of the beech, waiting for her to come round it and fall into his trap. He moved his arm off his knee, gripped the gun in both hands, lifted it to his eyes and trained it upwards to where he thought his hunter's body would be.

With infinite care she bent down, picked up a large twig and threw it over the branch which shielded him. It landed well to his right, and he whipped round in astonishment, still on one knee.

For the merest instant he lost his balance and used his left hand to steady himself. Cristal reached him in two and a half strides, skidded with her left boot to a near halt, and with the right lashed out at his stiff gun-arm. The crack as it broke was the loudest either of them had made since Vassily plunged to his death.

Bornin was almost too stunned to realise what had happened, then he let out a shrill howl that changed to a scream as Cristal reached for his shattered arm and used it to lever him on to his back. His fingers opened nervously and the gun lay on his open palm. She didn't even bother to kick it away.

The tears were springing from his eyes and his lips twisted in agony and the corners of his mouth were leaking froth. She took a slender knife from the sheath at her right hip and drove it cleanly into his heart. Then she stole everything she could find in his pockets, including the transistorized listening and recording device, and trotted back to rejoin the others.

Sleightley was waiting for her at the tower. 'From now on,' he said, 'you must be very, very careful. I don't have to remind you that if your cover is broken, and you are unable to repair the rent, your undoubted usefulness to the Department comes to an abrupt end.'

SEVENTEEN

Cristal was moodily fretful as the hired taxi raced back to Northolt, and Scott thought he knew the reason . . . she, of all people – and Scott himself, for that matter – should have spotted the TR7 tailing them from the airport to the shooting school. He guessed that she'd actually noticed the little sports car when they'd set out, but hadn't picked it up later. Sleightley's last remark to her had been a reprimand, as she well knew. He decided she didn't need or particularly deserve sympathy, and kept silent.

Their flight path for the journey home took them back over Holland and Holland's rolling acres, and he banked to get a better view of the main road. A large blue and white pantechnicon had pulled up on the verge near the abandoned TR7. His eyes followed the spur into the shooting school. The classy helicopter was still there, but the car park was empty of visitors' cars except for the British racing green Bentley and Sleightley's monstrous Panther de Ville.

Scott had always admired Department RE's skilful manipulation of people and events, but it never ceased to astonish him how they could arrange matters that when Sleightley and Pond wanted to shoot, the butts became magically untenanted, even though the place was stiff with legitimate customers anxious to demostrate their prowess. The explanation would have amused him: between them, Pond and Fanshawe had simply made it known that Sleightley's shooting was so erratic that anyone straying within unauthorized range of his guns placed themselves in mortal danger. Sleightley would have been mortified if he'd ever found out.

Scott saw that the butts were still unoccupied (Fanshawe hadn't yet figuratively hoisted the green flag). He thought

176

that Fanshawe, Pond and Sleightley must be lost somewhere beneath the thick screen of undergrowth and trees.
'I'm glad our masters are the ones who're having to sort out
what to with a couple of dead Russians in a sylvan paradise
dedicated to the leisure of English country gentlemen,' he
said to Cristal, nodding towards the ground. 'I'll be interested to see how those devious academic minds solve that
particularly nasty equation – if, that is, they can.'

He groaned inwardly as she turned to him, her eyes
blazing. 'I wouldn't, if I were you, assume that they can't,'
she said, tartly. 'Something like that will be child's play for
Dr Pond, and I doubt if he'll need any helpful suggestions
from you.' That, Scott thought, was distinctly unfair, since
he hadn't volunteered any, but he realised too late that he'd
touched another raw nerve – Cristal's affection for Pond –
so he joined her in a sulk, wrenching the Victa back on
course for Wales.

Cristal, of course, had been right. Pond's mind had been
working at full stretch since the moment Vassily's body had
tumbled out of the canvas tower. His immediate concern
had been the threat to Department RE's cover. He'd
instructed Fanshawe and Scott to drag the Russian's corpse
into the woods after sending Cristal to take the other man
they knew was lurking there. Then he'd searched Vassily
and found the car keys. He tucked his gun under his arm,
stuffed a handful of cartridges into his pockets, and set off
in the direction which – like a well-trained gundog, he
thought – she'd taken.

He was moving warily through the foliage when he met
her coming back. She told him what she'd done, and where
to find Bornin's body. 'You'd better report this,' he said,
and then loaded his gun. 'I'll go and see if there are any
more strange birds about.'

But there were not. A few minutes later he puffed out on
to the main road and saw the TR7. 'A two-seater car,' he
decided, 'means two agents – both happily accounted for.'
He selected the ignition key from the bunch he'd taken

from Vassily, and switched on the engine. It roared into life. Then he did the same to the multi-waveband receiver on the passenger shelf. It had been left tuned to the frequency Bornin was using to monitor Scott's arrival, and Pond gave a self-satisfied smirk. Now he knew the leak had been at Scott's end.

Someone in Wales must have suspected the agent, and had overheard him discussing his plans for the flight – and his destination. They'd passed it on to the Russians, and it would have been a simple matter for the Embassy to learn the details of Scott's flight plan and his ETA. Armed with the Victa's call-sign, all the two agents had to do was wait for him to land, Pond mused.

Unless the Russian agents had communicated with their base – and Pond deduced that they hadn't had time to – then Sleightley and himself had not been identified, and were completely in the clear. Neither of the men who controlled Department RE had ever made any secret of the fact that it was the security of Sleightley and Pond and their top agents on which the Department's very existence depended. Once that cover was broken, they were out of business.

Now Cristal and Scott – certainly Scott, who was under direct suspicion – had to be protected as well, Pond thought. The Russians were on to Scott, and would link the deaths of their two men with him no matter how cunningly plausible a scheme Pond could devise to mislead them. 'I'll make them work at it, though,' he said to himself. 'By the time we've finished with them, they won't even know which day it is.'

The crucial move, he decided, would be to establish that Bornin and Vassily were still alive long after Cristal and Scott had left on the return flight to Tredogan. He'd told Scott to get airborne as soon as possible, and sent Fanshawe to phone London for the men and materials he'd calculated they might need. 'When you get back to Wales,' he'd said to Cristal, 'go down to the pub and let everyone within earshot know what a pleasant and uneventful day you've had. What you quarrel about after that is your business. I've no doubt you'll think of something, my dear.'

Just as Scott's plane was disappearing to the west, Pond held a council of war with Sleightley and Fanshawe, whose call had brought from London two men identically dressed in blue and white overalls matching the livery of the big van parked at the roadside. Their names were Bill and Ben – but like the lately departed Hawker and Fielding, they were no joke. Each was a hardened criminal, paroled by Sleightley from maximum security wings of different gaols. Neither man knew or cared who his employers were, and they received lavish payment for the occasional acts of mayhem and destruction they were called upon to perform.

Through a gap in the trees, Pond could make out the elaborately scrolled lettering on the side of the pantechnicon that read SPEEDY AND EFFICIENT REMOVALS. It was, he considered, one of his blacker jokes, but it summed up precisely the tasks which Bill and Ben accomplished for the Department with, quite often, gratifying ingenuity.

Pond carefully avoided referring to Cristal or Scott by name in the presence of Bill and Ben. 'The two people we're anxious to protect,' he said, 'should be back in Wales by mid-evening at the latest. I have decided that we should arrange a rather unpleasant and undeniably fatal accident for our temporary guests to take place at – say – round about ten o'clock tonight. That will exonerate them completely.'

The three younger men waited for Sleightley to nod, then joined him enthusiastically. Pond, they knew, excelled at this kind of game, and Sleightley was only too pleased to leave it to him.

'Obviously,' Pond continued, 'the car must explode on impact and be burned to a cinder. That should conceal the cause – and, equally important, the time – of death from even the most thorough autopsy. It will happen at the end of what will seem to have been a long and unrewarding day. The Russians may suspect what they choose, but they'll not

179

be able to prove a single thing.'

'They'll still know it was us – or rather, one of us,' Sleightley objected, meaning Scott, 'because that's who they were after. However thick a smokescreen you throw over the incident, they won't be stupid enough to accept that it had nothing to do with their – ah – quarry.'

'I might, in that case, be able to help them,' Pond replied. 'The thing to do now is make sure the coast is clear and load the TR7 and contents on the van. We'll pretend it's broken down, and leave Ben to guard it. You and I – ' he turned to Sleightley ' – will go to London in your car. Henry, you'll come with us, and so will you, Bill. I'll explain everything once we're on the road.'

Scott cleared his plane for landing at Tredogan, and put down smoothly on the grassy runway. He taxied over to the hangar, and Cristal got out, stretched and yawned. she'd gradually mellowed during the flight, and now she grinned ruefully at him. 'Sorry I was bitchy,' she said. 'Sorry it's a bit cramped in there,' Scott replied. 'I don't take passengers very often.'

'Never mind,' she said. 'I expect I'm too big for the poor little thing.' She stretched again, and Scott coughed and looked away. 'Let's get off to the pub then, Ewan,' she suggested, 'and end what was getting to be a rather beautiful relationship.'

'Seriously?' he queried.

'I've enjoyed it,' she said, truthfully. 'Haven't you?'

'Need you ask?' he replied. 'People like you just don't happen very often – at least, not to me. I'd be an idiot if I pretended I was ecstatic at the thought of losing you. Oh, of course I know you've got to get into that hotel, and that we've got to split, and I'm being totally selfish – but as I said, you're special. Mind-blowing, I believe the current phrase is.'

'Well, in a few days when all this is over, I'll come back

here,' she said. 'You'd better alert the Fire Brigade.'

'What on earth for?'

'So that after, say, two or three weeks they can come and prise us apart,' she said, giving him an exaggerated wink and fluttering her eyelashes. 'God, you're not making it any easier, are you,' he said.

'Our Lord Buddha teaches us,' she said, portentously, 'that there is no easy path to Nirvana. And since Nirvana in this case happens to lie you know where, you'll just have to grin and bear it, won't you? The old boy probably knew what he was talking about.'

They settled in Scott's car and she put her finger on his lips and rested the other hand casually on the fork of his legs and said, 'that's Kismet, baby. Let's get dressed for our performance.'

The Ship was three-quarters filled when Scott unlatched the heavy walnut door and ushered Cristal inside. He had his hand on her arm and pressed it as she passed. She shook it off angrily and snapped at him, 'For Christ's sake don't maul me. How many times do I have to tell you? I don't like being pawed.' He recoiled in blank astonishment – until he saw that the charade had started. Cristal was a complete professional.

She pushed her way unceremoniously to the bar, and the complaints that sprang to the lips of the men she jostled turned to gurgled slavers of appreciation. The fury in her eyes only made her beauty more imperious and unbelievable. Behind the bar, Idwal Evan Christopher's wife moved the newly washed pint glasses out of his reach. He got his own back by asking her to serve the busy end of the bar, and made straight for Cristal. He stood before her, big, dark and beefy, with his thick arms folded and his capacious belly sitting snugly on the counter.

Warily he said, 'What'll it be then, Miss?' His astonishment almost equalled Scott's when she replied, 'A large whisky, please, and a large man to go with it. You'll do fine.' Idwal Evans pendulous lower lip slumped, and a

181

bridge of saliva spanned his wet mouth. He gulped and licked his lips, and it vanished. He shot a sidelong glance at his wife and said, 'Careful now, miss. You caused enough trouble when you was in here last night, and that's fighting talk, that is. I don't want no bother with your young man there.'

'He no longer is,' she replied. 'Neither mine, nor particularly young. Perhaps that's his trouble. He's good for buying drinks though,' she added brightly. 'I'm sure you'll get Mr Christoper a brandy, won't you, Ewan? I believe that's what you drink, isn't it – Idwal?'

'Evan it is, Miss,' Christoper replied, feeling his Y-fronts tighten warningly.

'You bet your life, sweetheart,' Cristal purred. 'That's just what it is. How did you guess?'

'N-no, Miss,' he stammered, 'I mean my name's not Idwal, it's Evan. The second name's the one, see?'

'A man by any other name feels just as . . . good,' she replied, her dark eyes boring into his, her voice husky with apparent lust. Christopher desperately pressed his body closer to the bar, and then turned half away from his wife's suspicious gaze.

'Are you serious?' he whispered. 'We close at half past ten, look and if you was to come round the back . . .'

'Just what the bloody hell d'you think you're up to, Cristal?' Scott demanded. 'You've got the poor guy so that he doesn't know his elbow from his weekend pass. And I find it distinctly insulting, apart from anything else. And here's another thing – he can buy his own bloody booze, and so can you for that matter.'

'Well,' she sneered. 'Who's a big boy, all of a sudden? Well let me tell you something – that suits me just fine. I'm deeply grateful to you, naturally, for permitting me to sit on my ass all day and watch you shoot earthenware ashtrays out of the sky. It really was one of the most interesting and rewarding experiences I've ever had. But now . . .'

'I asked you if you wanted a go,' Scott interrupted.

'And I asked you,' she flashed, 'several times, as I recall, if there wasn't 'something else' we could do, and if you didn't get my meaning then, you're unlikely to do so now. So as far as I'm concerned, you can stuff your shitty little cottage and your lumpy bed and your cracked mugs and beans on toast, and sod off and find a fourteen-year-old schoolgirl to screw, because that's about all you're good for. And if you'll be kind enough to pack my stuff and leave it outside the front door, we'll call it quits.'

Scott's eyes narrowed to points of blue ice. 'Thanks, Cristal,' he said. 'Thanks for showing what a dirty, man-hungry little tramp you really are.'

'Too big for you, Scott.'

'Get stuffed, then.'

'I intend to,' she said, coolly. He turned on his heel and stalked out of the now silent bar. Not a word had been spoken by anyone else during their quarrel, and every ear had heard what she'd said to him. Hardly a man in the room wasn't scheming how he could take Scott's place – with the exception of Idwal Evan Christopher, whose solid, pug-nosed and peroxided wife had now joined him at Cristal's end of the bar. A single look from her convinced him he was out of the running.

Mrs Christoper regarded the girl levelly. 'Unless you want another drink,' she said, 'I'd advise you to leave, before you start any more trouble.'

'I'd be glad to,' Cristal replied. 'If you really want to get rid of me, you could help by making a reservation for me at the – Carreg Wen, is it – hotel. Tell them I'll be there in about half an hour. And also a taxi to pick me up here.'

'As you told Mr Scott – outside the front door, Miss. You may be a beautiful girl – and you are,' Mrs Christopher admitted. 'But frankly, I think it's only skin-deep, and for myself I don't much care for either you or your language.'

Cristal smiled sweetly. 'Thanks for the instant homespun psychoanalysis. Do you want me to go now?'

'Yes, I do.'

'With pleasure,' Cristal said, 'but I think you'll regret it.'

She blew Idwal Evan a kiss and strolled unconcernedly through the open door. The antique clock on the wall facing the dart-board started to strike ten as she reached the penumbra of the pool of light outside, and twenty-one of the forty-seven men in the room had joined her by the time it finished its expectant count. The survivors were either too old (eighteen), not up to it (four), or queer (three), plus Idwal Evan Chrostopher, who was trying not to cry.

'Right then,' Cristal said to the nervously shuffling group of matadors. 'What are you going to do? Draw lots, toss up, or cut the cards? Whichever it is, when you've decided, let me know who's first.'

'I am,' said a voice coming from the open window of a faded pastel green Morris Oxford that had just pulled up outside the pub. 'Christ almighty,' moaned the skipper of The Ship's legendarily unsuccessful darts team,' it's Arfon bloody Jonas.'

'Taxi, Miss?' the voice, now accompanied by a pitted, pasty face under a battered peak cap, asked.

'Aah, never mind, fellas,' Cristal consoled them as she got into the cab. 'Some other time, perhaps. I'm sure you've all got gorgeous wives, anyway.'

They stood and watched, shaking their heads sadly, as the musty old taxi stuttered uncertainly away.

'What we have to do,' Pond said when they'd joined the A40 once more, heading east, 'is to convince them it's a genuine accident by involving another vehicle, the driver of which is also killed.'

There was uneasy silence from the other three occupants of the car. The Panther's progress along the main road slowed to a crawl. Sleightley drummed his fingers on the steering wheel and fumed restlessly against his co-sufferers in the traffic jam, whose only crime was daring to exercise their right to share the same stretch of road with him.

'How can we manage that, sir?' Fanshawe asked politely. Sleightley, Pond saw, was finding the strain intolerable. He was hunched forward in his seat gripping the wheel with gloved hands, and occasionally rocking his torso to and fro, as if to generate sympathetic impetus. Pond thought he looked rather like the Roman charioteer who drew pole position next to Ben Hur.

'They'll still smell a rat,' Sleightley growled.

'Agreed, but they must be convinced that even SIS – whom they surely imagine us to be – wouldn't ask one of their men to sacrifice his life merely to cover the killing of two enemy agents,' Pond stated flatly. 'They'd have to assume it was the real thing.'

What they needed, he elaborated, was another vehicle – preferably a van, which they could report as stolen – and another body, preferably stolen. 'Then,' he went on, 'we put all three bodies in the same van, and Henry arranges an explosion and a fire which destroys the van, the sports car and the corpses, and leaves only those traces we want to be found.'

'Which are?' Henry asked.

'I don't know yet,' Pond confessed.

'All three in the van, you say,' Sleightley muttered, shaking his fist at a small coupe which had had the temerity to cut ahead of him on the approach road to the M40.

'That's right,' Pond replied. 'It's easier to stage, and more confusing for the KGB.'

'I think what we'll do, then, is this,' Sleightley continued. 'Henry can get us some explosives and detonators and timers, that sort of thing, plus a couple of Czech machine pistols and a sprinkling of Armalite rifles, and . . .' he drove on to the motorway without looking to either side by the economic expedient of jamming his hand on the horn and his foot on the accelerator '. . . and we'll put 'em in the van along with the bodies. Then it'll look as if they'd fixed up an unscheduled meeting with the IRA or some other bunch of extremists, somewhere in the neighbourhood of

Holland and Holland, so they could keep their targets under surveillance, but unfortunately a bit of their hardware was dicey, as I believe the expression has it, and the whole damned show goes up. It'll cover their lateness and failure to report in, and it may even earn them posthumous awards of the Order of Lenin for intelligent deployment of private enterprise.'

He roared past the coupe which had dared so grievously to affront him a few miles back, and settled the Panther decorously into position a few yards ahead of the little car, reducing his speed to precisely seventy miles an hour, and leering evilly into the rear-view mirror.

'If that car attempts to overtake me again,' he growled over his shoulder at Bill, 'I want his number.'

Arfon Jonas kept up a meaningless patter until the car swept down the long, tree-lined drive to the Carreg Wen hotel, and Cristal had a sudden attack of nerves. The floodlighting at the front cast menacing shadows across the deeply recessed windows, and threw into relief the spiky peaks of the dormers on the second floor of the three-storey building. A number of the upper rooms, she noticed, were lit – five or six in a row at the extreme left of the hotel; while only a few had lights on in the floor below. Could the block of accommodation in the top storey, she wondered, hold Roger Ainley?

Gravel crackled under their wheels as the portico framed itself in the car window, and the Morris Oxford came to a rest. Cristal felt for the door handle beside her, and had just found it when the door opened from the outside. She started – but it was Arfon Jonas, performing as act of undisciplined courtesy which would have amazed his regular customers, who'd seldom seen him outside his cab. He also doffed the greasy cap he was wearing – a relic from his brother-in-law's brief reign as commissionaire at the Essoldo Palace, Tredogan – and gave her a wining close-up of the yellow fangs separating the gaps in his mouth. He remembered, however, to ask for the £3 fee negotiated with Mrs Christopher over the phone.

As the notes disappeared into a pocket of his shiny blue suit, he said, 'Ta then, Miss. I 'ope you can get in the hotel, see, because they told Beti Christopher they didn't 'ave much room, but they'd see what they could do.' She said, 'Thank you. I expect it'll be alright.' Then she shouldered the rucksack Jonas had retrieved from Scott's cottage, turned on her heel, and left the taximan picking his nose and feeling distinctly cheated. Still, he thought, he could add a few frills, like, for the lads at The Ship tomorrow night.

Cristal paused at the front door, which had taken on an entirely illusory menace. 'Ah well,' she thought, 'fools rush in . . .' She pushed open the door and walked through the large hall to the dark oak-panelled reception desk at the far end, next to a broad staircase. She tapped the pusher on the brass bell, and when nothing happened played a rapid peal on it until the white-coated figure of a surly young barman slouched through a door connecting with the service area to the lounge bar.

'I have a room booked by phone call half an hour ago,' she announced, not very graciously. 'Ya,' he said. 'I look.' He did, and found a name pencilled on a reservation slip. 'Miss Wengan, is zat so?' he inquired in his thick accent. 'Vengan' she corrected. 'Ya,' he replied. 'Wengan.'

A shadow fell across the desk from her left, and soft and well-modulated version of the same accent said, 'Miss Wengan. We are most pleased you could come.'

'I understood you didn't have much room,' she said. 'We don't,' he answered, 'but for so beautiful a young lady, we make room. By the way, I am the owner of the Carreg Wen, Paul Miernek. It means "white rock" you know. Carreg Wen.'

'In – um – Polish?' she hazarded. He laughed. Like everything about him, it was attractive both to look at and listen to. He was tall as she was, and looked Nordic rather than Slav, with muddy ash-blond hair, keen blue eyes, and showing an upper left snaggle-tooth when he grinned. He had small, pretty ears. Cristal wondered briefly what it would be like with him. 'No, Welsh,' he said. 'But you're quite correct, I am Polish. Most of us here are, though I've lived in England many years.'

The barman interrupted with a sullen 'Ickscuse me,' and pushed the hotel register across the counter at her. 'Where do I sign?' she asked. 'Zair,' he extended his left arm and pointed with his finger. 'And please also to fill in zis card.' He held it out to her. She picked up a pen from a stand on the desk – and froze. His fingers were small and dainty, his wrist slim, hairless. It seemed barely able to support the weight of the solid gold Rolex watch with the heavy alternating circlet and diamond-shaped chain-link band, which she'd last seen on the wrist of Roger Ainley.

She accepted the card with a murmured 'Thank you.' Her brain raced as she fought to keep calm and write her name and address in the book, and then on the self-important slip of pasteboard. Ainley was in the hotel . . . she'd been sure of that anyway. But he wouldn't have meekly handed over his watch to the first man who'd asked for it – unless he had no choice . . . unless he was being held prisoner and, officially or unofficially, Miernek's staff were dividing the spoils. If it was officially, then Ainley was already dead. But no, she decided, risking a sidelong glance at Miernek. It was unofficial. The handsome Pole's eyes were also locked on to the barman's wrist – and Miernek hadn't liked what he'd seen there. The barman must have stolen the watch practically as soon as Ainley'd been taken to his room – but Miernek knew whose it was. And now he knew that she'd recognised it, too.

She laid the pen down and asked which room she was in. It was Miernek who replied, 'Room 12, Miss Wengan.' There was an abrupt clang as the barman dropped the room key, with its heavy brass tag, on the counter. She pushed the card back to him. 'Is it on the first or second floor?' she inquired. Miernek smiled at her. 'All the guest accommodation is on the first floor. The second is private. For room 12, you turn right at the top of the stairs, follow the corridor along, and around the corner, and right to the end. Can you manage with your luggage?' He made as if to lift her rucksack, but she put her hand on his arm – both to restrain him, and because she wanted to touch him.

'It's all right, it's not heavy,' she said. 'I'll take it.' He replied, 'As you wish,' and watched as she stooped and once again hoisted the strong canvas bag easily up over her shoulder. He pursed his lips as her breast strained against the fabric of her shirt. Then she turned to go, and looked casually at the hotel key board fastened to the wall behind the reception desk. The top row of hanging keys was almost complete, starting with a block of six on the left. The bottom row had four spaces, including hers. 'So much for a hotel full of guests,' she thought. Miernek hadn't noticed. He was already hissing in Polish to the barman, and his large, powerful right hand reached out to grasp the younger man's fragile wrist.

Cristal grinned and made her way up the staircase. She paused at the top and listened . . . they were still talking, heatedly now, down below. She turned left instead of right and, counting the steps precisely, and noting the twists and turns, she arrived finally at what she calculated must be the branch leading to the corridor which housed the rooms where, she was gambling, Ainley was being held against his will.

The corridors were only dimly lit, and she pressed herself flat against the wall of the linking passage, and peered cautiously round the corner. There she saw what she'd wanted to see . . . the corridor ran past eight rooms altogether, and outside the fifth one along from her – that would make it the third from the end of the hotel – a man sat on a chair. That had to be Ainley's room.

She retraced her steps, memorising the route again, and

arrived back at the top of the front stairs. There was no sound from the reception area. She tiptoed along the corridor, pausing to listen for signs of activity from what were – according to Miernek – fully occupied rooms. But she could detect nothing.

She was about to take the bend into the dark passage leading to Room 12 when a barely audible creak of a floorboard made her stop in her tracks. Someone was walking towards her, moving almost as silently as she was. She froze – and the stealthy creaking abruptly ceased. Whoever was there had stopped too. She strained her ears, but there was no other sound. Fear coursed through her body and crept over her flesh. Then she shook herself and set her teeth and walked round the corner – almost into the arms of Paul Miernek.

It was nine-thirty, Pond noticed, as Sleightley swung off the A40 on to the good class secondary road which passed the shooting school of Messrs Holland and Holland. Sleightley had shown commendable restraint in keeping behind the anonymous black Commer 30 cwt van, bought by Bill an hour before from a second-hand dealer in Clapham, with a bundle of second-hand fivers plucked grudgingly by Sleightley out of a tatty violin case in the boot of the Panther. 'Really,' Pond had tut-tutted to him. 'You were quite upset when I suggested you ought to sport one of these.' Sleightley had replied, airily, 'Well, the more I though about it . . .'

Then two more calls – one to the Department's garage, where Fanshawe had assembled the terrorist arsenal (all confiscated from the Provisional IRA), and the second to an undertaker's in Shepherd's Bush, from whom they collected a bulky canvas sack, five feet eleven inches long and weighing 183 lbs. 'Well done, Bill,' Pond remarked, as they stowed their booty in the van. 'Your mortician friend does come in useful, I must say. Extraordinarily helpful chap, in fact, although I do wonder sometimes whether he actually buries any of his clients at all. Come to think of it, I doubt if he knows how to.'

By the time they got to Northwood, within striking distance of their destination, it was fully dark. Sleightley said, with a dry chuckle, 'This really is going to be most embarrassing for the Russians, you know. Heads, I shouldn't wonder, will roll.' The Commer van, with Bill driving and Fanshawe in the back, signalled that it was going to pull in, and parked near the Department's pantechnicon.

Pond checked that the road was clear both ways, and Sleightley drove past the two vehicles. 'Can't have the place looking like Piccadilly Circus,' he chortled. Then he sounded three long beeps on the Panther's flashy horn – the signal to Fanshawe to begin.

It took Henry, with Bill and Ben, just four minutes to transfer the dead Russians to the smaller van, slide out the ramps from the pantechnicon, and reverse the TR7 out on to the road until it was almost touching the Commer. Fanshawe waved Bill and Ben back into the cabin of the removal truck, and activated the 30-second fuse he'd connected to the tiny magnesium and gelignite bomb, which was itself linked to the 'captured' explosives and incendiaries in the van. The pantechnicon couldn't have been more than forty yards away, and still in second gear, when a muted 'crump' told them the blaze was taking hold.

Sleightley had motored on a fair distance before turning to come back, and they spotted the red glow in the sky at least a mile from the scene. When they reached the wreckage, the skeletal remains of both vehicles were still being licked by tongues of dull bronze flame. The interior of the van, though, was a radiant core of white-hot fire which could leave no trace of identifiable flesh.

'They might just about be able to decide how many people were killed,' Sleightley pronounced. 'But apart from that . . .' he shrugged – for him a most expressive gesture.

'I could write the headlines for you now,' Pond remarked dreamily. 'In fact,' he went on, getting out a notepad and gold propelling pencil, 'I think perhaps I will.'

EIGHTEEN

Cristal and Miernek collided briefly, and she gave a little startled cry and put her hand to her mouth. 'Forgive me,' he apologized. 'I came up to see if you were settled in all right, but you were not there.'

'No, no, it's my fault,' she assured him. 'I lost my way.' He still had his hands on her arms, and he was standing very close to her. She breathed evenly now as the fear receded. She was also, she discovered, a little embarrassed.

'Well – I suppose I'd better go to my room,' she said. 'Yes by all means,' he replied. He pressed back against the wall to let her pass, and her shoulder brushed his chest. She squeezed through the door marked 'FIRE' leading to twin, pitch-dark recesses, one containing her room. The passage was carpeted in dingy red and blue patterned pile, fastened with large brass pins. She stopped in the recess and knew he was still standing watching her, because even through the perfect fit of the fire door, she would have heard the corridor squeak again if he had moved. There was no sound. A light shone under the door of the room opposite hers.

She unlocked her own door, turned on the light, and sat on the bed, which creaked musically. She unbuttoned her shirt and was shrugging it off her shoulders when the phone rang.

'Cristal,' said Scott. 'Anything?'

'I'm sure I know where our friend is,' she said.

'And?'

'So I'll pay him a visit.'

'He'll be . . . accompanied,' Scott said, guardedly.

'So he'll be accompanied.'

'Watch it,' said Scott, anxiously. 'We don't want to lose you.'

'Ewan, it's very touching of you to be so concerned for me, but honestly – a couple of goons?'

Scott chuckled. 'OK,' he said, 'sorry love. Obviously you can take care of them. But – don't take any chances – please.'

She rang off and grinned at herself in the mirror. Her shirt had fallen completely off. 'Somebody cares,' she said.

She unzipped her jeans and kicked then off, rumaged around in her rucksack and pulled out a pair of black ski-pants. She put them on over her lemon-yellow briefs, and squeezed into a tight-fitting black top. She shook her head and her hair cascaded onto her shoulders. She crossed to an over-stuffed armchair in the corner by the window, and sat in it for the next half-hour. Then she slipped into the bathroom, cleaned her teeth, turned off the light and the main room light, and got between the sheets of the creaking bed. She shut her eyes and started counting, silently. At three hundred and forty-seven, she heard the snap of the switch in the room opposite, and a clunk as the bed took the weight of a man.

At a thousand and twelve (nothing special about round figures, she thought) Cristal stopped counting, slid over to the side of the bed, kicked the covers away, put her right hand on the floor and her left on the bedside cupboard, and vaulted out of bed as a gymnast would clear a fence. There was no musical creak.

She took the pencil torch from her pocket, lit her door-handle in the beam, walked silently over and, with exaggerated care, eased open the door. She left it slightly ajar and moved down the pitch-black corridor like a crab, her back pressed to the varnished wall and pine panelling, the balls of her bare feet treading the heavy carpet tacks. The corridor didn't squeak.

Once through the fire door she switched the torch on again, checked the time, and walked sideways to the stair-well. She climbed eight steps, reached a landing, then five more. Another landing, and she turned right. Thirty paces, a second fire door, and she came to the linking passage. For the second time that night she sidled up to the corner, and peered round. The guard – youngish, darkish and gently snoozing – was still sitting on the chair. A rifle lay across his lap.

She tiptoed up to him, holding her breath, and touched him lightly on the shoulder. He woke with a jerk and looked up at her, and she jabbed him cleanly at the base of the neck with the extended forefinger and index finger of her right hand. He gave a little cough and his head rapped back on to the door lintel.

'What's wrong? What's happened? You all right?' asked another voice from inside the room, in Russian. She gave a guttural moan, crashed against the door and slumped heavily to the floor on to her back, tight against the door with her right leg bent in front of her.

The key grated in the lock, and the door opened. The second guard leaned out into the corridor and tried, in the dim light, to make out what had happened to his friend. He didn't see Cristal until her foot caught him in the crotch. When he doubled over, retching, she trapped his head with both hands, put her feet against his chest, and wrenched his head viciously until his neck snapped. She put the first guard back on his chair and propped him up on his rifle, and hauled the second body into the room. She slung his Kalashnikov on to a chair, and walked over to the bed.

In the glare of the single naked bulb she saw Roger Ainley lying spreadeagled, his wrists strapped to the brass posts. He was bare to the waist and his chest was pitted with cigarette burns. He was unconscious, or asleep. She re-crossed the room and switched off the corridor light on the wall outside, leaving the door ajar, and then went to the window and opened it, fully.

There was a cup of cold water on the bedside table, and she threw it over Ainley and slapped him awake. 'No,' he whimpered. 'No. Please, no.'

Cristal said, 'I've come to help. But I must have the information if I'm to save you. It's vitally important.'

His eyes opened wider. 'You're not . . . with them?' She shook her head. 'No, I'm British Intelligence. I'm not saying it'll go easy with you, but at least you'll be alive.' Even as she spoke the words she knew it was a lie, but Ainley had to believe there was a chance of escape before he would tell her what she wanted to know. After that . . . he must die. There was not even a remote possibility of her being able to get him out of the hotel – and he had seen her face and knew what she was. He could not be permitted to live. But he was in bad shape, and she knew she wouldn't be able to kill him in completely cold blood . . .

He moaned and asked if she could release him. 'Not yet. No – don't worry,' she assured him. 'It's just that you must tell me what you know. Now. It's important,' she hissed.

'What is it you want?'

'How they're going to do it – steal the process. Why they wanted Canterwell. How this place figures in it.'

Haltingly, whimpering again, reeling under further slaps and straining at his bonds, Ainley told her. It was easier than with the Poles, because she believed him, whereas Miernek had not believed him, even under sodium penta-thol, and had given him back to torture from sheer frustra-tion. Cristal bent over him gently taking in every word as though her ears were magnetically recording what he said.

He finished and grinned weakly at her. 'That's all,' he said. To his astonishment Cristal brought her face close to his and kissed him lingeringly on the mouth. 'That's because of what you've gone through,' she said.

Ainley took the bait, as she knew he would. He saw the raven hair, the wet, parted lips, the flaring nostrils, the delicate ridge of her collar-bone and the beginning of the deep valley between her heavy breasts that brushed his face as she leaned forward to loose his straps.

He grinned like a thirties masher at a tea dance and said, 'What's a beautiful girl like you – '

' – doing in a place like this?'

'Something like that,' he said.

'I'll tell you later,' she whispered.

'Much later?' he leered. She grinned saucily; he'd given her the opening she wanted. 'I've always got time for that,' she said. He made as if to sit up, but she pushed him gently back down. 'Have this on me,' she said. 'Or rather, on you, and giggled.

She stood and pinched the jumper top between her fingers and thumbs and slowly peeled it over her head so that he drank in the jouncing globes of her breasts and the wild tufts of down in her armpits and, when she coyly wriggled out of the ski-pants, the spreading black mat at the junction of her legs. It was the hardest part she'd ever had to play in her life.

She slid on to the bed and felt him. He was hard inside his trousers. She moved up his body and unzipped him. She tried not to hurt him as her breasts stroked the angry red blotches on his chest. She held his sex tenderly and impaled herself on it, and moved her body slowly.

He gasped, and began to breathe faster, wailing as he started to climax. At that instant, Cristal pressed both thumbs deeply into either side of the big artery in his throat, cutting off the oxygen supply to his brain. He died finishing one of the most ecstatic, and undeniably the last, orgasms of his life.

Cristal slumped forward on him, and the tears coursed down on to his face and throat. Then a voice behind her said, 'Quite a performance, Miss Wengan.'

She jerked her head round and saw Miernek standing in the open doorway, a big, wicked-looking Luger levelled at her body. A tall scarfaced man with spiky grey hair stood alongside him. He, too, was armed. She gave a choking cry of rage and desperation and pounded the pillow with her fist.

NINETEEN

Miernek stepped into the room and picked up her ski pants and top and tossed them over to her. 'Get dressed,' he ordered. She lifted herself off the dead man and swivelled her body around, but went forward on her knees with her legs open. The Kalashnikov was still on the chair, six feet away. She had no chance of reaching it.

'Get dressed,' Miernek said again, uneasily this time. She was still naked, and the eyes of both men were riveted on her sweat-speckled body, wet from her sexual contact. She pouted, and disdainfully raised her arms and slipped the black top over her head, but she made no move to put on the ski pants. She felt with her toes for the iron-buckled belt that had fastened Ainley's right wrist to the bedpost.

'Put it on,' Miernek rapped. 'Now!' He made a threatening move towards her, and she raised herself up and her legs divided further under her emphatic mound, and her little toe found the belt. She sank back on her heels and laughed in Miernek's face.

'What's the matter?' she said. 'Getting a bit too hot for you?'

He retreated and turned to the scarred man to give him an order, and she swung the belt wildly overhead. The buckle shattered the hanging light bulb and in the same movement she dived off the bed on to the carpet.

Miernek yelled, 'The door!' and let off a shot which ploughed through Ainley's jaw and took away part of his face. The scarred man reacted sluggishly. He charged for the door and cannoned heavily into Miernek. Both men lost their balance and the scarred man crashed to the floor, dropping his gun. Miernek swore fiercely, picked himself off the wall, felt for the door opening, and blundered through to switch on the corridor light. He darted back into the bedroom and swore again. Cristal had gone.

The roofing tiles tore at her nails, but she clung desperately to her hold. Getting out of the window and climbing the eaves had been simple compared with this, she thought. The tiles gouged and scraped her legs as she squirmed upwards to clasp the chimneypot. Miernek's voice shouted, 'She's gone on the roof. She must have.'

Footsteps clattered along a bare section of corridor and up a flight of stairs. She twisted round and saw behind her, at the rear elevation of the house, the dark shapes of two dormer windows set about ten feet apart and six feet down from the chimney. She heard the sound of a little-used window being heaved protestingly up. But which one?

There was no time to choose, so she monkey-clambered along the apex of the roof to a point above the nearest window and gingerly eased herself down her own side to grasp a pair of tiles just under the ridge. She spread her legs and got a firm foothold, then eased her hand grips and put most of her torso weight on her left arm, leaving her right arm free. Whoever it was on the other side of the roof was climbing, as she'd gambled, straight up rather than at a slant. She crooked her right arm and the moonlight picked out the fluid swell of her muscles.

A hand holding a gun clawed at the ridge, less than eighteen inches from her eyes. It was tempting to reach for it, but it wasn't the gun she wanted.

There was a grunt and a spitting puff of breath, and the scarred man's head came up to join his hand. He peered cautiously over the top, levering himself on his arm.

He saw her almost at once, but he was too late. She siezed his tough, wiry hair and gave a mighty heave. With a strangled yelp of terror he tilted over the edge and hurtled past her. He did a kind of mid-air twist and the guttering caught him in the small of the back, tossing him well clear of the big bay window to bounce off a Volvo in the car park and lie shattered and crumpled on the gravel.

Miernek's voice came to her from the same window.

'Zoltan,' he hissed. And then again, louder, 'Zoltan.'

Cristal waited for a few seconds, then hearing no movement she felt her way across to a spot which she judged might be opposite the second window, climbed to the top and looked over, and there it was projecting darkly out beneath her.

She wriggled down to it, and was drawing back her fist to smash the glass, relying on speed and surprise to get away, when she noticed the shadowy forms of what appeared to be boxes stacked on the floor. It was obviously used as a storeroom, and the window was not only slightly open, but moved a great deal easier and more silently than its mate in the next room.

'Don't let it be a trap. Please don't let it be a trap,' she breathed – but there wasn't a sound or a chink of light anywhere. Then she did hear sounds – of footfalls on the tiles above; of a hoarse voice (Miernek's?) exclaiming in Polish; of more voices, more Polish, from the car park below.

She gave a sigh of relief, felt her way round a pile of boxes, and moved carefully to the door, and opened it. The corridor was in complete darkness, and the only light came from the moon shining through the window behind her. There were still noises from the roof and shouting outside, and somewhere the baying of a distracted – or enraged – dog, but the corridor was silent.

She elected to go left, rather than pass the room where Miernek had been. She pulled the door nearly shut, and she'd taken four faltering steps when the powerful torches snapped on and pinned her to the wall in a crossbeam.

Miernek was taking no chances. He had four armed men with him. She cowered miserably down and Miernek walked up to her and smashed her in the face with the barrel of his Luger.

'This time,' he said, 'don't bother to dress. It'll be easier the way you are.'

Gresson demanded, 'D'you know what time it is? Over.' when Miernek's urgent radio message got through to the rig.

Miernek said, 'It's bad news. I have to talk to him. Over.'

'No chance,' Gresson drawled. 'It'd be more than my life's worth to buzz the trawler at nearly three o'clock in the morning. You'd better tell me what's happened. Over.'

'It's that girl – the one I told you about. She checked in last night. The Welsh put us on to her – remember? She's with that guy who's always snooping around the village. You said it'd be OK for her to come here. Over.'

'Yeah, yeah,' said Gresson impatiently. 'What's she done, for Christ's sakes? Over.'

'She killed one of my men and put another in hospital, then she killed Ainley and got away, and killed another of my men before we caught her. Over.'

Gresson whistled. 'Lively, ain't she? Whose is she? Over.'

'I don't know. We haven't questioned her yet. She seems to be a British national. Over.'

'Yeah, OK. See what you can find out, but if I were you I wouldn't mess her around. Himself likes to do that himself, if you get my meaning. Give me a call in the morning, but not too early. The Colonel doesn't want to be woken until after ten. OK? Over.'

'OK. Base out.'

They had her in the hotel's television lounge and Miernek went into a bedroom and grabbed a sheet off a sleeping form to put round her middle.

She thanked him and he said, 'Talk.'

Blood was still seeping from her mouth and there was an angry welt on her cheek. She asked if she could bathe it, and Miernek sent someone for a medical kit.

When she'd finished she said, 'You know I killed Ainley because you saw me do it.'

'Yes,' Miernek said. 'It saved us the trouble, and your way was more interesting.'

'Thank you. You most also suspect that I'm Intelligence, and you're right, I am.'

'British SIS?'

'That's my business. As for the rest – how much I know, who I'm working with, what my plans are – I'd forget it, if I were you, because I honestly don't think any of you are good enough to get it from me.'

'We will have to see about this, Miss Wengan,' Miernek said coldly.

'That's right, you do that,' Cristal replied, brightly. 'Leave it to the man in charge, whoever he may be.'

'You might well end up wishing it was me.'

'Well, as you said, we'll have to see about that, won't we?'

'By the way, we have something belonging to you.'

'Oh?'

'Yes. A motorcycle. A big, black motorcycle. Ainley kept rambling on about a tall, slim man on a black motorcycle who killed the British agents on the sands at Marloes, and I didn't really believe him until a friend of ours spotted the bike outside your cottage in Trefynnon.

'That was careless of you, Miss Wengan, to leave it there, even if it was for only one night. We found it easily enough in the little lock-up garage you'd rented down the road, and our friend drove it up here. He's very attached to it. I may give it to him after . . .'

'I'm gone?'

'Something like that. So you see, Miss Wengan, we know you're not SIS , or you wouldn't have killed their agents, would you?'

'I suppose not.'

'Now, girl,' Miernek said, leaning over her on the settee, and seeing the four guns trained on her move fractionally forward with him. 'Now – would you like to tell me who you're working for, because I assure you it will be a great deal less painful with me than it will be with those above me.'

She gave the proposal some consideration, then looked him blandly in the eyes and said, 'No.'

Miernek slapped her hard on her bruised cheek, and she winced and grimaced, but stayed silent.

'Zoltan was my friend,' he said, harshly.

'What a shame, then,' she remarked, 'that you chose your friends with so little regard for either their charm or their stamina.'

Three of the guns lifted menacingly, but Miernek held up his hand.

'You're brave as well as beautiful,' he said, and inclined his head in a bow. She smiled winningly at him.

'Take her upstairs to 36 and play with her,' he said to the powerful, squat man with a badly designed face, standing by him.

'No rough stuff. No sex. No marks.'

The man nodded grimly. Cristal stood up, let the sheet fall to the ground, and gave a disappointed 'Aaah.'

Pond woke as usual at seven, and sat down to his Weetabix, scrambled eggs and streaky bacon half an hour later. He had the radio on and it gave him frequent time-checks, but still he kept glancing at the clock. A trendy Methodist flanked by unlikely and irrelevant rock music finished *Thought for the Day*, and he got up and paced the kitchen, willing the extension phone to ring. When it did just after eight o'clock he goggled at it, suspecting trickery.

He picked it up and Sleightley said, 'What did she say?'

'She hasn't called yet.'

'Which means she won't. Which means something's gone wrong.' Sleightley declared. 'Get hold of Scott, would you, please? Ask him to phone the hotel and go round there unless he can make contact Vengan. If she's been taken, she'll still be there, I would think.'

'Yes, all right,' said Pond. 'I'll let you know what happens when you get to the office.'

He rang off and dialled Scott's number, but there was no reply. Scott had left early for the airfield. His telephone link with Cristal was scheduled for ten o'clock, and he'd squeezed in a short service run so that he needn't waste the time before taking the call.

He got back with eight minutes to spare and they told him somebody from London had been on for him. He didn't want to tie up the line, so he delayed phoning for nearly half an hour, but she didn't call.

He rang the hotel and a girl connected him to Cristal's room and abandoned him to the unanswered internal dialling tone. He jammed his finger down on the receiver rest and redialled.

This time a man's voice said, 'Carreg Wen Hotel', Scott explained Miss Vengan wasn't in her room but he thought she might be somewhere around the hotel, and please could they look for her. The receptionist half-covered the mouthpiece and spoke quickly in a guttural foreign tongue (Czech, was it?) to someone else.

A second man's voice came on and said, 'This is Paul Miernek, the proprietor. Who is it wishes to speak with Miss Wengan?' Scott told him. There was another whispered conversation of longer duration. Then Miernek spoke again.

'I am told that Miss Wengan checked out, eh . . .' (he paused, and Scott said to himself, 'It's Polish; they're the ones who always say "W" for "V"') ' – at about nine o'clock. Her room had been cleared, and she left, I am informed, on foot. She did say she might be contacting us to see if there were any messages for her, so if you will leave me your phone number I will be glad to ring you in case it should be inconvenient for her to call you herself. It is no trouble, I assure you.'

Scott thanked him and gave him the Cambrian Helicopters number, then broke the connection. Almost immediately Miernek dialled the number and got them to explain slowly and carefully who and where they were before apologizing in an atrociously fractured accent for his mistake in calling them in the first place. He put the phone

205

down and looked thoughtfully across to the airfield and then upwards in the direction of the top left-hand corner of the house. He said to the clerk, 'I'm going to the radio room.'

When Scott told him she'd gone, Sleightley said, 'I don't believe it. You'll have to get over there and take a discreet poke around. Try to find Ainley's car, or better still, Ainley.'

'Yes. But look – I can't do it without breaking my cover. I'm due to fly two more service runs today. I've got to take a crew out to an American-Welsh rig, and some stores to an Irish one. If I don't do it, Cambrian are going to want to know why.'

Pond who'd been listening, chipped in with a suggestion that if Scott saw a rig flying the Soviet flag he should tell London without fail. Sleightley glared at him and said it was no occasion for jokes, and Pond fell moodily to filling in the remaining blank squares of Sleightley's copy of the *Times* Crossword puzzle with π to forty-eight places, in reverse.

'All right,' Sleightley said finally to Scott. 'Make it this evening, as early as you can, and telephone me at home. Good luck.'

Scott hung up, and because the roustabouts for the US-Welsh rig, OWAINCO Three, had been waiting nearly an hour already, he chose to take them off first, and then come back later to pick up the stores from the airfield for the Irish rig, TARACO FIVE.

Miernek got through to the rig again on the radio. They contacted the trawler, and a few moments later called him back. Gresson said, 'He wants the woman out here, *un*-harmed,' stressing the first syllable.

'Also he says if you've put any unauthorized drugs into her, he'll have your balls. Over.'

'No, we haven't,' Miernek said. And that at least was

true. 'Over.'

'And how is she? Over.'

'She's fine,' Miernek said quickly. 'Over.'

Gresson laughed. 'Quite a looker, isn't she? Over.'

'Gorgeous. Over.'

'See she stays that way. I guess The Man wants first bite at the cherry. Over.'

'Sure. She's fine. Over.'

'OK. Prepare her for shipment. Usual way. TARACO FIVE, out.'

There was no lift, and Miernek took the three flights of stairs at a gallop.

She was lying spreadeagled on the same bed they'd used for Ainley. Her arms and feet were chained and padlocked to the four brass posts.

He'd forbidden physical punishment, and the only attempt at rape had ended in humliating failure. She'd made such brutally candid comments about the young Pole who'd tried it, that his ardour collapsed, and even his ears turned pink.

In revenge, the imported muscle who was Miernek's nominal second-in-command – the dumpy gorilla called Francewski – had brought in a car battery and attached electrodes to her nipples and clitoris. She spat calmly and deliberately into his left eye.

When Miernek burst in, she was unconscious. He picked up a heavy torch and clubbed Francewski to the ground and kicked him savagely.

He seized the failed rapist by the shirt collar and hammered his head against the wall.

'Have you screwed her? Has anyone?' he shouted.

'No, I swear we haven't,' the man choked. The fear in his eyes told Miernek he wasn't lying.

'You'd better be right,' Miernek breathed. 'You and that filth there.'

He spun the young Pole around and flung him to the floor to join Francewski. One of the other two in the interrogation party, who'd been standing at the window with his arms folded, said quietly:

'Don't be too hard on him, Pavél. She's put Jan on the plane back to Warsaw. She killed Zbigniew, and now she's killed Zoltan. Did you expect us to treat her like our favourite little sister.'

'I said no rough stuff.'

The other man, who was older and who'd earned the respect of the rest as much for his brains as his fists, spat on the floor and said, 'We weren't rough. She's not been marked outside by us. Anything else she got, the fucking murdering bitch deserved.'

Miernek grunted and said, 'Clean her up, then tell Carla to get some clothes from the girl's room and dress her. I'll prepare the injection and the transit box. She's leaving in fifteen minutes.

TWENTY

Scott delivered his gang of boisterous roustabouts to the Welsh rig, and after a snack lunch he was back again at the controls of the S-61N heading towards TARACO FIVE at a steady hundred and twenty-two knots. He scanned the instruments automatically as the whirring turbines delivered their two and a half thousand horse-power to the slashing blades, and found his mind wandering, helped by the monotonous, muffled, 'flurp-flurp-flurp' sound as the blades cut through the air to keep an eighteen thousand pound load of men, machinery and fuel a thousand feet above the sea.

He normally took maximum pleasure from his flying. His initial enthusiasm had never waned. It was always just like that first time when, as a sixteen-year-old cadet in the ATC he had sat, mouth dry with anticipation, stomach slightly knotted, waiting for his first launch in an open glider. There had been the bumping over the rough ground, and then the instant, magical transformation into a state of smoothness and grace, and the explosion into his vision of a broader vista than he had ever seen or imagined.

Today his mood was reflected by the weather. Where Ireland lay, there was just a mist of cloud. No horizon, but an indistinguishable miasma of sky and the slate-coloured sea. Beads of rain formed on the perspex canopy, and the machine shivered as they passed through a squall. His eyes caught the white wake of a fishing boat – the only break in the total greyness around him. And inside him.

For he was deeply worried by Cristal's failure to phone. Had she checked out of the hotel? Was Miernek holding her prisoner? What could have happened? The anxiety gnawed at him. She'd sounded keyed up on the phone last night, but seemed confident she could handle any threat presented by Ainley's guards – if there were guards. Few people in the world, he'd come to realise, were more capable than Cristal in dealing with trouble from whatever quarter.

Yet even she wasn't invulnerable . . . he compressed his lips in a simulacrum of a mental shrug as the worry returned. She *must* be all right – she *had* to be. She planned her operations with such care and skill it was inconceivable that she could have been caught.

'Then why haven't you phoned? Why?' he ground out savagely to the sky and the seagulls, and his first officer, Terry Mason, said, 'Why haven't I what? . . .' Scott flushed and said, 'Sorry – thinking aloud.' Mason whistled 'Who were you with last night?' and then equally tunelessly, 'She was a dear little dicky-bird, cheep, cheep, cheep she went.' Scott laughed and said, 'Get stuffed,' and as Mason broke into song, '. . . sang to me 'til all my money was . . .' he added, 'And for Christ's sake shut up.' But good humouredly, for Terry was a loyal and valued friend.

The truth was, Scott had started to admit something he'd refused to allow before – that his anxiety wasn't solely the concern that one field agent felt for the safety of another. She was becoming . . . well – special to him. He whispered her name, and a sharp pang of remembrance caught his mind of that first time they were together in Trefynnon. When she'd taken him into her for the second time she'd asked him, as they lay joined, 'Could you love me?' It was said unsurely, falteringly, but with genuine curiosity, while her finger traced a path from his eyebrow to his nose, around his mouth, dipping in at the corner and delicately touching his teeth and his tongue, then wetly down to his chin, his neck and the hollow of his throat and stopping there though he'd ached for her to go on, and while all the time he moved carefully in her body. 'Could you?' she repeated. Had she wanted him to say yes, even just to nod? He'd said nothing, nor made any movement, but just buried his face in her hair. Now he knew that he could fall in love with her. But that, all the same, he'd make sure that he didn't.

The radio crackled into life with the latest weather report from the rig, jolting him back to reality. Checking his timings, he calculated that they were due to arrive in ten minutes. He called to Terry Mason to start the pre-landing checks, and strained against his seat harness to get a better view through the screen. So far there was no sign of the rig in the funnel of visibility below them. He checked the ADF to make sure they were on course, looked out again, and there it was, picked out by the watery flicker of its lights through the sparse rain. He pressed the RT button.

'TARACO FIVE, this Golf Alfa Romeo Whisky November. I have got you in sight.'

'Roger, Whisky November, you are clear to land. The QFE is one zero zero eight, and the wind is from two seven zero at less than five knots.'

Scott said, 'Roger, TARACO FIVE.' He adjusted the altimeter, took control from the first officer, and wheeled the helicopter into a long, sweeping descent to the tiny platform nine hundred feet down. As they landed, a group of men clustered near the platform hurried forward. The rotor blades slowed to a rest, and Scott and Mason climbed out.

'Look after the unloading and refuelling, Terry, could you, please?' Scott asked.

'Sure, Ewan,' said Mason. 'Going below?'

'Yeah, radio room. See you in a minute.'

'Sure. Right then, gentlemen,' to the loaders, who didn't answer. 'It's all yours,' said Mason. 'Do you know where it's got to go?' This to a man who looked as though he could be in charge. The loader looked blankly at him. 'The stuff. The stores,' said Mason. Then pointed to the crates in the Sikorski. 'The gear, for Christ's sake. Where does it go? WHERE DOES IT GO?'.

'Down the hatch,' a voice said. Mason turned, and a man who'd been standing near the diving-bell stanchion on the other side of the Sikorski's nose, strolled over. 'Down in the cargo hold. Sorry, you've got a dum-dum there,' indicating the silent loader.

'OK,' Mason answered, 'but I'm supposed to be in charge of this stuff,' waving a hand at the cargo, 'so . . .'

'No,' said the man, flatly, but not argumentatively. '*I* am. I'm the bargemaster, Mick Gresson.'

He wore the traditional oil-rig gear of tough white paper overalls, thick rubber boots and yellow plastic safety helmet. He spoke with a curiously in-place mid-Atlantic accent. Mason put his height correctly at six feet eight.

'Well, OK,' Mason said, brushing away with his hand the sudden frisson of fear that caught the hair at the back of his neck. 'But while they're still in there,' pointing at the Sikorski, 'They're my responsibility.'

'No sweat, pal,' the bargemaster replied. He came over to Mason, looking down at him. 'No sweat. Huh?' with just the barest hint of interrogative menace. Then he snapped his fingers, the sound cracked across the deck, and five men literally jumped into action.

They clambered on to the platform, and into the helicopter, siezed the more portable cases, and jumped down, still without talking.

'OK?' the bargemaster asked, not bothering to mask the bland insolence in his voice. The loaders were scurrying about like demented gerbils. 'Sure,' said Mason, and walked over to the main companionway to the crew's quarters and leant on the rail, trying to look as though he had urgent business there. He glanced down the steps, but Scott had disappeared.

Scott swung the raincoat off his shoulders that had given him protection from the drizzle when he was about halfway along the corridor leading to the radio operator's room slung, like the rest of the accommodation, under the main deck. There was so much external noise down below that his footsteps barely echoed on the metal flooring. You rarely, he mused, came across a piece of wood on an oil rig.

212

They all seemed to be built from steel, angle iron and acres of dun-coloured plastic partitioning. Then, as if someone had waved a wand, the internal clangour briefly ceased.

The door of the radio room was slightly ajar, and he was perhaps twenty feet from it when he half-heard the low tones of a conversation floating out to him. It wasn't in English, and some acquired instinct for dealing with unpredictable twists made him stop and stand rooted to the spot, holding his breath. It normally wouldn't have surprised him, because there were always foreigners on a rig. He couldn't catch much of what was being said, but of one thing he was sure: one of the men had twice spoken the word 'Spassi-boh,' once normally and then with sarcastic emphasis. Scott wasn't remotely in Cristal's class as a linguist, but even he knew the Russian for 'Thank you'.

He wheeled about and retraced his footsteps and then, with a heavier tread, and a careless, piercing whistle, he approached the door again. By the time he got there, the conversation was in English, a language the radio ops. would have to have as a matter of course in British (or Irish) waters. Scott pushed the door fully open and saw the two men, both probably in their late twenties. Radio operators, he thought, as though it were a sudden revelation, always seemed to be small, well-adjusted guys with short hair, thick glasses and excellent manners. These two were not. They had dull, square, chunky faces and their bodies were designed to stand up to a good deal of abuse. They could have been twins.

Neither was embarrassed by his arrival, so probably they'd been taken in by the back-tracking, and were satisfied they had not been overheard. Scott attempted with difficulty to give each of them a casual nod, then walked over to the control desk as though he was going to inspect the equipment or tap out a message. Four not so blank eyes followed him.

His mind raced furiously. Could the rig – *this* rig – have something to do with the rocket? Was it even the key to the whole business? And if not, why were a couple of radio operators on the rig talking Russian? The questions hammered at his brain.

Then he got a grip of himself, spun round as one of the pair said, 'Can we do anything for you?', and asked them for the routine forecast, which was why he'd come down anyway. He scarcely took in the details, said 'Thanks,' and then, 'Cheers,' and set off back down the corridor, trying to keep the urgency he felt out of his step. Now he had only one goal . . . to return to base and find Cristal or, failing that, inform London.

Back on the helicopter landing platform, picking up Mason on the way, who seemed relieved to see him, he called out, 'Speed things up, fellas,' to the fuelling crew, and inwardly cursed the loaders who were struggling to get one last heavy crate out from the Sikorski's main cabin. They manhandled it clumsily off the platform and plonked it unceremoniously on the metal deck.

Someone kicked over a trolley and three of the loaders moved forward to manoeuvre the crate on to it. The giant bargemaster shot an arm across the leading man's chest and he stopped in mid-stride. Alert now, Scott recognised him as the 'Post Office Tower' at Miernek's hotel, but said nothing. Gresson bent down, stretched his arms and huge, powerful hands into a rigid span, grabbed two of the rope carrying-handles and lifted the crate effortlessly off the ground.

Scott stood still with Mason, watching intently. None of the loaders had spoken, and Scott now knew why . . . they were the hired heavies. They didn't have to speak English. Gresson carried the crate easily to the main hold, and put it down. A little crane snatched it up, and it swung into the semi-darkness to lie with the other stores. At some stage, Scott thought, the bargemaster might be a problem.

'Thanks a lot,' Mason said. Then he indicated his friend and added, 'By the way, this is the pilot, Captain Ewan Scott.'

214

The big man's eyes narrowed, but then he relaxed, chuckled, and took Scott's hand. 'Gresson,' he said. 'Mick Gresson. Welcome aboard, Captain Scott.' And he laughed, but his eyes were cold.

One of the loaders secured the main door of the helicopter and Scott, wary but impatient to get away, nodded to Gresson and turned on his heel. He got up into the Sikorski and straight away started the pre-flight checks. Mason was distinctly more cheerful now.

Scott got the turbines under power, lifted the Sikorski off the pad, and streaked into the sky at very nearly the maximum rate of thirteen hundred feet a minute. He would have curbed his impatience had he known that the big crate in the hold contained Cristal.

Lift-off

TWENTY-ONE

The shadows were lengthening, and angry storm clouds massing to mask the dying sun, when Scott circled his corner of the airstrip, hovered briefly, and set the empty Sikorsky down as daintily as a falling sycamore leaf. He cut the engine and started to get out of the cockpit, and Mason asked, 'Hey, what's the hurry, Skipper?'

Scott sat down and fiddled indecisively with the control panel.

'Something on your mind, Ewan?' Mason said gently. Scott thought furiously and made his decision. It could well turn out that he'd need Mason's help, and Terry wouldn't fly blind into anything.

'A friend of mine may be in trouble, Terry.'

'You need help? You only have to ask, you know that.'

'Yes – yes, I know. And I'm grateful, Terry. But I must tell you . . . it could be hairy – very hairy.'

Mason regarded him quizzically. 'What sort of hairy?' he asked.

Scott pursed his lips, and allowed his teeth to roam along the lower lip, and said, 'Government business.'

Mason whistled, and said, 'You crafty old sod. So you *were* Naval Intelligence, and you've never really left it.'

Scott nodded. 'Something like that,' he admitted.

'Well, count me in, What's it all about anyway – and who's your friend?'

'The friend's a girl . . .'

'Aahh. Might've known sex was rearing its gorgeous tail somewhere.'

Scott grinned crookedly. 'Yeah, she's lovely. And I think she's been nobbled by the opposition.'

'Who are?'

Scott replied, 'Ivan.'

'The Russkies?'

'Uh-huh.'

Mason whistled again. 'Well, as I said, count me in.'

'Look Terry, you don't have to. I've told you, it could be nasty.'

'For you, Ewan, and the unknown beauty – anything,' Mason said, with a toss of his head and a cavalier twitch of non-existent moustachios.

Scott looked at him without laughing. 'Even if it had something to do with that big bastard on the rig today.?'

'Him?' Mason gasped, and then flushed. 'You saw, then.'

'Saw what?'

'That I was shit-scared of him – and for no reason at all.'

'You had plenty of reason, I think, Terry. He's very large, and I have a shrewd suspicion he's very evil as well.'

'Yeah,' Mason said and swallowed uneasily. 'There was something about him . . . you think your friend – what's her name?'

'Cristal.'

'Nice. You think she's on the rig?'

Scott considered the idea. 'I hadn't thought of that. But no, I don't think so. I think she's in a place not far from here.'

'So when do we leave?'

'You don't,' said Scott firmly. 'I'll spy out the land, and if you wouldn't mind going back to your place and sitting by the phone, I'll be in touch later.'

'As you direct, Mon Capitaine,' Mason said, his good spirits recovered. 'But you didn't tell me what it's all about.'

'No, Terry, I didn't,' Scott said. 'And I'm not going to – not yet.'

'You mean the less I know the better,' Mason bristled.

'I mean that if you don't know then you can't be made to tell.' Scott said, gravely.

'Oh – OK then. You'll ring me later?'

Scott nodded.

'Cheers, then' Mason said and walked off to pick up his car.

Scott watched him go, thoughtfully. Then he looked over at the broken quadrangle of Portakabins that made up the company's site offices. They were in darkness. He let himself into the main office and, with the aid of a pencil-torch, dialled London.

'It's Scott. I'm just about to go to the hotel, unless you've heard anything from her?'

'No, we haven't,' said Pond, who was at home. 'We fear the worst. We're depending on you, Scott. But be careful – if you're taken, too, we'd hesitate to send in someone else who'd be on absolutely strange ground. Do you follow me?'

'Yes, I do Dr Pond. What you're saying is, we're on our own. No lifeline.'

'I don't mean you're expendable, Scott. Just that we consider it would be – impracticable, to get you out.'

'I understand. Before you go, there's something else.'

And Scott told him of his suspicions concerning the ostensibly Irish rig.

There was a long pause. 'Talking Russian, you say?' Pond mused.

'Definitely.'

Another pause. 'An oil rig . . . What could they do . . . what *could* they do . . . with an oil rig . . . ? Unless?'

'Unless what?'

'I-I don't know. At least – that is, I'm not sure. I'll have to . . . I'm obliged to you, Scott. You've given me a great deal to think about. Now you'd better be on your way.'

Pond hung up. He thought for a while, then took a sketch pad and a set of pencils and coloured felt pens from the drawer of his bureau, and thumbed through the pages of an Atlas until he found one setting out in topographical and marine detail, the Welsh coast and the Celtic sea.

Half an hour later he arranged several pages of precise drawings and meticulously neat calculations before him on

221

the floor, sat on a cushion in front of them and called Sleightley's home number.

Scott climbed the airfield perimeter fence and circled through three fields to approach the extensive grounds of the Carreg Wen from the rear. The hotel, too, was fenced around; more securely if anything, than the airfield. Scott stood his wire-cutters on the ground so that they were earthed, and let them fall into the strong mesh fencing. They bounced off and hit the grass without causing a telltale spark of electricity.

He cut a large enough gap and crawled through. The undergrowth was wild at the spot he'd chosen, and he risked shining his torch. The large, gabled Victorian house, which he'd seen often during the daytime through binoculars, was to the front, and slightly left, of him. He was seeing it in the fitful light that remained, as a three-quarters rear perspective, about three hundred yards away. Nearest to him was the gravel car-park which occupied almost as much space as the hotel itself.

Further away to his left, the light from the front bay windows cast a faint glow over the stone pillars at the top of the steps running down to the big lawn, bisected by the drive, which started opposite the front door but then swept round in a question mark to avoid the bank. The iron gates leading on to the road were open.

To his right there was more dense undergrowth, and he could see against the skyline the tops of a broken row of trees which marked the boundary of the grounds for nearly a third of their length. He already knew the geography of the place fairly well from an aerial photograph he'd taken during a low pass in the Sikorski one day, on the pretext that the owner was a friend of a friend who'd asked him to do it as a favour.

Dead ahead were the beginnings of the hotel outbuildings – they seemed to be garages and storerooms – and it was through them that he hoped to gain access to the hotel.

A flash of light from a clump of bushes fifty or more yards to the right made him snap off his own torch and drop to the ground, stifling a curse. He wriggled to the cover of a tangled spread of gorse, fished out his gun and screwed on the silencer. The beam of light weaved an unsteady path in his direction, and as it passed him he pressed into the prickly bush and saw that the light came from a torch held by a man in a peaked cap with a rifle slung negligently over his right shoulder.

Scott swore silently at himself. He should have expected armed guards. In fact he had considered them, but he'd reasoned that whoever ran the place wouldn't want to risk showing their hand to an innocent guest taking an after-dinner stroll. Unless, he thought with a surge of alarm, there weren't any innocent guests – in which case they'd admitted Cristal because they wanted her to go there, in order to keep an eye on her. She couldn't have known she was under suspicion, so she'd walked straight into a trap . . .

He then walked – or rather, crawled – into one himself. The indolent guard was ten yards past him and Scott moved silently and swiftly out to the path, then crouched ready to break into a run and bring the man down, when suddenly the guard stopped.

He half-turned to his left, missed seeing Scott, and whistled. Scott froze while his mind raced for perhaps two seconds – but the realization, when it came, was too late.

The Doberman was on him, snapping and snarling. Scott lurched off balance, which probably saved him from death from both directions. Seeing a target at more or less its own height, the dog levered itself off the ground in a powerful, high-trajectory leap instead of rushing him as it was trained to. Just as a bullet from the guard's rifle thrummed past his head, Scott fell on his back, clamped the Walther in both hands, and shot the Doberman in mid-air through the throat, blasting off the top of its head.

He completed a backward roll and lay flat, face down,

arms extended in front of him holding the gun. Where was the guard? He peered into the almost unrelieved blackness.

Then the man's hoarse voice came to him, calling the name of the dog. 'Mannix. Mannix. Mannix.' Scott held his breath and stayed utterly still, and the guard hissed a fourth time, 'Mannix.' urgent fear in his voice now. Hearing nothing, he switched on his torch.

Scott's gun gave three dry, almost apologetic coughs as he placed a horizontal line of shots about eighteen inches above the beam and was rewarded with a strangled, choking gasp. The torchlight bobbed upwards and spiralled to the earth, and Scott heard two further dull thuds as the guard's rifle and then his body followed. The heaving and gurgling sound grew in intensity. 'Throat again,' Scott thought.

He felt around for the dog's body, and pulled it into the gorse. He was sure the bullet from the guard's rifle would have been heard in the hotel, and would bring men with lights and guns searching the grounds.

Then he ran over and picked up the still glowing torch and switched it off. Finally, he dragged the badly injured man and his rifle off the path into the deeper shadow of a laurel bush.

He gambled that if the guard was a Pole, like Miernek, he would also speak French. Scott bent his mouth to the man's ear, and said:

'You're hurt, I know, but I can save you. I will take you to a hospital, and the doctors will save your life. Do you understand? I am the only hope you have, because if you don't do as I say I will leave you here, and your friends won't be able to find you and you will die. Do you understand?'

He felt the man nod his shaggy head.

'The girl. The tall girl with black hair. Where is she? Is she in the hotel?'

The guard shook his head.

'Is she at sea? Is she –' he groped for the French for oil rig and made up a phrase – 'sur le gréement pétrolifère?'

There was silence, and no movement from the guard.

Scott shook him roughly, and repeated the question. The man was trying not to move his head but he was slipping fast. His chin dropped and Scott bent his own ear down, and as the blood dribbled out of the guard's mouth and throat, Scott heard him say 'Oui.'

Scott let the man's head drop to the ground, but a further bubbling moan came from his lips, so the agent placed the silenced Walther against his temple, turned away and pulled the trigger.

He dodged between clumps of bushes as he made his way to the back of the hotel.

Suddenly he heard more movement, and voices this time, and a light, behind him to his right. He stared into the night and saw more lights, fanned out in an arc, advancing not towards the hotel but away from it. Taking a chance, he slipped from cover and streaked for the nearest outbuilding. The last twenty yards or so were across the rear of the car park, which was quite empty.

He leaned against the wall, of what turned out to be a wooden hut, getting his breath back. Then a door opened from the hotel and at least two pairs of feet clumped in his direction. They halted in mid-stride, and one of the men said something to the other in a sharp and commanding tone.

Scott edged along the wall, and came to a flimsy side door fastened with a cheap, chain-store padlock. At the very instant that his wire cutters snipped through the locking crook, the entire rear of the hotel and most of the huge oak park and grounds were bathed in the glow of a set of powerful flood-lights. Scott shrank through the opening and shut the door softly behind him.

He sniffed motor oil, and since there were no windows in the shed, and plenty of light outside that would absorb any which might escape through chinks in the rough boarding, he decided it was safe to use his torch.

It was a garage – a large one. At the back end were two

Land Rovers side by side, in front of them a current registration black (or was it dark blue?) Rover saloon, and parked close to its front bumper was a hefty little pick-up truck equipped with a crane. There was another gleam of metal beyond the Rover car, but he couldn't quite make out its shape.

Scott checked the front doors first. Peering through the join he could see a formidably stout padlock sitting fatly on the hasp. There was no hope of cutting it, even if he could manage to stay outside undetected for long enough to try it. He looked round for oxyacetylene equipment, but reasoned that the line wouldn't reach. Besides, there wasn't any.

He was leaning against the truck gazing fruitlessly at the Rover when the realization dawned on him that it was Ainley's car. The number plate told him he was right.

'So what?' he thought, 'Cristal knew it was here.' Still, he decided to search it and he opened the door and climbed in, examining first the driver's side and then the unlocked glove compartment on the passenger's side.

He closed the compartment with a grunt of disappointment, mumbled 'What did you expect to find, anyway?' Then he got out of the nearside door, and almost fell into Cristal's Yamaha XS1000.

Scott gave a muted whoop of joy. Even without the key he could probably start it – but the key was in the ignition. He picked the big bike off the wall and wheeled it between the Land Rover and Ainley's car, checking the tank to make sure it had enough juice. He sighted the handlebars against the side door, and there was a clearance of about three inches either side. Spotting Cristal's smoky-visored crash helmet hooked to the luggage rack, he instinctively put it on.

He calculated that Miernek wouldn't want to have the floodlights on for longer than he could help for the same reason that he must try to keep shooting to a minimum. Both would be bound to attract the attention of the fire picket at RAF Tredogan, the Air force base just across the road. He eased open the door. The search was still continuing – with dogs brought in now – at the far end by the hotel fence. As if Miernek was obeying his every instruction, at that moment the lights went off.

Scott pushed back the door, climbed astride the Yamaha, and switched on the engine. It gurgled fluffily into life, and he worked the motorcycle through the door, gave it all the throttle it had, and exploded into the car park. The floodlights came back on.

The wheels bit deeply into the gravel as he flashed across the car park in a wide sweep, picking up speed all the time. Sporadic shooting broke out from the front of the hotel, which Scott hadn't expected.

A bullet zinged off the metal frame, and he took the steps between the stone pillars slantwise at sixty miles an hour, twisting the throttle to a banshee scream.

The Yamaha balanced itself in mid-flight and sailed majestically on to the lawn, landing on its rear wheel and gouging a great divot out of the turf. The bike bounced and tore its way across the grass, weaving between a group of birch trees, and scorched on to the drive in a spray of mud and tiny stones. Scott fought desperately to keep the Yamaha upright, and then opened the throttle again and shot out on to the main road, followed by a howl of rage and a last, despairing stray bullet. A blissful silence reigned at RAF Tredogan.

Scott left the Yamaha some distance from the airfield, telephoned Mason from a kiosk on the main road, and jogged the rest of the way to the watchman's hut at the entrance to the helicopter compound. The watchman, Gwilym Jenkins, was taking his time preparing for his rounds. Night duty was a routine and pretty boring task, and distractions – like a helicopter turning out for an air-sea rescue call – were rare. He yawned, but stifled it when Scott rapped on his window.

He buttoned his jacket, walked over to the door, and

opened it. 'Good evening, Captain Scott,' he said. 'Having trouble getting to sleep?'

'Wish I had the chance to,' Scott replied. 'I've had a call at home, Mr Jenkins. They've got an emergency out on TARACO FIVE. One of their executives visiting the rig is a diabetic, and he left his insulin in the chopper. If I don't give it to him, he could be in a coma by morning.'

'Oh, I see,' said Jenkins. 'I'll get the standby ground crew up, then?'

'No, don't bother. Mr Mason's on his way here, and if you can pull the GPU away for us, we can manage ourselves without bothering them. My machine's fully fuelled anyway.'

Jenkins left to switch the floodlighting on, and Scott strolled across to the Sikorski. Luckily, there was a Ground Power Unit parked close enough to plug in, and the big diesel generator started at the first touch. Scott could do no more until Mason arrived, so he asked Jenkins to watch the generator, and put in a call to Pond from the watchman's hut.

'Things are getting tricky at this end, Dr Pond,' he said. 'I was forced to be quite unkind to someone earlier this evening, and I now know for sure that Cristal's out on that oil rig I told you about. TARACO FIVE, the Irish one. I'm going out there now; I'll land by faking an emergency – engine trouble, or something like that.'

'The oil rig,' Pond said, triumphantly. 'I knew it, I just knew it. It's obviously some kind of huge transmitting station. I was right.' He was so elated he started babbling, 'They're going to attempt the most daring electronic theft of the century. There can be no other explanation. It can only be done on test because in actual flight the target's set on the computer and you can't stop it – but on test, Scott . . . on test, anything . . . *anything* could happen.'

Scott chuckled at his obvious pleasure, and Pond curbed his enthusiasm long enough to inquire if it was safe for Scott to fly to the rig. 'There must be quite a few people there, surely,' he pointed out.

'I'll take someone with me,' Scott assured him,' and our faked engine failure will give us time to sniff around. If we think we can handle the situation – OK. If not, you could sent a boarding party disguised as a maintenance crew in another helicopter. But give us until this time tomorrow before you act. I don't think they suspect me, so we'll have all day to see what's what.'

'Very well,' Pond said. 'I'll see to it that there aren't any more rocket firings from Tredogan until we're sure of being able to put the rig out of action.'

'Fine,' said Scott. 'One day you must tell me exactly what it they're going to do with this oil rig, because I'm damned if I can work it out.'

'Yes, I'll be pleased to, my boy. But for the moment – good luck.'

Pond rang off, and could hardly wait to tell Sleightley that his hunch had been correct. The Russians were going to use an oil rig as a kind of super-powerful, electronic lasso, and literally pluck an ORBITMAN rocket from the sky on the next trial run from Tredogan with a high-powered radio signal, while the Inertial Navigation was on stand-by. To all intents and purposes the rocket would have fallen into the sea, and the RAE boffins would write it off as a mechanical failure. They would, in a sense, be correct: the rocket *would* land in the sea – but it would home in on the oil rig's signal beacon, and Russian divers would be standing by to salvage it.

He dialled Sleightley's number, and they started methodically planning the continuing course of the wildest wild goose chase of their collective careers.

Scott ran to greet Mason at the gate. Soon they were seated in the Sikorski's cockpit running through the pre-start checks. 'How much can you tell me, Skipper?' Mason asked, as Scott reached up to the roof console to start the first engine. Scott waited for the tell-tale whine to confirm that the engine was running. Then he said, 'Only this. It matters like hell – and frankly, so does the girl. We've got a chance – a very slim chance – of pulling it off. But at least it's a chance.'

When both engines were running, and Jenkins had disconnected the GPU, they ran the pre-take off checks. Scott chose to fly the Sikorski himself; he revelled in the extraordinary series of actions that every helicopter pilot had to undertake when flying his machine; the sense of balance, allied to what the eye can see and the bottom feel, translated into commands by the brain which, through the infinitely complicated muscle and motor systems of the body, produces perfect co-ordination from the feet, and from both hands engaged in separate tasks.

Hovering about six feet from the ground, he held it steady, and slowly swung it around to face the airfield. The strip wasn't lit, and rather than risk hitting an unseen obstacle, he raised the collective lever to give then an almost vertical ascent to a safe height of several hundred feet. Then it was nose down, and full speed ahead for the rig.

The flight took about forty-five minutes. Mason spotted TARACO FIVE. Perhaps because she was no longer drilling, she was showing little more than the basic navigation lights. Scot tuned into the rig's radio frequency, and put in a call.

'TARACO FIVE, this is Golf Alfa Romeo Whisky November. Do you read?' He got no reply, and repeated the messsage. The receiver crackled into life.

'Station calling TARACO FIVE. Please repeat. Over.'
'TARACO FIVE, this is Golf Alfa Romeo Whisky November. We have engine trouble. We cannot make it back to base. We request an emergency landing.'

'Stand by, Whisky November.' Half a minute later, he came back. 'We shall switch on our landing lights at once. Over.' Obviously, Scott thought, whoever was in charge was aware that, however inconvenient their presence might be, to refuse a stricken aircraft was unthinkable. 'Roger,' he replied,' we are commencing approach now.'

The tiny disc of the helipad blazed with light, and Scott headed for it in a deliberately erratic fashion. While he was making his approach, Mason, on Scott's instructions, radioed 'Cambrian Ground' – their base at Tredogan – and got Jenkins on the transceiver in the watchman's hut.

'It's engine trouble,' he reported. 'Serious, the skipper said. Probably a turbine faliure. Could be ingestion. The Skipper says he knows you haven't got another engine at base, and that's what we need. We're landing on TARACO FIVE, and we're quite happy to sit tight here tonight and tomorrow while you get a new engine flown up from Bristow's at Redhill.'

Jenkins took a laborious and precise note, and promised to get things moving at first light. 'Here goes then, Terry,' Scott said, 'keep your fingers crossed.' And he set the Sikorski down with an awkward, jerking thump. They shut down the engines, made their way back to the door, and jumped down to the deck.

The fist man they saw – and he was unmistakable – was the giant Gresson. He saunted over, flanked by four other men including one of the pair Scott had heard talking Russian in the radio room. Scott and Mason glanced at each other. 'Sorry, old lad,' Scott said. 'I have a feeling they've got us cold.'

Gresson said, 'Engine trouble, sailor?' Scott replied, 'That's it. Like I said on the radio.'

'Yeah, sure,' Gresson drawled. 'I heard. I also heard your other call. Good thinking, that. Saves us the trouble of making you do it, and of hijacking tomorrow's flight.'

'What do you mean?' Scott demanded. 'What the hell are you talking about?'

The American wore a heavy ring on the little finger of his left hand, and it bit into Scott's cheek when Gresson smashed him back-handed into the arms of two of his waiting goons.

'Save it, pal,' he advised. 'You got more than engine trouble, baby. You couldn't have come at a better time. You and your girlfriend down below. And whatever that is' – nodding contemptuously in Mason's direction. The radio operator's hand plucked out Scott's gun and threw it over the side.

'Don't bother about the budgie,' Gresson said, glancing at the Sikorski. 'We got plans for it. And besides, you won't be needing it again. This rig is the last thing you're going to see, Skip. Either of you.'

TWENTY-ONE

Gresson and the Russians shepherded the pair across the platform past the derrick and down the main companion-way to the crew's quarters. The vivid overhead lighting picked out an opening, in the far corner, into an area that hummed with the sound of powerful machinery. 'Generating room,' Scott thought, trying to memorise the layout of this particular rig, since they all tended to differ in geographical details.

Gresson led them to the metal cage of a tiny three-man lift, and with a sinking heart Scott realised that they were going to be held prisoner in the one place on an oil rig from which there could be no possibility of escape . . . the underwater compressor room in the floating pontoon at the base of one of the rig's four gigantic legs.

'One at a time, now,' Gresson said, and pushed Mason into the lift with an armed guard. The minutes dragged by as it clanked slowly down, and came back with just the guard. Scott noticed how the men at the surface pointed their guns at the lift when it drew level with them, in case the wrong man came up.

Gresson followed his eyes. 'Happens every time, sailor,' he said. 'No chance that way.' Then he laughed. 'In fact, no chance any way for you. Get in.'

There was no gate at the bottom, and he stepped straight out into the compressor room. Cristal looked composed but dazed, and he suspected –correctly – that she was still suffering from the effects of a drug.

He kissed her several times and said, 'I've worked it out that it was probably *me* that brought you here.'

'In that case we're even,' she said, 'because I suppose it was me that brought *you* here.'

'Yes it was.'

'London won't like it – both of us in the bag.'

'No. They've already said they won't pull us out.'

'Have they?' she said. 'Then we'll have to manage by ourselves, won't we?'

He nodded. 'Any ideas?'

'No,' she said, which was a lie, because the sight of the lift making its repeated trips up to the top had implanted in her mind the seed of a desperate scheme, but one that she couldn't reveal because of the admittedly unlikely chance that the compressor room might be bugged.

'How've they treated you?' Scott asked, touching her bruised cheek tenderly.

'A bit roughly at the hotel. Not so bad here – so far.'

'Who's in charge?'

'Gresson appears to be,' she said. 'But he's only muscle. There must be a top man. I haven't seen him yet.'

Mason coughed politely behind him, and Scott turned and grinned. 'Haven't you met?' he asked.

'Not formally.'

'Terry Mason – Cristal Vengan.' They shook hands, and Mason started to say to her, 'What's a pretty girl like . . .' when she cut him off.

'Don't,' she said. 'Somebody asked me that in the hotel last night, and he didn't live long enough to find out the answer.'

Scott raised his eyebrows.

'Ainley,' she explained.

'Oh,' he said. 'You . . . ?'

'Yes.'

'Oh.'

She motioned him to come closer to her, and told him in a whisper what the Russians were planning to do.

'My God,' he said, incredulously. 'Does London know?' She shook her head. He let go of her and crossed the little room to stand facing her with his arms folded, a frown

234

lining his brow.

'Grim tidings?' Mason asked, as the lift alighted once again, and Gresson got out.

'The worst,' Scott replied.

'Don't you believe it,' Gresson said, looking down at them. 'Trouble's only just started for you.' He jerked his head aloft.

'The Man's arrived.'

Scott and Cristal were taken up singly with Gresson. Again there was a wary armed reception at the top, and Cristal's escape plan began to take shape. Gresson stepped aside to let her into one of the main cabins where only the sun streaming through the porthole provided light. A man was standing with his back to the room, gazing out on the sea.

Cristal's hand flew to her mouth to stifle the gasp of astonishment that barely escaped. Ivanovitch spun round to face her.

'Good, Miss Vengan,' he crowed. 'Very good. You recognised me even from the rear. You will obviously appreciate how much that tells me about you and your echelon in whatever Intelligence organisation you serve.'

Cristal flushed and bit her lip. Scott tried to keep a look of bland awareness on his face, but Ivanovitch read him like an open book.

'Something tells me,' he said in his deep, dark, rasping voice, 'that Captain Scott doesn't share your – er – intimate knowledge. Would you kindly inform him who I am?'

She said, 'He's Count Peter Nicholas Ivanovitch Orloff.'

Ivanovitch's brow clouded and the smile left his lips. The metamorphosis from benignancy to malignancy was instantaneous and overwhelming. Scott felt goosepimples rise on his arms, and Gresson shuffled nervously behind him. But Cristal bestowed on the Russian a radiant smile.

'You want to play games with me, child?' Ivanovitch asked softly. Then he snarled, 'Do you?' and Scott jumped

235

in spite of himself.

Cristal's face held an ingenuous grin.

'I'm sorry, Colonel,' she said. She ignored the menace of his looming bulk, less than a yard away now, and turned to Scott and explained.

'You see, Ewan, when he was a mere stripling in the late twenties, aristocracy became unfashionable in Russia, so Count Orloff dropped his surname and his newly inherited title, changed the lordly "Nicholas" to the more plebeian "Nikita" and joined the Young Communists' league. And that proved to be a very clever thing for young Niko to do, because now he's a full Colonel in the Red Army, *and* head of the Special Task Force of the KGB. You will observe, Ewan,' she continued, gesturing at the Russian as though he were a zoological specimen, 'that he is surpassingly ugly – apart, that is, from his teeth, which are quite beautiful.'

'I don't think the Colonel's amused, Cristal,' said Scott.

'On the contrary, Mr Scott,' Ivanovitch beamed, 'I find Miss Vengan most entertaining.'

The back of his hand across her face was like the crack of a stockman's bullwhip, and the second blow followed so closely on the first that they might almost have been one continuous sound. But that was on *Ivanovitch's* cheek, and whereas Cristal's face registered unbridled fury, the Russian's was a picture of almost delighted astonishment.

'One all, I think, Colonel,' she snapped.

'Mmm' he agreed. 'The trouble is, I'm the referee, too. Now which would you prefer, Miss Vengan – drugs, me or Gresson?' She said nothing.

'Captain Scott?' he asked, affably. Scott tried to clear his throat, but his mouth was too dry.

'I'll tell you what,' Ivanovitch said expansively, his good humour manifestly restored, 'have a little time to think it over. Gresson may be able to help you make up your minds.

'Anything you like within reason, Gresson,' he said to the

236

bargemaster, ignoring Scott and Cristal. 'But try not to damage Miss Vengan too severely, there's a good fellow. You know what I want to find out.'

Gresson nodded.

Back in the compressor room, Scott said to Gresson, 'Mason is innocent as far as this affair goes. He only got into it tonight, and he knows nothing. That's the first thing. The second is that if you harm Cristal in any way, I'll kill you.'

Gresson's answer was a sickening, slugging punch to the solar plexus. As Scott bent almost double, retching and heaving, Gresson caught his hair and jerked his head up. Holding him stiffly upright on his toes with one hand, at arm's length, the American puppet-marched him around the room, slapping his face cruelly with the open palm of the other hand, and with the return swing flicking it back in position for the next shattering blow. He did it perhaps forty times, and although at first Scott's arms and feet flailed out to retaliate, and some kicks actually landed, by the end it was only Gresson's grip on his hair that kept Scott upright. The giant hadn't even noticed the blows he'd received himself.

The side of Scott's face was a raw, ugly bruise, and his eyes were streaming tears, as Gresson contemptuously released his hold, and the agent folded to lie at Cristal's feet.

'Present for you,' Gresson said. He kicked Scott heavily in the ribs, then stepped over him and back-heeled him on the other side. Then back once more for a repeat dose . . . and again, and again, and again. Each blow tore a scream from Scott, and a whimpered, agonised plea, 'No more, no more.'

All the time it was happening Cristal kept her eyes on Gresson's face, her expression unaltered. The escape plan was now fully formed, and she realised that if it was to have any chance of success, she dare not interfere – short of preventing Gresson from actually killing Scott.

'I can easily stop,' Gresson said, punctuating the words with kicks. 'All you have to do is start talking.' But she didn't.

It was Mason who chose to act. However great his fear of Gresson, he couldn't stand by and see Scott murdered. While Gresson was in mid-air, stepping backwards over Scott's body, Mason launched himself off the wall and landed a savage kick just under the American's right knee. Gresson twisted around and howled, clasping his kneecap. Then he hopped back and massaged it gingerly.

His long, hard face was set in an almost detached look, his eyes dreamy and faraway, his hand mechanically rubbing his leg. A lock of dark hair fell over his forehead, and he tossed it away with a slow, fluid movement of his head. He tested the foot on the floor, putting his weight on it.

'No damage,' he drawled. 'Bit painful, but no damage.'

'He's going to kill you, Terry,' Cristal said.

'Then help me, for God's sake, help me,' Mason cried. 'Cristal, Ewan, please help me?'

Gresson limped unhurriedly over to him, and when Mason dodged out of his reach, turned patiently, almost resignedly, to face him again.

'You can't get away, little guy,' Gresson whispered, and then chuckled. 'You can't get away.'

Hysteria was mounting in the pilot, and when he was finally cornered in the lift he screamed like a hare falling to a pack of hounds as the giant walked slowly towards him, his hands splayed out, his mouth slightly open, his eyes vacant and unblinking.

'Three buzzes, Terry,' Cristal shouted. 'Three times and they'll close the gate and bring you up. You'll be shot, but it's better than this.'

If Mason even heard her he didn't show it. He was mesmerised, transfixed by the huge man getting closer to him. He shrank into the corner of the lift, unable to take his eyes off Gresson's face, repeating 'No, no, no, no,' in a pathetic falsetto, making himself as small as he could and finally buring his face in his arms and blotting out the sight of the big hands reaching for him.

Gresson made reassuring little noises as he picked up the quivering, then strangely still, bundle. He lifted Mason almost maternally, hoisted him above his head, and brought him back into the compressor room – and they saw his expression change. His eyes narrowed and hardened, his lips flattened in a snarl, his arms bent and he braced his legs and bellowed like a rutting stag, and Cristal knew he was going to smash the pilot against the far wall.

Gresson didn't realise she'd moved at all until he felt the searing, paralyzing pain in his upper arm. His roar changed to a cry of anguish and he dropped Mason to the floor where he rolled over and cannoned into the kneeling Scott. Gresson looked stupidly around him – at Scott, at Mason, and then at Cristal, standing with her hands held out in front of her, crossed and still and ready.

'What did you use?' the bargemaster asked, disbelievingly. He shook himself, muttered something, and walked over to Mason. Scott was cradling his friend's head on his lap. Gresson bent over to grasp Mason, and Scott spat blood out of his mouth and said, 'Don't bother. He's dead.'

'He can't be,' Cristal argued, and even Gresson seemed puzzled.

'Look at him,' Scott said. 'He died of fright.'

Cristal turned her eyes away.

Gresson pulled Mason off and sent him slithering across the floor, the ghastly rictus of terror fixed now on his face until his flesh rotted.

'You'll do,' Gresson said quietly, and yanked Scott to his feet. Scott swung wildly at the American's jaw, but Gresson brushed his fist aside and hooked him viciously in his bruised ribs. Scott yelped and his knees gave way and his legs turned to latex, his mouth contorted in agony, he beat the air futilely with his hands in the jerky, uncoordinated way of a frustrated child, and Cristal stepped in and said, 'Stop it. I'll tell you.'

Scott crawled away using the same swear-words mindlessly over and over again and fell forward on to the floor and beat his hands on the cold metal in shame and disgust.

She said, 'I'm CIA, but strictly unofficial. So's he,' pointing at Scott. 'Mason,' she still couldn't look at him, 'was nothing.

'Ainley told me about the ORBITMAN snatch, and about the rig, and the submarine. If you check with Miernek, you'll realise that I haven't had time to contact Washington, and Scott still doesn't know what I'm talking about, so neither has he told them. Ivanovitch was a surprise. That's the lot.'

Gresson folded his arms. 'Good girlie,' he said. 'I didn't even have to lay a hand on you. I'll go tell The Man. And I'll come back for you if I can, although things could be happening fast around here from now on.'

'I can hardly wait,' she said.

He stepped into the lift, confident of his power, masterful in victory. 'Play with yourself,' he suggested. 'It'll make it easier for what you've got coming.'

The ageing red Mini swept round a bend in the mountain road into a thick belt of clinging mist.

'I didn't realise we'd climbed that high,' Sian Griffith exclaimed.

'It's not mist, then?' asked Dafydd. Sian shook her head and changed down before the next bend, which she knew was less than fifty yards away.

'Low cloud,' she said. 'You don't often come up this far in the Prescellis, obviously.' They spoke in Welsh, because they preferred to.

'No,' said Dafydd. 'The little hills are good enough for me and the sheep.'

Sian laghed. 'You and your sheep,' she said. 'I sometimes feel you think more of them than you do of your friends.'

Dafydd grinned back. 'You know damn well I do.'

'Oh, and your precious dog, of course.'

'Sam?'

'Yes. Give him a big kiss tonight before you left, did you?'

'No,' Dafydd said. 'Actually, he seemed a bit upset. Not like Sam. They do say they know when something's going to happen, don't they? Dogs, I mean.'

'Second sight.'

'Mmm. Premonitions, sort of.'

'You had a premonition tonight, then, Dafydd' she teased.

'No, don't be daft,' he rejoined. 'Sam. I sort of . . . shared it, see?'

She was silent. Then, 'Nothing's going to happen Dai. We're just going to spread a bit of enlightenment, that all.'

'By knocking over a telly transmitter?'

'English telly, Dafydd. Not ours. Different isn't it?'

She bumped over a stone in the road and the little car rattled.

'Careful,' Dafydd cried, turning to peer apprehensively at the back seat of the car, as though his eyes could penetrate the upholstery to the boot, where the big bomb was strapped down.

'Don't fuss now,' she chided. 'It's all right. It's safe enough.'

'Did we need quite so much . . . stuff?' Dafydd asked.

'It's a television transmitter relay mast,' she said, patiently easing the Mini round another hairpin bend, and emerging from the cloud as quickly as they'd passed into it.

'Magic, isn't it?' Dafydd said. 'We're above it now.'

'And we're nearly at the transmitter. Look – see for yourself, Dafydd. It's big and well-protected. You need a lot of jelly to blow a thing like that up.'

Dafydd shielded his eyes from the glare of the sun and looked at the BBC relay mast. The aerial itself he judged to be about a hundred and fifty feet tall. As they drew near to the small track leading down to it, he saw that it stood in a compound surrounded by a high wire fence topped with a frieze of barbed wire. At the side of the track there was an angle-iron and wire mesh gate secured by a padlock and chain. Sian drove straight up to the gate; the relay station was not regularly staffed, and never early on a Friday evening.

She parked the car and turned to him and said, a shade too brightly, 'Ready, then? Let's go, boy.'

He looked shrewdly at her strong, almost beautiful face; at the long, thick chestnut mane wound into a tight bun; the green eyes in their nests of tiny crow's feet; the droplets of sweat beading the golden hairs on her upper lip. Her skin was soft, her cheekbones high and definite, and her mouth full and wet.

'You're frightened, too,' he said.

'No,' she denied. She was probably twice his age, Dafydd thought.

'Not scared. Nervous,' she added.

'Do we have to . . .'

'Yes, Dafydd, we do. You know we do. Action, Dai, action – this kind of thing. It's the only way to get things done – for the people. The language. They take notice of things like this, the English. And their Welsh poodles. More than all the speeches I or anyone else make. Don't you see, Dafydd? This hurts them.'

'Won't we just end up with the same bloody mess they've got in Ireland, then Miss?' Dafydd sometimes forgot to call her Sian, as though he'd never quite separated her from the classroom.

'No, boy,' Sian said, fiercely. 'We're one nation. And we're not blowing up people, are we? We're blowing up overgrown chunks of tin.'

He shrugged and chuckled, and she knew she'd got him again. It was a battle she'd fought many times before, with many people. Except that it was different this time . . . this was one she *had* to win. This one was for Russia – for world domination – for the defeat of the Americans – for the humiliation of Britain.

'Get the cutters then, love,' she whispered. 'And let's be about our work – huh?'

Dafydd snipped off the padlock and heaved the bomb across the grass. At Sian's direction, he set it on the concrete plinth at the base of the aerial. It was a 50 lb device, made with the help of a huge man who suddenly turned up at Sian's cottage with the explosives and detonators. He spoke with an American accent, and Dafydd had never seen him before. He'd also loaded the bomb into the Mini and put, as he said, the final touches to it. It had been neatly built into a small brown fibre suitcase, and no wires were showing.

'What do we do now?' Dafydd inquired.

'What do *I* do, you mean,' Sian said. And she showed him. 'I turn this key,' she pointed to it, 'in the left hand lock, and in precisely an hour from now, this mast will suddenly stop putting out English propaganda and Yankee trash. But by that time we shall be back at the pub having a hard-earned drink. Simple as that?'

'Go on, then,' Dafydd urged, 'do it.'

She reached down, gave him a quick, pretty smile, and turned the key.

Neither of them heard the deep rumble of the explosion or the echoes that raped the peace of the mountains and valleys because they were blown apart before either of their hearts could register another beat. There was a fleeting sensation of being cast into a stupendously solid wall at enormous speed . . . and then, nothing.

'No survivors,' Ivanovitch had told Gresson. 'No witnesses. She knows far too much. I cannot afford to take the chance that she might be caught. Anyway, a death will attract half the police in the county, and that will certainly keep them out of the way.'

When the police from Tredogan arrived, they found the abandoned red Mini – which they were slow to recognise –

243

the broken padlock, a pair of wire-cutters, and the twisted, smoking remains of the mast. There was no sign of a human being there, but the pervasive smell of death told them that the people who'd set the bomb had gone up with it.

TWENTY-THREE

They heard the lift trundling down again, and when it jarred to a halt, three men got out – two of Gresson's heavies and Gresson himself bringing up the rear. They were armed. Purely as a reflex action, Scott, who was slumped on the floor next to Cristal, started inching away along the bare metal to the far corner. But then he stopped. He stilled the quickening thump of his heartbeat and turned to face Gresson, driving the recurring subliminal imprint of the murder of Terry Mason from his brain.

Gresson noticed and jeered, 'I'm still saving you up for later.'

Cristal's iron self-control almost snapped, and her eyes narrowed to buttons of black hatred. She clenched her fists and her muscles tightened to knotted whipcord. She wanted to finish Gresson there and then – if she could. But she held herself back and breathed deeply until the red mist cleared and the killer hands relaxed. 'Your time will come,' she whispered. 'That's a promise.' He was *the* essential factor in her plan – the only one she had of escaping from the pontoon.

The goons had dragged Mason's body out to the lift, and she dimly heard it lurching skyward. At the same moment there came the sound of a dull, heavy impact from another part of the rig – but beneath the water, on their level. The image that came to her was the French poem La Cathédrale Engloutie, because it was like the sound of some ghostly hammer striking the bell of a ruined church long submerged by the sea.

Gresson cocked an ear to the dull clangour. He grinned, and then the lift's call system buzzed, and startled her. 'I'll be back later for you, too, honey,' he said.

'Oh?' she said.

He nodded. 'Yeah.'

'Really?'

'Yeah, really. And then . . .'

The lift on the rig diametrically opposite Cristal's prison reached the surface and the commander of the Red Navy submarine *Slavyanka* and a Marine Commando Major stepped out. They were shaken by the numbing peril of the docking link-up, but even more by the sight of the KGB Special Task Force Chief coming forward to meet them, a broad grin on his face and his arms outstretched as though he were greeting a brace of returned astronauts.

'Captain Zlansky,' Ivanovitch boomed above the machinery noise, 'Major Tchessorian. How good of you to drop in.'

'C-comrade Nikita,' the submariner said. 'I had no idea you'd be here.'

'Did you think, Captain,' Ivanovitch inquired, 'that I would miss the start of the most crucially important espionage operation launched by the Soviet Union since we – er – appropriated the atomic bomb?'

Zlansky looked dumbfounded. The Major smirked, knowingly. 'Yes,' Ivanovitch continued, 'that is precisely what this is. Major – you have your men ready and prepared?' The Major said he had. 'Then bring them up,' Ivanovith ordered. 'All of them. Come –' he gestured to the two men – ' come with me. We shall drink vodka – all of us. And Gresson, too. You haven't met Gresson, have you?' They shook their heads. 'You will, I promise you.

'While your men are coming up, Major, I'll tell the Captain all about our little escapade.'

'And then?' Cristal inquired, her genuine amusement barely masking her contempt.

'And then,' Gresson replied, 'I'll show you what a real man's like. You'll find it's a bit different from powder-puff there. And I guarantee you'll like it, you frigid bitch.'

He walked towards her as he spoke, and each word was a concentrated threat. She said, coolly, 'If you're man enough to show me whatever it is you've got, which I doubt, you won't keep it long, I'm telling you.'

Gresson towered over Cristal, cradled her chin in his hand, and rammed her head back against the wall. It didn't connect as he'd hoped, because she stiffened her body at the moment of impact, but it still hurt. Then with a downward slash he ripped the checked shirt apart, and caught both her breasts in a brutally strong grip, his thumbs digging into the inside slopes. He pushed, hard, and each breast flattened as if she were under the weight of a man.

She flinched at the pain. She couldn't struggle while he held her breasts, and she didn't want to disable him . . . not yet.

He forced her back against the wall, his arms straight out in front of him, maddened almost beyond control by her indifference and by the tight buds of her nipples pushing into the clefts near the base of the heels of his hands.

She waited for him to make a mistake. His gaze bored into her, and his lust mounted. He drew her to him by the breasts, then reched up to grab her shoulders and pull her in to take her, and her right knee drove sickeningly into his genitals. He gave an almost comical howl and doubled over clutching himself. A full two minutes passed until he looked up at her, his eyes watering furiously, and burning with pain and hatred.

'Now,' he ground out, 'I'm going to kill you, and you won't even feel what I do to you afterwards.' The buzzer on the lift sounded a second time its long, imperious rasp.

'It appears,' Cristal said sweetly, 'that they want you upstairs.' With massive unconcern she pulled the ruined shirt out of her jeans and tied it in a knot above her navel so that the material framed and supported her naked breasts,

247

thrusting them out insolently at him. 'Don't you think this style suits me?' she asked, blinking her eyes with feigned innocence. The buzzer sounded yet again, impatiently this time. Gresson dragged himself to his feet, wincing, and stood with his knees slightly bowed, so that he was almost on a level with her. He looked over his shoulder at the lift, as if willing the buzzer to stop.

'OK,' he said. 'There's plenty of time for you. Because after tonight we're not going to need either of you. So you're mine – both of you. You're first, sweetie. And he can watch, while he's still got his eyes.'

He limped over to the lift, entered it, and turned again to face them. 'I hope you can still do it then,' Cristal flashed at him. He jammed his thumb angrily on the button. The lift started to move slowly and loudly away, and Cristal tensed her body like a coiled spring. Gresson had told her what she wanted to know. Now . . . if he was mad enough, and the lift noisy enough . . . it started to disappear into the covered part of the shaft, and she leapt across the room, her feet smacking solidly on the metal floor as she launched herself into the air.

For a second the outstretched, groping hands met nothing, but then the fingers of her right hand fastened on what she knew must be there – the oily loop of a cable dangling from the base of the lift cabin. The fingers closed, and held, and she was drawn up into the air.

Cristal jerked like an animated pendulum until she managed to clamp her left hand on the cable as well, and clung there not knowing what to do next. She'd made up her mind that they'd have to get away before nightfall, and Gresson had confirmed what she'd already half-guessed . . . that the attack on the rocket base was to be launched within a matter of hours. He was to be the instrument of her escape. There was no point in going up in the lift to be met at the top by armed Russians, so the ascent had to be made when they weren't expecting trouble – and that could only be immediately after Gresson himself had stepped out of the lift at the other end.

The first part of the operation – including needling Gresson and sending him up in a bad temper – had gone well . . . but now what? Peering down the sheer steel walls of the shaft as the lift made its complaining way aloft, she calculated the drop would be more than a hundred and thirty feet by the time the cage reached the top. She shivered, and looked back up again. Was there room, she wondered, to squeeze up on to the roof of the cage, even if she could find the hand-holds to get that far?

She started swinging her legs and gyrating to try to get a better view of the side of the cage, but a bone-shaking jolt put an abrupt end to her acrobatics as the lift shuddered to a halt. One hand actually bounced off the cable as her body fought to counter the inertia. Then, heaving and gasping, she secured her double hold, and the panic swiftly died. She was annoyed with herself; she should have been prepared for the lift to stop, and she wasn't, and it was a nearly fatal error.

The top entrance to the lift was fitted with a safety gate to prevent anyone blundering into the mouth of the shaft when the lift wasn't there. Cristal heard the bargemaster slide it roughly back, crashing it on to its cushions of retaining springs and swearing as it bounced quarter of the way across again. He, at any rate, was still not in the best of humours. One of the guards waiting for him inquired if there was anything wrong, and Gresson told him to fuck off.

Cristal tut-tutted, giggled, and whispered, 'Who's a naughty boy then?' Her arms ached badly, but not intolerably. Not yet. To her immense relief, Gresson and, she guessed, both guards, walked away (the guards to join the submarine crew, although she had no way of knowing that). Why, after all, should the guards stay? The lift could not be operated from the compressor room.

When the sound of their footsteps died away she took stock of her situation. The cable which held her was one of a set that joined the lift at the front, disappeared down the shaft in a series of loops, and on the return journey bypassed the back of the lift to an eventual connection in the motor-room at the head of the shaft. She'd spent the couple of minutes the lift had taken to rise to the surface, climbing a few yards up the cable to get a more comfortable hold.

She now realised that she was trapped. Because she was on the cable leading to the front of the lift, rather than the one running up the back, there was no way she could get out of the shaft. There might be from the back . . . there certainly wasn't from the front.

She looked down – the bottom of the loop seemed impossibly far away, and even if she got there she'd have to climb up again the other side; she doubted if she'd have the strength. She glanced across at the return cables . . . the gap must have been all of seven feet. It might just as well have been seven hundred, because it was clearly beyond her reach.

She said 'Shit!' with immense feeling, and twisted her head round to see if there was any foothold on her side of the shaft that would ease the strain on her arms. It was as smooth as glass. Up? No. The cables disappeared into the floor, and there was hardly room for a drop of oil to squeeze between the lift and the safety door.

Even her excruciating pain was submerged in the tide of crazed, formless terror that swept over her. She was going to die. She, who had sometimes dispassionately brought death to other, now faced it herself. All the poise and detachment, the ice-cold confidence, disappeared, and she became a sobbing, choking halfwit. In her fury she pulled the filthy cable between her breasts and it smeared her body and face and hair with oil and grease, but she didn't seem to notice. Only the sheer, overriding will to live made her clamp her feet tightly together and keep the cable firmly lodged between her ankles, calves and knees.

Every nerve in her being was starting to tingle, and her pulses beat like drums. The roar of a helicopter taking off from the rig barely impinged on her consciousness. Then, despite the fierce and unyielding pressure from her knotted muscles, her whole body started slowly, slowly, to slide down the cable.

She gave a shrill, weary scream, and frustration and anger took over from panic. She wrenched and pulled at the cable as if she were fighting a gigantic black serpent, and thrashed out with her legs, not caring if she fell, because she was going to fall anyway . . . and her body began to swing towards the return cables.

Suddenly she woke up to what she was doing. She sniffed, blinked through the tears, stretched her legs out at the back until they touched the shaft, and kicked herself off the wall like a child on a swing. She brought her legs round again and kicked out to the front. Three times she did it, and three times she gained more in speed and momentum, though slipping fractionally down the cable with each mighty effort. Then her feet touched the opposite wall, and she wrapped then around the main cable and drew it towards her until both sets of cable were in her embrace, and she could haul herself over from one to the other.

The hysteria vanished and the adrenalin surged back and her power with it, and she practically swarmed up the cable before she stopped and told herself to calm down and conserve her energy. She relaxed, panting and bathed in sweat that traced meandering paths down her oily breasts as she allowed her body to form a bow, with the cable as its string.

Then she threw back her head, took several deep breaths, and saw, a few feet above her head, a metal arm. It projected from the corner of the lift to one of the guide rails at the rear, and Cristal cried again, only this time gladly, as she hauled herself up and curled her bare toes around it. She gratefully stepped off the cable to stand behind the lift, in a gap which was only just big enough for her, and pressed her burning face and hands against the cold metal.

She waited a few moments for her heart to stop thumping and her temple pulses to subside, and looked warily around.

Two pieces of angle iron were welded across the back of the lift, and her eyes glinted as though the bars of rusty metal were studded with diamonds.

She got a firm toehold on the lower bar, pressed her back against the shaft and snaked her way upwards until she could put both feet on it, and then followed the same drill again. Her hands found the top of the lift, she tensed her iron-hard stomach muscles, heaved up, dropped back, heaved again, and scrambled clumsily on to the first stretch of level ground she'd touched since leaving the compressor room.

Her 'home' on top of the little lift was four feet wide and gave a clearance of five feet to the winding gear. The walls were formed of wire mesh panels, at least one of which, she assumed, could be removed to give access for maintenance of the lift mechanism. Feeling rather than looking, because only a little light penetrated through the mesh from the few meagre bulbs strung around the generating room, she found what she wanted.

The panel measured perhaps three feet by two, and it was secured only by press fasteners. Cristal threaded her fingers through the mesh and gave a sharp push. All four press studs popped out at once. She almost dropped the panel and propelled herself into the generating room, but she braced her elbows against the neighbouring oblongs of mesh, turned the panel round and worked it back through into the inspection chamber. Then she went head first, face up, through the hole, gripped the mesh from the outside, pulled the rest of her long body clear, and dropped lightly to the floor.

TWENTY-FOUR

Ivanovitch handed each of the fifteen grinning Marine commandos and their officer a stiff measure of vodka, took one himself, and gave the last to Gresson when the bargemaster strode in.

'I've just been telling the Major here,' the KGB chief said, 'how important this mission is. Gresson,' he said to the commander, 'is responsible for the idea. Without him, none of this would have happened. The Trojan Horse would have stayed in the pages of the history books, or should I say "The Moscow Horse" perhaps?'

The marine politely lifted his glass in the American's direction. 'To your ingenuity, Comrade,' he said.

'To your courage,' Gresson replied. 'And the comrade Colonel's vision.'

Ivanovitch boomed a harsh belly laugh. 'I believe that's probably the nicest thing you've ever said about anyone, Gresson. You should be honoured, Major,' he turned to the Marine. 'Our big friend is usually neither so eloquent nor so complimentary. He must be in a rare good humour. Our "guests" had better watch out.'

'Shouldn't I be happy?' Gresson inquired, in English. 'With something as big as this about to begin?'

The Russian replied, also in English, 'Now there you're wrong.'

Gresson looked puzzled, and Ivanovitch said, slyly, 'It's already started.'

The explosion at the television transmitter had been merely the overture. The first act proper was commencing just off the northern tip of Scotland. The brilliantly conceived programme of diversions had started.

The pilot of a Russian Tupolev Tu-16 jet on patrol over

the North Sea made a course alteration that would take his aircraft just into British air space. He smiled as he imagined the reaction on the ground, and for a moment almost envied the British fighter pilots who would soon be shooting through the twilight sky at maximum throttle to warn him off. In the twenty minutes it took to reach his 'target area' he wondered why he was doing it – and who had ordered it. Then he shrugged. The complicated chess moves of Great Power politics were not his to fathom. They were for politicians, not for airmen.

Flight Lieutenants Tim Bell and Ian Brown were streaking down the runway at RAF Leuchars within minutes of the first report of a radar sighting. The flight controller who'd noticed the foreign blob rolled his eyes, heaved a sigh of resignation, and scrambled the Phantoms, as he'd done on countless days before. The ground reverberated with the thunderous crackle of two pairs of Rolls Royce Spey engines delivering maximum thrust, and a minute after leaving the ground the Phantoms levelled out at twenty-five thousand feet.

Radar guided them until they were in visual range of their quarry. Tim Bell grinned as he recognised the familiar shape of the Tupolev.

'Our old pal Badger,' he said over the intercom, for the benefit of Brown as well as Leuchars base, in case his friend hadn't got a perfect sighting. 'Badger' was the NATO codename for the Tupolev. The Phantoms took up station off the port wing of the Soviet plane, and just ahead of it. The pilots exchanged smiles and cheery waves, and the Russian's face registered baffled innocence as his navigational error was gently pointed out to him. He grinned again as the mighty aircraft veered slowly away to the north, trailed by the Phantoms to escort it officially off the premises.

At the Ministry of Defence Incident Room in London, the contact aroused only routine interest. Neither did the next surprise packet on Ivanovitch's shopping list of diversionary tactics cause more than a quiver of curiosity. It was a request from Search and Rescue Headquarters at RAF Mountbatten to dispatch a Nimrod to investigate an SOS from a Polish trawler nearly two hundred miles west off Land's End. The Nimrod pilot was setting out on his routine 'oil-rig slalom' up the Celtic Sea when the order to go finally reached him. The relief from boredom was ample compensation for the one hundred and eighty degree course change, so he needed no second bidding to soar into a steep turn and head off in the direction of possible excitement.

Ivanovitch, the choreographer of this precisely scheduled aerial ballet, glanced again at the watch on his thick, hairy wrist, and nodded to the Marine office. 'The moment,' he said, 'has come. You have your orders, and I know you will carry them out. All of them,' he added, meaningfully, and the man nodded. 'Goodbye, and may good fortune go with you.'

The Major saluted crisply, and rapped a command to his senior NCO. The heavily armed assault troops lined up on the deck. They climbed aboard the Sikorski, which stood on the helipad with its blades already turning. The special frame needed to carry an underslung load reminded Ivanovitch (who was thinking ahead) of a marsupial pouch. The great rotors threshed the air, and Gresson and the KGB chief stood side by side in the rushing wind and watched the helicopter climb away, its paintwork gleaming in the fading rays of the sun.

Ivanovitch turned to the American and, in a surprising gesture of intimacy, held out his hand. Gresson smiled almost shyly, took it, and briefly pressed it. The Russian said, 'I'll be in the radio room maintaining contact with the assault group if you need me – or if there's any trouble.'

'Nix,' Gresson replied. 'Not possible. How could there be trouble?'

Ivanovitch looked up at him – something he hardly ever

had to do to any man. 'I hope so,' he murmured. 'But be very careful. Cristal Vengan is a more formidable opponent, I think, than you take her to be. And Gresson, nothing, I repeat, nothing, must go wrong. For your sake as well as mine. I have plans for you when this is over. Big plans.'

Gresson nodded, patted the big revolver in his belt, and watched him walk away. Then his eyes hardened and his teeth bared and wheeled around and crossed the deck to the lift shaft – and Cristal.

Forty miles out from the rig, the Sikorski flew for its target in a wide semi-circle so that it could approach Tredogan from the sea rather than from the broken shoreline, where its cliff-hugging run could arouse suspicion. The pilot first of all maintained an altitude of a thousand feet, but when he spotted the distant shape of the land, with the unmistakable brightness of the rocket launch pad floodlights sparkling like jewels, he started a gentle descent to come in under the radar net. Soon the tense and silent commandos could watch the dark waters of the Celtic Sea slipping past barely twenty feet below them. By the time they reached Tredogan Bay the sun had gone and the helicopter cabin was in darkness.

On shore, Paul Miernek had been active, too. Francewski was sent to plant a small bomb behind a storage shed on the far perimeter of RAF Tredogan. It had been set to go off at 8.25, a couple of minutes before the raiding helicopter was due to land. Miernek knew there wouldn't be many ground staff on duty, which was why they'd fixed the original assault for a Saturday night. Bringing the operation forward by a day still meant the station was on weekend rosters.

The older and more reliable Pole, Stanislaw Kondrat, had taken the younger of the remaining two – the would-be ravisher of Cristal – with him to stage a later explosion at the base of a gigantic radar scanner, sited on the extreme inland

256

edge of the Royal Aeronautical Establishment next door. Then they were to break into a nearby underground inspection chamber and hack through the thick loom of telephone cables joining there.

Miernek himself set off fractionally after his men, travelling in a Land Rover painted in the identical dark blue and yellow livery used to distinguish vehicles bought by the Procurement Executive of the Defence Ministry. The road into the RAE was set between wire fences for a hundred and fifty yards, and Miernek halted before the single red and white striped arm of a traffic barrier, operated from a half-glazed police hut standing alongside.

The Pole had mounted a close surveillance of the Establishment, and he'd noted that while private cars were thoroughly checked entering and leaving, the vehicles in the privileged MOD colours were invariably waved through. It helped to keep the traffic moving, because the RAE was divided by a public road constantly in use from both sides.

Miernek's eyes dropped to the loaded gun on the shelf nearest his right hand. The duty policeman glanced up from the three-week-old issue of *Cambrian News* that camouflaged the current *Men Only* and, luckily for him, operated the mechanism raising the barrier. Luckily because, had he not done it, Miernck would certainly have killed him.

The Pole accelerated and passed under the colourful arm. He'd calculated that on a fine weekend in August there'd be no more than perhaps a dozen MOD police on duty – relying, as they always seemed to, on the detachment of the RAF Regiment based at the airfield, a mile or so away. Miernek looked at his watch. In a short time the RAF boys would have other things on their minds.

He pulled in behind the concrete building housing the electricity sub-station and stand-by generators – his first target. The window spaces were sheeted in green wooden louvred panels, and he crossed to the stout, matching door which bore a chipped white enamelled sign reading 'Danger' over a red zig-zag line; and below, 'Keep out – 11,000 VOLTS'.

He checked that he was alone, and levered off the padlock securing the door with a crow-bar from the land Rover. The door opened on a flight of six stairs. He closed it behind him, laid the crow-bar and padlock on the top step, and saw in the light of his torch the mains supply switches and the big diesel generators.

Miernek traced the grid supply cable to the point where it left the building, and rubbed his jaw thoughtfully. A break there ought to cause a complete power failure. He shone the torch on his watch. 20.21. He opened the black toolbag he was carrying, and prepared a small explosive charge. He wedged it into the outlet channel, primed it, and set the timer for five minutes. He hurried out of the sub-station, replacing the padlock on its hasp. As he did so, the last vestiges of sunlight disappeared. The helicopter, he knew, would be within striking distance of the base.

The Pole headed next for the concrete apron in front of the hangar where the rockets were prepared for dispatching to the launch platform. The hangar stood on top of the cliff, facing seawards, and twin steel tracks led from it to the railway which had been adapted to transfer the primed rockets a hundred and twenty feet down the gradient of the cliff to the launch platform, at sea level.

The platform and the cliff top were brightly lit, and Miernek drove slowly to time his arrival with the explosion which would cut the electric power. He'd switched off the vehicle's lights and selected the less noisy third gear. suddenly he pulled up with a jerk.

He swore in Polish, dropped to first gear, and stamped viciously on the accelerator, sending the Land Rover surging towards the pool of light. The thought that had struck him had come only just in time. If the power died, it would be impossible to raise the heavy door of the hangar to wheel out the rocket they wanted to steal.

Miernek hit the apron at speed, wrenched the wheel over and braked fiercely in the same movement. The manoeuvre spun the Land Rover through a semi-circle and brought it shuddering to a halt outside the lighted window of the guard post set into the wall of the hangar.

This guard wasn't going to be a pushover like the last one, Miernek thought. He leapt out of the driving seat and ran towards the door of the post as if he had an urgent message to deliver. The guard had already risen from his seat and was peering intently through the window. When he saw the official colours, his face lost some of the fleeting panic he'd felt at first, and he pulled back to open the door.

As the first chink of light appeared in the frame, Miernek launched himself against the door and knocked it almost from its hinges. The guard was catapulted off his feet and smashed against the far wall where he lay in a dazed stupor. Miernek's jump carried him over to the barely conscious man, and as he landed he drove his knee into the guard's stomach. The policeman doubled up, and Miernek brought both fists down on the back of his neck.

Without pausing to see if the guard was alive or dead, the Pole charged through the connecting door into the hangar, and jammed his thumb on the wall-mounted control button for the roller-slatted shutter.

The whirring motor set his teeth on edge, and he cursed the door frantically as it started to leave the ground with maddening slowness.

'More, more. Faster, faster,' he yelled, as though his frustration would increase the ascent by so much as a millimetre.

Then there was silence, and pitch blackness descended on everything. His bomb had gone off. But the impression left on the retina of his eye was of the door raised up at least halfway to the ceiling. It would be enough. The operation was saved.

An hour and a half had passed since Sian Griffith and Dafydd had blown themselves and the television transmitter to pieces. Up on the Prescellis the Tredogan and Fishguard police – who'd taken the better part of sixty minutes to locate the cause and site of the blackout and get to it – were joined by BBC engineers ruefully contemplating the destruction.

'Bastards,' muttered a grizzled, near-pensionable engineer grimly.

'Now, Bryn,' said another. 'We're all Welsh, you know.'

'That's what I said,' the older man replied. 'Poor bastards.'

'Can you get it going again?' a young policeman asked, indicating the shrunken, buckled transmitter, and got a glance of withering contempt for his pains.

Just as the Phantoms were touching down again at Leuchars, the Ministry of Defence Incident Room radar showed the Russian aircraft once more turning towards the coast of Scotland.

The monitors' eyes were glued in disbelief to the screens. 'I think,' the chief monitor said slowly,' that Ivan is playing silly buggers with us. Either that, or they're letting certifiable loonies take out their Badgers these days.'

'What do we do?' his deputy asked.

'I don't know. I just don't know. How's that other business down off Corwall going?'

'It's not,' someone else said. 'Our chap couldn't find the Polish trawler. He's asked us to check the position and we're still trying to raise her.'

'Something,' the chief monitor, who was a deliberate man in all he did, said deliberately, 'is going on.'

Miernek wiped the sweat from his face, and dashed back out to the Land Rover for the next phase of his back-up role. He started the engine. and engaged the little mobile generator with which it had been laboriously fitted on Ivanovitch's orders. Then he leaned over the seat and flipped a switch.

The vehicle was pointing away from the hangar, so he slipped out of the driver's seat and walked round to the back. When he pulled up and secured the canvas drape, the powerful searchlight mounted inside the Land Rover illuminated the entire apron and the cliff tip beyond, where the gleaming tracks disappeared.

The muffled roar of an explosion in the distance broke the eerie silence, and he knew the radar scanner had gone up on schedule at 20.28. The sound had scarcely died away when a manic chattering provided a ground base to an eldritch whining that swelled up from the sea and froze Miernek's blood. It grew intolerably loud and the Pole clapped his hands over his ears and involuntarily closed his eyes – and opened them again just as the great, silvery ghost of the Sikorsky crawled up the sloping rock face and danced into the rays of the searchlight.

The pilot hovered for a second or two, then set the helicopter down, perhaps a shade too firmly. The Russian marines jumped to the ground. Five of them, with their officer and the Sikorski's co-pilot, made straight for the hangar. The remaining ten spread out in a half-circle, defending the approaches to the apron. Without a word of command, they dropped to one knee and levelled their machine-guns at the grey half-shapes of the RAE buildings and the air base beyond.

The hangar party streamed under the half-raised roller shutter – and there, dead in front of them, was a long, sleek, shining ORBITMAN rocket, mounted on a trolley. It was already fitted with a lifting harness for its transfer by crane from the launch pad railhead.

The Major released the brake. Then he sauntered over to the co-pilot, cradled his Kalashnikov in his arms, and whistled a chirpy little Ukrainian folk song as the five commandos surrounded the missile and pushed it carefully out along the rails to the waiting helicopter.

Miernek was almost right about the number of MOD policemen on duty in the Establishment that night; there were fourteen, not twelve. Six were assigned to the permanent posts guarding the most important and sensitive areas, and one man rotated as a relief picket throughout the night. In case of trouble, their orders were to stay at their posts until the emergency was over. Of the remaining seven, four were dog handlers patrolling the four miles of perimeter fence, two went out on mobile patrol in a Land Rover, and the last one manned their general office, spending most of his time on the telephone.

By tradition, inclination and – finally – decree, not one of them carried a gun. Ever. Even though the buildings they guarded housed growing numbers of a weapon which could revolutionize nuclear warfare.

When the electric power went, each guard at a post followed the established drill and locked himself in. The Land Rover with its crew of two, and the relief man, who happened to be with them at the time, headed for the power station. So did two of the dog handlers. And of course their dogs. The man in the main office tried the phone, but somehow knew it would be dead. His hand moved to the direct alarm circuit, but before he touched the switch he knew that would be dead, too. He'd half risen when the radar scanner blew, and he fell back into his chair and topped heavily to the floor. It was, he thought, quite the best place to be.

The Land Rover party searched frantically for the site of Miernek's explosion, found it, and simultaneously hit the ground like scattered ninepins when the second, much larger, bomb toppled the big scanner less than half a mile away. Then all five of them (plus two dogs) crowded into the Land Rover and sped to the scene. Another dog handler beat them to it on foot, and so six men (and three dogs) stood helplessly in front of the crumpled metal lit by the glare of the Land Rover's headlamps.

It was one of the dogs which spotted and barked at the glow of light behind the cliff-top hangar more than a mile from where they were, and this time all the men and all the animals crammed into the Land Rover and bumped off down one of the network of small roads crisscrossing the station.

The roads didn't provide direct access to the rocket area, so by the time they were approaching the hangar, it was just before twenty to nine. A hail of bullets from the waiting commandos peppered the vehicle, lodging in the soft alloy of the body panels and smashing one of their headlights.

The Land Rover jerked to a halt and lurched into reverse, backing round into the shelter of the next hangar. Friday was the Inspector's night off, so the mantle of glory fell on the sagging shoulders of Sergeant Elwyn Prosser-Lewis.

'Well, boys,' he said, which seemed as good a way to begin as any. 'I don't know what the 'ell's going on, but we seem to be on our own, and the base is under attack. It doesn't look like old Dai in the office 'as been able to raise the RAF Regiment, even if he's thought of doing it yet, so we'd better do it for him. Handel Morgan?'

'Sergeant?' the youngest and quickest of his constables answered.

'Take the Land Rover, or what's left of it, and fetch the RAF, and for Christ's sake tell them to bring their guns. We'll stay 'ere and keep watch lads, at a safe distance, like.' The lads nodded eager assent.

'I'm not tangling with fire power like that little lot, and I should advise you not to, neither.'

'No, Sergeant,' they chanted, like the policemen in *The Pirates of Penzance*.

'Right, then,' Sergeant Prosser-Lewis decided, 'hit the deck, like they say in the pictures, and let's hope it's not some bloody stupid exercise, or we're all going to look a

263

bunch of right idiots.'

The NIMROD pilot was buzzing an intact but smoke-hazed Polish trawler at a position far removed from the one originally passed to him, and was happily engaged in an entirely unintelligible conversation with a radio operator from Lodz, which he'd just learned was pronounced quite differently from the way it was spelled. He was not to know that the spurious SOS had come from a Soviet submarine which had surfaced briefly to transmit, then dived and made off.

Flight Lieutenants Bell and Brown's previous good-humoured tolerance of the Tupolev pilot's map-reading was wearing a little thin as they headed north again to ease him back into no-man's-air.

When their covering troops opened fire on the defenceless Police Land Rover, the men trundling the rocket thought they were under attack, too, and dived for shelter behind the missile itself, ending in an untidy heap. A minute passed, and the danger with it.

'Get on with it,' the Major shrieked at them, and they jumped up and pushed and hauled the 2000-lb missile the last thirty or so yards to where the helicopter was standing.

The Sikorski captain lifted his machine off the ground, and his co-pilot lay on his stomach on the floor of the fuselage, with his head hanging out of the open cargo door, shouting instructions back to his skipper. It took five minutes for the helicopter to hover and trawl into position over the rocket, but finally the co-pilot waved to the Marines Major that he was satisfied, and the fifteen commandos stood breathlessly and rigidly at a distance while the tortuous business of winching the ORBITMAN up into the waiting brackets of the sling frame was accomplished.

The Sikorski remained at the hover while the missile was

attached, so a rope ladder was lowered to take the task force back on board through the cargo door, since there was no possibility of the helicopter landing again with the rocket hanging beneath it. After a progressive withdrawal, the commandos slung their weapons and shinned up the ladder, and finally only the Major was left on the apron. He waved to Paul Miernek, who'd stayed out of sight in the hangar during the first part of the loading operation, and had slipped over to his Land Rover when the helicopter left the ground to take on the rocket.

Miernek ran up to the Major and said to him, 'I think I spotted Kondrat and Francewski and the youngster over the other side of the hangar. They should have linked up by now, anyway, and I told them to break cover once the last marine was on board.'

'Is there anyone left at the hotel?' the Major asked.

'Yes,' Miernek said. 'One man. He's to get away if he doesn't hear from me by ten o'clock, and pick up the *Batory* at Immingham Docks tomorrow. It's get him back to Poland eventually.'

'How much does he know – about all this?'

'More or less nothing,' Miernek replied.

'And about Colonel Ivanovitch?'

'Nothing at all. Not even Francewski and the others know he's personally involved. Stefan – that's the one that's left – isn't even sure what it is we're stealing. We brought him along to serve behind the bar.'

'Right,' the Major said, briskly. 'Get your other three here, then. We want to get away.'

Miernek waved in the direction of his men, and first Kondrat, then the other two, started weaving runs across the apron. The Major climbed the rope ladder and heaved himself up into the Sikorski.

To the watching police, to the co-pilot still hanging out of the cargo-door, and especially to the Major of Marines, the apron, bathed in brilliant white light funnelling out from the incandescent circle perched on the Land Rover, looked like the ampitheatre of some vast, expectant stage, where the last act of a drama was about to be played. The puppet figure that was Paul Miernek, who had served his masters well and was now returning – perhaps for ever – to their homeland, mounted the rope ladder.

The Major of Marines said to the cold-eyed, impassive commando sergeant crouched beside him in the cargo door, 'Now, please.'

The sergeant sighted his machine-gun, and his first bullets cut Miernek almost in two. His body jerked and split and toppled from the ladder as though all its strings were being pulled at one time. The other three stood in stunned horror and amazement, and the sergeant took them in one practically continuous burst. He fired until the magazine was empty, and the three Poles were plucked off the ground and tossed backwards in graceless swan-dives, their blood spouting from a dozen holes, until finally they stopped twitching, and the Russian stopped shooting. The marine Major's mouth was dry with horror as the commando drew a hand-gun and cut the searchlight with a single shot, and the stage was in darkness and the tragedy was over.

The co-pilot, who didn't know what was going on, started to ask a question, but the Major cut him short.

'Orders,' he said. 'The Comrade Colonel's covering his tracks. And anyway, apart from you and from the skipper, the maximum number of men the helicopter can carry with this damned great thing – ' he gestured at the rocket ' – stuck up its ass, is sixteen. So . . .'

'Wasn't there any other way?' the co-pilot asked.

'Don't worry,' the Major of Marines said. 'They were only Poles.'

The Red Air Force officer's face relaxed into a grin of understanding and relief.

Police Constable Handel Morgan, his clear blue eyes radiating excitement, drove like a lunatic to the RAF Regiment lines, but then wasted four minutes finding the duty detachment, who were still on the far side of the airfield inspecting the damage to the stores buildings caused by Francewski's bomb. Morgan gasped out his story, and the flying officer in charge – a lad of about his own age – listened with mounting incredulity.

'Fifteen or twenty of them?' he said. 'Pushing a rocket? You're sure, are you?' PC Morgan said yes, he was sure.

'Not an exercise, is it – or some sort of elaborate joke? Funny lot of chaps they've got at the RAF.'

No, Handel said with as much patience as he could muster, the bullets were undubitably real. The young officer picked twenty armed men to give himself a shade of the odds, and they piled into a five-ton truck, with the officer and an NCO in Morgan's shot-up Land Rover.

The driver of the five-tonner didn't wait for the reluctant MOD guard to open the barrier. He splintered it with the front of his truck, leaving the policeman wringing his hands in despair, like a mother watching her only son go off down the mines. It wasn't, all in all, a good night for the MOD police.

Handel Morgan overtook the truck as they came within reach of the light bowl holding the apron. He parked next to the group of men headed by Sergeant Elwyn Prosser-Lewis who were keeping a careful, if discreet, eye on the proceedings.

'No, I still don't know what's going on,' Prosser-Lewis growled, even before Handel Morgan had asked him. 'And don't *you* ask me, neither,' he snapped to the flying officer.

'Don't worry, Sergeant,' the lad replied. 'We'll find out.'

He grouped his men in the cover of the five-tonner, and they looked with something like awe at the blazing basin of the apron, the helicopter suspended above the ground, and the tiny figures clambering up the swaying rope ladder.

'They're pulling out, sir,' his Flight-Sergeant said.

'In that case, we'll stop them. Take six men, Sergeant,

and head for the cliff top outside the range of that damned light. We'll use the hangar as cover and divert their attention. Get as close in as you can and shoot down that helicopter.'

'Right, sir,' the Sergeant said, and gathered a section around him. They were about to set off when another raucous burst of fire came from the Sikorski. All twenty RAF men dived for the ground and watched the slaughter, taking place, it seemed, on far-off, pint-sized television screen. Then a further, lone, shot rang out, and the brightness disappeared.

The young officer bellowed, his voice breaking with effort, 'Switch on the truck lights and get that fucking chopper!'

But as the driver flicked the headlamps on to full beam, the Sikorski's whine rose to a crescendo and then to a coda, and the big, beautiful machine slipped back over the edge of the cliff and out into the darkness of the sea.

The chief monitor in the Ministry of Defence Incident Room scratched his thinning thatch and drummed his fingers on the table.

'Don't understand it,' he said, to no one in particular. 'Is he coming in, or isn't he?'

All eyes were still on the screens, and they watched in bewilderment as the blob representing the trespassing Badger turned and headed back in the direction of Mother Russia. The other two blobs – the old firm of Bell and Brown – weren't even within range when the Soviet pilot unaccountably got homesick.

The helicopter co-pilot was feeling better now. The Sikorski had been airborne for some minutes on a dead straight course for the rig and the submarine. He adjusted his harness, and glanced up through the perspex canopy to admire the spectacular night sky.

His face took on an expression of mingled doubt and terror as he saw what was descending on them from the sapphire-studded velvet blackness.

TWENTY-FIVE

Cristal walked to the lift safety door, put her hand through the bars, and pressed the 'Descend' button, wondering if that was one of the words which even the stupidest of the Russians had been compelled to learn. She hissed 'Ewan' down the shaft, and then giggled, because obviously he couldn't hear her; the lift was making enough noise to awaken the dead. Anyway, he'd be bound to hear *that*, and when he saw it was empty he'd naturally come up in it.

She sensed, rather than saw, someone behind her, at the open door of the generating room. The machinery hummed powerfully and regularly around her. Without looking she knew it was Gresson.

'I don't know how you did it, sweetheart,' he said, 'but however it was, it's no good, because you're going straight back down.'

She turned and said, loudly and distinctly, 'Screw you, Gresson. As they say in the type of movie that no doubt formed your sole education – come and get me. If you dare.'

It worked, because he holstered the Magnum 44, which could have blown the lift apart, let alone her, and came in at a slight crouch, his huge hands curved, elbows parallel to the ground, muscles ballooning on his upper arms. The lift hadn't reached the bottom yet, so it would be ages before Scott could get to the surface.

'Christ,' she thought. 'He is big.'

She took up a stance before the lift gate and held herself ready, but he didn't rush in as she'd hoped. She knew he was a merciless and mindless killer, and she'd calculated that he held sway over his men because of his enormous size and strength, so he'd probably never had to develop beyond the status of superior rough-house brawler since no one

270

would have dared to challenge him. In that case, he would be no match for her. She was an exhaustively trained and superbly accomplished assassin, and she could kill equally well with either bare hand.

On the other hand, if she'd made a mistake and Gresson, too, was well-trained, it would be an error which she might never have the chance to live to regret.

She stalked him. His eyes were clear and level, and his gaze frankly amused. He was on his home ground, once again profoundly sure of his great bulk and the relentless power in his hands and arms. She stood still. He darted out first one hand, then the other; but she didn't move. Her breathing was even and controlled, her mouth slightly open, and she rocked almost imperceptibly on her heels and the balls of her feet. The terrible ridges of hardened muscle at the sides of her hands and the stabbing spears of her fingers which could rip out a man's intestines should have warned Gresson what he was facing, but he was looking her straight in the eyes and seeing nothing else.

They circled, and suddenly he leapt forward and slipped open the lift cage door. Now Scott couldn't come up to help her. She was alone. They stalked each other again and a spasm of fear contorted her face. Gresson saw it and his lips smiled but his eyes were hard and glazed with killing lust.

Cristal heard the lift clunk down in the compressor room, and the noise seemed to break Gresson's almost hypnotic paralysis. His gaze widened and she knew he was going to jump. He moved as fast as a charging panther, his teeth gritted and his lips pressed into a snarl. As his leading foot left the ground, she dropped to the floor like a padded stone, snapped out her right leg, dug the extended toes deep into his belly, flexed her knee, and then stiffened the leg and cantilevered him over her head into the open shaft.

His flailing arms and legs rapped the sides of the shaft and he gave a series of small, choked cries, piteous little sounds, as his great body plummeted down to crash on to the lift. The fall pulped his head and snapped his individual vertebrae as if they'd been part of a sardine's spine. She closed the steel gate and the lift started to ascend. He was still on the cabin, like a monstrous, squashed beetle, when it surfaced. Scott got out, bloody and shaken.

'Gresson,' Cristal said, nodding up at the corpse. 'He couldn't wait for the lift.'

Scott sat on the floor, leaning against the gate, his head in his hands. He looked up and gave a weak smile and said, 'Thanks. I feel better now he's gone.'

'Sure,' she said. He grinned, and she added, 'That's my Ewan. Now, lend me a shoulder.'

She stepped on him and felt around on top of the lift until she found Gresson's belted waist. She climbed down again. He looked inquiringly at her. 'We're still unarmed,' she said. 'Gresson's gun must be in the shaft.'

She walked to the door and peered cautiously out, then Scott saw her step into the open and heard her moving around. A moment later she came back, her face troubled and uncertain. 'There's no one,' she said. 'No one. It's empty. And I remember now – I think I heard a helicopter take off. It must have been yours.

'That means it's on. It's started. And there's nothing we can do to stop it. Have we – have we lost, Ewan? All this' – she flung her hands in the air – 'for nothing?'

He nodded, dumbly. While she'd been fighting for her life at the top of the shaft and he'd been slumped on the floor of the compressor room, his own Sikorski had lifted fifteen crack assault troops of the Red Army Marine Corps, fully armed for battle, to take from Britain a weapon which would give almost unlimited superiority to the Soviet Union in nuclear brinkmanship. And they were powerless to prevent the attack.

Cristal adjusted her weary spine to a vertical row of chunky rivets on a spray-painted bulkhead and felt an enormous lassitude steal over her. She closed her eyes and her body drooped and her spirit slumped.

'Hey,' Scott said, gently, shaking her arm, 'we must still

272

have some sort of chance.'

'What can we do?' she asked, listlessly.

'Well, for one thing, if the raid *has* started, from what you managed to tell me down there in the compressor room, right at this moment there's a submarine attached to a leg of this rig. The assault troops came in that way, and presumably the door's still open, as it were. So if we don't want a few dozen hairy submariners on our necks, why don't we go down and close it?'

She gave a rueful smile and said, 'OK, doc. Let's go.'

They scuttled furtively across the deck, using the big generators and scattered equipment as cover. The steady hum of the diesels was loud enough to blanket their footsteps, but still they felt compelled to move as quietly as possible. At the far side of the generating room, Cristal signalled to Scott to stop. She crouched behind a metal transformer cabinet, and looked sceptically at a large, closed steel door barring their way.

'Keep watch here,' she whispered, 'and follow me once I'm through the door.'

She pulled back the heavy handle and gave the door a mighty push. It swung so hard it hit the stop with a metallic clang and reverberated like the gong at the start of an old J. Arthur Rank film. She froze, but nobody came running, so she peeped through. There was no sign of life.

Scott crept up behind her and saw that the area of the rig they were in housed the filter beds used to separate samples of rock and shale bought back up the drill case by the iron pyrites pumped down in the drilling operation. The place was cold and rusty, and reminded him of the hulk of a wrecked ship.

Cristal pointed to the far corner. 'Isn't that another lift shaft?' she asked.

'Right,' Scott said. He looked back over his shoulder. 'It's the one opposite ours, I think.'

'Looks like it's in use,' she whispered.

'If it is,' Scott replied, 'I should think it's the one we

want.'

'Oughtn't there to be a guard?'

'Maybe they weren't expecting visitors.'

She stuck out her tongue at him.

'You've no idea,' he remarked, 'how divertingly dirty you are.'

She looked down at herself. Her torn shirt was still knotted above her navel, and the oil and grime and sweat streaked her face and smudged the end of her nose, and striated her breasts with filigree patterns as intricate as the marquetry on an Empireline escritoire.

She sniffed and drew her wrist and the back of her hand across her nose, which made the picture even more appealing.

'You're a lovely, grubby little slut,' he said.

'None of us,' she replied, loftily, 'can achieve perfection all the time. And get that bedroom look out of your eyes, Scott, 'cos we have work to do.'

She padded across to the lift and peered down the shaft. There was faint glow of light at the bottom. She looked around and spotted an isolator switch on the adjoining bulkhead. She flicked it to off and the light went out. She turned to Scott, winked, and tapped her temple with her forefinger.

The knurled head of the screw in the plate covering the isolator turned easily. She lifted the plate off and took out the two porcelain fuse-holders. Replacing the cover, she showed Scott the fuses, grinned idiotically at him like Tom the cartoon cat, trotted over to a porthole and tossed them into the sea.

'I'm sure that was the right pontoon,' she said.

'How do you know?'

'Well, the lift was down, and I saw a bunch of wires and temporary cables fed through at the back. I suppose they're drawing power from the generators to recharge the sub's batteries.'

'I think you're right,' Scott said. 'OK now. If there's

anyone else left on the rig – and there must be a skeleton crew – my guess is they'll be in the radio room. And the quickest way there is up the stairs and over the main platform.

'Dare we go unarmed?' she asked.

'You know where there's a gun?' She shook her head. 'Sharpen your fingers, then, because we can't stay here.'

When they reached the deck the contrast between the sea-fresh air and still bright sunshine of the late evening, and the dank, chilly prison they'd left, was startling and comforting. 'Eerie, isn't it?' Cristal said. 'Nobody being around, I mean.' Scott nodded. 'At least we hope no one's around.'

The rig trembled and murmured busily with the vibration of the machinery below, and they felt dangerously vulnerable as they crossed the open deck. The sun bounced off the windows of the toolpusher's cabin, and it was impossible to detect whether there was anyone inside.

The feeling of unease followed Cristal down the stairwell and along the gloomy corridor past crew cabins and mess rooms, until they turned a corner and saw the laundry and the sick bay and finally, at the far end, the door to the radio room. Twenty doors she counted, and any one could have opened behind them in an ambush. Yet the danger lay hidden not there, but far above them.

The lookout on the highest platform of the drilling derrick a hundred feet over the deck saw the two puppet figures leave the generating room. He returned to his paperback with a grunt, but looked back again when he caught a quicksilver slip of movement at the corner of his eye. One of the two had ducked behind a stack of drilling pipes, and the other remained stock still.

He grunted once more, picked up his binoculars and twirled the focussing control until he got a perfect head and torso of the leading figure. He swallowed hard. It could almost have been the body of 'Natasha the Naiad of Novgorod' whose exploits were so enlivening his uneventful spell of guard duty.

Then he swore, jerked upright on his precarious perch, and cursed again as Natasha fell from his despairing clutch and fluttered away on the stiff breeze. One of the captured agents was a woman . . . they must have escaped. His stubby fingers clapped the binoculars to his eyes, and when certainty grew he dialled the radio room on the lookout's telephone.

At the same instant, Ivanovitch picked up the tinkling handset of the field telephone connecting him with the submarine, and heard the communications officer complain that the lift was stuck at the bottom. 'We can't come up,' the officer said. 'Extraordinary,' the KGB chief replied. He slammed down the handset and listened stolidly to the radio operator's story of the escape of the captives.

'Impossible,' he declared flatly.

'The lookout's seen them, Comrade Colonel.'

Ivanovitch cracked his knuckes, and then ordered, 'Find the bargemaster. Arm yourself. Then go and check the docking pontoon lift. It's not working.'

The Russian was making for the door when it burst open and Scott hurled through, diving for Ivanovitch at the communications console. Cristal, behind him, casually slugged the radio operator on the jaw and the colour drained from his tanned face like beer poured out of a pint pot. Her hard, bare heel crashed against the side of his head as she skipped past his falling body, and his interest in the proceedings ceased.

A shot rang out and she automatically fell flat. The bullet ricochetted off a steel stanchion and lodged in the ceiling. It had come from Ivanovitch's gun, fired in his struggle with Scott – a battle that the huge Don Cossack was clearly winning. Until, that is, it unaccountably started to rain.

Ivanovitch's shot had neatly sheared away the fire sprinkler valve, and all three of them reeled under powerful jets of icy water. Then blue sparks and spitting, crackling flashes erupted from the radio desk and teleprinters, as the water sprinkler system behaved precisely according to its designated function and drenched everything within reach. In a matter of seconds, every single piece of communications equipment on the rig was useless.

Ivanovitch let out a howl of rage and despair as his link with the shore party disappeared in a puff of smoke, and Scott slammed his fist into the Russian's face and chopped viciously at his wrist. The gun fell out of his hand and slithered across the floor to rest at Cristal's feet.

She picked it up and shouted 'Break!' Scott stepped back like the gentleman he was, after craftily pushing Ivanovitch backwards over a tubular steel chair. The Russian sat on the floor with the water streaming down his face, looking like a gigantic, furious baby.

Cristal trained the gun at his heart, and with her free hand energetically washed the oil and grime off her face and body as she stood under the 'shower.' Her breasts shivered and jumped and the freezing needles of water stung the raised nipples. The eyes of both men were glued to the undulating globes until she complained, in pained exasperation, 'I'm cold, and wet. We are in danger of drowning. Do something.'

Scott obligingly stripped a soggy sweater from the radio operator and she said to Ivanovith, 'Out,' In the corridor she watched with raised eyebrows while Scott wrung the sweater out, and Ivanovitch rolled his eyes as she pulled it over her dripping hair.

He spread his arms and feet and leaned with his face to the wall to let Cristal search him. He didn't have another gun, but her probing fingers discovered, clipped to his belt, a little radio transmitter like a walkie-talkie, complete with telescopic aerial.

She handed it to Scott, who started to examine it curiously. Ivanovitch turned his shaven head, and frantic fear lit the cold grey eyes.

'Don't touch the switch!' he screamed. 'You'll blow us all to pieces.'

Scott let the transmitter rest on the flat of his hand. Cristal walked over to Ivanovitch, went down on her haunches, and raised the gun to eye level. 'Explain.'

Ivanovitch drew a sigh, and admitted, 'It's a remote control detonating device. We've got explosive charges placed to scuttle the rig when we leave. That' he nodded at the transmitter, 'is the switch that sets them off.'

Cristal rose and backed off and turned to Scott to ask him a question. The slight movement saved her life, because a revolver shot parted the air where the back of her neck had been. She dived to her left, turned in mid-air, and let off two rounds, but she was too late. The lookout had dodged back round the corner of the long corridor.

She heard a shout behind her and dimly saw Ivanovitch launch himself at Scott, who'd been bending to form a less available target. Scott landed heavily on her, and Ivanovitch jumped nimbly over his legs, wrenched open the door of the sick bay, and threw his big body into the room.

Cristal rolled clear, cursing, and lined up on the sick bay door, but two more shots came from the other end. She fired once at the lookout, and the bullet sang a shrill diminuendo along the metal wall. The lookout pulled back again, and they heard Ivanovitch slam shut the sick bay door. The stout double lock clicked into place.

'We're pinned down,' she rapped. 'Get into the nearest rooms.' They dashed further up the passage and chose doors on either side, facing each other.

Ivanovitch looked for another way out of the sick bay, and found it. A door in the far corner opened on to an iron catwalk, and from there a ladder bolted to the side of the rig led to the level of the helipad and the toolpusher's cabin. He had few physical weaknesses, but one was vertigo; he swallowed hard, gritted his teeth and shinned up.

Down below, Scott was in the laundry and Cristal was in the mess room next to the sick bay, with both doors slightly ajar. She had three bullets left in Ivanovitch's gun. She caught Scott's eye and pointed over her shoulder as an indication that she was going exploring for a back door. But there wasn't one. She heard another shot whistle down the corridor, and looked cautiously out of the messroom window. There was nothing to the left or right, and when she looked up she saw Ivanovitch clambering on to the helipad. The catwalk from which the ladder rose ended below the level of her window, and about three feet to the left. She stuck the gun in her waistband and waved to Scott, but he wasn't looking. She opened the window fully, and squirmed out until she was hanging from the sill by her clenched fingers. The metal bit into her hands, and she looked across. She was now nearly on a level with the guard rail, but still well short.

Gradually and painfully she inched her way along the window until both hands were clamped on the metal frame at the right-hand edge. She glanced down – and wished she hadn't. She was suspended like a fly on the smooth, vertical side of the rig, and the only thing beneath her was the sea, eighty feet away. One slip meant certain death.

She clenched the fingers of her left hand to tighten her grip on the window frame, and lunged desperately sideways, groping for one of the upright spars of the guide rail. He fingers touched metal . . . closed and held.

She grasped the slim bar firmly in her fist, breathed a quick prayer, and released her hold on the window. Her body swung out into the void – and her heart leapt into her mouth as her hand slipped agonisingly down the rail. Frantically she brought her left hand across and it made contact with a solid smack on the adjacent bar. She tensed her muscles, stilled her wildly swinging body, and pulled herself up, hand by aching hand, until she gratefully grasped the horizontal rail and hoisted her feet on to the catwalk.

Cristal scaled the ladder, peeped over the top, and saw the Russian about thirty yards away, with his back to her. He was leaning into the cockpit of a little helicopter on the far edge of the landing pad, and whatever he was doing occupied his attention entirely.

She looked in the opposite direction, and saw a staircase to the deck, beyond the toolpusher's cabin. Keeping her eyes fixed on the stooping form of Ivanovitch, she climbed on to the platform and crossed to the shelter of the cabin, then down the open tread staircase, and over to the top of the internal steps leading back to the living quarters.

She dropped on to her belly and pulled her body to the lip of the stairwell. Below, crouched peering around the corner into the corridor where Scott was still trapped, was the lookout, in a white sweater and dark trousers.

The corridor ceiling cut off a view of his head from her, so she put a single bullet into his back which passed through his heart and lodged in his rib-cage just below the left breast.

She leapt to her feet and dashed down the steps, calling, 'Ewan. It's all right. It's me.' They got to the corner at the same time, and he caught her and kissed her, and she was glad.

She told him Ivanovitch was on the landing pad 'doing something to a helicopter.' 'A helicopter?'

'Yes. A little one, parked on the far side.'

'Christ, he'll have a radio in it.'

'And he'll have heard my shot as well,' she said. 'There may even be more of *him*' – gesturing at the dead lookout – 'lurking in the ironwork.'

'I doubt it,' said Scott. 'You seem to have killed practically everything that moved.'

'What should we do?' she asked.

'Get to Ivanovitch – now,' he replied.

As they were running up the open staircase she said, 'What if he's got another gun in the little chopper.' Scott shrugged. But Ivanovitch wasn't armed. He was standing at the rail, heaving something into the sea, when they reached the platform. He didn't seem surprised to see them, and made no attempt at resistance. Maybe we've convinced him, Cristal thought, that fatalism has its attractions as a philosophy.

She covered him while Scott made for the helicopter. He was back a few moments later, looking crestfallen. 'He's sent his message and buggered the radio,' he said. 'The aerial's been wrenched off, and at a guess the thing that hit the water just now was the tuning module. There's no way we can raise anyone.'

Cristal thought for a moment, then she said, 'OK. Can you fly this thing?' Scott nodded, for it was a Kamov, and he had flown one before, although the Russian machine was rare in the west. 'Let's go then,' she said. 'We may be able to make it in time to do something at Tredogan, and anyway he' – nodding at Ivanovitch – 'might be a useful bargaining counter.'

'Sure, why not?' said Scott, though he was still depressed.

'We've also got that little toy you took from him,' Cristal added. 'We can set them back a bit by sending this lot sky-high.'

A look of consternation crossed Ivanovitch's face, but neither Scott nor Cristal saw it. Scott said, 'Yeah, OK. But I've been thinking. If they'd really wanted to dramatically cover their escape, they could have put charges at the well-head, too. That would certainly leave a gusher, and perhaps even an oilfield fire to keep everyone occupied. One hell of a mess, in fact. We can't take the risk.'

'How quickly can you check it?' she asked, reluctant to give the time to what she considered a mopping-up operation. Scott replied, 'It won't take long. But look – we really do have to do it. I don't think you appreciate what an oilfield fire can do.'

She nodded, and he crossed the whole length of the rig to the drilling derrick, and found there what he'd expected to find . . . a temporary cable running from a junction box. It disappeared over the edge of the platform and snaked down to the sea. He walked back over the platform to Ivanovitch. 'One you forgot to tell us about, Colonel?'

Ivanovitch looked innocently at him until Cristal waved the gun under his nose. 'I'm not an explosives man myself, Mr Scott,' he said, 'but I imagine the divers were both competent and thorough.'

There were no tools in sight, so when he was back at the derrick, Scott climbed on to the junction box, bent down, took the cable in both hands, closed his eyes, prayed, and heaved. The world didn't disintegrate, and the wires came up with his body, their exposed ends dangling free. 'Thank God for that,' he muttered. He doubled back to the helipad. 'The other end of that cable,' he explained to Cristal, 'was connected to charges in the sea-bed. If they'd gone up, the explosion would have taken off the head of the well as cleanly as you'd decapitate your breakfast egg. Then – ' he gestured at the oil-field in both directions ' – curtains.'

'Might have been fun,' she mused. He raised his hands in a Jewish gesture of despair and resignation, and climbed into the right-hand seat of Ivanovitch's helicopter.

'The rig itself will still blow, won't it?' Cristal asked. Scott nodded. 'I'll see if this thing will start. I haven't flown one of these for years. Welcome home, Ewan.' He leaned out and said to Cristal, 'Once I've got the engines started, bring him in through the other door. He can sit behind you. There's a hank of rope knotted through one of the cargo rings, and I'll cover you while you tie him to the seat. Then you take the co-pilot's seat. OK?'

He switched on the main electrics, and was relieved to find he had power. The fuel gauge registered full . . . great. He ran through the pre-start checks and operated the starter switch. The first engine roared instantly to life. 'Right,' he shouted to the girl. 'Get him on board.'

Scott started the other engine and engaged the rotor. Cristal pushed Ivanovitch through the port door, and he shot Scott a venomous glare as he squeezed to the back of the tiny cabin, bending his huge bulk almost double. Scott wondered whether the prize he represented as a capture was worth the weight he brought with him as a passenger. He

282

covered Cristal while she lashed the Russian's arms behind him to the tubular struts of the seat.

'Hold on,' Scott yelled – and they were airborne.

The Kamov fishtailed as it left the pad, and Scott straightened her up with the yaw pedals, and climbed steadily away at an angle of forty-five degrees, levelling out at about four hundred feet. At a little past a quarter of a mile he brought the helicopter round to face TARACO FIVE again, and shouted to Cristal, 'The transmitter's in my pocket.'

She took it out and looked steadily at the rig while her hand rested on the switch, and the Kamov hovered expectantly. A strangled scream of 'No!' from behind stayed her finger. She turned her head. 'Why not?' she demanded.

'You don't realise,' Ivanovitch said. 'If you do that, you could kill sixty men.' She looked blankly at him. 'The submarine,' he shouted. 'It may still be docked on to the pontoon. If it is, and the rig blows, so will the submarine. They won't stand a chance. Please, for God's sake – not sixty lives. You can't do it.'

'Put that thing down, Cristal,' Scott urged her. 'He's right, you can't do it. You couldn't even think of doing it.'

She hesitated, but still held on to the transmitter. A look of intense concentration came on her face, and then a sigh of resignation, as though she'd reviewed every conceivable course of action that lay before her, and had reached the only possible conclusion. She pressed the switch. Ivanovitch's mouth moved, but she didn't hear the Russian words. Her eyes were fixed on the rig. So were Scott's, drawn by the awful fascination of what was happening.

From the undisturbed sea there rose a white spout of water, obliterating the shifting shape of TARACO FIVE. It hung suspended on the wind for a second or two, then dropped lazily to the surface, leaving the rig visible again as the nucleus of an ever-widening circle of boiling, foaming sea.

For a moment they thought the rig had survived the

283

hammer-blows of the explosions, but Cristal realised with a catch at her breath that the structure was becoming truncated, stunted, its legs disappearing straight down into the ocean to its very bed, like some great, majestic dinosaur sinking into the morass of time.

It was a vision of horror. In less than half a minute, the Moscow Horse had gone, and there was no trace of it left.

Cristal dropped the transmitter into Scott's lap and said, 'Can we go now?'

TWENTY-SIX

Scott was horrified – shattered.

'My God,' he breathed, 'what are you? What *are* you? What kind of animal monstrosity can you be that you could send sixty men to their deaths without even turning a hair?'

'I don't have to explain my motives to you, Scott,' Cristal said, sharply. 'I am your field commander. Do not forget that.'

'No, Cristal,' he snapped. 'It won't do. I watched you press that button. You might just as well have been switching out a light for all it meant to you. Either it had to be done, or it was done because you wanted to do it. Now which was it.'

Her mouth was set in an unaccustomed straight line and her eyes flamed; she tossed her head haughtily and ignored him.

'Right,' said Scott, and banked the Kamov round in a tight turn, heading back the way they'd come.

'Where are you going?' Cristal demanded.

'To see if I can save any of those poor bastards you've blown into the sea.' Scott retorted savagely. Then the hairs at the back of his neck quivered as he felt the unmistakable pressure of a gun against his flesh.

'Scott,' her soft voice said, 'I'll kill you.' The metallic hiss of his headset underlined her menacing whisper.

There was a silence under the blast of the engine, during which Scott didn't change course by as much as a single degree. Then another voice spoke.

'Mr Scott,' Ivanovitch said, 'Don't be foolish, do as the lady says. First, because if you don't, she *will certainly* kill you. And secondly because she is right. The submarine had to be destroyed because without it we have no chance of taking the rocket back to Mother Russia. It is as simple as that. And if you need a third reason – how many of the poor bastards could you save with this little toy anyway?'

'Thank you, Colonel,' Cristal said. 'Ewan?'

Scott banked again and brought the helicopter round.

'Sorry, Cristal,' he said. 'I wasn't thinking. It just seemed – awful.'

She breathed a sigh of relief and tucked the gun back in her waistband. Had they but known it, their drama was for nothing. The suspicious submarine captain had ordered his divers to sever the link with the rig when communications failed, and the *Slavyanka* was already homeward bound.

'OK,' she said. 'Now will you please try to think of some way of stopping Colonel Ivanovitch's men getting their hands on our rocket at all, because they could still drop one smack on the deck of his trawler, couldn't they?'

Ivanovitch shot her a keen look of mingled respect and frustration, then he sank back in his seat and closed his eyes and started, slowly and with infinite patience, to move the rope binding his left hand against the sharp under-edge of one of the helicopter frame's cross-struts.

Less than two minutes had passed before Scott started to hum lightly through his scarred and puffy lips. Cristal, hunched forward on the seat next to him, was tense and wary. She picked nervously with her teeth at the pad of hard skin on one of her finger-tips – then shook herself crossly, grimaced and stopped. It had taken three years to form her hands into lethal weapons . . . and a chewed finger-tip wouldn't kill anyone. Ivanovitch was slumped like a question-mark, his huge head hanging in apparent resignation and defeat.

Scott was in a different mood. He had a plan.

His first job on leaving the Navy had been to fly for a small Swedish outfit that used the little Kamovs for aerial survey work. As he was taking off from the doomed rig he'd noticed the winch mounted on the side of the helicopter, but his brain had only just registered the fact and assessed its significance.

It was a special kind of winch designed for towing an aerial, and that meant that it had one unique property: if a sudden strain was put on the towing cable so that the safety of the aircraft was threatened, the cable would be automatically severed by a pair of shears.

His eyes flickered again from the controls to the light, compact winch and its strong, tightly-wound cable. The plan developed and matured in his mind.

Cristal, he guessed, was mentally limbering up for a pitched battle at the base, but Scott knew it wasn't on. Even flat out, the little Kamov was about forty knots slower than the Sikorsky's cruising speed. The rig party had a good start on them, and Scott accepted that the Kamov couldn't reach the base in time for them to be able to stop the attack. And if by some remote chance they did, he thought ruefully, they'd be unlikely to sway the battle when their only weapon was the hand gun they had taken from Ivanovitch. A squadron of Hunter fighters would be more to the point, and Scott amused himself by wondering briefly how he'd get on if he'd been able to call the RAF base at Brawdy and request one.

As the last traces of daylight faded, they were flying up the Cardiganshire coast just abeam of the village of Treddawen, fifteen miles from the rocket base, and Scott turned the machine inshore. There was a chance – a desperate chance – that he could square up the odds . . .

By now the shape of the village was picked out in twinkling lights, like a child's game of joining up the dots. Some were bright and some dim, but the pattern was dominated by a yellowish-brown area marking the car park of a public house and the boat-builder's yard next to it, where the pool of brightness created by the sodium floodlights was trying gamely to keep the night away. Scott had been often to the pub – The Harbourmaster's Arms: 'Fresh-cut sandwiches daily' (why did no one ever tell then it was freshly?), 'Try our mouth-watering Ploughman's Lunches' (Scott looked in vain for a ploughman to test them on), 'Gorge yourself on a Sea-Food Special' (they were genuinely excellent). He also had his sloop moored at the yard, and he knew the layout of both places well.

He lost height as quickly as he dared, and slid sideways over the harbour wall to position at the hover about thirty feet above the boatyard. Dry sand and dust, discarded crisp packets, greasy wads of fish-and-chips wrappers and a thousand other dejected particles of seaside detritus rose, fluttered, swirled and eddied around as he directed the power of the six-contra-rotating blades to hold the helicopter steady.

He said to Cristal through the co-pilot's headset, 'Keep the bastard covered, but use your other hand to operate that winch,' he pointed to the control. 'Then open the chopper door.' She looked at him in total bewilderment, and he added, 'Don't worry. I know what I'm doing. Just follow orders. Please.'

She nodded, glanced round at Ivanovitch, who didn't bother to return her gaze, then half-turned and quickly lowered the winch. Without looking at Scott she said 'OK?' into the mouthpiece, and heard him say 'OK'. She slid open the door, and part of the blast of air fanned by the blades whipped back her tresses and swept into the cabin. She saw the winch descend, touch the ground, and trail across the concrete boatyard.

The customers at the Harbourmaster's were roused from their sleepy conversation or solitary contemplation of their beer by the ear-shattering noise. They spilled into the car park, and almost with the precision of drilling soldiers formed themselves into a perfect arc, all looking upwards, hands shielding their eyes against the dust cloud. Several were shouting, but none could hear what his neighbour said.

Scott tilted the machine slightly to get a better view of the cable, then trawled sideways again, dragging the hook through a pile of rusty anchor chain which had littered the corner of the boatyard consigned to general junk for as long as he'd been going there. His heart leapt when he saw the hook engage a link. Just like trout-fishing, he thought.

Carefully he lifted the Kamov straight up into the air, trailing his cargo of clanking iron. Satisfied that it was safely attached, and hoping against hope that he wouldn't be too late, he swung around and climbed away as fast as the little helicopter would go. The crowd, now considerably larger than the normal evening clientele at the Harbourmaster's, said 'Ahhhh' as if it were the last set-piece in a firework display, and went back to find their beer even flatter than when they'd left.

At fifteen hundred feet, Scott hovered once more, peering into the darkness in the direction from which he expected the Sikorski to come at them. After what seemed an eternity, the dark clouds scudding menacingly across the face of the gibbous moon cleared, and he caught the gleam of light on metal. It was the Sikorski – *his* Sikorski – five hundred feet below, and more than three quarters of a mile away. The great silver disc of her revolving blades glinting eerily, she was running nose down flat out for the rig. Slung underneath was the rocket.

'Shit', Scott said. If the rocket hadn't been there, he wouldn't have had to do what he now knew he must. He had many misgivings about it, and one genuine regret: he was going to destroy a beautiful machine, an old and faithful friend and one that had served him well. He tried not to think of the people on board.

His hands clamped on the controls, his mind computed the complicated time and distance equation until he judged the moment to be right, and then he dived towards the oncoming Sikorski, whose occupants never once suspected that sudden death was hurtling down on them like a monstrous, flying scorpion with a fatal sting in its streaming tail. To Cristal, who's only just spotted the other machine, everything from then on seemed to happen in slow motion. As the Kamov levelled out and then started to climb steeply again, she saw the Sikorski vanish beneath them. The sharp, shuddering jolt when the winch cable, stretched to its fullest extent, tightened and then held, snapped her teeth together like a mouse trap.

Scott held on to the controls with all his strength, gripping the stick so hard he might have been welded to it. 'Jesus, it's not going to work,' he whispered. And shouted, 'It's not going to fucking – ', but then it did. A dull, metallic crack as the shears cut the cable, a fiercely vibrating twang as though the bass string had been severed from some gigantic guitar, and the Kamov surged powerfully upwards, its intolerable burden falling away.

Simultaneously, and above even the noise of their own engines, the man and the girl heard the hellish scream of tortured metal as first the blades, and then the rotor-head, of the Sikorski swallowed the flailing chains and destroyed themselves, wrenched off and borne away on the wind. Scott banked hard to see the decapitated body of the helicopter rolling, spinning, and toppling into the calm sea. He turned sharply in, and a white plume of water burst into the air as the carcase of the Sikorski hit the surface, and sank almost immediately. The foaming ripples melted away, the sea was calm again, and the moon slipped behind another cloud to restore a dark and dreadful peace.

It had all taken just twelve seconds.

Scott was beginning to relax before planning his route to London when, for the second time that night he felt the cold hardness of a gun barrel against his neck. He looked down into Cristal's lap. The pistol wasn't in her belt.

'Now it is I who want you to turn around, Mr Scott,' Ivanovitch said, raising his voice above the roar of the engines.

Scott heard the sharp hiss of Cristal's indrawn breath as she realised what had happened, and the curse at her own carelessness.

'My little helicopter had sharp corners,' the Russian continued. 'While you were – otherwise occupied, I managed to free myself and retrieve my gun. You didn't even notice it was gone, Miss Vengan. You were too busy enjoying yourself watching my men die.'

She hung her head in rage and shame.

'You will now,' Ivanovitch directed Scott, 'take me to the trawler, or I shall shoot Miss Vengan. I would hate to deprive the British Special Intelligence Service of a brilliantly gifted agent, but I have the feeling that mankind in general would be deeply in my debt.' His voice had taken on a sarcastic tone, but when he shouted the single command, 'Move!' Scott started to bank.

Cristal interjected 'No – wait.' She swung round to face Ivanovitch, and he drew a careful two-handed bead right between her big, dark eyes.

'Colonel Ivanovitch,' she began. 'OK, you've got us. But just think for a moment. Your mission's aborted – your men are dead – ' she ticked the indictment off on her fingers – 'you've lost the oil rig – you've lost a submarine – your British spy network is bound to be smashed. What kind of a welcome do you think you'll get from Mother Russia? A bullet? If you're lucky, that is.'

'I've still got powerful friends,' Ivanovitch replied. 'I'll take my chances.'

'As powerful as my friends?' she asked, slyly.

'SIS?' the Russian boomed, 'Vice-Admiral Sir Sacheverell Pink, KBE, DSO and bar? From Gorki Street to Queen Anne's Gate? Are you serious?'

'No – and neither are you, Colonel,' Cristal declared. 'You've known for a long time, haven't you, that I'm no more SIS than you are. You know SIS wouldn't do what I've done – couldn't kill like I do. You know they wouldn't sanction the sort freelance operation we've been mounting without Pink breathing down our necks. Come, Colonel, let us put our cards on the table, shall we?'

Ivanovitch assented graciously. 'By all means, Miss Vengan, if you wish.' But the gun trained on her was unwavering.

'There must be trust between us first.'

'Don't take me for a fool, child,' Ivanovitch grated. 'I am still more than half inclined to kill you.'

'The risk is all on my side,' she flared. 'Whether you decide to kill me or not, I could still lose my life if I tell you.'

'The decision is yours, then. It is I who have the gun.'

So she told him – everything. He was gratifyingly, and genuinely, astonished.

'I had no idea there was a Department like yours,' he admitted. 'None whatsoever.'

'Neither does Pink,' she said.

'Of course, I've known the names of Pond and Sleightley – particularly a man as brilliant in his field as Pond, but . . .' he needed say no more.

Cristal leaned on her arms on the back of her seat until her face was no more than three inches from the rock-steady gun. Even in the dim light of the Kamov cabin Ivanovitch could see her eyes begin to cross with the effort of looking round the muzzle at him.

He found the spectacle so ridiculous that he threw back his head and roared with laughter. Cristal couldn't repress a fit of hysterical giggling, and the gun was forgotten. Scott shouted above the noise, 'When you two clowns have finished, perhaps you'll tell me which way you want me to go.' He had in fact been flying in great circles while the argument raged alongside him.

Ivanovitch spluttered, 'Can we get to London in this machine, Mr Scott?'

'No,' Scott replied, 'but I do have a way. We can use my own aircraft, which I keep just down there – 'he pointed at the farm, which was bathed in bright moonlight. 'The thing is, it's only a two-seater, so Cristal will have to drive my car back. I left it about a quarter of a mile away, near the Carreg Wen Hotel,' turning to Cristal. 'The Colonel had better come with me, don't you think? In case the police have any road blocks up after this evening's excitement.'

She nodded.

'So be it,' Ivanovitch agreed.

'You'll find some money in my wallet in the glove compartment for the Severn Bridge toll,' Scott shouted at Cristal.

'Gee, thanks,' she screamed back.

Scott set the Kamov down alonside the hangar, switched off the engines, and got out to be greeted almost immediately by the farmer, who had been attracted by the noise.

'I've got problems with this thing,' said Scott. 'I'm going to have to use my Victa for a trip. Can you give me some lights for take-off?' The farmer said he could, and made off back to the house to switch on the primitive lighting system. Scott put his head back inside the cockpit and spoke to Cristal. 'Now's your chance to slip off and get the car.' He handed her the keys. 'See you in London.'

Scott had the Victa out of the hangar, with Ivanovitch uncomfortably installed in the passenger seat, by the time the farmer returned. He gave the advancing figure a cheery wave, turned on the power, and taxied rapidly out to the end of the field for his take-off. He congratulated himself, that nobody had yet got close enough to Ivnovitch to identify him. As he opened the throttle to full power, the thought ocurred to him that it seemed much more than two days since he'd bumped over the same ground at the start of his last trip to Northolt.

During the flight, Scott spent a great deal of time using the radio – not merely to progress their clearance to London, but also to arrange, in coded and on a reserved frequency, the kind of reception he wanted at Northolt. He was relieved, as they made their landing run, to see the large and venerable black departmental Rolls Royce parked on the apron in front of the terminal. The car had tinted rear windows, and Ivanovitch, he felt, would appreciate that touch. Sleightley and Pond, Scott reflected (not for the first time), were men of influence as well as taste.

When they got to Queen Anne's gate, Scott explained the travel difficulties they'd had, and estimated that Cristal should be back in London by two o'clock in the morning. Pond suggested that Ivanovitch should remain in the front office while Scott was debriefed. They would put off the pleasure of meeting their opposite number until they had all the facts.

The two men heard Scott out in utter silence. Then Pond said, 'So I had it wrong. Every little bit of it.'

'Not your fault,' Sleightley replied, briskly. 'We gave them credit for being cleverer, or at least more sophisticated, than they actually are, that's all.'

'I don't think so,' Pond went on, glumly. 'The Colonel,s scheme was brilliant in its simplicity, and totally audacious. We didn't get a smell of it. We just think that way.'

'He had a lot of luck,' Sleightley persisted. 'The whole Trojan Horse concept was sheerly fortuitous. If that loophole hadn't existed, neither would their plan. Anyway, now, thanks to you two, we have an unlooked for bonus. We can study the good Ivanovitch and learn to think their way, as well.'

'I suppose so,' Pond said, still unconvinced.

'Look at it like this, C.,' Sleightley said, gently. 'Because *we* think the way *we* do, and because we employ people like Vengan and Scott who think and act like *they* do, the Soviets failed. If they *had* been smart enough to do it your way, they might well have brought it off.'

Pond nodded, and buzzed for Ivanovitch. When the KGB chief came in, Sleightley studied the heavy, cut-glass chandelier intently, and said in faultless Russian, 'Comrade Colonel. Welcome to Great Britain and Department RE.'

Ivanovitch, who thought the ornate light fitting must be either a well-concealed camera or part of some arcane, possibly Masonic, ritual, contemplated the ceiling gravely, and said to the chandelier, in flawless English, 'I am most happy to be here, and I look forward greatly to working with you.'

Pond turned to the window and covered his face, and Scott went almost puce in his efforts not to laugh.

Sleightley looked sharply at the agent and picked up a small, shiny pasteboard folder fom his desk. 'I would not wish you to suffer any undue strain, Scott,' he said, 'so I suggest that if you have nothing better to do, you would do well to make yourself scarce for a few weeks. There is an airline ticket, money, and a passport in your new name in this packet. No doubt we shall hear from you in due course.'

Scott said, 'I'm sorry, Sir. Yes, of course.' He accepted the package.

'Send us a card,' said Pond.

'Quite,' Ivanovitch intoned.

Scott left the three to an earnest and exhaustive conversation that lasted until Cristal bowled up at the front door in the borrowed Lotus. She came into the office, and the men stood up. Ivanovitch bowed courteously.

'You look tired, my dear,' Sleightley said. 'Please go home to bed. We will of course have to deal with the remaining tiresome loose end concerning our political friend. A question of blocking a security leak, I'm afraid. Do you follow me?'

She inclined her lovely head, and said she did, and tried to keep a neutral expression in her eyes.

'Take care of it, will you?' Sleightley went on. 'It's late now, so I suggest you telephone me in the morning, and set the operation for Sunday.'

TWENTY-SEVEN

Canterwell woke at six thirty, from force of habit dating back to prep school and Charterhouse. Then the Army (five thirty in basic training, but as a National Service second lieutenant it was back to six thirty), and on to Cambridge, where it wasn't necessary, but suited his purpose and mood. He was one of those men who gave the clear lie to the attractive theory that Occidentals are evening people and Orientals morning people.

Somebody used this nonsense premise to him once to explain why Winston Churchill, summoned to the Yalta Conference table at 9am by a bustling, wideawake Stalin, made all manner of concessions before the first brandy of the day, but won them back with the last at midnight when the Russian was a burnt-out case. Canterwell considered the theory to be a plausible refuge for unsuccessful drunks. He need only an afternoon cat-nap to conserve his post-prandial resources, and his mind was diamond-sharp at both ends of the day.

He was an easy sleeper, so he patted his wife's rump when she stirred, and they both settled back down, because he'd realised it was Sunday, and his biological alarm shouldn't have functioned. But it was at best a fretful doze, and at 7.20 he reluctantly dragged himself out of bed, glanced at Eve, who still slept, with the sheet pulled up just past the tip of her nose, and slipped out to the bathroom.

He bathed and shaved and switched in the eight o'clock Radio Four news bulletin. The BBC had a mini-team of reporters in Cardiganshire to reinforce the Cardiff and Bangor-based regional staff, and they were just beginning to realise the full implications of the story.

This, he thought, was extraordinary, since they more

than anyone should have known something was wrong from the moment their transmitter in the Prescellis went off the air on Friday night. Now, however, they were catching up. They hadn't penetrated the cordon thrown around the base and Miernek's hotel by the police, but they'd hired a Piper Cherokee to investigate both areas of unusual marine activity reported by fishing smacks.

Canterwell anticipated – correctly – that before the day was out, the electronic media would have followed the Fleet Street papers in pulling the strands together, and producing a story hinting at Welsh Nationalist-inspired, terrorist-backed plot to steal an ORBITMAN rocket from Tredogan. The oil-rig – which they'd identified as TARACO FIVE – was to be linked to the raid in some nebulous way – it produced a consoling Irish connection as a bonus – but the secret of the Trojan Horse was never to be effectively unmasked.

In the weeks that followed, Yasser Arafat would blandly accept resonsibility because it was good for business. Only the Americans were ever to suggest Russian involvement, and Paulfrey was forced to issue a denial through his likeable young ambassador to Washington.

But that morning, as Canterwell finished his cooling tea, the Energy Minister was one of perhaps only a handful of people in England or Wales (or Russia) who knew even half the facts.

Not that he could reveal them, because there was no way that he *could* have known without being implicated to a far greater degree than anyone imagined (or so he thought). The absurdity of it suddenly struck him, and he chuckled. British politicians had been banished to obscurity for telling a single lie to the House, yet he, Lewis Canterwell, Her Majesty's Secretary of State for Energy and unofficial deputy premier, was now both a traitor and a murderer – unlikely, though, to be removed from office because to do so would risk a scandal of intolerable gravity.

He was still laughing when the phone rang, and Mark

Talmidge, his PRO, poodle and ferret, confirmed his burgeoning euphoria. Talmidge told him Paulfrey had called in the Service Ministers, the Home Secretary and the SIS Commander the previous evening.

'I know,' Canterwell said. 'The PM rang me. Said I needn't bother to come. He'd fill me in later.'

'Did he give you any details at all?' Talmidge asked.

'No,' Canterwell replied. 'In fact he sounded quite desperately mysterious. All I know is that it's something to do with the RAE at Tredogan and that – bloody oil-rig.'

'It's worse than that, Lewis. Philip told me as much as he knows. It's an incredible story – literally.' 'Philip' was Philip Ridgewood, Paulfrey's press secretary, and a man more powerful in the Downing Street hierarchy than he should have been.

'The Russians were behind it, they think. And you're right – somebody was using an oil-rig . . . well, you know, *that* bloody oil-rig – like a number ten bus. Apparently they didn't get the rocket, but no one knows what really happened.'

There was dead silence. 'Lewis?' Talmidge asked, anxiously. 'Are you still there?'

'I-I-I'm sorry, Mark,' Canterwell stammered. 'Yes, it's just that – I don't know what to say. This is awful – terrible. God Almighty, Mark. The Russians. And I licensed the oil-rig. I made it possible. Mark,' he whispered, hoarsely. 'They don't – they can't surely suspect . . . Mark, I swear before God I had no part – no idea – '

'Of course you didn't, Lewis,' Talmidge expostulated. 'And of course no one believes for a moment that you could have known, or even half-suspected. You – Lewis Canterwell? Not for a single moment, believe me, Lewis.'

His reassurances, Canterwell thought, sounded too fervent, too committed. The slimy little bastard does suspect, he mused. But not Paulfrey. No.

'What about Paulfrey?'

'Philip says he's completely happy.'

'What the hell does that mean, "completely happy"?' Canterwell exploded. 'Happy that the bloody Russians damn near got away with our top secret weapon? Happy that they were stopped but no one seems to know how or by whom? What's he got to be happy about?'

'No, not that,' Talmidge said, as soothingly as he could. 'Happy, I mean, that no word has got out – ever . . . nor could it . . . of any involvement of you in the affair.' Canterwell remained silent, and Talmidge took it to mean he was still unconvinced.

'Look, figure it out,' he went on. 'There was no earthly reason, was there, why the Department shouldn't have granted the drilling licence to that firm? For God's sake, no one knew they were a Soviet front.' His voice took on that note of sly, conspiratorial mendacity which, though he was unaware of it, was the principal reason why Canterwell took him on as PPS.

'I mean,' he said. 'Even if you – or the Department – caught the tiniest bit of stick . . . well, you can always blame it on Lindstrom, can't you? He was, après tout, bent. And now he's dead.'

'Yes, I suppose you're right, Mark,' Canterwell conceded. 'There'd be no grounds for suspecting me, would there?'

'No. Look, the official version's this: there was an attack on the RAE at Tredogan by Welsh Nats with foreign backing – probably the Arabs, they'll say, who won't deny it, and anyway who'd believe them if they did? – and it was defeated by good old British guts and ingenuity, with the SIS coming out of it smelling like fiercely scented roses.'

Canterwell sighed. 'All right, Mark,' he said. 'Whatever happens, I'm deeply grateful to you, for your help and support. You know I won't forget it, don't you?'

'Yes, I know, Lewis,' Talmidge said, softly, insinuatingly. 'Now look, why don't you have a completely restful day. Go sailing with Rodney, or have a run with Pongo in the park. Get Eve to make a picnic. Why not? They say it's going to be another fine day.'

Canterwell said, 'Oh yes, what a good idea, it would help to take his mind off it, how could he ever thank him enough' – and hung up. Talmidge, of course, he mused, knew – or suspected – too much. What a loathsome little shit, he was – and what a problem he would have with Paulfrey getting Talmidge a junior ministry. But Mark must be paid his price . . .

He pushed the cup and saucer back as Eve walked in. 'You're up early,' she remarked, brightly but unnecces-sarily.

'Yes,' he replied. 'I woke up at the usual time, and I couldn't get back to sleep, so I thought I'd make a cup of tea. I'd have brought one up to you but I didn't want to wake you.'

'It's OK,' she said. 'You're forgiven. I couldn't sleep either.'

'Rodney and Jane still well under, are they?'

'You know them, especially Jane.'

'She was late last night, wasn't she,?' Canterwell asked.

'One, or thereabouts,' Eve replied. 'I think she was round at Sarah's. Someone brought her home, anyway. I heard the car door slam.'

Canterwell looked at her as she talked. Eve was safe and confident and competent and serene, and she'd stand by him, no matter what. She didn't mind the other women (and she didn't know about the occasional boys). She was irrationally proud of his supposed integrity, his principles, his – uncorruptibility? Yes. Even if he told her himself that he'd helped sell out his country to the Russians, she wouldn't believe it.

She decided he looked a little peaky, and suggested they'd have cooked breakfast – which she knew he liked – for a change. Jane wandered in, her short nightie riding up her puppy-fat plump thighs as she stretched and yawned.

Canterwell noticed stubble patches under her arms. She was fifteen, and her body was lissom and enticing. With no

300

encouragement at all, he thought, she could become a problem. Rodney, nineteen and going up to Oxford in October, was slothful by nature, except on the rugger field. The smell of frying bacon, eggs and sausages was one of the few things that could get through to him in bed.

Breakfast was eaten, the picnic established, and the children did the washing-up – badly, as always; they were sullen, argumentative, and bored. Canterwell left them to it, and decided that another of Talmidge's suggestions might prove acceptable. He whistled up the family Golden Labrador, and five minutes later he was throwing an oddly compressed tennis ball around Kensington Gardens . . .

Cristal woke at nine on the dot. She lifted her head from the pillow, and let it fall again. She closed her eyes and enjoyed a few more moments of pleasant half-sleep, then kicked the duvet off her body, rolled over, sat up, and slid from the huge bed on to the soft sheepskin rug. She sat completely still with her legs wide apart and crossed, the heels tucked under her naked rump. The yoga regimen she performed then was demanding, the exercises notoriously taxing. She liked best the fifty press-ups, when the fine strands of the rug played with her nipples every three seconds for two and a half minutes.

She squeezed four oranges into a glass, drank it, and ate an apple and half a bar of roasted almond dark chocolate. Then she showered and dressed, and read the papers. All three quality Sundays had the Tredogan story on their front pages. Each account was different, and each had got it wrong. *The Globe* had perhaps the best spread, an intelligent pull-together of local correspondents' and Press Association copy, collated with the stuff their own man on the spot had managed to get (he was the only one to inquire why it was that Miernek's totally empty hotel was so closely guarded by the police), and the whole fabrication was rounded off by the inspired guesses the Defence Correspondent had produced on the bedside phone of the News Editor's ex-mistress.

Cristal dialled the Department's number for that day, and the phone rang three times on Sleightley's desk. There were several clicks and a B flat major bleep from the music tone, and the call was automatically rerouted to Sleightley's weekend cottage on the border of Wiltshire and Dorset.

'Good day,' he said.

'Nothing happened to make you change your mind?' she asked.

'I don't think so, no.'

'I'll go ahead then.'

'Please do. Shall we see you in the morning? You ought to have some leave.'

'Yes,' she said. 'Eleven?'

'Eleven will do,' he answered. 'Good day.'

TWENTY-EIGHT

Pongo showed no sign of tiring. As he wiped the wet, sticky, elliptical tennis ball on the grass for the umpteenth time, Canterwell did a gruff and rather accomplished bark at the big dog, and Pongo jumped joyously into the air and started a sympathetic echo of barking from carefree dogs over an area of several square acres. The Energy Minister grinned and nodded at someone who'd recognised him, looked at his watch and saw that it was coming up to noon, and whistled for the labrador as he turned to recross the park on his way home.

The girl who'd smiled at him was going his way. She had a small, sulky Jack Russell terrier on a lead. She was taller than Canterwell, with wild black hair and deep blue eyes and magnificent breasts.

'Freed from the cares of State, Minister?' she asked, as she swung into step. Her finger, looped through the thong of the lead, tightened to bring the terrier to a disconcerted halt. It yapped at Pongo, who sniffed at its rear end and resolved that though it was indisputably female, anything that resulted would be at best an unequal contest.

'Well, you know, all work and no play . . .'

'That's a lovely dog,' she said. 'What's his name?'

'Pongo,' Canterwell replied.

'Hello, Pongo,' she said, bending to pat him on the head. 'I'm Cristal.' Pongo barked and licked her hand.

'He likes you,' Canterwell remarked.

'Dogs do,' she replied.

'Not only dogs, I imagine.'

'Perhaps. Do you mind if I walk along with you, or would that be unwise?' Cristal asked.

'By no means,' Canterwell said, and laughed. 'It'll do my

image the world of good to be seen with someone lik
you.'

She smiled in genuine pleasure. 'You flatter me, M
Canterwell.'

'I couldn't,' Canterwell replied. He looked at her; sh
was careful to stay several feet away from him so that th
disparity between their heights was less noticeable, and h
liked that. He had no way of knowing that normally i
would have given her real pleasure to stand as close as sh
could to him and watch him draw himself on to his toes t
lessen the distance between their eye levels. But today sh
didn't . . . today, Canterwell was special.

So they walked on the grass at either side of the narrov
path, and Cristal tactfully kept her terrier and Pongo in th
middle, using them as an excuse not to be next to him. H
asked the terrier's name. Cristal had anticipated th
question. She'd borrowed the snappy little brute from
neighbouring lady of remarkably similar disposition, who'
been only too glad to get rid of the terrier for a couple o
hours, but feigned desolation when Cristal swept off witl
her.

'Jane,' she said.

'Jane?' he asked, irrationally thinking of his daughter.

'Yes,' Cristal replied. 'She's a Jack Russell, you see, so
call her Jane . . . Russell?' she finished, lamely.

Canterwell's eyes flickered to the bitch's rudimentar
mammaries, then up to Cristal's all-too-opulent pair, anc
decided it would be best to say nothing at all. 'Ha,' h
remarked, equally lamely. They come together as the patl
joined the main exit from the Gardens, past the Alber
memorial.

'You live around here, then,' he observed.

'Not far from you,' she said, slyly. He lifted his eye
brows. He had a strong and undiscriminating sexual drive
and a sadistic streak of which Eve (probably mistakenly or
his part) had never been the beneficiary. This big, cool
beautiful girl was getting to him.

'How far?'

'Sorry?'

'I beg your pardon. How far from me do you live?'

'Literally just around the corner,' she said. 'In one of those . . . very private little streets.' She gave the words an audacious wealth of double meaning.

'The Regency flats with the little courtyards and walled streets? Yes, I know them. Very pretty. Would you . . .'

'Permit you to walk that way with me? I think you know I would.' He glanced surreptitiously at his watch. 'But of course,' she added, 'not if you don't have the time.'

'Oh, I do,' he assured her. 'I don't have any pressing engagements – just a family picnic.'

'Perhaps I could offer you . . . an aperitif?' she said. Canterwell's breath quickened, and so did his step. He almost leered at her as they crossed the main road. He really is an arsehole, she thought.

She allowed herself to be led in the opposite direction from his home – and hers – for reasons which benefited both of them; he didn't want to risk Eve or the children spotting them, and she wanted to elude his Special Branch man, whom she knew to have strong sweat glands and incipient halitosis. They made polite, meaningless conversation, which Cristal usually managed to steer delicately in the path of sex.

A large black car with tinted windows passed them as they turned left to complete a circuitous route to the quiet little street that housed the exclusive private estate where she lived. She looked casually up and down the road – which he appreciated – before opening a wrought-iron gate into one of the courtyards. The trees, shrubs, and old-fashioned trellised climbing roses almost formed a pergola. The roses were yellow and white, and matched the mellowed cream of the buildings.

She walked through the arch, and put her hand on his chest to stop him following while she checked the windows of the flats through one of the occasional gaps in the overhead canopy of intertwined branches and leaves. 'OK now,' Cristal said. Her warm fingers burned on the flesh at the 'v' of his open-necked shirt.

She turned her head and looked at him with her lips half parted and lust in her eyes. With her back still half to him she allowed her fingers to trail down his body. She took a silk square from the slim, snakeskin belt at her waist and dabbed at her mouth.

He licked his lips and started to say her name, but she interrupted. 'Sorry. Would you like to go ahead? I'll close the gate.'

Pongo tugged at the lead. Canterwell said, 'Sure,' and started to walk past her.

Her right arm was swinging back as he took the first step. The square of silk formed a pad over the quarter-inch steel circlet shielding her knuckles. The movement of her body was scarcely a blur, and all her massive strength went into the blow that landed on the back of his head with unendurable force. Her fist penetrated beneath the ridge of bone at the base of his skull. The brain haemorrhage was instant and bloody, and he died before he hit the ground. The price for treachery and murder had been paid. Pongo barked, and Cristal patted his head and whispered to him until he stopped.

She spoke into a tiny pocket communicator. The black limousine with tinted windows cruised into the street, and pulled up on to the pavement by the courtyard gate where, since there were no garages to the flats, car-owners often parked. She glanced up at the house windows again, and said 'Quick!' to the peak-capped chauffeur. They dragged Canterwell's body into the car and she shooed the two dogs after it. The scent of the roses went with them.

The black car made two more turns to reach Canterwell's street. They paused to let a little Italian sports car disappear, and the chauffeur nodded when Cristal told him to get the limousine's number plates changed that afternoon. They went by the Energy Minister's home to a spot a hundred yards or so up the road in the direction of the park. The chauffeur parked a foot away from the opposite kerb outside a pair of blackened, stately and empty Georgian houses, sporting the name-boards of fashionable Belgravia estate agents.

The door handles of the Rolls Royce Silver Wraith were set close together on either side of a narrow central pillar, so when Cristal and the chauffeur opened the doors to an angle of sixty degrees, they effectively shielded a sizeable triangle of road from view. The previous owner of the elderly car but one, had used the space to allow his equally elderly mother-in-law to perform her vital functions when they were on a motoring holiday in Scotland, using a portable commode which he called a 'Traveloo'.

Canterwell's body toppled out, and Cristal deliberately slammed the back of his head against the edge of the pavement. The sharp stone bit deeply into the bloody pulp and collected a satisfying smear of crimsoned hairs. She picked up Pongo and placed him at his master's feet. He sat there, whining uncertainly. 'Good boy,' she said, and patted his head again.

She took Canterwell's thick, plaited dog lead, still fastened to the Labrador's collar, looped it round the dead man's left leg, pulled it tight, and clenched three fingers of his right hand through the thong.

'Sorry about this, Pongo, old chap,' she said. 'I'm afraid you're going to get the blame. 'Bye now.' Pongo barked and wagged his tail, and she blew him a kiss as the big car purred out to the main road and joined the sparse traffic heading east.

It was eighteen minutes to one, and Canterwell was nearly half an hour overdue. Eve, peering anxiously out of the open window of the drawing-room, heard Pongo's yelps, and saw the body. She had a pretty china basin of mashed red salmon in her hand, and it fell and shattered on the window ledge. The salmon plopped out on to the floor and the seasoned vinegar dribbled down the radiator. Pongo's barks changed to a despairing howl.

Postscript

The limousine dropped Cristal at the office, and Pond was waiting there for her. 'Is all – well?' he asked. She said, 'Yes.' He crossed the room and sat at his desk, and she perched on the 'difficult' Chesterfield. 'Good,' he said. 'I expect you'll want a holiday now.'

'I think I would, unless you want me for anything.'

'Not at the moment, although Colonel Ivanovitch is being most helpful and cooperative, and certain matters are becoming somewhat clearer to us now.'

'Interesting,' she said.

'Very,' Pond agreed. 'By the way, we've taken care of that little helicopter Scott left at Tredogan. It's sitting in the pantechnicon at Wapping. I'm afraid you've lost your motorcycle, though. The police have discovered that the Road Fund Licence was, unhappily, a forgery,' – his eye roamed to a pad of pristine licence discs on the desk – 'and the registration number apparently belongs to a Post Office van in, I believe, Lanarkshire.'

'And Scott?' Cristal asked.

'We've sent him to Brazil for a while. He says you can keep his Lotus.'

'I'll write and thank him.'

'What a good idea.'

'May I go then, please?'

'By all means,' said Pond. 'Will you use the Montego Bay villa?' Cristal said, 'I was thinking of it.' She rose and held out her hand. 'Goodbye then, Dr Pond. And say goodbye to Sir Marcus for me,' glancing at Sleightley's desk. 'Yes, I will,' said Pond.

She turned to go, but he raised his hand. 'There is just one small thing. It may have slipped your mind, but it so happens that your – ah – contract with us expires while you're going to be away. It was, of course, only an initial, temporary arrangement. May I take it that you wish to stay with the Department, and regularize the situation?'

'Yes,' she said, without hesitation.

'Splendid.'

She grinned in the spontaneous, affectionate way she had, and left the office, and Pond was acutely conscious that she'd gone, because the room became dull and ordinary again. He crossed to the far corner and typed a programme on the computer keyboard. There were a few energetic clicks, and a section of the oak panelling behind his desk slid open. On a silver salver held by extending steel brackets stood a goblet of thirty-five-year-old port wine, chilled to 41 degrees Farenheit.

He lifted the glass to his lips, and sipped the amber liquid. Then he walked to his desk and opened a file. It was headed: VENGAN, the Hon. Victoria Emmaline Cristal. He inked a red rubber stamp pad and impressed across the name the one word, 'CONFIRMED'.

Pink was playing a four-ball and had sliced his tee-shot atrociously at the twelfth when Swaine tapped him on the shoulder and gave him the news of Canterwell's death. It wasn't, Swaine said, an accident, and explained the circumstances. They'd decided, though, not to contest a likely 'Death by Misadventure' verdict.

'Let sleeping dogs sleep, eh?' Pink chuckled. 'Something like that, sir,' Swaine replied, looking pained. 'I do believe you're in a bunker, Admiral,' pointed out Savage, who was on the opposing team and rarely lost a round of golf. 'Rubbish,' Pink declared absently, hooking the ball out with his foot. Savage sank a thirteen-foot putt while Pink stood, head bowed, lost in thought.

At the end of an uncomfortable ten minutes with Paulfrey at Downing Street the previous evening, he'd asked the

Prime Minister point blank if there could be a clandestine but enormously powerful arm of British Intelligence, of which even SIS and the Government were unaware. Paulfrey had considered the suggestion carefully, and replied, 'Impossible, Admiral. Utterly impossible.'

But somhow Pink knew, with total conviction, that he was wrong – or lying. And that one day all the pieces would interlock. But in the meantime there was one obvious and appalling explanation which he had to consider – the possibility that Paulfrey had called in the CIA, that the Prime Minister didn't trust his own Secred Service machine and was running Britain's counterespionage operations himself – with American help. He resolved to keep a closer eye on Paulfrey in the future.

At that precise moment, over a mid-afternoon sherry at Chequers, Miles Paulfrey determined that Admiral Pink had been lying to him when he pretended ignorance over the Tredogan affair. 'It has to be Pink and the SIS,' he said to himself. 'It couldn't be anyone else. What is he holding back from me – and why?'

Paulfrey resolved to keep a closer eye on Pink in the future. He might, he thought, even seek assistance . . . the CIA? Why not? It wouldn't, after all, be the first time . . .

Three weeks later, Pink's theory that an outside agency was working against him had grown in his mind to virtual certainty. He confided his suspicions to the trusted and impressively discreet Senior Civil Servant whom he had invited to luncheon at his club.

'It must be that,' Pink growled. 'And it must be the Americans. I'm sure of it. Sure of it.'

'I shouldn't be a bit surprised, Admiral,' Sleightley said, 'if you're not absolutely on the right track.'

SWAP

Walter Wager

The toughest way to pay a debt.

I've only got six months, captain, which means you've got less. I'm asking you to go into the Soviet Union, a police state with some of the most heavily guarded frontiers in the world, and bring out the girl – illegally.'

Vietnam veteran David Garrison had a debt to pay – and the price was high. Bring a very special person out of Russia.

But a dying man's dream and an orphan girl's future had to be bought. With another human being.

Fast, tense and violent, the action sweeps from Washington to Tel Aviv, from Moscow to Paris in a Cold War confrontation of horrifying dimensions.

WOLF MOUNTAIN

Peter Lars Sandberg

'You can have any one you want except the Major and the one I picked out for my own. You can even have her when I get done.'

On a desolate mountainside in Colorado a party of teenage girls and their climbing instructor are terrorised and violated by two psychopaths. Their only hope of survival is an ex-air force major who must first engineer their escape, then outwit two lethal enemies to lead them to safety.

One is the mountain itself with its treacherous rock faces, snowfalls and freezing fog.

The other is a pair of killers armed with high velocity rifles.

'A book that propels the reader through it non-stop.' *Publishers Weekly*.

'Intense high velocity plotting . . . Hitchcock himself might like to get his hands on the film rights.' *Bestseller*.

ARCH OF TRIUMPH

Erich Maria Remarque

Erich Maria Remarque's most powerful novel since
ALL QUIET ON THE WESTERN FRONT.

A man hunting for his Nazi torturer . . . A woman on
the run because her lover has died . . . A city on the
brink of war . . .

Paris 1939, waiting for the long summer to explode into
war, seethes with refugees fleeing from the inferno of
the Third Reich. Among them Ravic, a German surgeon
eking out a living in the shadowy backstreets while he
looks for the Nazi who tortured him and killed his wife;
Joan Madou, the tragic girl Ravic fell in love with; and
somewhere in the heart of Paris, von Haake, the
Gestapo torturer and murderer whom Ravic must find
and kill.

THE DEFECTOR

Donald Seaman

'EXPERTLY CONSTRUCTED THRILLER' *Daily Express*

From the author of THE BOMB THAT COULD LIP-READ, a second brilliantly realistic thriller – THE DEFECTOR.

A vital Russian scientist leaves the Soviet Union in order to save his wife from torture and imprisonment. In Britain their faces are changed by plastic surgery and they learn to play the roles of Mr. and Mrs. John Stevens. It is the perfect defection, until John Stevens shoots and kills a housekeeper and becomes the pawn in a deadly struggle between the English courts of law, British Intelligence and the KGB.

'A slow-fuse thriller that GRIPS FIERCELY' *Birmingham Post*

The Minotaur Factor

Stuart Stern

The cause:
THE BIRTH PILL

The symptoms:
LETHAL CATATONIA

The result:
CERTAIN DEATH

A young woman goes berserk at a party and mutilates three people with a knife before collapsing into a coma. She dies and acute lethal catatonia is diagnosed as the cause of death, an unstoppable and incurable chemical malfunction of the brain.

Sir George Upton, head of the medical team investigating the epidemic, discovers that it is linked with a brand of birth pill. But what is the link? In desperation the team selects a group of human guinea pigs for a series of experiments as deadly as the disease itself.

THE MINOTAUR FACTOR is a terrifying extrapolation on the theme of the possible long term effects of the birth pill – effects which are still not wholly known.